THE NIGHT MARKET

JONATHAN MOORE

An Orion paperback

First published in Great Britain in 2018
by Orion Books,
This paperback edition published in 2018
by Orion Books,
an imprint of The Orion Publishing Group Ltd
Carmelite House, 50 Victoria Embankment
London EC4Y 0DZ

An Hachette UK Company

1 3 5 7 9 10 8 6 4 2

A CIP catalogue record for this book is
available from the British Library.

ISBN 978 1 4091 5977 3

Printed and bound by CPI Group (UK) Ltd, Croydon, CR0 4YY

www.orionbooks.co.uk

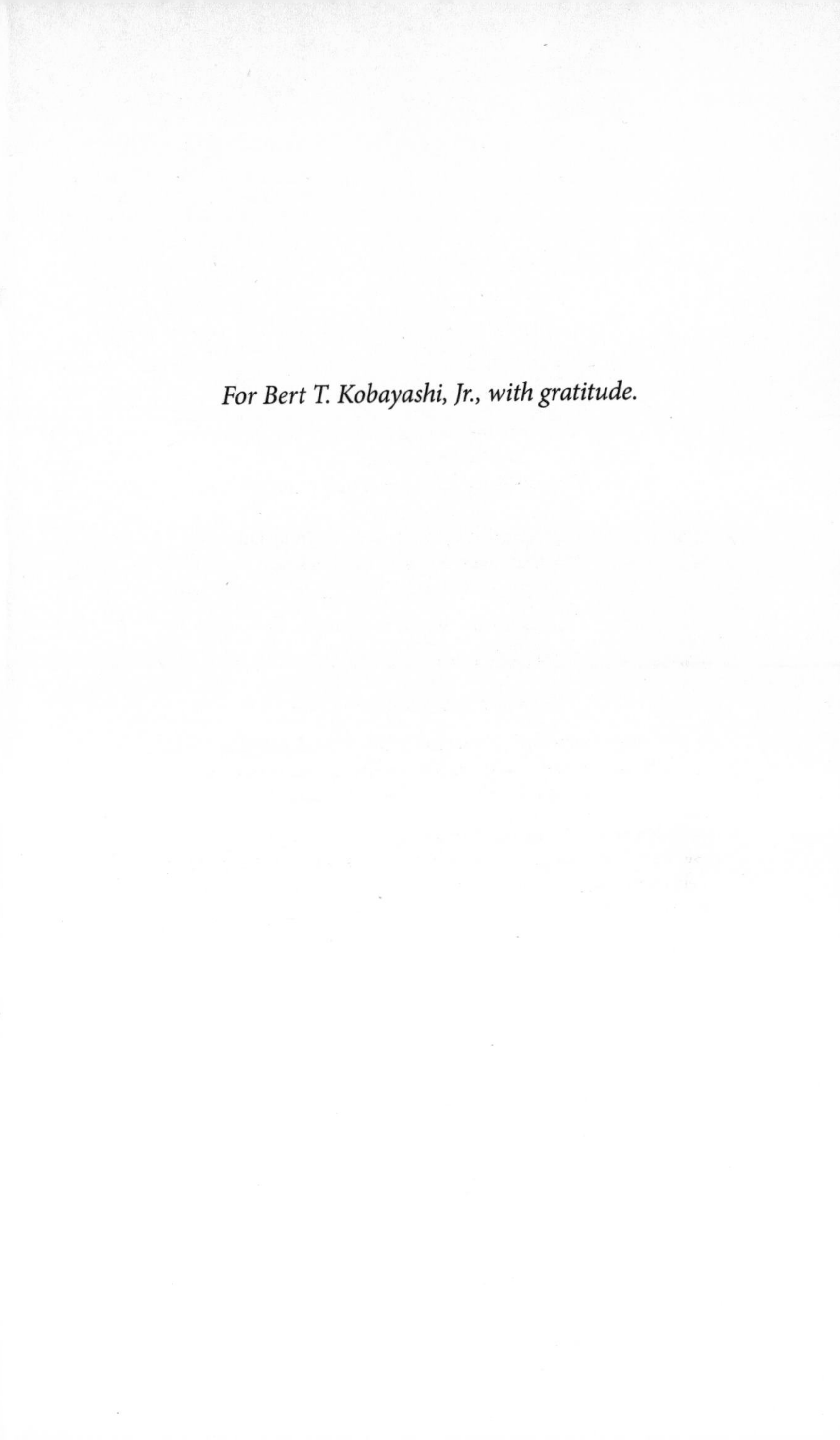

For Bert T. Kobayashi, Jr., with gratitude.

THE NIGHT MARKET

1

CARVER PULLED TO the curb behind the chassis of a burned-out car.

Across the intersection was the billboard, six spotlights along the bottom. They shined upward, lighting the sign, throwing its shadow across the vacant building behind it. The rest of the neighborhood was dead. A moonscape of abandoned warehouses, everything picked over twice. Walls punched in with crowbars, wires and plumbing stripped out. Even the streetlights were gone; in Bay View and Hunter's Point, copper was worth more than light. Kids were creeping in from the edges to steal bricks now. They could take them by the bucketload to the salvage yards south of town and trade them for day-old bread. He knew about that from last night.

But no one had touched the sign. Maybe it made them feel better, having it lit. He turned on the windshield wipers so he could see it clearly. He thought about getting out of the car. He'd be able to see all of it if he walked to the middle of the intersection. He'd almost done that last night, too, when he'd been lost in the dark, driving back from the scene. Shaking still, from the gunfire. Tonight he'd driven this way just to see it again. He didn't have any business here. No one did.

The sign was brand new, but he couldn't imagine who would have put it here. A place like this? They might as well have buried it in the desert.

It was selling perfume, a fragrance called Black Aria. The woman in the ad was an actress. He knew her face but not her name. His grandfather might have known. Elizabeth something? Or Audrey, maybe. She lay on her stomach, her chin propped in her hands. Her knees were bent so that her bare toes pointed straight up. She was surely nude underneath the black sheet that was draped over her, covering no more than it had to. Sheet or not, every curve was there, defined in bare skin or beneath the indents and contours of satin.

It was all digitized, of course. Just another seamless fake. The real Elizabeth, or Audrey, wouldn't have posed like this. Not back then, whenever she was alive, and not to sell perfume. People used to have standards. But those were gone now and they weren't coming back. Like the burned-out car, like the whole of Hunter's Point. The bottle hovered above her bare shoulder blades, the crystal vial so thick it looked like ice. The liquid inside was the color of old blood.

The warmth started while he was looking at the sign. It began somewhere near the base of his skull and followed along his spine until it had spread through him entirely. Then the feeling inverted and his skin went cold. The hair on his arms stood straight out. It was thrilling, ranking right up there with the rush he'd felt last night after the shooting had stopped and he'd realized he hadn't been hit. If anything, it was better.

It was so quiet that he could hear the low hum coming from the billboard's spotlights. Six slightly different tones combining into a curious chord. It might have been engineered to draw him closer.

He remembered television advertisements he'd seen as a kid. A Saturday-morning parade of things he'd wanted desperately and then forgotten about. He didn't think he was going to forget about this. Of course, he had no use for perfume. He didn't wear it, and he had no woman to give it to. But that didn't seem to matter, because what he was feeling was far beyond desire. It was the crushing need a drowning man has for another breath.

He stepped out of the car and looked across the intersection. A flock of small birds, sparrows maybe, came swirling out of the darkness like a storm of leaves. They landed in unison on the roof of the scorched car, then turned toward him. He heard tiny claws tapping on the steel, felt a hundred pairs of black eyes watching him.

He was standing in a neighborhood that was waiting for a wrecking ball. Bulldozers had been idle on its perimeter for months. When the last condemnation orders came, they'd lower their blades and roll. The demolition teams meant to wipe away everything the thieves hadn't already taken. They would knock down row houses and wire C-4 into century-old factories to make way for the sparkling future. He'd seen the model in City Hall. White concrete and black glass transforming the neighborhood into an autonomous shipping center. An unpopulated city from which driverless delivery trucks would glide north on pavement so smooth, their tires would barely whisper. Drones would hum upward from rooftop landing pads, packages dangling beneath them as they sped over the blocks of unlit tenements and into San Francisco. In City Hall, he'd seen no plan in the models for the residents who would be displaced. Maybe they were supposed to sell bricks.

He reached into the car and switched off the headlights, and then the street was blackout dark. The ruins around him disappeared. There was just the sign.

Finally, he let himself walk out into the intersection. He stared up at the dead actress and the perfume she'd been enlisted to sell. It wasn't just the woman, wasn't just the suggestion of her naked body under the sheet. It was the bottle and the lettering and the way the spotlights fell onto the black background, making something so bright out of a void. As if he'd struck a match in a mineshaft, and diamonds in the thousands came glittering back from the walls.

He couldn't say where the peace came from, but he knew exactly what it was doing. It was cleansing him. Each swell took away a layer of darkness. In a moment he'd be bare; last night would be gone. He stood in the rain and savored that.

He only turned away when his phone rang.

2

HE ANSWERED IT in the car, wanting to be out of the sign's reach before he spoke to anyone.

"It's me."

"You coming, or what?"

It didn't matter what Jenner was saying. He could be dictating a form over the phone, or telling a kid to drop a gun. His voice never rose above dead calm. That made Jenner the kind of man people usually listened to, but the kid last night hadn't. He hadn't dropped his gun, either.

"I lose you, Carver?"

"Sorry – on my way."

"Call came in and we're up," Jenner said. "You knew we were up again, right?"

"Sure."

"Where are you?"

"Close to last night's scene," Carver said, after a pause. "There was something I wanted to see again. The call, it came just now?"

"Just now. I hung up, I called you."

"Be out front in five. We'll go in my car."

"You were out there?" Jenner asked. "You got questions about last night?"

"Not about you – you did just right. Plus there's video," Carver said. "So don't worry about it."

"Okay."

Carver could see the expressway ahead. No one had stolen the wiring up there – the commissioners and the mayor could ignore Hunter's Point until the redevelopment was done, but not the new expressway. Its art deco streetlights glowed in a curving run toward the city center, where there was enough midnight light to make a false dawn beneath the fog.

"Tell it to me," Carver said.

"I talked to the lieutenant first. It started with 911. Some lady called from Filbert Street. Said her neighbor's screaming. Patrol comes, front door's locked."

"Okay."

"When she tells me this, the lieutenant, she's got the patrol guys on hold. So she patches them in, and they tell me from there," Jenner said. "I got it straight from them. They'd knocked on the door, shouted *Police,* the whole thing."

"Nobody home?"

"Nobody."

"What time was that, they knocked? We could establish—"

"Jesus, Ross, you told me to tell it. I'm telling it. You want to let me?"

"Go ahead."

"You're throwing me off," Jenner said. "They knock just after midnight. How do I know? They radio dispatch at twelve oh five. Say they're getting out of the vehicle, going to the door. They make enough noise knocking and yelling, and after five minutes the neighbor lady comes out."

Carver steered onto the entrance ramp. The pitted asphalt gave way to the new expressway. It was like driving on a black mirror.

"The lady tells them she's never heard anything like it," Jenner said. "The screams, I mean. Said he was so loud, it was like he was in the room with her."

"She know him?"

"Ross, I don't know. I'm telling it. I'm not leaving anything out," Jenner said. "So, he's screaming. Like a madman, she says. Makes her blood go cold, all that. She goes to her window, peeks through the curtain. It's dark over there, across the street. But she sees someone in an upstairs window. He's beating on the glass. Naked and bloody, and beating on the glass."

"Just one guy? Not two?"

"She just sees him, the one guy. So when patrol hears this, what she saw in the window, they come off the porch and go back to the street. One of them gets the spotlight out of the vehicle, and asks her which window. She points, and they light it up. Then they see it."

For the second time that night, Carver felt his skin tighten, felt his hairs stand up. But this time, it wasn't good. He took his foot off the accelerator and slowed down. He knew what Jenner was about to say.

"The window, it was covered with blood," Jenner said. "Handprints – he'd been slapping it with his palms."

"Trying to get out."

"That's right," Jenner said. "Trying to get out. Thick glass, I guess."

"We'll see when we get there," Carver said. "How thick it is. But . . . so now they go in."

"They see the blood, they figure it's time to go in. They get the ram out of the trunk, punch down the door. And you'll like this: The door was on a chain. Locked from the inside."

"Okay."

"They clear the downstairs first. Nobody's home. There's a basement, but it's empty when they scan it. Windows are locked from the inside. Same for the back door," Jenner said. "So then they go up. They find him in the front bedroom, second floor."

"And –"

"He's dead," Jenner said. "But these two are smart. They're not staying in patrol forever. They back the hell out. They don't touch anything. They secure the place and call the lieutenant from the front porch. She calls me."

"When they say *dead* – how'd they know, if they didn't touch anything?"

"I asked them," Jenner said. "You think I wouldn't? They said I could take their word for it."

"Take their word."

"They said I should get down there," Jenner said. "See for myself. You almost here?"

Carver rolled up to the old headquarters on Bryant Street, and there was Jenner, under the cone of a streetlight. He'd turned his trench coat's collar against the rain. When Carver slowed, Jenner shielded his eyes with his hand, then got in.

"Took long enough."

He slammed the door. The rain was running off his smooth head.

"Five minutes," Carver said. "What I told you."

"In this, that's long enough."

Jenner took a white handkerchief from his jacket pocket and used it to wipe down his scalp.

"Some people have hats," Carver said. "You could look into it. Where we going?"

"Filbert Street. Near Telegraph Hill. I know the place."

They crossed Market Street, broken glass glittering back from the pavement and then crunching as they passed over it. They were at the edge of the Financial District, which had been smash-and-grab territory for as long as Carver could remember. But now it was empty. Even the shops that still had glass in the windows were closed. An advertising kiosk at a bus stop lit up as they went by, triggered by their motion. It treated the vacant sidewalk to poster-sized images of a tropical beach. Neither of them asked where everyone was, but Carver guessed they were both wondering.

They didn't see a single pedestrian until they crested Nob Hill, and then they found the missing populace. At the top of the rise, they had to slow to pass through a standing crowd. Men and women were stretched in a three-block line to get into the Fairmont Hotel. Its marble-columned façade had been draped entirely in black fabric, the gauzy cloth tied in place with red silk ribbons that circled the building. Strings of Chinese paper lanterns weaved through the grounds, and ten thousand people stood in the rain, waiting. Some of the men wore black capes, and most of them carried paper lanterns. Scattered inside the crowd were homeless men. Barkers and distributers, hired part time to hand out glowcards advertising whatever they'd been paid to hawk tonight. Most of the women were holding baroque carnival masks to their faces. Jewels flashed all around their eyes. Carver could smell the perfume, the scented skin powders.

"What is this?" Carver asked.

"I don't know," Jenner answered. "It's not your usual mob. Push through — there's a gap to the right of this guy."

Carver put his hand on the horn to clear a way forward. The crowd parted, but one man remained in the middle of the street. He was holding a brass candle-lantern in his cupped hands, and he stood staring upward, his face as blank as the orange-black fog.

"Unbelievable," Carver said.

He steered around the man, then accelerated past the crowd.

"And not a patrol officer anywhere," Jenner answered. "You think I ought to call it in?"

"You think?"

Instead of reaching for his cell phone, Jenner folded his hands on his lap and leaned back.

"That's right," Carver said. "Not our thing."

Coming down the hill, they saw a straggler on the sidewalk, the strange silhouette of his plague-doctor mask extending from the outline of his tricorn hat. He carried a silver-tipped cane in one hand, a white globe lantern in the other. The neighborhood was dead for two blocks after that, until they came upon a lone streetwalker struggling up the incline. She wore white patent heels, and little else. She didn't try to signal them as they passed, and kept her head down. By then they'd entered a dark block. Smudge pot oil lamps burned in a few of the tenement windows; unlicensed and unlit drones flew in and out of the broken windows at the top floor of one of the buildings like oversized flies. They were taking pictures, following people. Ferrying goods that weren't fit to be seen on the street.

The streetlights picked up again a minute later, and Jenner leaned forward.

"Hang a right on Filbert," he said. "Place is two, three streets past Washington Square."

Carver made the right turn.

"I see it."

It would have been hard to miss. An SFPD cruiser was double-parked in front of the house, its rooftop lights pulsing blue and red. There was an ambulance on the other side of the street. The two paramedics were just sitting in the back looking at their phones.

An officer in a black slicker came out of the shadows and aimed a flashlight at Carver, who came to a stop next to the man and rolled down his window. When the patrol officer leaned down and looked into the car, rain slid off the top of his plastic hat cover and dripped onto Carver's arm.

"Carver and Jenner, Homicide."

Carver took his badge from his jacket pocket and handed it to the patrolman, who glanced at it and handed it back. He pointed ahead.

"You can park behind that car, sir. House is right there. We were the first officers on the scene. I'm Roper and my partner's Houston. She's watching the back door."

"Anybody been inside besides you?"

"No, sir."

"Is the medical examiner here?"

"No, sir."

"What's with the ambulance?" Jenner asked.

"We didn't ask for it. Dispatch must've done that on its own, when the lady called in the screaming."

"But the paramedics didn't go in?" Carver asked.

"We didn't let them. They weren't happy about it."

"That's fine, Officer. Have Houston come through and meet us on the front porch."

Carver put up his window and drove to the parking space Roper had pointed out. He popped the trunk and went around the rear to get their crime scene bag. He looked around the neighborhood again, but saw no faces in the windows. Sparrows perched on the power lines. Hundreds, maybe thousands, of them. They never used to come out at night, but the last few years, he'd been seeing them all the time.

"We'll suit up out of the rain. Talk to the officers before we go in."

"Fine with me."

Carver lifted the bag out of the trunk before Jenner could help him with it. He wasn't about to let his junior partner carry all the weight.

"Let's go."

Roper and Houston looked like a couple of high school kids dressed up as cops, but that was hardly new to Carver. Most rookie patrolmen these days looked like they'd just cut class. Roper straightened up and saluted when Carver stepped onto the porch.

Instead of saluting back, Carver took off his hat and shook the rain from it.

"Stand down, son."

"Yessir."

Carver looked them over. Houston was maybe two years younger than her partner, and much better-looking, but they had the same bearing.

"Army?" Carver asked.

"The Marines, sir," Roper said.

Houston nodded.

"I'm Inspector Carver, this is Inspector Jenner. Jenner told me what you told him on the phone. You did good work."

"Thank you, sir."

"You find out whose house this is?" Carver asked.

"Yes and no. Houston, she found the deed online. It's titled to a corporation—"

"Something called the MMLX Corporation," Houston said.

"—but it's not registered in California—"

"Nevada," Houston said. There were beads of water in her dark hair, and they caught the revolving lights from the patrol car.

"—so we just have an agent of record, and that's a corporation too," Roper finished.

"In other words, no idea whose house it is. No idea if the dead guy belongs in it," Carver said.

He was looking at Houston's wet hair, the way it was reflecting the lights from the top of their cars. He thought of the jeweled masks he'd seen on Nob Hill, the women in their finery waiting outside the Fairmont. Why would someone wrap an entire hotel in silk?

"Yes, sir."

Every night in the city was like a long-running dream. He couldn't remember the last time he'd stood outside in the sunlight.

He shook it off and looked at Roper.

"What about the neighbor, the one who called 911?" he asked. "She around somewhere?"

"In her house, across the street," Houston said. "Asked her to sit tight till someone comes to talk to her."

"Anyone else come forward? Other neighbors?"

"No, sir," said Roper. "Seen them looking through the curtains, though. So there's people around."

"Anything you want to add before we go in?"

"No, sir," Roper said. He looked at his partner, who nodded at him and made a signal with her hand, cupping her fingers to her lips.

Roper turned back to Carver and Jenner.

"Except, you'll want to suit up. Masks, gloves. Houston and I, we were in Kinshasa on an Ebola operation. Two outbreaks ago. Never saw anything worse than what's upstairs."

"You want to elaborate?"

"It's just, the guy looks like he got cooked," Roper said.

"And eaten," Houston added.

"We can't explain it any better than that," Roper said.

There was a wooden bench and a potted rosebush next to the front door. Carver put the duffel bag on the bench and unzipped it. He and Jenner stood next to each other while they donned the garments of their trade: plastic shower caps and clear safety goggles, blue latex gloves and cellophane booties to go over their shoes. They slid on paper surgical masks and clipped pen-sized cameras to the sides of their glasses so they could record what they saw inside.

"You check the whole house before you pull back?" Carver asked.

Roper looked at Houston, and she looked at Carver and then shook her head.

"We never went to the third floor," she said. "We found the body on the second and that's when we pulled out."

"You go in the basement?"

"We just scoped it from the kitchen – nothing."

"All right," Carver said. He pointed to the Ønske thermal scope on Houston's utility belt. "Mine got smashed last night. Let me borrow that."

She unclipped the scope from her belt and handed it to Carver. He switched it on to check the battery level.

"Good," Carver said. He looked at Jenner. "You ready?"

"Let's do it."

Carver hadn't gotten a good look at the house from the outside, but when they stepped through the splintered door and into the entry hall, he knew it must belong to someone very rich. Anything on this street, in the shadow of Coit Tower, was worth a fortune. That was a given. Because of that, most of the row houses were subdivided into condos. But this place was an undivided three floors, plus whatever was in the basement.

The floors were made of book-matched koa planks, and the walls were some kind of stone. Alabaster, maybe. Spotlights mounted flush with the floor illuminated a row of gyotaku prints on one wall: octopi dipped in their own ink and pressed in death poses on ancient rice paper. On the far side of the entryway, Jenner was standing in front of an oil painting that took up most of the wall. It showed the beach across from Golden Gate Park on a fog-bound day. Everything blue-gray, like smoke in the winter.

"That a Laurent?" Carver asked.

"That's what I was thinking," Jenner said, turning around. "I think it's stolen."

"When the Legion of Honor got hit, ten years ago," Carver said. "I remember that."

Jenner nodded.

"Ballsy, putting it by the front door. Or the guy didn't expect a lot of company."

"You want to look around down here, or go up?" Carver asked.

Jenner answered with his eyes, looking to the ceiling.

They moved to the staircase, their cellophane-wrapped feet crinkling with each step. The stairs were wide enough to climb side by side. At the first landing, where it got dark, they stopped and turned on their flashlights. Then they rounded the corner and ascended into the shadows.

"You think Houston and Roper are an item?" Jenner asked.

"I don't know."

"They finish each other's sentences," Jenner said. "Makes it likely, in my book."

"Sometimes you finish my sentences."

"You know what I'm talking about. Plus, you saw the way he was looking at her. And her at him."

"I think it's none of my business," Carver said. "I can tell you that. Forget what the policy says. Who cares, if they're doing good work."

"I think it'd be really nice," Jenner said. "You know? A partner you could spend time with. Someone who really understood you. Who could be gentle with you."

"You want to put in for a new partner, I think Ray Bodecker's looking for one."

"I said gentle."

"Tough shit, then," Carver said. "Here, look at this."

He moved his light along the wall at the top of the stairs. There was a bloody handprint on the wallpaper. Carver pictured a man running up the stairs, stumbling at the top, and catching himself against the wall. Shoving himself off and sprinting in a new direction. The blood was laid on thick enough that it ran to the wainscoting.

They climbed the rest of the way to the second story.

"I don't see any on the floor," Carver said.

"Any what?"

"Blood – if he had it on his hands when he was running up, you'd think there'd be some on the floor."

"Maybe he was covering a wound till he got to the top. Holding his hand over it. There's a light switch," Jenner said. "Want me to hit it?"

Carver looked up and saw where Jenner was pointing his flashlight.

"Don't," he said. "House like this, who knows what it might do? I don't want to turn on a fan, stir things up."

"Make a wall swing around, send out an army of robot vacuums. That kind of thing."

"Now you get it," Carver said. "When the techs come, they'll have lights. Until then, let's stick with these."

Jenner aimed his light on a spot farther down the upstairs hallway.

"There's your blood on the floor."

"Hold up," Carver said. "Make sure you don't step in any."

"I'll go behind you. That way, we step in it, it's your fault – but what's that?"

Jenner's flashlight was illuminating a lump on the floor, ten paces ahead of Carver. They went up to it and stopped.

"A sparrow?" Jenner asked. "Whatever it was, it got stomped on."

Carver crouched, holding his light close to the small bird's broken body. Its left eye had been smashed. A thin steel ring was visible in the back of the socket. Tiny shards of black glass lay on the floor near its beak. Its feathers were threaded with shiny black strands that Carver guessed were photovoltaic filaments. There was no blood.

"I don't think it's a bird," Carver said. He didn't touch it, whatever it was. He thought of the sparrows lining the power lines outside. They'd all been facing the same direction, staring into the house's bedroom window.

"Then what is it?"

"We'll bag it later and take it to the lab. But if you want a guess, someone really wanted to keep an eye on this guy," Carver said. He stood up and looked down the hall. "Let's go find him."

• • •

Before they went to the front bedroom, Carver took Houston's thermal scope and switched it on. He put the viewfinder to his eye and did a slow scan of the second floor, then looked up at the ceiling. Houston and Roper hadn't gone to the third floor, but after they'd backed out of the house, they'd been watching the front and rear entrances. They'd kept the stair landing in sight, so anyone coming to the entry level would have been in plain view. If anyone was hiding in the house, that person could only be on the second or third floors.

"How's it look?"

"There's a hot water heater right above you. Good size on it," Carver said. "But nothing else. No one's up there."

Carver clipped the scope to his belt and led the way forward. After they came into the bedroom, their flashlight beams picked out the blood marks on the walls, the thick smears on the window. The dead man must have hit it fifty, sixty times to get that many prints on it.

"You smell that?" Jenner asked.

They were all the way into the room now.

"Yeah," Carver said. "I don't know what it is, though."

He could smell blood drying on the Persian carpet, could smell the fresh linens on the four-poster bed. There were vanilla-scented candles on each nightstand, and he could smell those, too, even though they weren't lit and their wicks were clipped flush to the wax. With each breath, he caught the usual scents of fresh death. This early, they weren't so bad. Urine and bile, mostly. But another smell was braided in, a single thread so intertwined with everything else, it was almost impossible to pick out.

"Like ozone," Jenner said. "You know? Out in the country, when a storm's coming."

"Maybe," Carver said.

But it wasn't right at all. It was like saying that rage was red. That your first love was clear and cool, like a drink of water from a springhead. Some things couldn't sustain a comparison, and this smell was one of them.

"Roper said the dead guy was between the bed and the window," Jenner whispered.

"All right," he said. "Let's check it out."

They moved around the end of the bed, letting their flashlight beams rove the floor and the walls.

"There," Jenner said. "You see that? Holy shit."

Carver let his light slide along the body. From the head – or at least, what he thought was the head – down to the feet, and back. He swallowed once behind his surgical mask.

"What time did the lady call?"

"Midnight," Jenner said.

"Roper and Houston, they rolled up at twelve oh five?"

"That's right."

"Lady saw someone beating on this window at midnight?"

"That's the story."

"Holy fuck," Carver said. He wanted to sit down, but he didn't want to touch anything in the room. "You getting this? With the camera?"

"I'm getting it."

Carver had to stop his gag reflex. He brought his gloved fist toward his facemask, then thought better of it. He dropped his hand back to his side, and spent ten seconds working his throat and clenching his teeth.

"You okay?" Jenner asked.

Carver nodded and breathed in slowly.

"The lady," he said. He swallowed. "She say anything about him being covered with that stuff, whatever it is?"

"Just saw a guy in the window. Said he might be naked. That he was bleeding."

"That's it?"

"That's it," Jenner said. "Nothing about this. This doesn't even look like what Roper and Houston described."

"Cooked and eaten."

"Maybe last month," Jenner said.

"Don't touch anything."

"You couldn't make me, Ross. Not with a gun to my head," Jenner said. "What is it? I mean, what the fuck?"

"I don't know."

They heard a knock from downstairs, and Roper called up.

"Inspector Carver?"

"What is it?" Carver yelled back.

"The paramedics say if you don't need them, they've got better things to do."

"Let them go, Roper," Carver said. "We don't need them."

"We definitely don't need them," Jenner added, low enough that only Carver would hear it.

Their beams converged on the body. Just an hour ago, this had been a man. Now he looked like gray moss. Like a carpet of it spread across a rot-shrunken log. Carver could see the bones of his fingers, could see the riverine fissure marks in his skull where patches of scalp had been eaten away.

"Is that—"

He stopped and bent closer. Whatever it was, it was moving.

He thought of an old time-lapse film he'd seen of a coral reef, the brain corals expanding at night as they put out their tentacles to feed, then contracting by day. All of this sped up, a year or more of days and nights flickering by in half a minute. The corals pulsed like breathing things, growing infinitesimally between cycles. He edged closer to the body, holding his breath.

"Jenner, you see that? You see what it's—"

The sound of shouting stopped him. Voices from below, boots on the stairs.

"Jesus, now what?" Jenner said.

Carver swung to face the door. Already, Jenner had his gun out, balanced over his flashlight. Carver reached beneath his jacket and drew his weapon, unclicking the safety as he went to a firing stance on his knee. He saw the lights coming up, and put pressure on the trigger as he called out.

"SFPD! You're coming into a crime scene and you want to back the fuck off!"

The footsteps stopped. The cold glow of the intruders' lights went still.

"Yeah?" The voice was muffled, as if it came from behind a window. "We're FBI, and we're coming up. So you want to stand the fuck down."

The men on the stairs didn't wait for an answer before they started moving again. They came to the second-floor landing, six of them in full biohazard suits, their faces invisible behind reflective glass plates. They came down the hall without speaking. Just their boots on the floorboards, the hiss of positive pressure venting from behind their helmets. When they were at the threshold of the bedroom, Carver's light found the letters stenciled on the point man's chest.

FBI.

He holstered his weapon, then turned to be sure Jenner was doing the same. Carver stood.

"Inspector Carver, SFPD. This is Inspect—"

"I only give a shit about one thing—how close did you get to him?"

It was hard to tell which of them was talking. They had gathered six abreast inside the bedroom door, and now they were moving again, advancing on Carver and Jenner. The LED lights built in to their fully enclosed hoods picked out dust motes floating between them. The air was thick with them, but there hadn't been enough light to see until now. They were the same color as the moss growing on the dead man. The FBI agents were dressed to weather a night on Venus. Looking at them, Carver felt naked in his thin gloves, his cheap paper mask.

"How close?" the suited man repeated.

"What?"

"Goddammit, the *body*. How close?"

"Four, five feet."

"You can see it in the air," another voice said. "Like it's gone full bloom."

It was hard to tell, because of the suit, but the point man seemed to nod his head. He turned to his men.

"Get these assholes out of here. Decon truck," he said. He turned back to Carver. "How long were you in here?"

Carver and Jenner looked at each other. Jenner's face was gray and drained.

"Thirty seconds," Carver answered. But even as he said it, he wasn't sure it was true. He had no idea how long they'd been standing above the body, repulsed and transfixed in equal measures.

"Longer," Jenner said. "A couple minutes, in this room. Five in the rest of the house."

"Then you better get moving. And fast. If you're lucky, there might still be time," the suited man said. He turned back to his team. "Take them."

A man grabbed Jenner by the elbow and yanked him forward.

"Decon truck?" Jenner said, looking back to Carver.

The man put his rubber-gloved hand between Jenner's shoulder blades and shoved him forward.

"Just *go*."

Carver followed. Behind his surgical mask, his lips were numb. His earlobes and fingertips were tingling.

"What is this?" Carver asked, over his shoulder. The remaining men in the room had fanned out. One of them was kneeling behind the bed; another was pulling drawers from the dresser. "Who called you guys?"

"Down the stairs."

"You're walking all over our scene," Carver said. He could feel a tickle at the corner of his eyes now, like the first touch of hay fever. "You can't—this is a crime scene."

"You'll be part of it if you don't get to the truck. You want to look like that? Give it half an hour."

They came into the entry hall. A man in a spacesuit was coating the walls with decontaminant. Orange and yellow hoses snaked through the front door to the pressure sprayer in his hand. He shot a mist of liquid at the Bridget Laurent painting. The paint bubbled up, then melted and ran toward the bottom of the canvas in a blur of wasted color. Carver could only guess what the spray did to fingerprints, to DNA.

He turned to the man behind him.

"There'll be nothing," he said. "Nothing left."

"Out."

He pushed Carver onto the porch. Houston and Roper were gone, as was their patrol car. His car was gone too. Down the hill, a pair of unmarked semitrailer trucks sat in the middle of the intersection with Grant, the only place in the area level enough for them to park. A black bus idled behind them. Sawhorses blocked both streets, yellow lights blinking in the rain. There were men in white spacesuits setting up lights on tripods, carrying chemical sprayers. Others were bringing out enough plastic sheeting to tent the block. Carver thought again of the Fairmont, all covered up in black silk. The man behind him gave him a push and he nearly stumbled on the stairs going down to the sidewalk.

In the street, a man in a heat-resistant, aluminized biohazard suit was strapping on a backpack frame holding compressed gas cylinders. A hose led over his shoulder to a nozzle gun. He passed Carver, adjusting the belt as he went.

"Carver?" Jenner said. He was rubbing his fingers together, as if they were asleep. His face was puffy. And gray.

“I don’t know,” Carver answered. “I got no idea.”

A set of metal stairs led from the street to an open door in the white truck’s trailer. There was a sign just inside the door, but its letters were washed out by the white light pouring from the truck.

“Up,” the FBI man said. He gave Jenner another push.

Carver watched his partner head up the stairs. Shivering, clutching his arms to his chest. When Jenner was up, Carver climbed the stairs too. Before he went into the trailer, he turned and looked back at the house. Two more men in spacesuits were going through the front door. He looked up toward the bedroom window. The bloody handprints were silhouetted against a blaze of firelight. They were burning it. Burning the man on the floor, and everything in his room. Cleansing with fire.

The man who’d rushed them out of the house reached up and slammed the decontamination unit’s door. Carver turned around. He was looking at a plain white wall, adorned only with a sign pointing men to the left and women to the right. He could still hear the chaos on the street, but it was muted by the trailer’s walls.

“Move to the left.”

A woman’s voice came from above, and Carver looked up. An intercom speaker was mounted in the ceiling next to a surveillance camera.

“Let’s go, Jenner.”

He took his partner’s elbow and led him along the wall to the left. Jenner was hot, and the sleeve of his jacket was wet with sweat. They stepped through the narrow doorway, marked STAGE 1. This room was the size of Carver’s bathroom. A lidded metal bin against the wall was marked with an orange biohazard symbol. One wall held a sliding steel hatch, like the night deposit box at an old bank. When they were all the way into the room, the door closed behind them automatically. Carver felt the air pressure change as it sealed.

“Undress,” the woman’s voice said. “Clothes in the bin.”

Carver looked at the ceiling but wasn’t sure whether to address the camera or the intercom speaker.

“What happens to them?”

“Incinerator,” the speaker said.

“We’ve got our service weapons, our badges. Wallets and phones. What about those?”

“Those go in the wall locker, for sterilization.”

Jenner looked at the bin and the wall locker, and then turned to Carver. His eyes were red and watery.

"This shit's for real?"

"I think so," Carver said. "Real as it gets. I think we better hurry."

They undressed, dumping their clothes into the incinerator bin. Carver saw Roper and Houston's clothes lying at the bottom. Dark shirts and pants. Rubber-soled shoes. Caps with their plastic rain covers still on.

"That clinches it," Jenner said, shivering. "They're definitely a couple."

"Must've moved them through here like a car wash," Carver said. "Like cattle in a chute."

"How long were we upstairs?"

"Five minutes."

Jenner nodded. Unbuttoning his shirt, he had to stop twice to scratch his face.

"Try not to," Carver said. "You'll get it in deeper. Whatever it is."

"It's like it's eating me, Ross."

"I know it," Carver said. It was too easy to imagine how it would go. The two of them thrashing around the trailer, beating on the locked door with bloody hands. In an hour, they'd be moss-covered lumps, barely recognizable as human beings. The air would shimmer with metallic gray dust, their bodies bursting into full bloom. "Just hurry. Try not to think about it. The guy said there was time."

They pulled off their latex gloves and their surgical masks, and stood naked in the small white room, beneath the camera's eye. Carver looked down at his chest. It was prickled with red dots, like a heat rash. On the opposite wall, there was a second air-locked door. STAGE 2. It hissed as it unlocked, and then it swung open.

"We supposed to go in there?" Jenner asked.

"Yeah."

They went over the threshold and into the second room. It was empty except for a stainless-steel column coming from the middle of the floor. Four shower nozzles pointed down from its top. The door closed behind them and then showers came on, blasting water and steam at the already wet floor.

Carver put his hand into the spray, then smelled his fingers.

"Not just water," he said. "Bleach, maybe. I don't know."

“Shit’s gonna make me look like you,” Jenner said.

“Could be worse.”

They each stepped beneath a nozzle. The liquid coming out stung on Carver’s skin, around his eyes. When he breathed in, the chemical steam burned hot in his nostrils, then inside his chest. He used his hands to scrub himself, checked that Jenner was doing the same. Toward the end of the shower’s cycle, pure water started pouring from the nozzles, a clean rinse unadulterated with disinfectants. Carver held his face close to the showerhead and let the water pummel his eyes and nose. His heart was beating so hard he could feel its pulse behind his clenched eyelids.

When the water switched off, he and Jenner stood across from each other, looking at the locked doors and the swirling steam. A set of dryer vents kicked on above them. They stood beneath the rush of hot air, using the sides of their hands to brush the water off.

Jenner had stopped shaking.

“Think that helped,” he said.

“Yeah.”

“It was getting to me,” Jenner said. “I don’t know what it was.”

“You okay now?” Carver asked.

“I don’t know,” Jenner said. “You saw what was up there.”

The door marked STAGE 3 hissed and swung open. Jenner watched it and shook his head.

“Feds,” Jenner said.

“They hadn’t come, it might’ve been you and me beating on that window. Same as the guy we saw, trying to get out.”

“But how’d they know?” Jenner asked. “How’d they get here so fast? They were just in the neighborhood—fifty guys with space-suits and flamethrowers? A decontamination truck? And what is that shit?”

“I don’t know,” Carver said. “I don’t know anything about any of this.”

They went into the third room. There were metal benches there, with plastic-wrapped bundles of hospital clothes lying on top. Carver took a packet and ripped it open. Pajama-style pants and a matching V-neck, short-sleeved shirt fell out. There were paper slippers, the kind you’d get at a teahouse in Japantown. They sat opposite each other and dressed. They had just put on their slippers when the fourth airlock opened. A person wearing a biohazard suit stepped through carrying a tray. The suit's faceplate was made of reflective glass, a silver-black void.

"Your guns and badges are in the sterilization unit. Your phones, too."

Carver realized it was the woman from the intercom.

"Are you a doctor?" Carver asked. "Or FBI?"

"Both," she said.

She set the tray on the bench next to Carver. It held two paper cups, each brimming with a yellow-brown liquid. There was also a hand towel, but Carver couldn't tell what was under it.

"Here," she said, handing Carver a paper cup. "Drink it."

"What is it?"

"You need to boost your immune system."

"That's what this does?" Jenner asked.

"Yes."

Carver sniffed it, then took a sip. It tasted like metal, like water that had spent years inside a dead radiator.

"You drink it all at once, it's easier."

"Fine."

"And you should hurry. The sooner you drink it, the better. You saw what happened to the man in there, didn't you?"

"We saw."

"Not many people see that without a suit and live. You're lucky. So drink."

This was madness, but there wasn't anything to do about it. Carver lifted his cup toward Jenner.

"Cleve."

"Ross."

Each of them drank. They set their empty cups down. Carver coughed twice; Jenner leaned forward, his hands on his knees and his head down. He shuddered and knocked his empty cup from the bench.

"What's in that house?" Carver whispered. "What does that to a person? Less than an hour, and he looks like that."

"A disease."

"What kind of disease does that?" Carver asked.

"And who called you guys?" Jenner added. His head was still

down, and he was speaking through clenched teeth. "Since when does the FBI contain outbreaks?"

"You'll want to sit on the floor," the woman said. "Your backs against the bench."

Carver searched the mirrored faceplate for any clue to her identity. But all he saw was his own face, Jenner huddling against himself as the drink worked into him. She wasn't going to answer any of their questions. She wouldn't tell them what was up there, or how they'd gotten here so quickly. He thought of the sparrows again, and that thing that they'd found upstairs. Carver had thought it was a bird until he'd gotten close enough to see its disguise.

"What'd you say?" he asked. "The floor?"

"So you don't fall," she said. "Hit your head on something. It'll be thirty seconds."

"That stuff up there," Jenner said. He'd taken his hands off his knees and was holding his clenched fists against his eyes. "We washed it off. Right?"

"Thirty seconds, more or less," the woman said. "And then you'll feel it."

But Carver could already feel it. The drink had tasted like liquid steel, but it wasn't any kind of metal. It was epilepsy in a cup. Spasms and chattering teeth. He slid off the bench onto the floor. Jenner had beat him there, was now bringing his knees up to his chest and opening his mouth in a silent scream as his body began to shake. Carver watched his own hands jerk against his chest, felt his jaw pop as his teeth snapped together and released, a dozen cycles in the space of a few seconds. The woman lifted the towel from the tray and picked up a jet injector inoculation gun.

"Nothing to it," she said.

She stepped behind Carver and pushed his head forward. His muscles were locked in a fight against themselves, his body a conduit for an electric charge that came from nowhere and went back to nothing. When he felt the muzzle of the inoculator against the back of his neck, he couldn't do anything.

"Really, it's just a little sting."

She hit the trigger three times.

3

CARVER LAY UNDER a blanket and listened to the voice.

He'd been aware of her for an hour, maybe two. She'd been reading aloud to him for most of that time. He was unmoored, adrift just above the rippling surface of a dream. Her voice was throaty and calm, beautiful in the pauses, when she breathed between sentences. He didn't recognize it, this voice, but was glad for it.

"The purpose is simple," she read. She drew a slow breath and turned the page. *"And it is this: to make a man do that which he would not otherwise do. To change his course; to alter his mind; to realign the world as he sees it, so that it is no longer his course, his mind, or his world – but ours."*

Behind her voice, there were other sounds, and with them, Carver placed himself. There was the steady whir of a space heater, the rattle of cables and wheels as an elevator moved unseen between floors. Fingertips of rain tapped against the window. He was in his own bedroom. The only thing out of place was the voice. The last woman who'd had a key to this apartment had slipped it under the front door on her way out. That was eight months ago.

"With some minds, and for some subjects, accomplishing the task is as simple as presenting the opportunity. But we need not concern ourselves with easy cases. This is a study of persuasion in extremis. Think of a young bride, seduced by a stranger in the apse of the chapel where, a minute hence, she is to be married. Forget whether this is a moral goal – obviously it is not – the question is one of tactics."

Carver opened his eyes and looked at her without turning his head. She'd rolled the leather armchair over from his desk, and angled the reading lamp on his bedside table so that it lit the pages of the book in her lap. He couldn't see her face in the shadows above the lamp, but he could tell by the shape of her silhouette that she was lovely. Behind her, through the slits in the wooden blinds, he could see the neon sign of the hotel across the street.

"How is the seduction accomplished, by what measures do we ensure success with each new bride—"

She looked up, then closed the book, keeping her thumb inside it to mark her place.

"You're awake."

"What's that you're reading?"

He'd never felt his mouth so dry.

"Letessier," she said. "The essays on persuasion."

"Never heard of him."

"Her."

"Her, then," Carver said. "Should I know you?"

"We're neighbors?"

He still couldn't see her face, but now he understood. She'd moved into the apartment directly across the hall from his three months ago. A week later, he'd gotten a letter meant for her box. Just a piece of junk mail. A catalog from a grocery subscription service. But it was hers, and he'd slid it beneath her door.

"You're Mia," he said. "Mia Westcott. You live in six fifteen."

"That's right."

She glanced toward the window and he saw her eyes narrow in focus. There was a bird on the ledge outside. Mia reached across and flicked the glass with her fingertip; the bird disappeared into the rain. She took the wooden rod and twisted it to close the blinds.

"What are you doing here?"

"I saw them carrying you in," she said. "When they brought you back. You didn't look good, and they were just leaving you—dumping you off, really—so when they came out, I asked if you were all right."

"You asked who?"

"The people who brought you back. I thought they were with the police too."

He nodded. The motion hurt. He'd been a boxer in high school and college. There were good fights and bad ones, and then, toward the end, there were fights he should have stayed out of altogether. This was like the morning he woke up and knew he'd never put on his gloves again.

"They were cops?"

"I don't know. They weren't in uniforms. I just figured, since you're a detective, and since they had you . . . You understand."

He didn't ask how she knew he was a detective. Maybe she'd seen a piece of his mail; maybe she'd caught a glimpse of his holstered gun. He pushed himself until he was leaning against the headboard. Under the covers, he touched his hip and leg. He was wearing pants. That was it.

"They say what happened?"

"You don't know?" she asked.

"I'm just waking up. Coming to, and seeing you here. You know what's going on, say it."

"You were poisoned. But I heard them say you'd be okay."

"Poisoned how? And with what?"

"That's all I heard. I heard them say it, in the hall."

"Nothing else? Was there an accident?"

"They didn't say. When I first saw you with them in the hall, I thought maybe you were drunk. But when I got close to you, later, you didn't smell like you'd been drinking. You smelled like chemicals. Not on your breath, but coming right out of your skin. Like metal, when it gets hot."

Carver wondered how close she'd been to notice a thing like that. He let it go.

"They told you to watch me?"

"They didn't tell me to do anything," she said. "I came out and asked if you were okay. They said you were fine and they left. But they left your door unlocked. So I went in, to check on you. And then I decided it'd be best to stay."

"When was this?"

"Friday morning. Around seven. That's when I heard them with you. I came out to see what was going on."

"Friday morning," Carver said. "Now it's what?"

"Sunday night."

He brought his hand to his face and touched his cheek with the backs of his fingers. Normally he shaved every morning, but he felt days of rough stubble.

"You've been watching me for three days?"

"Friday, Saturday, and today."

"You could've called 911, gotten me off your hands."

"I thought about it. But you told me not to."

"I told you?"

She nodded.

"Mostly you were sleeping. I read books. I'd go across the hall to my apartment for tea. Dinner and a glass of wine. I didn't mind."

She reached over to the nightstand and pushed the reading lamp back. Now he could see her better. She was sitting cross-legged in his chair. Jeans and a white button-up blouse. No shoes. Her dark hair fell across her scarf, which she wore in the Parisian style, wrapped and loosely tied at her throat. Before today, the half-dozen times she'd seen him on the far side of the lobby, she'd glanced away, and then looked back with a hint of a smile.

In return, he'd ignored her.

He'd worried if he didn't, sooner or later, she'd invite him in. There might be a bottle of wine, and that would just be the opening. He was good at starting things, but not so great at seeing them through.

And look at her: she didn't need to be broken. It would be a disgrace to do that to anyone. But with her it would be a travesty, like spraying acid on a painting. He studied her, weighing his next question. With the light beside her, she seemed to be glowing. Unbidden, he pictured her stretched nude beneath a black sheet. He looked away, ashamed of himself.

"You say I was sleeping, mostly—but I was talking, too?"

"Yesterday you were up a little," she said. "You drank some tea and asked me to help you stand. You walked to the bathroom on your own. I went across to my place, gave you half an hour, and then came back. You were in bed again, but awake. We talked a bit."

She opened her book long enough to see the page number, and then shut it again and set it on the nightstand.

"You don't remember any of it, do you?"

"No."

"I didn't think you would."

"When I said not to call 911, what did I say?"

She looked at her lap and Carver saw a touch of color on her face and her throat.

"I'm sorry," Carver said. "I gave you a lot of trouble."

"You were really out of it," she answered. She didn't look up. "You said I was beautiful. That I shouldn't call 911, because you wouldn't get better if you weren't with me."

She looked up at him.

"And you didn't call 911 right that second?"

"You weren't yourself," she said. Her face turned serious again, and she leaned forward. "You also said if you went to a hospital, they'd know. That it was safer for you here."

"I said that?"

She nodded.

"Did I say who I was afraid of?"

"No."

"The people who dropped me off, can you describe them?"

"Three men and a woman," she said. She looked at the ceiling and closed her eyes. "Late thirties or early forties, all of them. Two of the men and the woman were white. The third man was Asian. Japanese, maybe."

"Anything special you remember about them?"

"They were all business. I guess that's why I thought they were police."

"What were they wearing?"

"The men were in suits. Black, charcoal gray. The woman had a navy blue jacket, a matching skirt."

"If I found some pictures to show you, you'd recognize them?"

"Of course – you have pictures?"

"Not yet."

Mia's description would fit half the people at the Bryant Street headquarters, but it didn't match anyone on Homicide Detail. Jenner was black, in his fifties, and built like a pile of bricks. Ray Bodecker was sixty-four, and looked like he belonged in a back room playing poker. He'd spent half his life undercover because no one ever took him for a cop. And Lieutenant Hernandez wore navy blue blazers, but she was a long way from her late thirties.

If he could find pictures, maybe he'd have a start.

"What about you?" Mia asked. "What's the last thing you remember, before it goes blank?"

He had to think about that. He watched the space heater. The chimney in his apartment had been blocked up, but the old fireplace was still there. He'd put the space heater where the andirons had been. It cast an orange glow onto the firebrick behind it. It took him a moment to find the memory, and then another moment to place it. Once he had his hands around it, though, it didn't get away.

"Wednesday night," he said. "My partner and I were in Hunter's

Point. A couple kids got in a fight over bricks – kids out there, they steal bricks, to sell them. They trade them for food, sometimes. That's how bad it is, out on the edges of the city. They're squabbling over a plastic bucket of bricks, and this kid shoots his friend. When we get there, he's standing over the dead boy, and he's holding the gun to his own head."

"I know."

He looked away from the heater and met her eyes.

"I must've told you yesterday."

She nodded.

"You said Jenner tried to talk the kid down," Mia said. "Told him to drop the gun. But the kid didn't listen. He took three shots at you, and then he shot himself."

"That's right," he said.

He wondered what else he'd told her.

"And after that, what do you remember?"

He looked at the space heater, its orange pulse a lousy stand-in for a gas fire, which he couldn't afford.

"Nothing," he said. He remembered the kid's eyes, the flash of calm as he turned the pistol to take the barrel in his mouth. "That's the last thing. After we cleared the paperwork, I came home."

"You came here," Mia said. "I was still awake, reading. I heard you come in."

He looked at her book on the nightstand. It was about three inches thick and bound in leather. No one had books like that anymore. Even a paperback was a rare thing. The title, embossed in gold, was in French. He wondered if she'd been translating it as she read it aloud to him.

"When you got home," she asked, "you went to sleep?"

"Eventually."

"Do you remember what you did when you woke up?"

"No."

"Close your eyes," Mia said.

"Why?"

"Just close them."

He closed them. The floorboards creaked. She was moving the chair toward the bedside, coming right up to him. He felt her palm on his forehead. Her skin was cool. He was running a fever, probably. She was checking that, watching over him still, as she had been for three days. She kept her hand on his brow. He could have fallen asleep again, could have let another day or two slide away beneath him.

"What do you see?"

"Nothing."

"You can relax," she said. She smoothed his hair back from his forehead, then increased her palm's pressure. It was like being gently pushed underwater. "Please? Just relax."

He was too tired to fight her off. Moving away from wakefulness was like climbing down a ladder, rung by rung, toward the darkness. He stopped before he went all the way, holding himself in the between-space where he could always find the flickering film of images that played just before sleep.

"Ross?" she said. "What do you see?"

"The Fairmont Hotel. It's wrapped in black silk, the whole building. Tied up with ribbons, like a present. Chinese lanterns in the gardens. Red and white."

"What else?"

"Nothing," he said.

"Take your time," Mia said.

She hadn't moved her hand yet. It was still cool. The heat boiling out of him had no effect on her.

"A fire. There's a house on fire."

"Were you in the fire?"

"No."

"Do you want to sleep some more?"

"I think so."

"Do you want me to come back?"

"Please."

When he woke, it was still dark outside, but the reading lamp was on. He looked to his right. The chair was empty. He lifted the covers off and then sat up. He was wearing blue pajama bottoms that he'd never seen before. He looked at his wrists, expecting a hospital admission band. But there was nothing. When he stood, he used the chair for support. His bare feet felt tender on the floor, as if they'd never felt his body's weight.

In his bathroom, he found his phone on its charger. Someone else must have put it there. He normally kept it in the kitchen. He switched on the screen with a flick of his thumb and was surprised there were no missed calls. There was a text from Jenner, though.

Call when you're feeling better.

It was two thirty in the morning, but that didn't matter. Jenner would be up. Carver went back into the bedroom. He needed to eat something, needed to drink about a gallon of water. But those needs weren't priorities. Jenner was the priority. They'd always worked that way.

He sat on the chair and dialed his partner's cell. Jenner answered on the first ring.

"Ross – how are you?"

"Been better."

"I got the memo. Must've been some flu."

"What memo?"

"Hernandez sent it, after she got your note. Your email."

Carver swiveled the chair and looked through the gaps in the blinds. The neon hotel sign was blinking, descending one letter at a time in a flashing chain of red and blue light that led down the corner of the building.

Red and blue. Like the lights on a squad car.

He closed his eyes and put his hand on his forehead the way Mia had. He thought of red and blue pulses, racing against the dark. He thought of the city, fogbound in the night, each street curving away to a mystery. He remembered standing on a porch, seeing the siren light reflected in a young woman's hair. Beads of rain clinging to her, the colored light shining back like so many jewels.

"You there? Ross?"

"You were saying about the memo?"

"Bodecker and I, we were gonna come see you," Jenner said. "Bring you a casserole or something. But then we got the memo. Hernandez said you were strictly off-limits. Contagious, you know? We're running lean, we can't afford –"

"The email I sent her, you read it? Did I c.c. you?"

"Never saw it."

"Somebody told you about it."

"The memo," Jenner said. "It sounded like you and Hernandez were emailing back and forth. You okay, Ross?"

"I've been running a fever," he said. "I haven't been all here."

"You coming out of it?"

"Just about," Carver said. "Listen—when was the last time I came in?"

"Wednesday," Jenner answered. He lowered his voice and added, "The night with the kid."

"I've been sick since Thursday?"

"Unless you've been faking it," Jenner said. "How bad was it? Are we talking last-January bad, coma-in-a-hospital kind of thing?"

"Forget it—I'm getting better. You came in Thursday night?"

"I was in Chinatown. Thursday night, into Friday morning. Got a sit-down with Patrick Wong, finally. Talked about his uncle."

"I didn't call you?"

"First I heard about it was the memo."

Carver squeezed his temples between his thumb and his forefinger. This wasn't anything like last January. He couldn't see a way to reconcile what Jenner was telling him with the story he'd heard from Mia. He'd trust Jenner with anything, but Mia hadn't struck him as a liar. If she'd been telling the truth, he couldn't have been emailing Hernandez all weekend.

There were too many gaps here. And his memory was no help.

"Sorry I left you hanging with Patrick."

"Hey, I got it. Patrick, he was easy. But look, I can't talk. I'm stuck with Bodecker till you get back. You know how he is. So rest up."

Jenner cut the connection.

Carver stayed in his chair and looked at his phone. He turned it around and studied its polished chrome back. It was surely his phone, but it was cleaner than he'd last seen it. No fingerprints on the screen or the case, no pocket lint in the charging port. He brought it to his nose. It smelled like bleach and melting iron. Like some kind of disinfectant.

Ozone, he thought. *Out in the country, when a storm's coming.*

The thought came like a spider, scurrying from nowhere. He ran his hands along his chest, then down each of his arms. He wasn't sure what he was afraid of finding on his skin. It was pallid from three days in bed, but otherwise it was fine. He rested a moment longer, then braced himself on the windowsill and got up.

4

CARVER STEPPED INTO the hallway outside his apartment and looked both ways down the hall before shutting the door behind him. He'd found his keys on his kitchen table, in a pile with his badge and gun. His wallet and watch had been in the bathroom. He locked his door, then leaned against it to gather himself before crossing the hall.

There was a light on in Mia's apartment.

He could see it under her door, a thin glowing bar, and then he saw the shadow of her feet as she came down the entry hall. She must have heard him turn his deadbolt, which meant that either her hearing was exceptional or she'd been waiting for it. It was four in the morning, but when she opened the door, he saw she was still dressed.

"You're looking better."

"Showers help."

"You're okay to go out?"

"For a bit," he said. "I was going to look for my car."

"I'll come with you," she said. "If you want."

He nodded. There were things he wanted to ask her, and he was glad he hadn't had to knock on her door and wake her up.

"One second — I'll get my boots and a coat."

She went back into her apartment but didn't shut the door completely. From the hall, he saw polished cherry floorboards. There was a Chinese vase balanced on a lacquered stand. He wondered if she rented the place or owned it. This was an expensive building. He could only afford his apartment because his parents had left it to him. If Mia had a job, he couldn't guess what it might be. This was her fourth morning looking after him, and she didn't seem in a hurry to do anything else. In a moment she was coming back, her boot heels clipping the hardwood floor. She stepped out, locked the front door, and then put her other arm through the sleeve of her leather trench coat.

They went down the hall to the elevator, and she kept pace with him. She didn't take his arm, but he was worried she might if he went any slower.

Once they were in the elevator, he leaned against the rail to catch his breath.

"Do you ever sleep?" he asked her.

"Some," she answered. She buttoned her coat, then fixed her scarf, using the polished brass elevator door as a mirror. "I got a lot on Saturday. Sleep, I mean. On your couch."

"You strike me as someone who wouldn't mind some company," Carver said, though he wasn't sure loneliness quite explained the story she'd told him. She had to have some other reason for helping him.

The elevator doors opened and they stepped into the lobby. In the light, he saw that the color had come up again from beneath Mia's scarf, touching her cheeks and her ears.

"It's that obvious?" she asked.

"It was just a guess."

He took her elbow, turning her to him. They'd come to a stop under the chandelier, across from the security desk. If she wanted to keep him close, then he wanted her closer. It would have to be that way until he figured out who she really was.

"I'm sorry I didn't talk to you sooner. I should've. It's my loss I didn't."

"It's okay?" she asked. "What I did?"

"Of course it is."

"Then let's go find your car."

The guard was watching them, his glasses lit blue by the video monitors built flush beneath the desk's glass surface. He'd come back later, to talk to him. But he'd do that without Mia.

They crossed Grant Avenue, and Carver led them into a narrow alley between the Neptune Hotel and a bank. A hundred feet down, it ended in a brick wall.

"You're looking for your car down here?"

"There's a parking garage on the other side of that building," he said. He took his key ring from the pocket of his coat. "One of these opens that door."

At the end of the alley, Carver found the key that fit the lock in the steel door. He tried to open it for Mia, but could only pry it back ten inches. She took the edge of the door and swung it back effortlessly, then held it for him.

"You need to take it easy, Ross."

They stepped through the door into a concrete stairwell. The light fixture on the wall buzzed and flickered. Carver went to the first step and then leaned against the handrail before starting up. His whole body was sore, but in the shower he'd found no visible wounds. His skin was softer than usual. He seemed to be missing some of the hair from his arms, even more from his chest. There was no way to prove it; it was just a feeling. Mostly, he was exhausted, and had to stop to rest at every landing.

When they reached the third floor, Mia opened the door and he led them into the rows of parked cars.

"It's here?"

"Down at the end," he said. "The black Ford."

He started down the length of the garage, keys in hand.

"We're going somewhere?"

"I'll need to rest first. Unless you want to drive."

"I don't know how."

He stopped and turned to her.

"What— Seriously?"

"I'm from New York," she said. "No one in New York knows how to drive."

"That doesn't stop most of them."

They finished the distance, and then Carver stood behind the car. It was in his stall, over the charging plate embedded in the concrete floor. He knew he hadn't parked it himself. Its rear faced out. But Carver didn't do that. He was never in a hurry coming home, but he was often in a hurry when he left, so he always backed into his space.

"What is it?"

"Nothing," he said. "But stay there a minute."

He pulled back his jacket and unclipped the flashlight he kept with his shoulder holster. He switched it on and shined it under the car's front bumper. He wasn't sure what he was looking for. Tracking devices were so small now, he'd never find one on his own. Bombs hadn't gotten any smaller since he'd joined the force, but he didn't think there'd be anything like that. If someone had wanted him dead, he'd already be dead. They wouldn't have brought him back to his place, wouldn't have put his car in its stall.

He aimed the light through the windshield. The curved glass sparkled like the face of a fine watch. They'd washed it before bringing it here. Detailed it. He stepped to the driver's door and lit up the seat. The upholstery had been cleaned so thoroughly, it looked factory new. There wouldn't be any prints inside, no physical evidence at all. On the other hand, they surely wouldn't have cleaned it so well if packets of plastic explosives were wired into the batteries.

Switching off the light, he turned to Mia.

"It's okay."

He took out his remote and unlocked the car. Mia came around to the passenger side and they both got in and shut their doors.

"That smell," Carver said. "You said it was like hot metal, coming out of my skin. This is the same?"

"Yeah."

Everything he'd carried had come back with the same scent—his phone, his gun, his wallet. Now his car, too.

"You must've driven somewhere," Mia said. "To wherever it happened."

Carver nodded.

He powered up the car, scanning the gauges as the console lights came aglow. The batteries were full. Carver waited for the GPS to come online, then swiped through the menu with his fingertip.

"Jesus."

"What?"

"When I'm driving, I keep the tracking on," he said. "It's department policy. It makes it easier to testify. We can go back, figure out where we've been, and when."

He pointed at the screen. It displayed a blank map of San Francisco. A blue dot pulsed off Grant Avenue, showing their location. But there were no track lines tracing the history of his past routes.

"They cleared the memory," Carver said.

"Now what?"

"Start with what we know. The one thing we know."

"The Fairmont."

He nodded and slid the transmission into reverse, but he didn't take his foot from the brake. He leaned against the headrest and closed his eyes, his hands on the wheel.

"Ross?" Mia asked. Her fingers alighted on his shoulder.

"I need a minute. But there's some stuff I've got to ask you. You mind?"

"Go ahead."

"You watched me three, four days. You sat with me, read to me," he said. When he turned to her, she looked away. "For all I know, you bathed me. Dressed me. I don't know why."

"You said it already," she said. "You nailed it. I need a friend."

"Why me?"

In the long silence after the question, he could see the reflection of her face in the window glass, could see the tiny movements in her eyes as she worked through it. He wanted to give her another chance to lie to him. The more she talked, the more she might begin to contradict herself.

She turned to face him.

"You've been around a cat?"

"Sure."

It wasn't what he was expecting, but nothing ever was. Night after night, he talked to people while the blood was still wet on the walls. Questions in tenements and warehouses. On rooftops and in the backs of ambulances. No answer ever came directly back at what he'd asked. There was always something askew.

"You like them?"

"Cats?" he asked.

"Yeah."

"Not especially."

"Neither do I, but that's not the point. You go to someone's house — a dinner party, maybe — and there's a cat. Ten, fifteen other guests, and they all like cats. After dessert, when you're all in the living room having a brandy, where's the cat jump?"

"On me," Carver said, guessing where she was going with this. "My lap."

The last time he'd been to a dinner party like that, he was about twelve. His parents were the ones having brandies. His father had gone with other men to a library or a study. A gun room, maybe. His father's friends lived in houses with that sort of thing. Someone would have given Carver a club soda.

"Why's it pick you?" Mia asked. "Every single time, it picks you."

"I don't know," he said. He wanted to let her finish, let her try to explain it.

"Because you're not looking for cats," she said. "So you don't pay attention to them. You don't blow kisses at them, try to call them over with your fingers. You just ignore them, like they're not there. And in a cat's mind, that makes you the safest person in the house."

Her eyes held steadily on his now, and he hadn't expected that either. Most of the time, when his witnesses deflected a question, they'd look away. So her eyes were as interesting to him as anything she'd said. He lifted his foot from the brake and let the car slide from its space.

The rain eased for a moment as he steered out of the garage. A garbage truck was blocking all of Sutter Street as it wrestled with a dumpster, so he went farther down the hill until they were driving past some of the finer blocks close to Union Square. There were restaurants where you could still find a good steak from cattle that had walked on grass, the sun on their backs. The wine on offer was genuine, not counterfeit swill made of lab-grown grapes. They passed a jeweler's showroom built like a Greek temple, its marble façade held aloft by bare-breasted caryatids. Aphrodite and Themis, selling diamonds. Across the square, there was an SFPD roadblock. Red and blue lights pulsed and glittered on the shattered glass that blanketed the street and the sidewalk. He slowed to look at the crowd of uniforms.

"We'll go around up here," Carver said. "Skip past all that."

"What is it?"

"Smash and grab."

He pointed at the Vendôme, the marvel of mercantilism that had taken over the Macy's when he was a teenager—part of the ever-spreading Ønske empire. Every display window on the first floor was gone. A stripped mannequin tilted through a newly shattered opening, her plastic hand gesturing to the gathered patrolmen. Glass lay everywhere, the aftermath of an ice storm.

"That happens a lot?"

"In this neighborhood, a couple times a night," Carver said. "Sometimes more."

He took a right on Powell and accelerated up the hill.

"Before you got on Homicide, that's what you did—dealt with those?"

"Things were different when I was on patrol," Carver said. "We had other problems, in other places."

"How long ago?"

"Before you were born, I bet."

"Maybe."

Above Bush Street, they passed into the new blight between Union Square and Nob Hill. Carver could remember when this used to be a nice street, all the way up. It had been glittering windows and filigreed stonework, building toward the final extravagance atop Nob Hill. Now liquor stores with blacked-over windows anchored the corners. A string of underground clubs stretched between them, all marked by their red-painted doors. A girl in an open silk robe and black panties leaned against a parked car at the mouth of Fella Alley. Pulses of purple light and bass-heavy music slipped like smoke from an open door.

As they went up the slope, Mia turned to look down the side street, but Carver didn't need to look. He was here whenever the men got out of hand in the basement clubs. There was always something to get them started. The drinks were laced; the girls were underage. Once the knives came out, the men usually finished each other down there, tucked inside the cordoned-off private rooms. Sometimes they'd lurch up and end it on the sidewalk. Then he and Jenner would come, if it was their draw. Had they marked the outlines with something indelible, by now these blocks would be a collage of human anatomical possibility—spread-eagle bodies, men curled up like shivering infants, young women sliced into their constituent parts and scattered.

It hadn't been anything like that when he'd been a patrolman. Sex clubs tried to minimize the number of on-premises murders because the city would shut them down. So as a consequence, he'd walked his first beats in the sunshine. But San Francisco lived under a shadow now. Maybe everywhere else, too. He was too busy to get out and check.

He turned to Mia.

"When you were watching me, did you use my computer?"

"Of course not."

"Did I ask you to send any emails?"

"You asked me not to call 911. You didn't say anything about email."

"Did you see me send any emails?"

"You couldn't sip from a cup with a straw. You weren't typing anything."

"The people who brought me back, did you see them in my apartment, see what they were doing?"

Carver came to a stop at a red light. The rain started again and he turned on the wipers. As they swept across the glass in front of him, he felt a warm rush of longing. It bloomed in his chest, its delicate petals unfolding in the dark behind his ribs. He didn't understand it, couldn't fathom how a few raindrops and the arc of the windshield wipers could set this off.

"The light?" Mia said.

"What?"

"It's green."

He started through the intersection.

This wasn't just déjà vu. That was an illusion, some kind of mental stutter. Revenants of true memories blowing past in the storm. This was physical, and as distinct as a lover's fingertips in the dark.

He stared at the windshield wipers, waiting for the feeling to come again. Hoping it would come again – that slow-rolling wave of peace, carrying a desire as urgent as thirst – so that he could catch hold of it and place it.

He saw that he'd stopped the car, that he'd pulled to the curb. Mia was watching him.

"What was I asking you?"

"The people who dropped you off," Mia said. "I didn't see what they were doing inside your place. Two of them – the woman and one of the white men – were with you in the living room. They had you on the floor. The others were back in your bedroom, maybe. I couldn't see."

Carver started driving again.

"You saw all that through the peephole?"

"That's right."

"Someone used my computer," Carver said. "Or got into my email account, anyway."

"How do you know?"

He decided to take a risk. To give her a little information and see where she ran with it.

"I talked to my partner—"

"Jenner."

"—and he said our lieutenant sent a memo. I had the flu, is what it said. I was off-limits, contagious. And Jenner said I'd been emailing back and forth with Hernandez, the lieutenant. Giving her updates."

"Updates?"

"On my condition—how I was feeling."

"You've checked your email?"

Of course he'd checked his email. It was the first thing he'd done after getting off the phone.

"They were in my Sent folder. Like Jenner said. One on Thursday, three on Friday. Last one's from Saturday afternoon."

"You didn't email anyone Friday or Saturday. I was with you the whole time."

"That's what you said."

"Who'd do that?" Mia asked.

"I don't know."

"You'll report it? Tell your lieutenant?"

He shook his head.

"Why not?"

"Someone wants me to forget," he answered. "Wants me to think I was out with the flu. That I was delirious, writing emails in a fever. And it worked. I forgot it, whatever it is I'm not supposed to know. But they weren't perfect. They made mistakes, left a trail."

When she didn't respond, he slowed the car and looked at her.

"You were there, and they didn't count on that," Carver said. "And if I tell anyone what I know, they're going to start wondering if someone like you exists."

"Is it dangerous?" she asked. "For me . . . for either of us?"

She must have already known the answer. The real question was whether she knew more than he did.

"Not so long as I play along," Carver said. "Go about my business."

"That's just what you think."

"What I think," he said.

"Not what you know."

"At this point, I don't know anything," Carver said.

5

THEY CAME TO the crest of Nob Hill and saw the Fairmont Hotel rise above them. It was not wrapped in silk, nor was it tied up with red ribbons. There were no strings of Chinese paper lanterns winding through the boxwood hedges, hanging from the manicured cypress trees.

Carver turned onto Mason and then came to a stop beneath the hotel's porte cochère. He stepped from the car, putting his keys in his pocket as the valet approached.

"Sir?"

Carver flipped his badge holder open and held it out for the man. "I'm leaving this here a couple minutes."

The valet looked at the empty street, and then at Mia as she got out of the car and freed her dark hair from the fold of her scarf with a flip of her hand. Carver watched him think through a range of remarks. He must have thought better of all of them, because he finally turned his face down and addressed Carver without meeting his eyes.

"Go ahead," he said. "Sir."

Carver came around the front of the car and then walked with Mia to the hotel's main entrance. A uniformed doorman let them inside, murmuring good morning to Mia as she brushed by him. What they stepped into, when they passed through the brass door, was a jewel. A time capsule, shimmering like the evening star of the Gilded Age. Somehow that star had never set, as if the hotel and the city moved through time on different tracks. Just blocks from here, there were buildings without power, wary inhabitants navigating the fire stairs with candles and knives. But marble still stretched across this lobby floor, and gold leaf set off the coffered ceiling. Carver spotted a concierge desk between a pair of matched Corinthian columns, each column a single piece of stone the size of a redwood trunk.

"There," Carver said. "Let's talk to her."

The concierge was the only person in view, and she was asleep in a leather wingback chair, her hands folded across the front of her cream-colored suit.

They walked over to the desk and sat in the guest chairs across from the concierge. He watched her sleep a moment longer, waiting to see if she might wake on her own. Then he leaned over and rapped his knuckles twice against the desktop. The woman started awake, then smoothed her hair with her hands.

"I'm sorry – yes?"

"I'm not a guest here," Carver said.

He showed her his badge, putting it flat on the desk so she had to lean across to look at it. He watched her eyes, saw how they focused and started to scan it, then put it back inside his jacket.

"I have a couple questions," he said.

"Something's happened, here in the hotel?"

"Right now this is just background. Tracking down something I heard."

The woman looked around. The doorman had stepped back outside. The registration desk was empty. Helpless, she looked back to Carver. She was waking up fast.

"We'll help if we can."

"Of course you will," he said. "Something came up about one of your events. You decorated the hotel, wrapped it in black cloth?"

The woman breathed out and sat back. She smiled for the first time, not one of those joyless professional smiles, but something stirred by pleasure.

"Everybody knows about that. It was huge. But we didn't do it ourselves, the wrapping. That was an artist."

"When was it?"

"This past Thursday night. G. Franklin Pan – the artist – he and his crew started Monday morning. Then we had the ball on Thursday night. I was up seventy-two hours straight, handling it. But we pulled it off. It was unforgettable."

"There was a ball?"

"The Black Aria Ball," she said, enunciating the words so that he could hear the capitalization of each one.

This was beyond reverence. She might have been whispering to her lover. Then she blinked, as if she'd forgotten for a moment that Carver was there.

"The launch party," she said. "For the new fragrance?"

"That was here, on Thursday night?"

She nodded.

"Thursday night, and into Friday morning."

"I'll need any pictures you have – anything showing the hotel, with the wrapping."

"You want to see pictures?"

"To see them. To keep them. Whatever you have."

"I'm sure they're all over the internet. Everyone's been talking about the ball."

"Then we'll wait," Carver said. "While you go back and print them."

The woman looked at him, then turned to Mia. But Mia stared back coolly, not giving her any help. Finally the woman pushed her chair back and stood.

"I'll be right back, Officer."

"Inspector," Carver corrected.

She went to the registration desk and then disappeared through a door behind it. When she was gone, Mia reached across and touched his wrist.

"You must have seen it," she whispered. "The Black Aria Ball. You must have been here Thursday night."

"Or I went past it on the street – this lobby's not ringing any bells," he said.

He looked around again. He'd seen it as a ten-year-old, had managed to drink half a neat Glenlivet when his father wasn't watching. That was the only memory that stood out. He hadn't been back since. He was sure of that.

"You heard of it?" he asked her. "The ball?"

"I wouldn't hear about something like that."

"Why not?"

"I try not to go out much," she whispered. "I keep to myself."

Carver started to answer, then stopped. She didn't look like a shut-in. If she wanted, she could go to a black-and-white ball, a Black Aria Ball, and blind everyone she met. But thinking back, he'd mostly seen her in their building's mail room. Or near the front doors, where sometimes she'd hide in the shadow of a potted palm, waiting for a deliveryman. Before tonight, he'd never seen her dressed to go outdoors in the rain. Because the California current had collapsed along with the rest of the Pacific, it had been raining the entire time she'd lived in San Francisco.

"Looks like she found the pictures," Mia said.

Carver glanced up and saw the concierge coming around the registration desk with a manila envelope in her hand. After she sat, she slid the envelope across the desk.

"That was fast."

"Press handouts," she said. "We had a few left over."

Carver held the envelope open with his thumb and forefinger and looked at the first print. He nodded his thanks at the concierge and then turned to Mia.

"Let's go."

It was a quarter of five when he parked in his stall again. He and Mia retraced their path through the stairwell and the alley, then across Grant Avenue to the front door of their building.

"Go ahead," Carver said. "I need a word with somebody."

"Knock, later, if you want some tea," she said.

She had to understand he was sending her away, that he didn't want her around for this conversation. He wanted to have a private word with the security guard, but he was just as interested to see how she would handle a dismissal. She started for the door, then turned back to him and took his wrist.

"I could make you eggs and toast. Or if you'd rather have dinner, I could heat up a cassoulet."

"Seriously, Mia – do you ever sleep?"

"I keep my own hours."

She squeezed his wrist once more and then went through the door. She stood with her back to him, waiting for the elevator. When she was gone, he went in and checked his mail. A bundle of junk, the size of a brick, was waiting for him. He remembered nights standing here, shoulder to shoulder with his neighbors, each of them looking through the day's offerings: stacks of postcard-sized disposable screens, images lighting up and soft music playing at the touch of human fingers. Gemstones and real silk. Scotch whiskey casked a hundred years ago. A subscription service that could send cuts of meat, the bones still in to prove it was real. Tap the screen to your wallet and enter your PIN code, and if you had money left to spend, any of it could come to your bedroom window by drone. More than once, he'd looked up to see trembling hands beside him. Tears on his neighbors' cheeks; his own vision hot and blurred. But today he didn't have time for it, as if all desire had been scorched out of him.

He took the ads and dropped them in the empty recycling bin.

The guard put down his newspaper when Carver came out of the mail room. He stood up, taking off his reading glasses as he rose from his chair.

"What's up, Glenn?" Carver said.

"Mr. Inspector Carver," the guard said. "Where you been?"

"Flu," Carver said.

"You still got it?"

"I'm better."

"Not so you could tell," Glenn said. "What's going on?"

"Morning I got sick, I came home somehow. But I don't know how, and I need to know."

"Must've had it bad."

"You see me come in?" Carver asked. "I'm talking Friday, around seven."

"I was here – Friday, I was here. But I don't remember you coming through."

"I'll owe you, if you do a couple things."

"Say it."

Carver pointed at the ceiling, to the glazed-glass dome covering a security camera.

"The feed on that – it stores on a hard drive somewhere?"

"Off-site." Glenn nodded. "But I can access it from here. Every hour, it makes a new file."

"Can you email me a couple hours' worth?" Carver asked. "Six in the morning Friday, till about eight?"

"Easy," Glenn said. "Done."

He pulled a notepad from his breast pocket and started patting his other pockets for a pen. Carver leaned over the desk and took the notepad.

"You don't need to write it down."

"Okay," he said. "That's fine – I'll remember."

Carver handed the notepad back and the man put it in his pocket again.

"There was something else?"

"The woman I was just with," Carver said. "Mia. You know her?"

Now Glenn sat in his chair, its springs creaking alarmingly as he leaned back.

"I figure, that makes you the last."

"The last what?"

"Last man in this building, married or single, to ask what I know about her."

"They ask because you know, or they just, like, to ask?"

"I know a little."

"Then fill me in."

"She keeps to herself," he said. He was whispering now. "She talks to me, but it's just to ask favors."

"What favors?"

"I look things up for her sometimes – online? And I order things. She pays me back with cash. She doesn't like computers. Doesn't have a credit card."

"You're buying her what, exactly?"

"Groceries, mostly," the guard said. "I don't think she even has a phone."

"She asks you to make calls?"

"Takeout places, things like that. A repairman, once."

"That's it?"

"Pretty much. Listen, I didn't tell you this, all right? She trusts me, as far as that goes. But she's wary."

"Wary?"

"I'm serious, Ross. You can't tell her."

"You didn't tell me anything," Carver said. "And I didn't even ask. But you'll send me those files?"

"Before you get upstairs."

"Thanks."

He took the elevator to seven, then came down one flight of the fire stairs to his own floor, so that the elevator wouldn't chime in his hallway. There was still a light on under Mia's door, but she didn't come out. He knew he'd see her later, and that was fine. He'd surely have more questions for her, after he watched the videos. So far, nothing he'd learned proved that she was lying. How long that would last, he couldn't guess.

6

CARVER WAS IN the old study overlooking Bush Street, in the chair that had belonged to his father. He was tapping his fingers against the armrests, staring at a computer monitor marked along its bottom edge *Property of the SFPD.*

He scrolled the video backwards, to the spot he'd marked, and started it again. He saw the lobby, the security camera's fisheye lens getting most of it in the frame. Glenn sat off to the right, head down as he read something. The digital time stamp at the bottom of the image showed 7:03:58. Carver watched the front door. It opened at 7:04:01, and the woman in the blue jacket came in. She was holding a cellphone to her ear with one hand, and was using the other hand to shield the mouthpiece. When she came to the middle of the lobby she stopped and seemed to listen. Then she looked up for the first time and scanned the room quickly, but Carver couldn't see her eyes; she was wearing sunglasses.

Between the dark lenses and the way she was using her hands to cup her phone to her face, Carver couldn't make out any of her features. And that was surely the point. He froze the screen when she was staring directly into the camera. He'd watched the whole thing already, so he understood what she was doing. She'd needed to know where the camera was. She had to figure the angles.

He started the video again. The woman looked away from the camera, and then crossed the lobby toward Glenn. Now her back was to the camera and she was holding the cell phone in her right hand, beneath the level of the security desk. Seven seconds into their conversation, Glenn began gesturing. He pointed toward the door, then counted along the fingers of his left hand with his right index finger. One, two, three. Both hands went into the air, palms down.

Giving her directions, maybe. The image quality was too poor to read Glenn's lips.

Carver paused the video.

Of course it had no sound, but he thought an audio feed wouldn't have made any difference this time. She wouldn't have said anything worthwhile to Glenn. She was just distracting him. He looked at her right hand. She'd changed her grip on the phone, was holding it like a flashlight. Its thin edge was pointed directly at the camera's lens. He wasn't exactly sure what kind of phone it was, or pretended to be. It had to be linked with the sunglasses, though, and the laser inside it must have been powerful. A camera on the phone, feeding to a heads-up display in the sunglasses. It was the only way to explain what she did next.

He'd talked to inspectors who'd worked art burglaries, to FBI agents who ran counterintelligence. They had stories. The tech firms in San Jose and Palo Alto might have run out of ideas a decade ago, content to repackage the same goods in brighter boxes. But somewhere there were still active research labs. They just didn't make anything for the public. If you could believe the rumors coming out of the FBI, there were little autonomous bugs that could crawl through a building's air ducts and into its secure servers, rewiring and reprogramming them. There were drugs that could make a man talk and then forget what he'd said. A camera-killing laser disguised as a cell phone wasn't that hard to swallow.

He toggled the slide bar at the bottom of the screen to adjust the playback speed, dragging it all the way back. Then he hit play again, and watched her. The video crawled frame by frame. She never turned her head, never looked away from Glenn. But with her right hand, she was fine-tuning her aim. Once she had it locked in, she didn't move a finger. She must have triggered the laser with her eyes, selecting the switch with a glance on the heads-up display, pushing the button with a practiced blink behind her dark lenses.

Glenn wouldn't have seen anything.

And after she switched on the laser, Carver couldn't see anything either. In the last visible frame, she was leaning against the desk, talking to Glenn. The next frame was pure white. The camera's photosensor was about to burn out.

Carver backed up the video and replayed the second before she turned on the beam. This time, he didn't focus on her hand, didn't try to read Glenn's lips or make sense of his gestures. He watched the brass door. In the two frames before everything washed away to white, he saw that it was opening, saw the shadow gathering at the threshold.

Then the screen went white, and it stayed that way for twenty-nine seconds, which was just long enough. Three men could have dragged Carver across the lobby, hit the elevator button, and stepped into the car. There weren't any cameras in the elevator. At the security desk, the woman had Glenn's full attention.

Carver sat and watched the white screen, watched the seconds tick past. When the colors came back, the woman still faced away from the camera. She was leaning on the security desk, talking to Glenn. She must have made a joke, because Glenn started to laugh. Then she turned, bringing her cell phone back to her ear, covering half her face again as she pretended to shield the microphone with her hand. She crossed to the elevator without looking at the camera, and twenty-five seconds later, the doors opened and she stepped out of view.

Carver scrolled to the beginning and watched it again.

He woke at eight o'clock in the evening, still in his father's chair. He couldn't remember falling asleep, but now that he was awake again, he understood what he had to do. The lost days clung to him, as persistent as the smell of hot iron seeping from his pores. Maybe that was why he'd been moving so slowly: the poison hadn't fully left his system. But he couldn't wait any longer. He needed to go in. The only way out of the dark was to talk to Jenner and Hernandez and then follow it from there. There'd been a crime and a cover-up. It wasn't so different from what he saw any other day, except that this time, it had happened to him.

7

WHILE PULLING OUT of his narrow parking space, Carver's hand bumped something between the seats. He hit the brakes, then shifted the transmission to park. Before he even looked, he knew what he'd touched. It shouldn't have been there. He unclipped the thermal scope from its mount and turned it around to examine it. After a moment, he switched it on and put it to his eye, scanning around the garage.

The concrete walls were too thick to get a read-through, but he could tell a handful of the cars had been driven recently from the glow of fading warmth radiating from their electric motors. The scope worked, and that was all he needed to know it wasn't his. He didn't need to check the serial number. He'd shattered his on Wednesday night, diving for the asphalt, the kid's bullets ricocheting off the pavement and whining into the dark like bees. The last thing he'd done that night was drop the pieces off with Equipment and fill out the paperwork for a replacement. So this couldn't be his. But when he brought it back up and smelled the textured metal grip, he knew it must have been with him on Thursday night.

It was cool to the touch, but it smelled like an iron skillet hot enough to smoke. It didn't make any sense at all, but at least it fit the building pattern.

At the Bryant Street headquarters, Carver made it through the first floor and to the elevators without talking to anyone but the Ønske Corporation guard the commissioner had contracted to run the backscatter x-ray. The man set down his magazine long enough to check Carver's badge and wave him through. As soon as he got to the Homicide Detail's corner on the fifth floor, he knew Jenner was in.

There was a light behind the frosted glass window of their shared office. As he came closer, he caught the murmur of a radio. A throaty torch singer, the kind of stuff Jenner liked to see at the club on his nights off. Carver turned the knob and put his shoulder to the door – it hadn't fit properly in its frame since last year's earthquake – and stepped inside. Jenner looked at him, then glanced sideways at the three-foot stack of files leaning from Carver's chair.

"I'll clear that."

"I can stand," Carver said.

"Sure," Jenner said. He switched off his radio. "But you'd better sit."

Jenner came around his desk and put the files on the floor. He wheeled the chair across the office and didn't speak until Carver was sitting.

"Sorry for that."

"For what?" Carver asked. "Carrying my weight the last three days?"

"I don't know," Jenner said. "I don't know how much I carried. You remember what I said about Patrick Wong?"

Carver nodded. His neck was still stiff. He twisted his chin left, then right.

"You got a sit-down with Patrick," Carver said. "Had a talk about his uncle."

"Last night, when we talked – when you and I talked – I remembered it clear as anything."

"But now?"

Jenner tapped his fingertips against his temples.

"Now I got nothing. And I can't find my notes."

"That's what this is?" Carver asked, pointing around the office. "You're tossing the place, looking for the notes?"

There were stacked binders on both desks, and leaning columns of folders along the walls. The drawers to the filing cabinets were open and empty.

"Any interview, I always take notes," Jenner said. "During and after."

"You remember taking them?"

"Taking them, sure. We were sitting in the lounge. That booth in the back, by the fish tank?" Jenner looked up, waiting for Carver to nod before he went on. "I had the notepad on the table. Took a napkin, swiped the table before I put the pad down, so it wouldn't get grease spots. But what I wrote? I can't remember that at all."

"That ever happened before?"

"Not like this," Jenner said.

"You think someone came in, took your notes?"

"I don't know."

"You don't remember what he said?"

Jenner shook his head.

"Ross – it's not just that. I don't even remember what I asked him. But I know I talked to him," Jenner said. "Me and Patrick, in the lounge. After closing. I talked to him."

Carver tried to understand. He'd never seen his partner's eyes turn to the floor to avoid a glance, had never seen him rub his fingertips into his scalp as if searching for the hair that had abandoned him a decade ago. If Jenner had been on the other side of the table in the interrogation room, Carver would have known what to do. When his suspect started acting like that, it was time for the kill.

But this was Jenner, so Carver stepped back and gave him space to breathe. Besides, Carver knew something about this kind of memory, lost thoughts that slipped out of reach like an animal in the underbrush.

"The lieutenant in?" he asked.

"Left already," Jenner said. "Dinner with the commissioner."

"That's what they do now? Have dinner?"

"Between soup and dessert, maybe they'll come up with a way to privatize everything else in the building. Why stop with security? We could have coin-operated elevators, corporate sponsors for the urinals."

"You tell her about Patrick?"

"As soon as I got in, the next evening – Friday night."

"A written report?"

Jenner shook his head.

"Just the two of us talking, either side of a desk. Then she tells me to partner up with Bodecker until you're back on your feet."

"After you talked to Patrick, then what?"

Jenner was massaging the bridge of his nose with his thumb and two fingers.

"It was late. I went around for dinner, then home."

"Dinner at that place of yours?"

"Nothing like that. I didn't get drunk, if that's what you're asking."

"I'm just asking," Carver said. "What about the morning? How'd you feel when you woke up?"

"Like hell."

"Like you'd been in a fight?"

Jenner looked up, taking his hand away from his face.

"A fight?" He lifted his shoulders, then dropped them. There was a shiny patch on his dress shirt where his holster strap usually rode. Right now he wasn't wearing it; the gun was on his desk. "Maybe it was just a delayed thing. Reaction to the kid, to getting shot at. I don't like seeing it, kids like that."

"You remember going to bed that night?"

"What are you driving at, Ross?"

"I'm just trying to figure it out. Six weeks, we've been trying to get Patrick to sit down."

"You're saying it like I don't know. Like I'm not trying."

"I'll tell you what," Carver said.

"What?"

"We'll get my car, ride over to Chinatown," Carver said. "Grab a booth in the San Lung Lounge and see if Patrick Wong's around. If he showed his face on Thursday, maybe he'll do it again."

"All right."

"Find us a couple coffees first. I need one. I'll log in, make sure I'm caught up. Then we'll go."

Jenner nodded and stood. After he left, Carver waited until his partner's footsteps went all the way down the empty hall, and then he went to the desk and lifted Jenner's gun from its holster. He brought it to his nose, closed his eyes, and breathed in. It smelled so strongly of burnt iron and bleach that there were only hints of gun oil and spent powder from firing on the range.

Jenner had been with him that night. Whatever it had been, they'd seen it together.

He put the gun back where he'd found it, then sat at his computer and went through the motions of logging in. He entered his password and then leaned to the pin-sized camera for the retinal scan, but he was thinking of Jenner, and remembering waking up with Mia by his side. He was grabbing at the swishing tail of his own lost dream. The Fairmont Hotel, wrapped in silk, candlelight, and fog. That had been real: he had photographs of it, newspaper articles about the Black Aria Ball. It could be that Jenner's dream had been real too. But Jenner couldn't account for all his time between Thursday night and Friday morning. Maybe he'd been with Carver outside the Fairmont Hotel, maybe he'd been poisoned somehow and brought home by the same group Mia had seen. If that was the case, then Jenner had gotten back on his feet a lot faster than Carver had. That wasn't too surprising—Jenner was younger, and more cautious with himself. He didn't end up in the hospital once or twice a year.

Carver leaned back and stared at his computer screen. He didn't know if there were cameras in Jenner's building, wasn't sure he'd be able to casually get the video feeds if they even existed. There had to be some other way into the case, a path that would lead straight to its heart.

"You sure you're up for this?"

He looked up. Jenner stood in the doorway, holding two cups of coffee.

"I was ready five minutes ago. You get lost or something?"

Jenner handed him one of the coffees, then stepped to his desk and strapped on his gun. He pulled his jacket off the back of his chair and eased into it. Then he unsnapped the holster and put his hand on the gun's grip, tugging it halfway out to be certain there was nothing catching it, slowing his draw. He looked up and saw Carver watching.

"Patrick won't be jacked to see me again," Jenner said. He reseated the gun in its holster but left it unsnapped.

"Maybe he doesn't remember either."

"That'd be good."

Carver parked in front of a fire hydrant at the corner of Grant and Washington. It was raining again, but that didn't seem to bother the crowds of people walking deeper into Chinatown. Vertical signs clung to the buildings, advertising stores and wares in calligraphy Carver couldn't read. He looked at Jenner and caught him staring at the strings of red paper lanterns crisscrossing Grant Avenue. His hand was still on the car door and his throat was working like he was holding something in.

"See something?"

Jenner shook his head and turned to Carver.

"Nothing," he said. But he turned back once more to the lanterns before he closed his door.

"All right," Carver said. "Let's go see this place."

Jenner reached beneath his jacket again to check his gun. Then he and Carver walked down Grant Avenue to the San Lung Lounge. Three women were taking shelter from the rain beneath the bar's awning, their faces lit by the paper-thin glowcard advertisements they held. Every few seconds, one of the women would tap a glowcard against her cell phone to consummate a purchase. Discarded screens pulsed like LED embers around their feet, twinkling with soft music and looping videos. The ads were hawking perfume and jeweled watches. Vacations to artificial islands built on the ruins of bleached reefs. The women stood close together, but each had fallen so deeply into her collection of screens that it occurred to Carver he might be able to carry one of them off without the other two noticing. He hadn't bought anything since he'd woken on Sunday night. He hadn't even felt the urge. Now he recalled, with shame, how often he'd looked like this. Standing on a sidewalk between home and nowhere, lost in the cold glow while everything else slipped by.

They stepped past the women and came up to the San Lung's door, which was rimmed by three stone dragons curled into a half-circle. The steel gate was closed and padlocked. Behind the gate, a crack of light came from between the twin doors.

Jenner put his hand on the gate and gave it a hard shake.

"Patrick!"

"No way he can hear you."

Jenner shook the gate once more.

"Patrick Wong! Get your ass out here!"

Carver looked over his shoulder. One of the women had roused herself. She looked at Carver, then nudged her friends into the rain. They went up the sidewalk in a huddle, but only until they reached the next awning. Jenner didn't pay any attention to them. He was focused on the door behind the gate.

"You hear that?" he whispered.

Carver stepped closer, leaning against the gate's wet bars. He heard the slap-thud of a heavy cardboard box hitting the floor. Silence spread like a bloodstain. On the sidewalk, the glowcards the women had dropped began to dim out, their music fading along with the light. They were programmed to save themselves in the absence of human touch. Then, from behind the door, there was a shatter of glass. A wet-hollow pop, like a beer bottle falling from a shelf.

"They're cleaning the place out," Jenner said.

"There's an alley, runs past the back."

"You want to watch this door?"

Carver reached behind his back and pulled the spare set of handcuffs from his belt. He locked them above the gate's padlock.

"It's covered. We'll stay together."

They walked back to the intersection, turned left, and then hooked into the alley that ran parallel to Grant. There were storefronts even there. A furniture repair shop, a half-dozen jewelers. Carver could only guess at the trade of the others because he couldn't read the signs. The windows were dark and gated, and there were no people moving through the alley. But there was a white delivery truck parked at the curb in front of the San Lung Lounge's unmarked back door.

"I'll get the plate," Jenner said.

They paused while Jenner used his phone to snap a picture of the truck's rear bumper. Carver looked along the alley beyond the truck. One of the buildings had a recessed doorway next to its main entrance, probably leading up to second-floor apartments.

Jenner scrolled through a menu on his phone and hit a button.

"It's a rental, from Serve-All. That dump by the airport."

"We can hang back over there," Carver said, pointing at the sunken doorway. "Watch a bit, while you make the call."

"You okay, Ross?"

Carver nodded. "Could stand to catch my breath, maybe."

They hadn't walked more than five hundred feet, but he was winded. He thought of Mia. If she were here, she'd take his arm. She'd tell him it was time to go home.

Carver watched the back door of the San Lung Lounge from the sheltered alcove on the other side of the alley. Jenner stood farther back, where the light from his phone would be invisible as he spoke to the night clerk at the Serve-All Rentals desk. Beneath them, the shadows stank of urine. There were flattened cardboard boxes and blankets against one wall, where someone had built a nest. But that person was gone. Carver leaned against the wall and watched the back door, waiting for the spots to leave his vision. If this had been any kind of ordinary sickness, he'd have stayed at home another day or two.

Behind him, Jenner ended the call.

"Rented this afternoon. Guy's license said Joseph Lin. Same name on the card he paid with. One night only, returns it tomorrow."

"Nice," Carver said. He didn't turn away from the door. "You know someone down there?"

Jenner shook his head.

"But I can fake it."

The door opened and a man emerged. He wore pinstriped black pants and a white dress shirt, and was walking backwards, pulling a dolly loaded with cardboard boxes. He was built like a bantamweight boxer. A very young woman in a slim black dress came next, her hands steadying the top boxes, her high heels unsure on the broken pavement. They came to the back of the delivery truck and the man jumped up on the bumper and lifted the rolling door. Then he leapt down and started heaving boxes into the truck. He was done in less than a minute, and the two of them went back into the building without saying a word. When the door closed, Carver turned to Jenner.

"Recognize them?"

"The boy," Jenner said. "He tends bar. The girl I've never seen. Would've remembered her if I had. Too bad we don't have a scope. It'd be nice to see who else they got in there."

"Yeah," Carver said. He'd put the thermal scope in his glove compartment so Jenner wouldn't see it. He wasn't ready for questions he couldn't answer, and the thermal scope was near the top of the list of things he couldn't explain. "I think we're looking at a two-person job. A girl dressed like that? If Patrick Wong had a whole crew waiting inside, they'd have sent someone else to load the truck."

"All right," Jenner said. "You ready?"

"No, but I'm coming."

They crossed the alley and went to the door, which stood slightly ajar on a wooden wedge. Jenner pulled the door back and stepped through, his hand inside his jacket on the butt of his gun. Carver followed, letting the door slide shut against his shoulder blades so that it wouldn't make any noise.

They were standing in a storage room. There were empty metal shelves against the walls, dead cockroaches and rat traps on the floor. Everything that had been here a day ago was probably in the back of the truck now.

Ahead of them, in the bar's main room, the young woman spoke in Chinese. The kid answered her in English.

"Just shut up and hold the light."

She said something else in Chinese. Her whisper was sharp and quick, like a blade in the dark.

"I'm sorry. *Duibuqi.* Okay?" the kid said. "Please just hold the light. *Hao bu hao?*"

"Hao ah," she answered.

Jenner and Carver stepped out of the storage space and into a short hallway. The door to the men's room was propped open with a yellow mop bucket. Someone had used a crowbar or a claw hammer to rip out the drywall and tiles behind the urinals. Debris was scattered across the floor. They moved past the restrooms and came to the end of the hall. A curtain made of bamboo beads separated them from the bar. Jenner went through it and Carver followed.

A line of booths clung to the wall. In the center of the barroom were high, round tables. Some of the stools were knocked over, and others had been pushed aside to make a clear path for the dolly. Carver and Jenner scanned the room in opposite directions. The light came mostly from exit signs, and from a string of white Christmas lights wrapped around the empty liquor shelves. No one was in sight, but the voices had come from this room. Jenner glanced toward the bar and Carver nodded. The kid and his girlfriend must have been kneeling behind it, out of sight.

Jenner went up and leaned against it, like a man about to order a whiskey. He rapped his knuckles twice on the bar top.

"This place open, or what?" he said. "Patrick told me to come by. Said y'all make a *mean* mai tai. Real pineapple slice and everything."

The girl cried out and the kid stood up and whirled around, reaching for something behind the bar. Carver took three steps to the left and drew his gun.

"Don't," he said.

"That's right," Jenner added. He took out his pistol and laid it on the bar, his hand on top of it. "Easy now."

The kid raised his hands and looked at the ceiling, his eyes closed.

After a while, the girl stood up and raised her hands, too. She was looking at the kid, and her face was burning. She was holding a flashlight in one hand. Its beam shook across the paper lanterns hanging from the ceiling.

"You see what he was reaching for?" Carver asked.

"Crowbar. In the sink."

"Right."

"Why don't y'all come out, have a seat at a table?" Jenner said, his voice as low and as reasonable as ever.

But neither of them answered, and neither of them moved. The kid looked at Jenner. The girl never stopped staring at the kid.

"Come on," Carver said. He was holding his badge in one hand and his gun in the other. "I know at least one of you speaks English."

He aimed his gun at the young man's chest.

"What's your name?"

"Joe."

"That sound right to you, Jenner?" Carver asked. "His name's Joe?"

"Don't know. Maybe we'll have to run his thumbprint. Get this incident into the system."

"You know we can do that, right, Joe?" Carver asked. "Run it in a couple seconds, make a permanent record?"

The kid didn't answer.

"Come out and take a seat," Carver said. "And tell her to come with you. Or doesn't she speak English?"

"She speaks it."

"Just not to me, huh?" Carver said. He looked at her. "Ma'am, you can put the flashlight on the end of the bar when you come through. You don't want anything in your hands right now."

The bar was a U-shape that cut into the middle of the room. There was no swinging gate in the bar top, so to get out, Joe and the girl had to duck and crouch through a passageway near the wall. The girl went first. She chose a table near Carver and sat with her hands folded together. Joe came and sat next to her, but she leaned away from him and looked at Carver. Carver spoke to Jenner without taking his eyes off the girl.

"Want to check what they were doing back there?"

"I'm on it."

Jenner came around the bar and went through the tunnel. When he stood, he picked up the girl's flashlight. He aimed it at the floor, gave a whistle, and ducked out of sight for a moment. When he came up again, he shook his head and looked at Joe.

"What you got?" Carver asked.

"Kid pried up some floorboards with the crowbar. There's a safe underneath, set in concrete."

"That right, Joe?" Carver asked.

The kid just looked at the tabletop.

"Looks like he wanted to open it but didn't know the combination," Jenner said. "Got a stethoscope on the floor. Some steel wedges and a hammer."

"Really, Mr. Lin?" Carver asked. He saw the way the girl's eyes shifted and knew he'd scored a point on the name. "You can open a safe with a stethoscope? That's a neat trick."

"He can't," the girl said. When she looked at Joe, her nostrils flared and her face flushed red again. "He doesn't know what he's doing."

"Stop it," Joe said.

"I don't have to stop it. I don't have to do anything."

"That's right," Jenner said. "You work here, ma'am?"

"He does."

"What's your name?" Carver asked her.

"Samantha."

"What'd he do to get you into this?"

"Sam—"

"Shut up, Joe," she said. She turned back to Carver. "His boss left. Disappeared. Joe ran the bar without him, for as long as he could. He called tonight, asked me to help him pack it up. I came over, soon as I got off work."

"What else was I supposed to do?" Joe said. "I can't pay the vendors. I can't schedule anything. No one's paying me. Customers buy drinks with their phones, and the money goes straight into the boss's account. I had to shut down two nights ago. Let our cook and the waitresses go."

"Why not go cash only?" Carver asked. "Run everything straight out of the till?"

"Why not just hang out a sign that says 'Drink Somewhere Else'?" Joe said. "Who carries cash? How much cash do you have on you?"

"So you decided to clean it out," Jenner said. "You own this place?"

"Not him," Samantha said. "His boss."

"That'd be Patrick Wong," Carver said.

She looked at Joe, and Carver caught the question on her face. She didn't know his boss's name. That was good for her. Good for Joe, too: if he wasn't talking about Patrick when he was out with his girlfriend, then he was either very cool or he didn't know anything about the man who paid him. Carver looked the kid over and knew which way he'd bet if he could roll the dice on that.

"Yeah," Joe said. "Patrick."

"When's the last time you saw him?"

"Four – I don't know – maybe five weeks ago."

"You worked every night since you last saw him?" Carver asked.

"Yeah."

"That includes Thursday night?"

The kid nodded. Carver glanced at Jenner and then looked around the room. There was a booth in the back, near the fish tank. The koi were floating upside down at the top, and the glass surfaces were nearly opaque with green algae. They'd been dead a lot longer than a few days, but Jenner had mentioned them when he'd talked about his late-night Thursday chat with Patrick.

Jenner couldn't like where this was pointing.

Their eyes met again and Jenner shook his head, then nodded with his chin toward the kid. He wanted Carver to go on, wherever the trail went. Carver loved him for that.

"Patrick got family?" Carver asked.

"I don't know."

"Ever meet his uncle, Johnny Wong?"

"No."

"How about his business partners?"

"I don't know."

"Anyone tell you it was okay to strip the place? Punch out the walls and pull up the floorboards?"

"But – Patrick's *gone*. He owed us."

"That makes this yours?"

The kid shook his head and looked back at the table.

"You know where Patrick lives?" Carver asked.

"No."

"What if you need to get in touch with him? How do you do it?"

"Cell phone. He wants a face-to-face, he'll just turn up."

"You've tried calling?"

"The first two, three days. Now it just goes to voice mail."

"You said you can't pay the vendors, can't schedule deliveries. Patrick handles that?"

"Used to handle it," the kid corrected. "But not anymore."

"Business mail comes here. Bills and bank statements?"

"No."

"They get mailed where he lives?"

"I don't know."

"Who delivers the kegs? What company?"

"Golden Gate Beverage."

"That's here, in town?"

"In the Mission," Samantha said. "Everybody uses Golden Gate. They're fast."

"You can call any time, they'll bring it over?" Carver asked.

"Any time if you've still got credit," Joe said. "We used ours up. Patrick wasn't paying. So they stopped coming."

Jenner took his phone from his pocket and walked through the bead curtain. Carver heard him open the back door and step into the alley. The closing door cut off the first words of his call. Carver looked back at Joe and Samantha.

"You seen my partner come in here before?"

"Couple of times," Joe said. "I figured him for a cop."

"He was here Thursday night, Friday morning?"

"Last I saw him was Tuesday."

"You sure about that?"

"Cop comes in, I remember."

"You know why we're looking for Patrick?"

"Everyone knows about Hadley," Samantha said. "But Joe was still manager at the House of Shields when she was singing here."

"That right, Joe?"

The kid nodded.

"I wasn't here," Joe said. "But it got around—I heard the cops wanted to talk to Patrick. So he started coming less and less. If he came at all, it'd be through the back. We'd talk in the storeroom. Then he stopped coming at all."

"He ever talk about it? The girl, or why we're looking for him?"

"Never."

"You both work in bars," Carver said. "You and Joe."

Samantha nodded.

"You ever see the singer – Hadley?"

"No," Joe said.

"I did," Samantha said. "She had a two-week set, at my last job. Up near Nob Hill."

Carver pulled a stool away from the table and sat on it. He put his gun on his knee.

"What'd you think? About her singing. About her."

"She was good. And she was pretty. A lot of men would come to watch. A lot of the same men, each time."

He knew how true that was. There'd been two dozen men to investigate, and almost half looked like good suspects. Some of them were sick enough, they probably would've killed Hadley Hardgrave if they'd gotten the chance. But he and Jenner had patiently winnowed it down to one man. Johnny Wong. He wasn't just sick; according to the rumors coming out of Folsom, he'd had a motive. And Joe's boss, Patrick Wong, was the only key they had to finding him.

He looked up. Samantha had asked him something, but he'd missed it.

"What's that?" he said.

"Is it true?"

"Is what?"

"She looked like the Black Dahlia, when they found her. All cut up like that."

"The black what?" Joe asked.

The girl shook her head at him and looked at Carver. Her hands were still folded on the table, but she was leaning on them.

"It's true," Carver said.

"Even the face?"

She traced her fingertips along her cheeks, from the corners of her lips back to her ears.

"That, too," Carver said. "He did that to her."

He thought she might have shivered. She should have, if she knew what they were talking about. Joe tried to take her hand, but she swatted him away.

The three of them sat in silence for half a minute, and then Jenner came back. He stepped through the bead curtain and touched his temple. Carver glanced at the kids, and then toward the back door. Jenner nodded. Carver wanted to cut them loose, and Jenner didn't have a problem with it. It was Patrick they wanted, and Johnny. Not these two. But they were too good to let go without some kind of warning.

They deserved at least that.

"I'll tell you what," Carver said, to Joe. "You may not know anything about Johnny Wong, but I do. And Johnny Wong is not the kind of guy you want to rob. That girl, the singer, she found that out—"

"It was *him?*" Samantha asked.

He ignored her. He focused on Joe, because that was what they would expect of him. But he knew it was Samantha who would make the decision.

"He may not own this place. Not on paper. But he owns it in his mind. A guy like him, what's in his mind is all that counts. You can do what you want. But if I were you, I'd take the shit in the truck, and I'd put it back. Right where I found it. I'd lock it up tight and clear out. I wouldn't want to give him a reason. Not that he needs a reason."

They watched in silence as he took one of his cards and dropped it on the table in front of them.

"Call me if you need to."

He stood and started for the curtain, but stopped halfway. He turned and looked down at Joe.

"If you're still not sure what to do, ask Samantha. Ask her about the Dahlia. She'll tell you."

He thought of the way she'd traced her fingers along her finely drawn cheeks, toward her ears. He thought of the body in the moonlight at the edge of the redwood grove in Golden Gate Park. Her black smile, showing teeth as far back as the molars. Her pelvis and legs a meter or more away from her torso, the ants making a carpet on the grass.

He nodded again at Joe and left them that way, their hands on the table, their heads turned to watch him go. On his way through the storeroom, he heard them speaking in Chinese. Samantha was doing most of the talking. Fast and desperate. He didn't understand a word of it, but he could guess. He wondered if they'd take his advice. If they didn't, he hoped they'd make it through. He kicked the wedge from beneath the alley door, then pushed it closed behind him, feeling it lock from the inside.

They were safer with a bolt between them and the street. He wanted that for them, wanted them to have the thirty seconds it might buy. He looked up and saw Jenner standing with his hands in his coat pockets, the rain running off his bald head.

"You sit in the car," Jenner said, "and I'll go get your cuffs off the front. You could use some rest."

"The address – you got it?"

"I got it," Jenner said. "In the Richmond, down in the avenues. It'll take us fifteen minutes. We can go right now, if you want."

8

THE ADDRESS JENNER had gotten was at the corner of Twenty-Third and Geary, opposite Our Lady of Fatima. Half the signs in the neighborhood were in Cyrillic, but the church and the school beside it might have been built by Spanish missionaries.

"That's it," Jenner said, pointing at a building on the opposite side of the street. "Third floor, I guess."

Carver nodded but didn't slow the car. There were empty spaces along the curb in front of the church, but he didn't pull over. He wanted to watch the building before they went up and knocked on the door, and he didn't want anyone looking out an upstairs window to see a couple of cops idling a car and checking the place out. He went another block, turned north onto Twenty-Fourth, and found a parking spot alongside the St. Monica School.

"There's a good spot to watch, from the door of the church," he said.

"I saw it."

They got out and went along the sidewalk. Some of the streetlights were dark, and Carver noticed the access panels at the post bases had been pried open. The thieves must have ripped the copper wiring out. He wondered how much they could get for it.

"That can't be where he lives," Jenner said. "Guy like Patrick. Or else, why do it? Why work for Johnny Wong?"

Carver looked across the street at the building. The top two floors were apartments, maybe only two units per level. The curtains were dirty and the light from behind them was dim. There were shops along the sidewalk: a Chinese bakery, a Russian toy store that doubled as a notarial service, a dry cleaner.

"We even know what else he can do?" Carver asked.

"I was just making an observation."

"So was I," Carver said. "What do we really know about him? What do we really know about either of them?"

Jenner pointed at the church's front entrance, where there were deep shadows from the pilasters on either side of the door.

"That where you figured on standing watch?"

"Yeah."

They went up the steps and stood in the darkest places they could find close to the stucco wall. Carver knew that most detectives would have just parked at the address and walked straight to the building. But he was five years short of mandatory retirement—too old to walk into anything without finding out about it first.

"You see how to get upstairs?" Jenner asked.

"There's a gate. Between the toy shop and that Chinese place. Glass door behind it, probably opens to a stairwell or an elevator."

"Got a lock on it?"

"Yeah, but I can't see what kind."

"Here."

Carver looked down. Jenner was offering him the pair of compact binoculars he kept in his lapel pocket. He took them and looked back across the street at the gate.

"It's old," he said. "The lock, I mean. Looks like a pushbutton combo job. No electronics."

"Figures."

A modern gated building would have electronic keypads coded to open with a squawk from a police radio, or a close swipe of the RFID chip in a detective's badge. Even older buildings were upgrading. But that took money, and Carver didn't have to make a hard study of this building to understand its owner's plan. He was going to wring what he could get from it, then walk away.

"But you're pretty good with those," Jenner said. "You've got a way with locks."

"Sometimes," Carver said. "Which floor?"

"Third."

"And the unit?"

"It's three-oh-one," Jenner said. He leaned out, looked at the apartments, and pointed. "That'd be the corner, above the intersection."

Carver studied it. Three bay windows faced Geary, and three looked across Twenty-Third Avenue. All of them were lit. Carver brought the binoculars to his eyes. He found the windows and twisted the dial to focus. When the image resolved itself, and he could see the movement on the glass more clearly, he took a quick step back, nearly tripping over Jenner. He pushed the binoculars against Jenner's chest.

"Jesus," Jenner said. "What is it?"

"Flies. On the glass. Thousands of flies."

They were crossing the street, walking as fast as Carver could go. Jenner was in front, talking over his shoulder.

"You get us through the gate," Jenner said, "and we'll go up to the door and knock. No one lets us in, we'll pick it open or kick it down. Whatever happens once we're in, the DA won't jump on our asses. Exigent circumstance."

"She's probably never seen a case where the exigent circumstance is flies."

"I bet she's never seen that many flies. Shit, Ross. Nothing else, we've got probable cause on a health code violation. A serious fucking health code violation."

"I don't disagree."

They reached the gate and stopped. Jenner stood with his back to the building, watching the sidewalk in both directions. His hand slipped inside his coat, and Carver thought again that there was a reason they were the longest-lasting pair of inspectors working homicide. He could get up after a beating, and Jenner was usually smart enough to avoid whatever got thrown his way.

"See if you can't open that thing," Jenner said.

Carver crouched in front of the gate and used his flashlight to illuminate the lock's face. There was a row of ten brass buttons. Any engraved numbers had long since worn off. But he'd seen these locks before. Zero was on the left, and nine was on the right. You hit a four-digit code and felt a click on the last button, and then the gate would swing out when you pulled it.

"You got any ideas?" Jenner asked.

"I don't know."

He reached to the numberless lock and punched what he guessed was *8-0-0-0*. Something clicked behind the faceplate. Carver pulled the gate, and it swung out.

"How the hell?" Jenner said.

Carver stood, feeling his knees pop as he came up from the crouch.

"The old Richmond District police station," he said. "Used to be at Sixth and Geary. That was its phone number – the last four digits."

"That's how they did it back then, to let the cops in?"

Carver nodded. He held the gate back for Jenner.

"After you."

"Put the junior guy on point," Jenner said. "Sure."

"Wiseass gets shot at a few times, he'll get perspective."

"There you go."

Jenner opened the glass door and they stepped into the small lobby. A plastic plant and a metal trash can flanked the elevator. There was a stairwell, but the door was locked when Carver tried it. Jenner was standing in front of the brass mailboxes.

"No names," he said. "Just numbers."

"Anything in it?"

Jenner poked his finger through the metal slot.

"It's full," he said. He hooked his finger farther into the box and began fishing out the top piece of mail. "We'll just take a look, put it back."

"Fine."

What Jenner slid from the box was a postcard-sized Interruption of Delivery Notice. He handed it to Carver and the flexible glowcard screen lit up. Patrick Wong's name flashed in bright red print.

"The mail has to stack up three weeks before these go out," Carver said. He passed it back.

Jenner turned it over and looked at the time stamp.

"It went out last Thursday."

"So we're looking at a month, maybe," Carver said.

"Fits what the kid told us."

"Let's go see."

They stood outside the door to 301 and listened to the flies buzzing on the other side. Carver could hear them tapping against the wood. He looked down. Someone had sealed the outside of the door with clear packing tape, covering the gap at the bottom and then going all the way around the jamb.

"That's a new one," Jenner said. "Keeps the smell in, I guess."

"Hard to make it look like an accident or a suicide if it's taped from the outside."

"You'd think his neighbor would've said something."

Carver looked down the hall.

"I don't think his neighbor's saying anything."

Jenner followed Carver's glance, saw the tape wrapped around the neighbor's door.

"Shit," he said, then turned back to 301 and hammered on it with the side of his fist.

"Patrick Wong!"

The buzzing reached a crescendo, as if ten thousand flies had taken to the air. Carver and Jenner looked at each other. The only sound from the other side of the door was the flies. No one was coming in response to the knock. They went to the neighbor's door and tried there, too. If anything, the flies in 302 were louder.

When Jenner was finished photographing the tape seal, Carver took the leather kit from the crime scene bag and knelt with it in front of the doorknob. He looked at the lock, then selected a metal forcing tool and a pair of vise grips from the kit's selection of picks. The first tool didn't fit the lock, but his second choice did. When he held it with the vise grip and twisted, he could feel the deadbolt sliding back. His stomach was sliding too. The flies were humming behind the door, and though he couldn't smell anything yet, he knew what was coming.

"Okay," he said.

He stood up and put the kit back in its place. He was already wearing latex gloves and a surgical mask. He'd wiped menthol cream under his nose.

"You rolling?"

Jenner tapped the side of his safety glasses with his fingertip. The pen-sized camera was clipped to the frame.

"Rolling," Jenner said. "Started with you opening the lock."

"All right."

He checked his own camera and then turned to the door. The taped seal broke in a prolonged rip, and then the flies were swarming out into the hall. They were fat and had shiny, green-black bodies.

"Blowflies," Jenner said. "Corpse eaters."

Carver brushed a dozen of them off his arm and then stepped into the apartment. The smell inside was as thick as the flies. Carver's eyes blurred with tears and he heard Jenner choke back a cough. They left the door open and walked into the apartment, letting the flies billow out. The death smell was so strong that it seemed to color the air. They'd entered into the living room, which was lit by table lamps, and there were flies moving across the lampshades. Every surface crawled with their shadows. There was a red and white Chinese carpet on the floor. It might have been valuable once, but definitely wasn't anymore.

There were two dead bodies on it, laid out side by side. They were probably nude, but it was hard to tell – because of the flies, and because of what the flies had done to them. The woman had been cut in half at the waist, and both their faces had been carved with Glasgow smiles that reached their ears.

"Did Patrick Wong have a wife?" Carver asked. "A girlfriend?"

"I don't know."

"Maybe both," Carver said. He took one step closer and looked down. "He's wearing a ring, but she isn't – you think that's even him?"

"Could be. Body's about the right size."

A fly landed on the inside of Jenner's safety glasses. He swatted it away, knocking the glasses askew on his face.

"Fuck this," Jenner said. "We need moonsuits. We need the ME van and a camera crew."

"We'll check the rest of the place first, and then the next apartment. We should at least tell Hernandez the right number of bodies when we call it in."

Jenner nodded, and they went back to work.

9

THEY'D SPENT HALF an hour going over Patrick Wong's apartment, and then they'd picked the lock on 302 and found Patrick's neighbor.

She hadn't been cut in half or sliced up: she'd just been shot once in the forehead. They'd found her in her bed. There'd been a lump under the blankets, near her side. They'd lifted the blankets back, releasing flies and all sorts of wriggling things that had never until that moment seen light. They stood looking at the woman and what had died next to her. There was a photograph of a dog on the woman's nightstand, but the body was too decayed to know for sure if that was it. The flies were everywhere. Crawling on their faces, trying to get under their masks.

They'd called Hernandez and then stayed on the scene to coordinate with the ME and the forensic technicians. They'd gone downstairs to wake the neighbors. No one could remember when they'd last seen Patrick. No one knew anything about the woman who lived with him, or about the woman down the hall.

Now he and Jenner were changing into their workout clothes in the Bryant Street headquarters. The three bodies were downstairs in the morgue, waiting in the cold storage chamber for their turn on the autopsy table.

It was four thirty in the morning when Carver's cell phone rang. He picked it up and glanced at Jenner.

"It's Hernandez," he said.

"Then you better."

He swiped the screen to take the call.

"Carver," he said.

"Jenner's with you?"

"Yeah."

"You back in the building?"

"In the locker room."

"I need you both in my office."

"Give us five minutes."

"I'll give you one."

She hung up.

"You catch that?"

"Yeah," Jenner said. "Here it comes. The shitstorm."

They finished dressing without saying anything else, and then they came out of the locker room and went to the elevators.

Carver tapped twice on the frosted-glass window. Hernandez's name was printed on it in gold letters, the paint almost new.

"Come."

He opened the door and they went in.

"Good morning, Lieutenant," he said. He looked to his right and saw the chief medical examiner in the chair opposite Hernandez's desk. "Dr. Alexander."

"Come in and close the door," Hernandez said.

He stepped the rest of the way in, and Jenner followed. There was only one free chair, so they stood with their backs to the door.

"Dr. Alexander was just giving me some preliminary findings. And I wanted you to hear it," Hernandez said. She looked at the ME and said, "Tell them what you just told me."

When Erika Alexander turned to them, Carver understood the position she was in. She was smart enough to know something was wrong, but she didn't have enough facts to know what it was. *That makes two of us,* Carver thought.

"I haven't done the autopsies yet. But I already got an ID on the male. Patrick Wong had a DNA profile on the system. A sexual assault, ten years back. So the lab ran that."

"A match?" Jenner said.

Dr. Alexander nodded.

"I haven't identified the women. But the man is definitely Patrick Wong. And then the other thing I mentioned to the lieutenant was time of death. You know I can't be exact with that. But it's got to be at least a month. The forensic entomologist will tell us more, but at these temperatures, blowflies take around four hundred hours to develop from an egg, through the maggot phase, and into a fly—you figure two weeks, per generation."

"There was more than one generation?"

"Three, maybe. And another one well on its way—I understand the room was full of flies?"

"You got that right," Jenner said.

"So we know it's Patrick Wong, and we know he's been dead at least a month," Hernandez said.

"Correct."

"Thanks, Erika," Hernandez said. She pointed to the door. "I don't want to keep you."

Once she was gone, Hernandez motioned for Jenner to shut the door again. She nodded at the empty chairs, and they took them.

"Okay, Jenner," she said. "You heard her, and you know what it means. So explain yourself to me."

"I can't."

"Can't, or don't want to?"

She waited for him to answer, but he didn't.

"On Friday, you told me you spent Thursday night talking with Patrick Wong about Johnny Wong."

Jenner nodded.

"Does Patrick have a twin brother?"

"No."

"You've seen Patrick before. Interrogated him, even, after some of those old arrests. You remember what he looks like?"

"Yes."

"So if you were talking to a guy on Thursday who wasn't Patrick Wong, you'd know it, right? And you couldn't have been talking to Patrick Wong on Thursday because he was dead. Really dead."

Jenner nodded again.

"I want to see your notes. Did you even take any?"

"I don't know," Jenner said. "I thought I did, but I can't find them."

"You can't find them? Did this even happen? When you talked to me on Friday, were you lying, or just hallucinating? I mean, it's got to be one or the other, right? And neither's good for a man who walks around the city with a gun."

"I wasn't lying," Jenner said. "I told the same thing to Carver on Sunday, and he—"

"We'll get to Carver. We'll get to him right now."

"What about me?" Carver asked.

"Where to even start?" she said. "You say you're sick. You email Friday morning, but no one saw you on Thursday night, even though you and Jenner were on duty. You've never taken a sick day unless you're checked into a hospital. Not once, in thirty-five years."

Now it was Carver's turn not to answer. Like Jenner, he couldn't explain himself. And like Jenner, he didn't want the lieutenant to know how deep the rabbit hole went. He didn't know whom he could rely on. He'd worked with Hernandez for only the last year and a half. She was a fine lieutenant, but he didn't know enough about her to trust her.

"So I start to wonder: What are these guys up to?" she said. "And luckily for me, there's an easy way to check. I remote logged in to your car's GPS, to find out where you've been."

Jenner looked up. "You're allowed to do that?"

She ignored him.

"Do you know what I found?"

"The memory was cleared," Carver said.

"That's against policy, and you know it," she snapped, raising her voice for the first time. "How am I supposed to convince anyone—the commissioner—that you're not covering your tracks?"

"I didn't clear it."

"Then who did?"

"If you can log in to it remotely," Jenner said, "it could've been anyone—it could've been you."

She leaned back in her chair and put her palms flat against her desk blotter.

"You're two of my best inspectors. I don't think you're killing off gangsters, a couple rogue cops. I don't think it, but I don't know it. I *do* know you're not telling me something, and I know I'm not going to get it out of you. And the commissioner isn't giving me any breathing room here."

"There are seven commissioners," Carver said. "In case you forgot."

"And only one matters," she answered. "But maybe you don't appreciate that."

He appreciated very little about Lyndon Ivies. He'd seen the black motorcades going north over the bridge, shadowed from above by helicopters. He'd watched the other commissioners and the mayor turn into nodding sycophants, diminishing a little more each year until they were as thin as the papers they rubber-stamped. A river of money must have been flowing through the city government, but Carver didn't know where it was coming from or what it was buying, aside from cops and limousines. There were stories around the station, of course. If you wanted to moonlight, and if you could keep your mouth shut, you could do well for yourself. There were guys thirty years younger than him, still in uniform, buying new condos in the high-rises south of Market. But none of those men were too clear about who they were working for, or what they were doing to earn their upgraded lifestyle. If Ivies had a patron, Carver didn't know who it was. Not that he'd pressed hard, or made much of a point of trying to learn. If he started getting answers, then he'd have to make decisions.

Maybe he'd been too complacent about the way things were. He was just Inspector Ross Carver, Homicide Detail. He wasn't dirty, but he got his hands bloody now and then. Whenever he did, the City thanked him for his good work. No one ever sat him down and gave him the big picture, and that was just fine. He could come home, and sit in his father's chair, and not have any regrets. Until now, that had been enough.

"It was Ivies, wasn't it?" Carver asked. "He told you to check the GPS."

She shook her head.

"I'm not going to say yes, and I'm not going to say no. But I'll tell you one thing he did say: If you two don't have a rock-solid explanation for everything we just talked about, I'm putting you on administrative suspension. So I'll have that story, right now, or I'll have your badges and weapons. I don't like it any more than you do, but there it is."

"Is this a real suspension?" Carver asked. "Because it sounds more like something Ivies cooked up. Unless we get a hearing."

"Forget the union and your hearing. This will be real enough once I have your badge."

Carver looked at Jenner. They didn't have a story that would satisfy Hernandez. They didn't even have a story that satisfied themselves. It was like every interrogation room he'd ever seen: if they opened their mouths, they'd make it worse. Jenner's nod was almost imperceptible. At least they understood each other. They always had. This time it was especially easy to agree; there was no other choice.

Carver's gun was underneath his hooded workout sweatshirt. He unholstered it and set it on Hernandez's desk. Then he put his badge next to it. Jenner did the same, and they went to the door.

Carver turned and leaned in before he closed Hernandez inside her office.

"Call me when you need us back," he said.

They were in the parking garage behind the entrance to the morgue. They had stopped in a dark circle where one of the overhead lights was broken. Carver couldn't remember the last time he'd been outside his apartment without the small tug of his gun on its holster.

"You want to go somewhere, get a cup of coffee?" Carver asked.

Jenner shook his head.

"I need to go home and cook breakfast. Rosaline's dropping Cora off at seven. I get her today – she spends the night. I can't fuck it up."

"Then I'll call you tomorrow. I might know more by then."

"You know something I don't?"

"Maybe."

"You gonna call Henry Newcomb and get his take on the bodies?"

Henry Newcomb, the former chief medical examiner, was the father of an old friend of Carver's. His son was gone, but Henry was where he'd always been, shuffling around his house on Bay Street and breathing oxygen through a tube.

"I never call him – we only talk face to face. And before I bother a ninety-year-old man, I'll see if my lead pans out," Carver said. "Something happened to us on Thursday night. I don't know what it was, or if it's tied to what we saw tonight. But we're going to find out."

"You think the lieutenant's part of it?"

"I don't know," Carver said. "Maybe it happened to her, too. You smell it in her office?"

Jenner looked up, recognition and relief on his face.

"Like burnt metal," he said.

"You've been smelling that since Friday?"

"Yeah."

"Me too," Carver said. "It's on everything."

"It was on the crime scene bag," Jenner said, quietly. "Not just on it, but *in* it. There's only one reason we'd have had that out."

"We were at a scene," Carver answered. "We had a body. And then something happened. We'll figure it out. But when we meet up next, be on your toes—and just go with me on it. You're going to walk in on the middle of something, and you'll have to figure it out. You get me?"

"I get you."

"See if you can pick up a couple of burners. We'll need a way to talk."

"All right."

Jenner held out his hand and they shook.

Carver stepped into the hallway outside his apartment at five thirty. The winter sun wouldn't be up for two hours. As he was putting the key into his lock, he heard Mia's door click open. He turned.

"Ross," she said. She was leaning from behind the door, and he couldn't tell if she was dressed or not. "You've had a long night."

He pulled the key from the lock and pocketed it. He didn't know what to say to her.

"Why don't you come inside?" she asked. "I still have the cassoulet. I'll open a bottle of good burgundy."

For the last two hours, he'd heard nothing but the ceaseless buzz of flies, but all that faded when he looked at her. God, she was lovely.

"All right."

"It's rich, the cassoulet. With duck. And with the wine, it'll be perfect."

She opened the door for him and stood in full view. She was wearing a long white robe, made of silk. He came in and waited while she shut and locked the door behind him. He set his duffel bag on the floor by the door and then went with her into the living room. The layout was the same as his apartment, but that was as far as the similarity went.

She had cherry floors and exposed brick walls, and art that could hang alongside anything in the Legion of Honor. The curtains drawn across the windows were so heavy that they blocked not only the light but most of the sound from the alley. He saw no TVs, no computers, no telephones and no radios. Instead, she had books. Hundreds and thousands of hardback volumes on shelves built throughout the apartment. It smelled like the Rare Books room of the San Francisco Library — aged leather and the exotic musk of dry paper. He could also smell the violet water she must have touched to her neck. He thought she might have used a cedar comb on her hair; when she passed him to step into the kitchen, the air that moved with her smelled like the forests up north. The forests that had been there when he was a boy, before the ancient groves had been wiped out by the years of drought that preceded the rains.

She pointed him to a stool at the island bar in the kitchen.

"Sit," she said. "I didn't even ask if you like red. I also have a chilled white Bordeaux."

"I'll have what you're having."

"Then we're having red."

She knelt at the wine cabinet under the counter and came up with a dark bottle. She set it down next to the stove, and he looked at it while she opened a drawer to get her corkscrew. The bottle didn't have anything on it. He could see the glue marks on the glass where the label had once been, but someone had washed it off.

She came back with the corkscrew and a paring knife to cut the tin capsule from the bottle's top.

"How do you know what it is, without a label?"

She tilted the bottle so he could see its bottom. There was a small sticker there. On it, in neat script, was written: *Côte de Nuits, '96.*

"Why take it off?"

"It's the wine I want, not the label."

She turned to a cabinet and brought out a pair of glasses. She poured a splash of the wine into one glass, lifted it by its stem, swirled it, then passed it to him. He took it and brought it to his nose, closed his eyes, and breathed in. Then he drank the sip she had poured, letting it glide onto his tongue and rest there. He opened his eyes and gave the glass back to her.

"That's wonderful."

He'd never had anything like it. He could taste the grapes and the earth they'd grown out of, and the sun that had ripened them through the end of a dry summer.

"Good."

She poured wine into both glasses and then held hers up to him.

“Thanks for coming in.”

He touched his glass to hers.

“Let me get the oven going,” she said. “Then we can drink wine and you can tell me what’s on your mind.”

“Who says there’s anything on my mind?”

“Me,” she said. “I’m good at faces.”

She turned to the oven and lit it, then went to the refrigerator and brought out a lidded clay pot. She put it on the counter and pointed with her wineglass into the living room. There was a pair of wing-backed leather chairs facing the fireplace. A low walnut table sat between them.

“Let’s sit in there. We’ll be more comfortable.”

He followed her to the chairs and sat. Everything about the night seemed far away now. Stepping into Mia’s apartment was like traveling to another continent, in another time. She put her glass on the table, knelt to light the fire, and then sat down opposite him. She folded her legs underneath her in the chair and balanced her wineglass on her right knee, one finger keeping it upright.

“I’ll start,” she said. “What did I do tonight? I sat in this chair and I finished Letessier. I made breakfast at seven and had lunch just after midnight. Now I’m going to have dinner with you. This is my first glass of wine.”

She brought it to her lips and sipped. Then she looked at him and waited. He was sure he could knock on every door in the city and not turn up a single other person like her.

“I went down to the station and met Jenner,” he said. “The last six weeks, we’d been trying to find this guy. Patrick Wong – a small-time crook who’s connected to a big-time crook. We wanted to ask him about a girl who got murdered. When I called Jenner on Sunday, he told me he’d talked to Patrick on Friday.”

“While you were with me.”

He nodded.

“But when I saw him at the station, Jenner couldn’t remember what they’d talked about. He couldn’t find his notes. And his gun smelled like everything else does. Like hot metal.”

“You think he was with you. That whatever happened to you happened to him.”

“Yeah.”

"Did he remember the Fairmont?"

"Maybe a little – I didn't ask him. But I saw him staring at the lanterns over Grant, in Chinatown. Just standing there staring, like he was hypnotized. Or remembering something."

"You were in Chinatown tonight?"

He told her the rest then. At one point, Mia let him keep talking while she got up and put the clay dish in the oven. Then she came back and he finished the story of his night.

Talking to her was easy. He'd felt sick since waking up on Sunday, but his head had been clear. He could focus, could scan a scene and see all the details. With Mia, it was even better. It wasn't just her. It was the space she'd created around herself. Her apartment was a shelter from the rain and the wind. A place where you paused and found your breath, and thought that perhaps it wasn't so cold after all. Perhaps you could carry on, once you'd had a moment to gather yourself.

They ate dinner at the granite bar in the kitchen. He thought she might excuse herself and change out of her robe, but she didn't. Before she sat down, she turned her back to him and drew the robe closer before cinching the sash tight. That was all, and then they ate.

He'd never had anything like her cassoulet, and he wasn't ashamed to tell her. She thanked him, but didn't say how she'd found a woodland duck, or olive oil that wasn't adulterated with synthetics, or herbs he hadn't seen since he was a teenager. When they were finished, he took the plates and washed them at the sink, and then he followed her back to the chairs. She'd put the bottle of wine on the table between them and carried over their glasses.

He sat and looked at the fire, and then at the curtains. There might have been a little light out by now, but he couldn't see it, and that was fine with him. He let the silence stretch out as long as it was comfortable, and then, the wine loosening him up a little, he spoke aloud the first thing that had been on his mind.

"I've never been in an apartment like this."

She leaned forward in her chair.

"Never?"

"At least not since I was a kid – a young kid, at that."

"What about it?"

Words failed him as he looked around. Part of it was shame at how he had been living; more of it was awe that it was possible to live some other way. He looked at her and shook his head. He couldn't answer.

"Do you ever wonder why that is? Why every change has been for the worse?" Mia asked.

She was sitting cross-legged in her chair with her wineglass cupped in her hands.

"Come again?"

"It's just, it wasn't always like this," she said. "Do you remember how people used to be? Not just other people, but us, too. Do you remember when you could take a walk in the park and not buy anything? When you could make love to someone and not get up to check your phone? The streets weren't always covered in glass."

"Things change," Carver said. "Years go by, some people get harder. Others break. And the ones who break make things worse for everyone. That's your smash-and-grabs, those clubs on Powell."

"There's more to it than that," Mia said. "It's not just time going by. It's not just the world growing up."

"I don't know."

"I do."

She drank the last of her wine and reached for the bottle. She refilled her glass and then leaned over and poured the rest of the wine into his. There wasn't much.

"This reminds me of when I was a little girl," she said.

"In New York?"

"That's right. A little girl, in New York. Just off Central Park West. Six, seven years old, and my friends would come over to my parents' apartment for a sleepover. We'd stay up all night, talking. There were chairs, like this, in my dad's study, and we could close the doors, so no one would hear us. We'd talk the sun all the way around and back up again. Then when the light was gray and sleepy, we'd get pillows from the couch, and blankets, and bed down on the carpet in front of the fire—but who does that anymore?"

"Not little girls?" he asked. He drank the rest of his wine.

"They don't, and they haven't for a long time. They're lost in their screens, or out on the streets, in the shopping districts. Like moths to a flame," she said. She looked at his glass. "There's another bottle of the burgundy, if you'd like it."

"I shouldn't," he said. "I should get some sleep, I think."

“When you wake up, you’re going to try to find out more, aren’t you? You’re going to try to track it down.”

“Yes.”

He hadn’t told her any more about that than he’d told Jenner. But he’d come close.

“Knock on my door if you want someone to come with you.”

He nodded, and stood up. She didn’t rise from her chair, but she held her hand out to him. He took it and squeezed her fingers lightly. Then he showed himself out.

10

CARVER CHECKED EACH room of his apartment. He didn't think anyone had been in it since he'd left. It was nearly eight in the morning, and there was a hint of light from behind the wooden blinds in his bedroom, but he made no move to open them. Instead he sat at his father's desk and opened the duffel bag. The thermal scope was on top, wrapped in his gym towel. He turned on his computer, found the number he needed, and dialed it.

"Equipment, Hollis speaking."

"Hey, Hollis. This is Inspector Carver, from Homicide. Can you help me out?"

"I can try."

"I was at a scene on Thursday night. Typical government clusterfuck. Paramedics, cops, firemen. Witnesses milling around. We got it squared away, but someone left a thermal scope in my scene bag. A patrol model, an Ønske. If I give you the serial number, can you tell me whose it is?"

"Read it out."

Carver gave the number to Hollis, and then waited. He could hear tapping on a keyboard.

"Just a sec," Hollis said. "I need to pull up a different table."

"Fine."

Carver closed his eyes and held his temples between his thumb and middle finger. He thought of Mia. She'd been gorgeous in the firelight, her legs tucked beneath her and her wine glowing like a garnet. She'd asked him if he thought something was wrong with the world. It hadn't felt like a casual question. He was certain she knew something, and he sensed she was trying to lead him to it.

"Here we go," Hollis said, more to himself than to Carver. "Officers Kimberly Houston and Winton Roper. They're Metro Division, out of Central Station. You want their badge numbers?"

"That's okay," Carver said. "And listen, don't mention this. I don't want to bust their asses or anything. I just want to get it back to them."

"You ought to bust their asses. Shouldn't just leave stuff like that lying around."

"It was a complicated scene."

"So they should've kept their gear in order," Hollis said. "Of course, I'm talking to the guy who smashed his scope last week. At least you reported it."

"They haven't reported theirs?"

"Not that I can see. Maybe they don't even know they lost it. Christ, what would that say about them?"

It was possible they didn't know. But Carver was putting his money on a different story: they knew it was missing, but they had no idea what to write on the report. They were taking their time, trying to trace their own steps back to last Thursday. If that was the case, then it would say a lot about them. It would mean they were his kind of cops.

"Thanks, Hollis," he said.

"Anytime."

He hung up, and thought about how he should come at Central Station. He didn't like calling the desk officer because he didn't know who would be on duty. Calling to ask for the work schedules of two patrol cops might raise more than an eyebrow. It wasn't beneath reporters to call the front desk and pretend to be someone on the force. The desk officer might ask for Carver's badge number, and then run it on the system to see if it checked out. If Hernandez had put a suspension hold on his file, he wouldn't last thirty seconds.

He dialed the main line and a kid's voice answered on the first ring.

"SFPD Central Station, this is Officer Yardley."

"Good morning, Officer," he said. "This is Inspector Ray Bodecker, SFPD Homicide. My badge number is 2524. I need a favor."

He could hear the desk officer typing, looking him up. He hoped Ray wasn't standing at Central Station's front desk. The kid cleared his throat and shouted something to someone in the lobby. Carver couldn't tell what it was, because the kid had covered the receiver with his hand. Then he was back on the line.

"What can I do for you, Inspector Bodecker?"

He must have passed the test.

"You got a pair of patrol officers on your roster, and I need them. Houston and Roper. When's their next shift?"

"Can you hold, please?"

"Sure."

"I got a situa—"

The officer transferred the call to hold, and Carver sat listening to a recording. The SFPD wanted him to remember the new tip line. It wanted him to remember: *If they're ripping copper, call in a chopper.* Probably plenty of people called. Nobody liked it when the lights went out. The recording cut off and Yardley came back on the line.

"Inspector?"

"Still here."

"Roper's been out since Friday. Flu, sounds like. Houston's on a shift that started ten minutes ago. She comes off at eight."

"Thanks."

"You want me to have dispatch call her with a nine-oh-four?"

Carver thought about that. Yardley was offering to have the dispatcher broadcast an instruction to meet another officer. It would be the fastest way to meet her, but he couldn't have Bodecker's badge number going out on the radio.

"How about a note on her locker?" he asked. "I'd rather keep it off the air."

"She in trouble?"

"Not at all, son. I'm just working something and need to keep it close. I think she can help me. That's it."

"Yessir. What should I put on the note?"

"Tell her to meet me at Hideo's. Tell her it's about Thursday night, what she saw. If she can't make it, have her call my cell."

He gave Yardley his cell number, thanked the kid again, and hung up.

In the shower, he noticed he was feeling stronger than he had been. Mia's meal was keeping him warm. He thought of what she'd said about the gray light at dawn, pictured her as a little girl, rolling out her bedding in the library of a townhouse on the edge of Central Park. Gray light and snowflakes on one side of the window; fire and books – and Mia – on the other. He liked that image, and liked even more that she had shared it with him. He knew there must be more that she was keeping back, but perhaps she meant to give him small things first, to see how carefully he could hold them. When she trusted him enough, she would give him something larger, more delicate.

He toweled off and put on a pair of boxer shorts. The blue pants he'd woken up wearing on Sunday were in the hamper next to his dresser. He looked at them and wondered where they'd come from. Then he pulled back the covers and got into his bed.

He'd told himself to wake at six in the evening, and he opened his eyes within a minute of that time. He'd never owned an alarm. He rolled out of bed and went to the kitchen to make coffee. While it was brewing, he shaved and dressed, and then he took the first mug and went to his study to see what else he could learn about Kimberly Houston. It didn't take much effort to find a photograph. She was in her SFPD uniform, a pair of flags behind her. She might have been half Chinese, but he was no good at that kind of guessing. Her dark hair was wrapped in a bun. If she let it down, it might reach her shoulders. He tried to picture it that way, to see if it stirred any memory. The wooden blinds in the study were open, and he looked out at the Neptune Hotel's neon sign, the red and blue lights blinking in the rain.

"Houston," he said. "Officer Houston. Officer Roper."

Saying the names didn't bring any familiarity to them. Looking at the picture stirred something, but it was more a feeling than a memory. The feeling was fear, but he couldn't connect it to anything. Until right then, he'd never been afraid without having something to be afraid of. It hadn't even occurred to him that fear could be a free-roving agent, a dark thing that walked wherever it chose. He closed his eyes and tried to see the first thing that flashed behind his eyelids – Mia's trick. But there was nothing.

There was still an hour and a half before Houston's shift ended. When she got back to Central, she might have paperwork, and she'd likely want to shower and change before she went to her car or walked to a MUNI station. All that could add an hour. More, if her shift had been a bad one.

He took his coat from the hook by the door and stepped out of his apartment. He'd handed his department-issued weapon to Hernandez, but he had a personal nine-millimeter automatic in his holster. Without a badge, he had no right to carry it. Until today, he'd never considered he might need a concealed carry permit. But that wouldn't matter if nobody knew. He crossed the hall to Mia's door and knocked. When he heard her boot heels come down the entry hall, he knew she was dressed already. She opened the door and leaned against the jamb. She was wearing blue jeans and a knit sweater underneath a leather coat; not only had she been waiting for him, she'd been waiting with an expectation that he'd ask her to come.

"I'm going to meet someone," he said. "I don't think it's dangerous, but I don't know that for sure."

"Where?"

"A Japanese place," he answered. He'd chosen it because it was walking distance from Central Station, but it wasn't a cop hangout. "Less than a mile from here."

"Will I need to do anything?"

"Sit with me," he said. "Follow my lead. Be disarming."

"I can do that."

"You ready?"

She stepped out and turned the lock, then pocketed her keys and took his arm.

In the parking garage, he gave Mia his flashlight, and she held it for him while he knelt next to his car's open door. The car belonged to the city, and if Hernandez hadn't taken his keys when she was collecting his badge and gun, then she must have wanted him to have it. He didn't like that at all. He reached under the dash console, searching for the fuse panel under the steering wheel. He found it, had Mia point the light, and then pulled out one of the fuses. He tossed it into the back seat, then came around the car and opened the passenger door for her.

"How did you know which one?"

"I looked it up."

"With a computer?"

"With my phone."

He came back around the car and got in. He tried the GPS and nothing happened. He'd found the right fuse. Hernandez couldn't follow him that way, but he knew it was impossible to disappear from her altogether. She could track his phone, if she got a subpoena. Or she could just put a two-man tail on him and he'd never know it if they were any good. Maybe that had been her thought all along. She knew he was going to move around the city no matter what she did, so she meant to keep him in a vehicle she recognized. He'd have to think about that, weigh whether it merited some kind of response.

He drove out of the garage and down into the wet street. After looping to Kearny, he followed it north. Mia never looked out the window. She was either watching him or looking at her lap.

"Except for the two times you've gone out with me," he said, "have you left the building since you moved here?"

"I try not to."

"Why is that?"

"When I'm at home, I feel like I'm myself," she said. "I'd rather be alone, and be myself, than be with other people and lose everything."

None of that made sense to him, but he went with it.

"What about when you're with me?"

"If we're in my apartment, it's fine. More than fine. If we're in your apartment, it's okay. Not as good, but okay. When we're out here . . . I don't know."

"You don't know what?"

"How much I can handle," she said. "I thought I'd be okay, when we went to the Fairmont. But it was hard. It took time, after, to get back to myself."

They passed an Italian boutique. Purses and leather goods glowed beneath spotlights behind its tall display windows. A mob of women jammed its entrance, pushing to get in. Off-duty cops moonlighting as security guards were trying to force the crowd into a line along the sidewalk. Carver changed lanes to avoid the women who'd fallen into the street, and he saw Mia glance up when she heard the shouting. She looked away quickly when some of the uniformed men raised their nightsticks and started to swing at the women nearest the door. A cry went up, then faded as they went on. After they passed Columbus Tower, they entered the new red-light district that had metastasized from North Beach. There were Thai massage parlors and flashy sex clubs. Yellow cabs unloaded men at every corner, adding to the existing crowd. Flyers littered the sidewalks, their flexible LED screens running looped videos of girls in the unlicensed brothels.

"Tell me about the person we're going to meet," Mia said. He glanced at her and saw she'd closed her eyes.

There wasn't much he could tell. He was finished before they reached the station. The first parking spot he found was five blocks away, in front of a takeout pho shop. This was a quieter street, but when he came around the back of the car and joined Mia on the sidewalk, he turned in the direction she was facing and could hear the men hollering from outside a club on Columbus.

"I'm going to take your arm," Mia said. "If I hold on tight, and lean on you, it's because I'm closing my eyes."

"You're okay?"

She nodded fiercely but didn't say anything. When she took hold of him, at first she was trembling. He moved her arm around his waist, then took her shoulder. He didn't understand it, but she'd told him what she believed: There was nothing wrong with her. It was the world that was the problem. Frankly, it was hard to argue against that.

He led her to Vallejo, and then past Central Station. She never closed her eyes that he could tell, but when they passed lit-up storefronts, and back-lit advertisements at the bus stops, she looked away.

"We're here," Carver said.

They were across from Hideo's. Mia looked up and must not have minded what she saw. She didn't look away. The building's façade was finished with untreated cedar. The sign was in kanji characters, carved into the wood and painted black. It wasn't quite past eight. Up the street, he saw signs of the shift change at Central Station. Uniformed officers were coming and going from the building, and both sides of the street were clogged with parked squad cars.

"You think she'll come?"

"She might test me first," he said. "I've got an idea she's careful. But she'll come."

They crossed the street. She let go of him and walked by his side, slipping on a cloak of confidence he hadn't yet seen. For a moment, Carver was ashamed that he'd brought her. He'd told himself that he needed to keep an eye on her. With her at his side, he could see what she noticed, how she reacted. But there was another reason, too. She was like a lens that bent any light that touched her. People would see them both but would only remember her. He understood this would cost her something, though he still didn't understand what. It would take her a while to come back to herself.

They reached the door. The hostess opened it for them before Carver could even take the handle.

"*Irashaimase,*" she said. "For two?"

"For three. One's not here yet. I've got a reservation."

"Your name, sir?"

"Ray Bodecker."

The hostess went behind her podium, checked her list, and then gestured for them to follow her. She led them down a dimly lit hallway, lined on each side with sliding shōji doors. At the third door she stopped and motioned with her open palm to a bench and a shelf beside it. They took off their shoes and put them on the shelf. Carver looked along the hallway and saw that the room opposite them had shoes, but the rooms on either side were empty. Then the hostess opened the sliding door and showed them into their room. They settled onto cushions around the low table.

"The waitress will be back with your tea."

"Thank you," Mia said. When the hostess was gone, she looked at Carver. "Now what?"

"We wait," he said. "Welcome to police work."

Carver's phone rang at 8:35, when they were into their second pot of tea. He lifted it from the table and answered.

"Yes?"

"I got your note."

Houston's voice was harder than he'd expected from the department photograph. But then he thought about what she'd been through in the last several days. She'd hidden it, had swallowed it like poison, and come back to work. Of course there'd be an edge.

"And I've got your thermal scope."

"What scope?"

"Come on, Officer Houston, you know—"

"*No.* I don't know anything."

"We could help each other figure it out, maybe."

"If I didn't hope that, I wouldn't have called," she said. "But I'm not walking into that restaurant until I see you."

"Tell me how you want to do it, then."

"Come outside, onto the sidewalk. Go to the curb and turn all the way around, slowly. Don't try to look for me. Keep your head down. Then go back inside."

"All right."

"And don't hang up. Keep the phone next to your ear. Put your other hand on your shoulder."

He nodded at Mia, then stepped out of the tatami room and closed the door behind him. He sat on the bench next to the shelf.

"I have to put you down a minute," he said to Houston.

He didn't wait for Houston to answer. He slipped on his shoes, tying them as quickly as he could.

"Sir?" The hostess was coming down the hall from her place behind the podium. "Is everything—"

"I just have to take a call," he said, picking up his phone.

The woman bowed and turned away. He came down the hall and exited the front door. He walked to the curb, eyes on his feet. He wanted to look around for her, scan the stores on the other side of the street. Or maybe she was up the block, near the intersection. But she'd told him not to look, and he knew she could be anywhere. She might be on top of the police parking garage half a block up, with a clear view of him. When he finished the turn, he went back inside the restaurant.

"Did you see me?" he asked her.

The hostess looked up at him, and he shook his head and pointed to the phone.

"I saw a guy come, turn around, and go back in," Houston said. "But that guy wasn't Ray Bodecker. I looked him up, and you're not him. So who the fuck are you?"

"Ross Carver," he said. "I'm an inspector, Homicide Detail. I couldn't give the desk officer my name and badge number because Lieutenant Hernandez suspended me last night. My partner, too."

"Why?"

"Why do you think?" Carver asked. "You think it's not going to happen to you? How long can you cover it up? How long can you cover for Roper?"

"You said Carver? Ross Carver?"

"That's right," Carver said. "Look it up. I'm going back to my table. We'll be waiting for you."

"Wait—who's we?"

"My friend," Carver said. "I brought her so you'd know I don't bite."

"I don't have to come."

"And I didn't have to tell you about your scope," Carver answered. "But I did, and I kept it between us. Look me up, read my record. We'll be waiting."

Carver hung up. He knew she was going to find his SFPD bio, and then she would come. And she'd come in knowing he wasn't alone. She wouldn't be taken by surprise. Carver didn't like surprising people with guns. He went back down the hall and took off his shoes, then let himself into the tatami room. Mia was kneeling behind the table and began to get up when the door opened.

"It's just me."

"Is she coming?"

"She's coming."

"Okay."

Mia curled back into her cushion. Carver sat, then refilled their cups. Houston's cup was still upside down on its wooden tray. He turned it upright and poured her some tea.

A moment later, he heard their footsteps coming down the hall, and the hostess slid the door back.

"Your third guest has arrived," she said.

11

FOR A MOMENT, they just looked at each other. Houston stood with her back to the rice paper door, her hands behind her. She'd changed from her uniform into jeans and a UCSF sweatshirt, and her hair was down. She was probably over twenty-five, but she could have walked into a college classroom and wouldn't have been out of place. Still, Carver knew she'd tucked her service weapon into the waistband of her jeans, and her hands were close to it now. He kept his hands on the table and didn't take his eyes from hers.

Her eyes moved from Carver to Mia, and then back. If she made a decision that she was safe with them, he didn't see her make it. She sat down and looked at the teacup.

"This one mine?"

"Yeah."

"Thanks," she said. "I could use it."

She drank the tea and Carver refilled the little cup for her. Then he took the thermal scope from under the table and put it next to her.

"This is yours too."

She didn't touch it.

"Where'd you find it?"

"My car, Monday night. I woke up on Sunday but couldn't get back to work until the next night."

"Why's that?"

"I was sick."

She looked past him at Mia.

"Who are you?"

"His neighbor. I took care of him."

"You're not a cop?"

"No."

"Take a look at me and think," Carver said. "Have you ever seen me?"

"I haven't." She shook her head and looked at her tea. "There's something, maybe. When you came out of the restaurant – when I first saw you – it was there. Like when you think of the way something smells, and you breathe in through your nose and almost catch it, even though you know it isn't there. But it was just for a second, and I couldn't hold on to it."

"What's the last thing you remember?" Mia asked.

"Why should I tell you? You're his neighbor, not mine. You took care of him. Not me, not Roper. I don't even know your name."

"It's Mia," she said. "I just want to know the last thing you remember."

"Why?"

"Because I care about Ross. Because I want to know what happened," Mia said. She might have been acting, playing the role that Carver had given her. But it didn't sound like a role. Maybe she'd been rehearsing it a while now. "So what is it? The last thing?"

Houston poured herself another cup of the tea.

"Wednesday, sometime," she said, after she put the empty cup down. "I was in court, waiting to testify. I should've been on patrol Thursday night – but if I was, I don't remember it."

"Did you check your body camera?" Carver asked. Every patrol officer had a shoulder-mounted camera that filmed everything they did.

"The memory's cleared," Houston said. "If someone files on me for anything from Thursday, I'm fucked."

"And someone's messed with your email, your patrol logs?" Carver asked. "Cleared your GPS history?"

She nodded.

"I found stuff I don't remember sending – and wouldn't have sent. I managed to see the roll logs. We both made roll call for Thursday's night shift. Roper and I. But we didn't check in at the end. I found emails, though."

"Saying what?"

"Telling our sergeant we were at UCSF, in the emergency room. Waiting to talk to the complaining witness on a domestic."

"What about dispatch?" Carver asked. "Did you report it there?"

"I don't know," Houston said. "I can't think of a way to get in and see the dispatch logs."

Carver shook his head.

"If there's just the email, and no radio call, you know what that means."

"You don't have to tell me."

"What are you talking about?" Mia asked.

"Houston's on patrol," Carver said. "So she's tied to her radio like she's married to it. If she'd been in a hospital waiting to talk to a witness, she wouldn't have been emailing her sergeant on her cell phone. She might have done it, but that's not all she'd have done. She'd have called dispatch on her radio, to report a ten-seven-I—"

"Out of service, investigating," Houston said.

"She never goes anywhere without saying where she is. That's the policy."

Houston nodded.

"Okay," Mia said. "Maybe you broke the radio protocols. And you probably never sent the emails. But what's the next thing you do remember?"

"Sometime on Friday, I woke up," Houston said. "I do four days on, three off. Friday was the start of my off days. I was in my apartment, in El Cerrito. But that's not where I usually spend the night. It's just the address I use, until I can break the lease."

"So if someone took you home but didn't know anything about you except what he found in your wallet, you'd end up there," Mia said, and Houston nodded before she was finished.

"Where do you stay?" Carver asked.

Houston's eyes dipped down toward her teacup, and Carver understood.

"You're living with Roper," he said.

"Maybe it's good you're on suspension," Houston said. "You can't bust me."

"After you woke up, you went to him."

"I was so sick, it took me an hour to get to Winton . . . to Roper. But at least I could move. When I first found him, I thought he was dead."

"Why didn't you take him to a hospital?" Carver asked.

"Why didn't she take you?" she asked, looking at Mia.

“He told me not to,” Mia said. “He begged me—when he was awake.”

Houston nodded. “I’m not crazy, Carver,” she said. “But I look at all this, and I don’t know what to think.”

She picked up the scope and brought it to her nose. She sniffed it and grimaced.

“And there it is,” she said. “That smell’s on everything.”

The door slid open and the waitress came in.

“Something to drink?”

“A beer,” Houston said. “Kirin, or whatever.”

“Hai,” the girl said. She turned to Carver and Mia. “And for you?”

“I’ll stick with tea,” Carver said.

“Same,” Mia said.

When the waitress was gone, he looked back to Houston.

“Roper’s still out?”

She nodded.

“But he’s better than before,” she said. “Not so touch and go. He can’t walk without getting dizzy. He’s sleeping fifteen, twenty hours a day.”

“He’s okay on his own, while you’re working?”

“Yeah,” she said. She didn’t sound as if she liked it, the necessity of leaving him.

“You’re checking in with him, though?” Mia asked. “By cell phone?”

Houston nodded.

“Good,” Mia said. “Keep doing that. Did he have a fever?”

“It’s been hovering around ninety-nine. Highest I saw it was a hundred and one, but that didn’t last long. I crushed up some aspirin. Gave it to him with water.”

“How’s his speech? Slurred? Slow?”

“Both. When he can even talk.”

“Do his eyes track yours? Or is he looking off at something else?”

“Somewhere else—Listen, are you a doctor?” Houston asked. “Who are you?”

Carver watched Mia. He knew her reactions well enough by now. He knew the downward glance and the inward tuck of her shoulders as she thought of how to respond to a hard question. He knew if he unwound the scarf from her neck and tilted her chin up with his fingers, he’d find that her blush extended past her throat.

"I took care of Ross," Mia said. "I saw what it looked like. So I'm trying to find out what Roper's got."

It was a good response, Carver thought. But Mia hadn't answered either of Houston's questions. It occurred to him for the first time that Mia might have done more than simply watch over him; perhaps she felt comfortable not sending him to a hospital because she'd known all along what she was doing.

The waitress came in then with Houston's beer. She set down the bottle, put a small glass next to it, and poured the glass half full. Then, using tongs, she passed each of them a warm hand towel.

"Are we eating?" Houston asked.

"If you want," Carver answered. "It's coming either way."

He saw how tired she was. It was hard, on a rookie's salary. To live at all, she had to stay in El Cerrito, in the East Bay, which meant she spent a good part of each day either on the road or on a train. And then, because she really lived with Roper, she had the added expense of keeping an apartment she didn't even need, except for the cover it gave her from the department. There wouldn't be anything left over, unless she worked side jobs, like the cops they'd seen managing crowds outside the leatherwork store.

"What are we supposed to do?" Houston said. "I can't keep this up forever. If he misses another shift, they'll want a doctor's note. My sergeant thinks I'm holding out, not telling him something about Thursday night. He was looking for me after roll call, and I dodged him. But I won't always be able to do that."

"You've got to stay ahead of him as long as you can," Carver said. "We'll have a better time of it if you're not suspended."

"More access, you mean."

"Access, resources. Official cover."

"What about your partner?" Houston asked. "He's part of this?"

"Whatever it was, he was there."

"But he's suspended too."

Carver waited for her to go on. He liked Houston just fine, thought he could work with her. But he didn't plan on explaining himself to her.

"Wint's hardly walking," she said. She looked at Mia. "You're not a cop. So what are you guys going to be doing?"

"How long have you been on patrol, Officer Houston?" Carver asked.

"A year."

"Before that, you were in the Marine Corps."

She nodded, and moved the sleeve of her sweatshirt up to hide the small tattoo on her forearm.

"How many homicide scenes have you gone to in the past year?"

"Four."

"That you know of, you mean," Carver said.

Mia had perched herself on the cushion so that one hip rested against it, and her knees were tucked away to her left. She was watching him closely.

"What are you talking about?" Houston asked.

"I'm a homicide inspector. Jenner, too. That's all we do. So if we were there, and if we had our scene bag out, then we were there for a dead body."

The waitress came back with a tray. She knelt on the cushion next to Houston and served them the first course of the *omakase* that Carver had ordered. When the waitress left, Carver picked up his chopsticks and rubbed them together. The fish was probably farm-raised, but a farm was better than a lab. Even Mia was picking up her chopsticks.

"Let me give you a hypothetical."

"Okay."

"Someone hears shots fired, and calls 911," Carver said. "You and Roper are the nearest unit. How do you get the call?"

"Over the radio."

"Then what do you do?"

"We respond."

"You go to the scene. Dispatch gives you an address over the radio, tells you it's a two-sixteen – shots fired. You check it out. And you find a dead body," Carver said. "What's the first thing you do?"

"Secure the scene."

"And then?"

"I'd call Homicide, on my cell. The radio's an open channel. Anyone with a police scanner can listen in."

"You call Homicide to give the details on a private line," Carver said. "Sure. I get that. But you're married to the radio, right? You've got to say something to dispatch, or it's your ass. What do you say?"

"If Roper and I found a body?"

"Yeah."

"I'd call in, give my twenty, and tell dispatch I had an eight-oh-two. And then I'd call Homicide on the private line."

"When you call that eight-oh-two, that goes out on the public channel."

Houston nodded.

"So your unit number, location, and the fact that you've got a dead body – all that goes out over the public channel," Carver said. "And anyone with a police scanner can listen in."

"I understand that," Houston said. "But I don't see how it'll help us."

"If we had the dispatch logs, we could find out where you went that night, and why they sent you. There'd be a callback from you, saying what you found. You can't get the logs, and neither can I. But what if there's another log out there?"

"Is there?"

"Anyone with a police scanner could make a log."

"You think you can find someone who's got one," Houston said. "You and Jenner. And Mia."

"That's right."

"What do you need?"

"Your unit call sign. For when I get the log."

"Adam-Five-David," Houston said. She poured the rest of her beer into the little glass and drank it off. "What else?"

"Just try not to get suspended," Carver said. "Keep your ass one step ahead of your sergeant's boot. Do you know the Irish Bank?"

"The bar?"

Carver nodded.

"It has a private booth, the one in the old Catholic confessional. That'll be our next meeting place. But we have to be careful how we set that up. If someone could send emails from our accounts, they might still be reading them. Same goes for our cell phones."

"So how do we contact each other?"

"I'll call from a pay phone. I'll say I've got the wrong number, and hang up. Then we'll meet an hour later."

"If I can't come?"

"Then you can't come."

"All right."

"And let me know if anything changes with Roper," Mia said. "Use a pay phone to call Ross, and set up a meeting."

"What for?"

"If he gets worse," Mia said, looking at Carver, "he can bring me out. Right?"

Carver nodded.

"And then maybe I could help."

Houston looked at Mia, and Carver watched the distrust and caution fade from her face. She looked relieved, but she didn't acknowledge it to Mia, except by lowering her eyes. After a moment, she turned to Carver.

"I gotta go – it's a long ride back, and he needs me. I'll be in touch. But don't leave yet. I don't want anyone to see me within a mile of either of you."

She got up and showed herself out.

12

WHEN THEY GOT back to the car, Carver let Mia in and then stood on the sidewalk a moment, using his phone to look up an address. He had an idea Mia would be more comfortable if he didn't use it in the car. She was in the passenger seat, her hands folded on her lap and her face turned down. She'd been fine in the restaurant, fine with Houston. She clearly hadn't shut herself off in her apartment because she was afraid of people. She didn't seem to be a recluse by nature.

He looked at his phone's search results and found the address he needed. He got in the car and put the phone away.

"This guy's a cop?" Mia said.

"Was a cop," Carver answered. He checked his mirrors and then did a U-turn from his parking spot. "He quit five years ago and became a PI. Most of his clients are defense attorneys."

"That's how you know him?"

Carver nodded and took a right onto Broadway.

"He's got a bone to pick with the city – with the department. He'll take any case if he thinks he can score one against us."

"What makes you think he'll help you?"

"We'll see – maybe he won't."

"You weren't friends?"

"Not even close."

The address was at Noriega and Forty-Fifth, in the Sunset. They parked up the street and looked at it from the car. It was a townhouse that had been small to start with, and now was broken up into apartments. Dave Fremont was in what used to be the garage. The rolling door had been paneled over with pressboard. There was a narrow door to the side.

"You want me to come, or wait here?"

"If you're willing, I'd like you to come."

She unbuckled her seatbelt and started to open the door, but he put his hand on her wrist to stop her.

"I like to watch a minute or two before I go up to a door and knock."

"Okay."

She pulled her door closed and turned back to the windshield. They watched the house together for five minutes, but saw no movement in Dave Fremont's windows. There was a TV in one of the upstairs bedrooms, and there were lights on in the houses on either side, but nobody moved into view. Nobody was out walking and they only saw one car pass. Its taillights quickly disappeared into the weather.

"All right," Carver said. "We'll go see if he's home."

They were only four blocks from the ocean, and Carver could smell it when he got out of the car. Curtains of mist gusted down Noriega. A block down, a Japanese karaoke bar and a pizza parlor faced off on either side of the street, their neon signs the only lights shining against the night.

They went up to Dave Fremont's door and Carver knocked. He was standing in front of the peephole, with Mia next to him. She took hold of his arm when they heard footsteps come to the other side of the door. The outside light flicked on, an old incandescent bulb inside a glass and tin cover. There was a pause, and then Fremont spoke through the closed door.

"Ross Carver?"

"That's right, Dave."

"The hell do you want?"

"To hire you."

"Who's the woman?"

"A friend."

Fremont switched off the light, then twisted the deadbolt and slid the chain off its catch. He opened the door and stepped out. His hair was whiter than it had been the last time Carver had seen him, and there was less of it. But he was still a big man, taller than Carver and heavier than Carver and Mia combined.

"You're still lifting weights, I guess," Carver said. When Fremont just looked down at him, his back resting against the door, Carver added, "Aren't you going to ask us in?"

“I let clients in,” Fremont said. “And I let my friends in. Speaking of, no hard feelings about Tipton. Right?”

“None from me,” Carver said. “You caught them, and they deserved what they got.”

“And since when did the SFPD hire me?”

“It’s not the department. This is just me. I’m suspended—as of last night.”

“Suspended? You?”

“Jenner, too.”

“You should get a lawyer,” Fremont said. “For the hearing. You need a name?”

“If they have a hearing, I’ll talk to the union guys and see what they say. I know your guy must’ve been good.”

If Fremont noticed the dig, he didn’t show it.

“What do you mean, *if*? They’ve got to give you a hearing. You should talk to the union now.”

“Later, maybe. But I need your help first. Actually, I’m here because of Tipton—you still making those recordings?”

Fremont nodded. “It’ll cost you.”

“I didn’t expect favors,” Carver said. He’d stopped at an ATM on the way, and his wallet was as fat as he’d felt it in a long time. “How much?”

“Depends on what you want.”

“Twelve hours. Last Thursday night, starting at six, into Friday morning. How much for that?”

“For all districts?”

“Southern, Central, Park, and Northern.”

Fremont looked at Carver and then glanced at Mia, trying to gauge how much this was worth to them. There were no set prices in this market.

“A thousand.”

“Five hundred.”

“Seven fifty,” Fremont said. “That’s final.”

Carver put out his hand and they shook.

“Now can we come in?”

“You’re still not a client. Not till you give me the cash.”

Fremont left them on a coffee-stained couch in his living room while he went into his bedroom to transfer the recording files onto Carver's memory card. Mia looked around the little room, taking it in. There was a weight bench against one of the wood-paneled walls, facing a TV mounted close enough to the ceiling that Fremont would be able to see it from his back while doing presses. The kitchen was just a sideboard in the rear of the room. A little sink, with barely enough counter space next to it to hold a hotplate. Her gaze paused at the shelf above the sink. It was made of unfinished pine, and had twenty-five bottles of Kinclaith scotch whiskey on it, all but one of them unopened. She looked at them for a moment, then turned back to Carver.

"Who's Tipton?" she whispered.

"A kid, went to trial two years ago for shooting a store clerk. He was probably good for it, but he walked."

"Because of—" She lowered her voice to nothing, and glanced toward the bedroom.

Carver nodded. He remembered everything about the trial, especially the look on Fremont's face when he took the stand.

"Tipton's lawyer thought one of our guys was lying—this kid from patrol testified in the preliminary hearing that he saw Tipton go into the store five minutes before the shooting. Said he recognized him from a prior, so he remembered it. The lawyer heard it and called bullshit. But she didn't cross him at the preliminary."

"Because she didn't have anything yet," Mia said.

"That's right—but before trial, she subpoenaed transcripts of the dispatch tapes. They didn't disprove anything. The cop could've been there, could've seen what he claimed."

"I don't get it. How's that—"

"Because she didn't believe what she saw on the transcript any more than she believed the cop," Carver said. "So she hired Fremont, because she knew he recorded the scanner feeds. And his recording wasn't doctored. It put the officer on the other side of town, serving a no-knock warrant. Exactly when Tipton was supposed to be pulling the trigger."

"They changed the transcript?" Mia asked. "They didn't think his lawyer could find her own copy?"

It still shamed him, just thinking about it. As he'd watched his case fall apart, he'd realized that the men above him had known all along. They'd fed him a lying witness and a garbage transcript, and when they got caught, he was the only man from the SFPD standing in front of a camera.

"We looked so bad, it didn't matter how guilty Tipton was. The jury acquitted him to convict us."

"You know he wasn't guilty," Fremont said, coming out of the bedroom. "Or why'd they do it?"

Carver stood up, pointing to Fremont's closed left hand.

"That it?"

"Twelve hours, starting Thursday night," Fremont said. He tossed the memory card in the air and caught it, palm down. "You don't find what you're looking for, come back and we'll deal."

Fremont gave Carver the memory card.

"You didn't say why you got suspended," Fremont said.

"And I won't," Carver answered. "Thanks for this."

Mia followed him to the door.

They were driving back to their building, rolling east down Lincoln with the park a dark blur to their left. The streets were busier and better lit as they came deeper into the city.

"Do you know Kinclaith?" Mia asked. "What Fremont had in there?"

"I know it's a scotch."

"It's what they call a silent still," she said. "The distillery's gone, so whatever's left gets more valuable any time someone takes a sip. When it's gone, it's gone."

"You know a lot about scotch?"

"My husband knew scotch."

"Okay."

He wasn't sure what else to say, or where she was taking this. He wanted to know more about her husband, what he might have had to do with Mia's decision three months ago to cloister herself in an apartment. Haunting the lobby, peeking out at the street from the windows without ever going outside. But he didn't want to interrupt her train of thought.

"What I'm saying," she said, "is those things are valuable. A bottle of Kinclaith might go for ten thousand dollars. More, maybe. We might've just seen the entire world supply of Kinclaith on a homemade shelf in a garage apartment in the Outer Sunset. An ex-cop who takes work sometimes as a PI but looks like he's scratching for it — and he's got his retirement tied up in scotch. Does he have something going on the side?"

"Not that I know of."

"Then you have to question his financial decisions."

He understood what she was getting at, but his mind went first to his own cabinets and closets. There were watches he never wore, bottles of bourbon that belonged in a railroad magnate's library but not in a police inspector's kitchen. A year ago he had sold his parents' wedding rings for the weight of their gold; he couldn't remember what he'd bought with the money. It had seemed important at the time.

"What are you thinking about, Ross?" she asked, quietly.

"Sleeping."

"You just woke up."

"I know."

He thought she might invite him in, or ask to come into his apartment so she could listen to the radio calls with him. But she didn't. Instead, when they got to the space between their front doors, she took his hand in hers and then held their interlaced fingers against his chest. She leaned up and kissed his cheek.

"Thank you, Ross," she said, drawing away without releasing his hand. "I'm glad I came."

"Should I —"

"Yes," she said. "Knock tomorrow."

"All right."

She let go of him and unlocked her door. He didn't turn to his own apartment until she was gone.

13

CARVER PUT THE memory card into his computer, opened the file, and hit play. He turned up the volume and switched the feed to the wireless speakers so the audio would play in every room of the apartment. Then he went into the kitchen and put coffee on to brew. The dispatcher on duty sounded young, but she spoke calmly and patiently, moving officers throughout the city to keep up with an incident board that only she could see. She was busy, but she was good, and he could tell the squads liked her for it.

It sounded like the beginning of any other night in the city. A homeless person on the corner of Post and Mason was trying to burn passersby with a lit cigarette. Dispatch sent a foot patrolman. A man outside a bar on Columbus had cornered a woman in the doorway of the abandoned liquor store next door and was badgering her for money and sex. The dispatcher sent a radio car and noted that the victim was not a 647b — it shouldn't matter if the victim was a prostitute or a schoolgirl, but the dispatcher knew her job. She could get patrol moving.

After two hours, the young dispatcher wished everyone a good night and signed off, and a new woman came on the air. Her voice was different but her demeanor was the same, and the night plowed forward, each incident reported and recorded over the radio. The hours grew stranger — and more dangerous. Carver made a second pot of coffee and listened as dispatch sent units to an armed robbery on Russian Hill, to a smash-and-grab in Japantown, to a stabbing at Embarcadero and Market. In the Stockton Tunnel, a naked man with a wooden club was blocking both lanes of traffic and shouting in a language no one understood.

After three hours, he heard Houston's voice for the first time.

"Adam-Five-David—we are ten-seven-M at one fifty-seven Columbus."

"Adam-Five-David, ten-four," the dispatcher responded.

They were calling in their dinner break, which reminded him he hadn't eaten in hours. He went back into the study with his coffee and paused the recording, then called an Italian delivery service he sometimes used. After he ordered, he hung up and called Glenn, asked him to ring up when his food arrived.

For the next half hour, he listened to the dispatcher run the board. Adam-5-David called in toward the end of that time, reporting a 10-8. Their meal was done and they were back in service. The dispatcher sent them up to Nob Hill to monitor a crowd gathering outside the Fairmont Hotel.

He paused the recording again when Glenn called, and went out to pick up his meal. There was a light from beneath Mia's door, and on an impulse he knocked. He didn't hear her coming down the hall, didn't hear anything from her apartment at all. If she'd come out, then she must have done it very quietly, because he'd never heard her front door open. He took the elevator down to the lobby, and paid the deliveryman. The couches were empty and so was the mailroom. There was no one behind the potted palm. Glenn looked up when he came to the security desk.

"She go out a little while ago?"

"She?"

"Come on."

"I haven't seen her," Glenn said. "You came in together, and went up. And that's the last I saw. Everything okay?"

"It's fine."

Back in his apartment, he restarted the playback and sat at his kitchen counter to eat. Everything he'd eaten since his dinner with Mia had tasted like cardboard. The uniform white cubes in his tagliatelle had the flavor of chicken, but lacked the texture of real meat. The top of the takeout box was quietly flashing with an LED boast that everything inside was organic and free range. That was an obvious lie; everything in the box had been hatched in a test tube and grown in a vat. On the plus side, at least no chicken had died to become this. He tossed the container into the trash and washed his hands.

He didn't know what to make of Mia. He'd knocked hard enough that she'd have woken, if she ever actually slept. Usually she was on her way to the door before he'd even had a chance to knock. Maybe she'd been in the bath. Or maybe she had some way of leaving her apartment without opening the front door, without walking past Glenn.

He laid his hands on the table when he heard the next call.

"Adam-Five-David, what's your twenty?"

"California Street, across from Grace."

"Proceed to four fifty-seven Filbert for a nine-eighteen. Complaining witness is in the house across the street, at four fifty-six A."

"Ten-four," Houston said, and Carver heard the siren kick on before she finished transmitting.

He stood up and went to his study, thinking of the radio code the dispatcher had just used: *918*. Someone had heard a person screaming for help. He sat at his desk and pulled up a map of the city on his computer, zooming in to 457 Filbert Street. It was about a mile from Grace Cathedral, but Houston was driving with her sirens and flashers on. She must have hit air on some of the hills, because her next call was barely a minute later.

"Adam-Five-David, we are ten-ninety-seven and will be ten-seven-I."

"Ten-four."

They had arrived at the scene and were exiting the vehicle to investigate. Carver stood up and began to pace in the study. It would probably be several minutes before their next call. Meanwhile, the dispatcher was busy with a dozen units from the Tenderloin to the Golden Gate Bridge. Outside the Fairmont Hotel, the crowd was still growing. There were reports of men in hooded black cloaks, women carrying lanterns and wearing masks. But the dispatcher couldn't keep any units in the area. The night was too busy for it.

"Adam-five-David," Houston said. "There was no answer at the door at four fifty-seven Filbert. We are proceeding across the street. We'll talk with the caller at four fifty-six A."

"Ten-four."

For the next five minutes, Carver stood behind his chair, gripping its back tightly while he waited. He stared at the computer screen, watching the seconds tick past. Five minutes turned to ten.

He started to pace again, and then sat in his chair. The radio calls proceeded at the same relentless pace, the dispatcher refusing to tire and never getting confused. But Houston and Roper were off the air and out of the game.

"Adam-Five-David —"

Carver snapped back to attention.

"— we have an eight-oh-two at four fifty-seven Filbert," Houston said. "We have spoken directly to the lieutenant at Homicide, and inspectors are ten-ninety-eight to our location."

"Adam-Five-David, ten-four. Do you require an ambulance?"

"Can you call me on my cell?" Houston asked.

"Give me the number."

Houston said it and the dispatcher read it back. Carver paused the recording and started to pace again. Whatever the dispatcher and Houston talked about on the phone, it wouldn't be on the recording. Houston had either wanted to convey something too sensitive to go out over the air, or too complicated to explain without tying up the airwaves for the entire force. But she'd found a dead body, and was so sure it was dead that she'd called Homicide and hadn't asked on the air for an ambulance. That wasn't standard procedure, but Houston was a rookie. She must have spoken to Hernandez. He and Jenner were on their way now, maybe edging past the crowd surrounding the Fairmont, the Black Aria Ball imprinting itself on their memories.

Whatever had happened to him that night was going to happen soon, but it probably wouldn't go out on the radio.

He restarted the audio, and then pulled up a street-view image of 457 Filbert. It was a beautifully kept house, set in a row that climbed the steepest block in San Francisco. It was striking, if for no other reason than what it must have cost. Carver could count on one hand the number of times he'd investigated murders in homes like this. But looking at it didn't stir anything.

"Adam-Five-David," Houston said.

She followed up with something else, but it was too garbled to catch. The dispatcher didn't get it either.

"Adam-Five-David, I am ten-two," the dispatcher said. "Can you repeat?"

Carver leaned closer to the speakers. The next transmission was scratchy, and there was wind. She was standing outside, talking on a handheld unit. She spoke slowly, carefully enunciating each word.

"Homicide inspectors have arrived. They are on scene. We are at the front and back doors."

"Do you require assistance?"

"Negative. Thank you."

After that, Houston and Roper disappeared again, and the dispatcher handled other calls. She sent three units to Pier 38 to respond to a sexual assault in progress. There was a drug overdose in a bar restroom in Chinatown. A 647b was in a loud fight with a man in an alley behind the Coburn Arms Hotel.

Carver hadn't carried a patrol radio and listened to these dispatches in years. It sounded as if the city and its people were sinking into an eternal night. But still the sun rose every morning, and they swept the glass off the streets and sprayed the blood off the sidewalks, so that by dusk the cycle of darkness could begin again.

He went back to the kitchen, then remembered that he'd tossed his meal into the garbage. He made more coffee instead.

Twenty-two minutes later, Adam-5-David made its final transmission of the night.

"Dispatch, this is Adam-Five-David – do you copy?"

"Go ahead, Adam-Five-David."

"Inspectors are in the house. They say they can take it from here. The eight-oh-two was a false alarm. Roper and I are no longer required at this location. Do you copy?"

"Thank you, Adam-Five-David. Proceed to your original twenty at the Fairmont Hotel and give me a ten-thirteen on that crowd."

"Will do."

Carver stopped the recording and backed it up, then played this exchange twice more. He thought about Houston's confident radio manner compared to the unsure voice in this last transmission. The woman talking now wasn't used to using a police radio. The signal was weak and the recording was distorted, but Carver was sure of one thing. The woman who made the last call wasn't Houston.

Carver listened to the rest of the recording, but Houston and Roper had disappeared into the night's static. They never checked in with dispatch to state their arrival at the new location. They never reported on the crowd outside the Fairmont Hotel. After thirty minutes, the dispatcher made the first of four requests for Adam-5-David's status. They went unanswered. Finally, after an hour had passed, Houston's patrol sergeant came on the air and asked dispatch to call his cell. He must have gotten the first email from Houston, telling him that she was at a hospital waiting to speak with a witness. He'd want to let dispatch know the unit wasn't lost or in trouble, but would also want to keep it off the air so that his officers' odd behavior wouldn't be broadcast to the entire force.

It was a good move on the sergeant's part, handling it quietly like that. But Carver saw the jam Houston was in. If she and Roper were lucky, they could convince their sergeant to chalk it up as a rookie mistake. Once Houston listened to the dispatch audio, she'd know everything the sergeant had heard, and she could make up a story that fit. She and Roper might get a dressing-down, or screwed on their shifts, maybe assigned to new partners. But they might not get suspended. A patrol sergeant was so busy trying to hold a lid on the nightly chaos that a mistake like this might never get dealt with at all.

He looked up at the window. Gray morning light was pushing at the edge of his wooden blinds. He made a new audio file, using his notes to grab the relevant exchanges from Fremont's memory card. When he'd sent it to his phone, he went into the kitchen and knelt at the liquor cabinet. He poured himself a bourbon and took it to bed. He didn't have as many bottles of Van Winkle as Fremont had of Kinclaith, but maybe he just drank it faster.

14

THIS TIME, MIA opened her door before he even knocked. She was dressed already, in black jeans and boots, and a cashmere shawl.

"Can I come in a minute?"

She stood back and held the door open for him.

"Please," she said. "I've put some things out already."

He could smell the scones in the oven as he walked in. On the kitchen counter, she'd laid out a pair of plates, and a pot of tea. There was a small dish of marmalade, and a bit of butter. He stood looking at it, and then turned to her.

"Mia –"

"It's not much."

"I was going to tell you not to come tonight," he said. "That's what I knocked on your door to say."

She came around him, pulled out a stool and held the back for him while he sat. He looked down. Next to his plate was a manila file folder, and it was open.

"And I was going to try to talk you out of it," she said. "But maybe I don't have to."

A thin stack of documents lay inside the folder. The top page was a glossy photograph, but it was nothing he could place. White and gray blurs evaporated like ghosts into a black background. It was an x-ray, maybe. Some kind of medical scan. She'd written notes on the open side of the folder's cover.

"I'll get that out of your way."

She closed the folder and slid it to the other side of the counter. There was nothing furtive in her movement. Her face showed no guilt or dismay that he'd seen the papers. She was just making room for their breakfast. She reached across him and poured their tea, then went to the oven and brought out the scones.

"What was that?" Carver asked.

"The folder?"

He watched her set the baking sheet on the stovetop. She took a scone with a pair of tongs and set it on his plate, then served another to herself.

"That's tomography, from Sloan Kettering," she said. "It's why I left New York and came here."

"Those are your scans?"

"Mine," she said. "Right in here."

She tapped her temple, then came around the counter and sat. She took a butter knife and cut her scone in half, shaking her fingers afterward.

"Watch out," she said. "I should've taken them out earlier, let them cool on a rack. They're really hot."

"Mia – are you all right?"

He put his hand on her shoulder and she turned to him, lowering her eyes. He thought, later, that if he had leaned toward her just a little more, if he had carried the momentum instead of holding back, she would have come all the way to him.

"I'm all right, Ross," she said. "I've got to come to terms with it – with several things. You probably knew that."

He moved a strand of hair from her face.

"You can tell me, if you're ready," he said. "Maybe I could help."

"You already are," she said. "But let me come tonight. Okay?"

"Okay," he said.

"Tell me what you found on the recording," she said. "I know you were up a long time, listening to it."

He cut his scone in half, and breathed the steam that rose from it. The last time he'd met someone who could bake, he'd been a patrol officer. As green as Houston. He took a dab of the butter onto his knife and spread it on the scone, and then topped it with marmalade. He wasn't sure, but he guessed she'd made the marmalade herself, and maybe the butter, too.

He put his knife down, took a sip of his tea, and told her everything.

The Irish Bank was in the alley behind their apartment building. Before they stepped inside, Mia looked at the Gaelic street signs bolted to the white brick wall, at the outdoor tables warmed by gas heaters.

There were white lights interwoven with the vines on the trellises. Then she turned to look up the alley at their building. Cast-iron fire escapes zigzagged down its brick walls. He could see her heavily curtained windows.

"You didn't know this was here?"

"No idea," she said.

Carver opened the door for her and they stepped into the pub. It wasn't as crowded as it might have been. There were a dozen men and women at the bar, and twice that scattered at the tables and booths. Carver looked across to the confessional, which must have come directly from a Catholic church before its installation here. After some refurbishing, it held a small booth behind its purple curtain. A sign hung next to its door: RESERVED.

Carver led Mia to the bar, and the woman behind it came over.

"How you been?" he said. He tilted his head toward the confessional. "Jenner called?"

She nodded. "All yours," she said. She turned to Mia and examined her with some curiosity; he'd never come here with anyone but Jenner. "I know what he wants, but—"

"Whatever he's having."

"Go on," the bartender said, to Carver. "Confess to each other. I'll bring it."

"Thanks, Cathleen. Add one for Jenner and our other friend."

They went to the confessional. Carver held the curtain aside for Mia and watched as she slid in. He started to sit on the bench opposite her, but she motioned him around.

"With me," she said. "I've never met Jenner."

"All right."

He sat next to her on the narrow bench, her hip pressing against his. With the curtain closed, the light in the booth came only from the small window of yellow frosted glass. He could smell the cedar in her hair and the jasmine rising from the warmth of her throat. She took his hand and turned it over on the table so that his palm faced up. She spread out his fingers and traced the lines on his palm.

"You were working the case of the singer—the girl who got murdered."

"That's right."

The girl's name was Hadley, but that was just a stage name. They'd never learned her real name, and she hadn't been on any biometric database that Carver or the ME could access. As far as Carver could tell, she'd been living hand to mouth on cash from her singing gigs. No bank account, no family, no boyfriend. It was as if she'd swum ashore from some other country and had invented herself in San Francisco: Hadley Hardgrave, the nightclub singer. Her past was a mystery, and her future was gone. Her whole life might have taken place in the three months she wandered through the bars.

"They'd cut her face," Mia said. "While she was still alive. After she bled to death, they cut her in half."

"Yes," he said.

He'd told her about the autopsy, and he could tell it bothered her. She wasn't like Samantha, in the San Lung Lounge, who'd been as fascinated by the darkness as she had been afraid. For Mia, it was simple terror. But still, she wanted to talk about it. She was interested in Hadley Hardgrave, and that interested him.

"The same person might've killed the man Jenner thought he'd talked to?" she asked.

"Yes. Patrick Wong."

"And his girlfriend, and the neighbor who might've witnessed it."

"Some of that wasn't reported. The cutting, especially. That's why we think it might be the same person who did it."

"And you think it's Johnny Wong."

"I think Johnny killed Hadley. That puts him in my sights for Patrick and the other two."

"Does that have anything to do with what happened Thursday night?"

Carver shook his head. "Whatever it was, by the time it happened, Patrick had been dead a month. And Hadley was dead maybe two weeks longer than that."

"Jenner remembered meeting Patrick in Chinatown," Mia said. "But it was a dream, right? We'll call it a dream. But we could also call it a hallucination—"

"What Hernandez called it."

"Or we could call it a suggestion," Mia said. "But for now we'll just say it was a dream. We know he was dreaming because it couldn't have happened. Right?"

"That's right."

"So why would he have dreamed about that?" Mia asked. "Of all the things he might've dreamed about?"

"Maybe it was on his mind," Carver answered. "It's not all that odd – you dream about the things that take up the space in your day."

"Maybe," Mia said, though Carver could tell she wasn't buying it. "If he hadn't had that dream, would you have pushed so hard? Would you have found Joe and the girl, and then the liquor supply company, and then Patrick and the other bodies?"

"We'd have found them sometime."

"But would you have gotten suspended?"

The curtain drew back, letting the barroom's light shine into the booth. He thought Mia would pull her hand away, but she didn't. Then Cathleen was there, with a tray. She leaned in and put down coasters, then set four pints of Harp on the table.

"Jenner's outside, on the phone," she said.

"Thanks."

"You bet."

Cathleen closed the curtain and Mia let go of Carver's hand.

"Would you have?"

"No."

She nodded, but Carver wasn't sure what point she thought she'd proved.

"How much does Jenner know about this?"

"None of it," he said. "I just phoned him, told him I'd buy him a drink at the usual place. I didn't want to say more, and I didn't say anything about you. I don't trust it, the phone."

"Not long and you'll be like me."

"Then what'll we do?"

"We'll need an island, maybe," she said.

There was a knock on the outside of the confessional.

"Ross?"

Jenner's voice turned his name into a low growl.

"Come on in."

The curtain parted just enough for Jenner to step inside. He nodded at Carver and looked at Mia a moment before he slid onto the opposite bench.

"How was Cora?"

"Glad to see me. Can't say as much for her mother," Jenner said. He picked up his beer and took a sip, looking from Carver to Mia. "Who we got here?"

Before Carver could begin to explain, the curtain opened again.

Houston squeezed onto the bench next to Jenner and then pivoted to slide the velvet back into place, sealing their privacy.

"What is this?" Jenner asked.

It took him an hour to answer. He kept his eyes on his partner's, making sure that Jenner understood. At the end of it, he brought out his phone and laid it on the table. Jenner and Houston leaned toward it, their elbows on either side of their empty glasses. Carver brought up the audio file he'd created, and played the exchanges between Houston and dispatch that had led Adam-Five-David to the house on Filbert. When it was done, he put the phone back into his pocket and they all sat back.

Houston was the first to speak.

"That wasn't me," she said. "The last transmission, that wasn't my voice."

Carver rolled his pint glass between his palms, watching the bubbles in his half-finished beer. He looked up, checking each of their faces. They were waiting for him to decide.

"We can't just go to that house, the four of us, and knock on the door," he said. "It's too dangerous. We can't be seen together. If anyone's watching us, they'll know we're following their trail. Maybe they won't be as nice the second time around. Take us home, tuck us in."

"They didn't tuck you in," Mia said.

"But they didn't cut us in half and take a razor to our faces, either," Carver said.

"Then what do we do?" Houston asked.

"You and Roper are still on patrol," Carver said. "We talked about access? This is it."

"What's your plan?" she whispered.

The four of them leaned toward the center of the table, and Carver told them what he'd been thinking about.

15

HOUSTON LEFT FIRST, anxious to get back to Roper. Jenner gave her a good lead, then slid back the curtain and stepped out of the confessional, heading toward the bar. Carver fixed the curtain so that it was tight against the doorway.

"What now?" Mia asked.

"We wait a bit. I'll go out and pay the tab. Then you and I walk home."

"And after that?"

"Houston and Roper aren't up till tomorrow night," he said. He put his fist in front of his mouth to stifle a yawn. "So there's nothing to do until then."

"You're tired again."

He nodded.

"It's still in you," she said. "A little bit of it, maybe. Do you have that flashlight?"

He reached into his coat, slipping his fingers past the gun's grip and finding the flashlight where he always kept it clipped. She took it from him when he handed it to her.

"What is this?"

"I'm just checking," she said. "Here – let me sit across from you."

She slipped over his lap and came around the end of the table. Her hair brushed his face, but otherwise she passed over him without touching him at all. He'd known she was graceful, but he hadn't realized she was so willowy, or so fast. When she settled on the bench where Houston had been sitting, she picked up the flashlight again and patted the table in front of him.

"Lean across," she said. She switched on the light and held it off to the side, aimed at the confessional's low wooden ceiling.

He did as she asked, and then she came across the table to meet him. Their eyes were five inches apart.

"Good," she said. "Like that. Now just look at my eyes."

"Okay."

She brought the light up and let it shine into his right eye. Suddenly the booth was split in two, a diagonal slash of light and shadow. He lost her face in the glare, and could just make her out by the hazy penumbra of her hair.

"Stay still, Ross."

"Okay."

Her left hand gripped his.

"Come back – don't lean away."

She swung the light to his left eye and let it linger a moment. Then she switched it off.

"You can close your eyes now," she said. She let go of his hand.

He lowered his head and shut his eyes. The flashes and the sudden switch from one eye to the next had left him dizzy.

"What was that?"

"I was checking. It's better now – your eyes react to the light, like they should."

"You did that before? When I was sick?"

"I did," she said. She was still right across from him. "Keep your eyes closed now. Can you feel me touching you? Don't look."

"Yes."

"Where am I touching you?"

"On my fingertips," he said.

"Good – that's good."

"Now on the back of my hands," he said.

He could feel her tracing the tendons there, a brush so light she might not have been touching him at all. He might have just been feeling the heat of her fingers, a premonition of the skin.

"And now?" she asked.

"You're not touching me," he said. He wished she would.

"I'm not?"

"You're not."

She turned his hand palm up and put the flashlight back into it.

"You're a lot better," she said. "But you still must be tired."

He opened his eyes and looked at her. He'd trust her completely if it were just the two of them, somewhere far from here. But it wasn't that simple and he knew it.

"I'll go pay the bill," he said. "Just wait here a second, till I come get you."

"Okay."

He left the booth and closed the curtain, then walked around to the other end of the bar. Cathleen left the customer she was with and came over to him. He handed her a paper bill, and she looked at it as if she hadn't seen one in a long time. If Hernandez was remote-logging into his car's GPS, he didn't want to use his credit card here. When Cathleen came back, she gave him change, and a plain white envelope.

"From Jenner," she said, quietly.

She slid it across the bar and he took it and pocketed it, knowing what it contained by its weight and bulk. Cathleen's eyes tilted toward the confessional, and then back to him.

"He said if she—"

"That's okay," he whispered. He pushed the change across the bar. "I know what he said."

Jenner hadn't wanted Mia to see the envelope. He went back to the confessional. Mia came out when he opened the curtain, and she took his arm.

When they were in the elevator, making their slow and rickety rise up to their floor, Carver leaned against the brass rail and closed his eyes. Mia touched his shoulder.

"You're all right?"

"I'm okay."

"You probably need some sleep," she said. "Do you want me to knock, later? Tomorrow evening, before we start?"

"Please."

"I'll knock," she said. "I'll come a little early, and have things ready."

He nodded, and the elevator car jerked to a halt as it reached their floor. The doors shuttled open. He opened his eyes and went down the hall with her. She waited while he opened his door.

"Good night, Ross."

"Good night."

She turned to her door and slipped the key into its lock. Carver watched her over his shoulder until he was inside his apartment. Then he shut the door and quietly turned the bolt.

He went into the living room and took the envelope from his pocket, ripping it open and letting the phone slide into his hand. It was a burner, the kind you could get in Chinatown for less than the price of lunch. There was a piece of masking tape on the back, with a number written in pencil. He dialed it and brought the phone to his ear. It rang once and the line picked up.

"That you?" he whispered.

"Good," Jenner said. His voice was almost too deep to register on the phone's tiny speaker. "You got it."

"You out front?"

"That's right. Listen – do you trust that girl?"

"I don't know."

"You want to. I know that."

"But I don't know if I can," Carver said. "Why do you think I brought her?"

"You were making a big noise, to see what it flushed out."

Carver leaned against the wall and cupped his hand around the bottom of the phone to keep it quiet.

"You're still thinking."

"And you haven't gone soft – I was worried."

Carver went to the window and looked through a crack in the blinds. The street was wet. It glistened blue-red beneath the Neptune's sign. Above the rooftops, the night was lined with streaks of electric rain. He couldn't see Jenner, but that didn't surprise him. Any one of the shadows might hold Jenner, and that made all of them seem less menacing.

"But that was a big risk, Ross, letting her in so far."

"We're in a corner and we need to know who our friends are," Carver whispered. "So it's not like I had a choice. Look – if she comes out her front door, then she has to go to the elevator or the stairs. Either way, I'll hear her."

"So?"

"Once she gets to the lobby, the only way out is through the front door – what you're watching."

"How else is she going to leave?"

"There's an old fire escape around back. It connects to her windows."

"I'm on my way—call me if she's headed for the front."

Jenner hung up, and Carver watched out the window. Somewhere down there, in the dark, his partner was on the move. But he saw nothing. After a moment, Carver went around his apartment turning out the lights. At the last switch, he stood in the dark and checked the phone to make sure it was on silent mode. Then he went to the entry hall and was settling down to wait near the door when Jenner called again. He answered it and brought it to his ear.

"You are not going to believe this."

"Tell me."

"She's on the move. The window just slid up and she's coming out."

"You're in a safe spot?"

"She won't see me."

"She's still on this floor?"

"Shutting the window—now she's on the ladder."

If she was on the fire escape, she wouldn't hear him leave. He went for his coat, switching the phone from one hand to the other as he put his arms through the sleeves. Then he took a hat from the hall closet and went to his front door.

He headed to the elevator at a trot, aware he might have Mia to thank for his strength. When he'd set up the meeting at the Irish Bank, when he'd laid out his plan for Houston and Jenner, he'd brought her along so she would hear everything. It had been a gamble, a willing risk of their momentum to see if she would lead him to someone bigger. But he hadn't expected it to work. He'd wanted to believe she was on his side. He hit the elevator button and stood waiting for the car, remembering the way she'd used the light in the confessional to check some reaction in his eyes. The way she'd touched him, her fingers as soft as a whispered word.

The phone vibrated and he answered it.

"You better hurry," Jenner said. "She's already down to the third floor."

"On my way."

The elevator doors parted, and Carver stepped into the car.

"She's hitting the ladders like—"

The call cut off when the doors shut. He didn't need Jenner to finish the sentence. He could already picture it: Mia, in her black jeans and leather coat, sliding down the ladders without touching the rungs, gliding across the narrow wrought-iron walkways to kneel at the next trapdoor. Her movements silent, her body sovereign over the space beneath her, over the metal in her grip.

When he thought how far she'd gone to lie to him, he had to hold on to the brass rail.

The elevator bounced to a halt, and the doors opened. He pounded across the lobby, empty except for Glenn. He dialed Jenner as he pushed outside.

"Where are you?"

"Just got out front," Carver said. He stopped at the curb. "What's going on?"

"She's in the alley. She used a rope to climb down the last bit," Jenner said. "She's tying it off now, out of the way – to get back up, I guess."

The fire escape's lowest landing had a weighted ladder that would swing down from the horizontal as someone began to climb out on it. It would rotate back to its resting position when the person stepped off, so that it remained out of reach from the alley. But from what Jenner was saying, Mia was bypassing that ladder altogether.

"She's moving," Jenner whispered. "Headed toward me ... hold on."

Carver moved away from the building's front entrance to where he could stand in the shadows.

"Shit," Jenner said.

"Did she see you?"

"No – but she's moving. Fast."

"Which way?"

"Toward the Irish Bank."

"She's gonna hang a left with the alley, come out on Bush?" Carver asked.

"That's right."

"I'll head up there, cover where it meets Bush – where's your car?"

"A block south, on Sutter."

The alley was an L shape, with entrances on Bush and Grant. They could do this if they stayed mobile, but Mia was the hardest kind of person to tail. She knew their faces. They'd have to stay far enough back that she wouldn't see them at all.

"Go out the way you came in," Carver said. "Make sure she doesn't double back. Soon as I see her on Bush, make a run for your car."

"Got it."

Carver went up the hill toward the intersection with Bush. On the other side, where Grant led up into Chinatown, the Dragon Gate was lit with red lanterns. He thought of Mia stepping from his car at the Fairmont Hotel, reaching under her collar and scarf to free the spill of her hair. He'd seen this coming from the moment he'd heard her voice, but he hadn't wanted to believe it. It was too easy to be with her. He took a right on Bush, running now, and stopped at the entrance to a brasserie, where he could stand in the alcove and watch the alley.

"You got her yet?" Jenner asked. His words came in between hard pants.

"Not yet," Carver answered. He was breathing at least as hard as Jenner. "Wait—I see her."

"I'm going for the car," Jenner said. "Keep talking to me. Don't hang up."

She was directly under the Irish Bank's sign, her dark clothes blending with the sooty bricks. She was looking down Bush Street, watching the traffic as it passed, and Carver turned to follow her line of sight. Across the intersection, a line of cars waited for the light to change. A delivery van, a couple of scooters, and a taxi had the front positions. The light changed and they started to roll in unison.

Carver figured out what Mia was doing the second before she started to run.

"Shit, Jenner," he whispered. "Make it fast. She's about to catch a cab."

"Thirty seconds."

Mia came out of the alley and crossed the sidewalk to the curb, her hand raised toward the cab. It put on its signal and swerved to the right lane, stopping in front of her. The driver rolled down the passenger window and she leaned in to speak with him.

"Jenner?"

"I'm coming," he said. "Where are you?"

"On Bush, between Grant and the alley. We're about to lose her. She's getting in right now."

Mia's right boot disappeared into the cab and she shut the door. The driver put on his left turn signal, waiting at the curb for a clear path to the far lane. All Carver could do was stand and watch as it rolled to Kearny, signaled a left, and made the turn. Then, for just an instant, he had a clear view of Mia in the back seat. Her head was down and she was holding her fingers to her temples, so that her palms would block her sight on each side.

16

JENNER SLAMMED TO a stop in front of the brassiere, not even bothering to pull to the curb. Carver ran out and jumped in.

"Which way?" he asked, moving again before Carver had closed the door.

"Left up here – on Kearny."

Jenner checked his mirror, then changed lanes, cutting off one car and slicing behind another. Horns wailed from two directions, and Carver braced himself through the turn.

"You got the plate?"

"I see it. It's up there – slow down, or she'll make us."

He pointed through the windshield. The cab was caught at a red light at the intersection of Kearny and Pine. It was in one of the middle lanes, but as they watched, it made an illegal left on red and disappeared down Pine.

"You got it?"

Jenner answered with his foot on the accelerator. They made the turn and the taxi was one block ahead, passing the Ritz-Carlton. It cleared the intersection with Stockton and the light changed to red behind it. They watched it pass Dashiell Hammett Street and take a left on Powell.

"She's going in circles," Jenner said.

"Run this," Carver said. "They won't see us now. Run it."

Jenner looked up the hill to make sure nothing was coming, then ran the light. He accelerated all the way to Powell, and braked through the left turn. The car skidded on the wet trolley tracks, then found its grip again on the asphalt as they went down the hill. There were half a dozen cabs in front of them now.

"You see it?"

"There," Carver said. "Crossing Bush. She's headed to Union Square."

"How smart is this girl?"

"Smart."

There was an opening in the traffic, and Jenner could have closed the gap between them. But he held back, leaving three cars as a buffer. The hill was steep enough that they could still see the taxi clearly. Mia's shoulders and head were illuminated by the car directly behind her. She still had her head down, almost as if she were trying to curl inside herself.

"You think she's talking to the cab driver?" Jenner asked. "That she meant to meet him?"

"No way," Carver said. "She caught it by accident. If he'd been expecting her, he was in the wrong lane – Mia saw a chance and she took it, to make this hard."

"Make it hard on us, you mean."

"On anyone."

"Who else would be chasing her?" Jenner asked.

"That depends on what she knows."

They watched the cab pass through the intersection ahead. It swerved to the left curb and stopped. Jenner didn't have any choice except to pass it. As they went by, Carver looked out the rear window. He saw the cab and the lights of Union Square behind it. The sidewalks were packed with shoppers. Uniformed patrolmen stood in front of the display windows and at the shop entrances with their batons out and ready. And then there was Mia, sliding into the throng on the sidewalk, meeting the driver as he climbed from his seat.

"She's paying – I'll get out at the corner, double back."

"She goes into the Vendôme, it'll be a zoo."

"That's why she picked it," Carver said. "Let me out."

"Keep your phone close."

Carver raised it, to show Jenner he had it in his hand. Then he stepped from the car, came around its rear bumper, and pushed into the crowd. He didn't look up the block until he was close to a shoe store's display window. Mia was weaving through the crowd, and then she vanished past the corner on her way to the Vendôme's main entrance. All he saw was the spill of her hair over her shoulders, and the back of her black coat. But that was all he needed.

As soon as she was out of sight, he began to jog, dodging through knots of shoppers until he reached the corner. He slowed when he got there, then rounded it and stood as if he were looking in the shop window. The mannequins on the other side of the glass looked back at him with empty eyes, their hands open and welcoming. He looked to his left and saw Mia stuck in a mob waiting to pass through the Vendôme's revolving doors. He waited until there were five people packed behind her, and then he started along the sidewalk toward the doors. He called Jenner, who answered immediately.

"You still got her?" Jenner asked.

"For now," Carver said. "She's going into the Vendôme. Try and park on O'Farrell, watch the back doors."

"I can try," Jenner said. "Cop comes, it's not like I can flash my badge. I might have to keep moving."

"See what you can do."

He stopped again, this time in front of the window that had been shattered the night he and Mia first drove out. The yellow tape was gone, and there were no glass shards underfoot. The newly installed pane sparkled like the facet of a diamond, and behind it, the mannequins had been switched out. It was all perfect, the crime erased. But it was that way wherever there was money – nothing aged anymore. The wealthiest parts of the city regenerated each night. It was another story out at the edges, time and desperation grinding entire neighborhoods to sand.

A whirl of movement drew his eyes back to Mia, to the mob she was joining at the entrance. Carver started toward her, thinking it was a stampede toward the door. He saw the off-duty cops rushing into the crowd with their batons up, and he began to run toward them. He was thinking only of Mia. Sprinting now, his one blind thought was that if he could pull her away in time, she might not be hurt too badly. But before he reached her, the commotion resolved itself and he knew she wasn't yet in any danger. He stopped running and faded back toward the display windows, walking sideways, then backwards to keep his distance in case she turned around.

The cops converged on the shoplifter. She was a young woman, a teenager probably. She'd made it through the doors before she'd been spotted, and she was struggling with a plainclothes guard who'd come out after her. She broke free of him and punched into the crowd, but by then the off-duty cops had converged on her. The crowd cleared back, giving them a circle of space on the sidewalk. Everyone knew what was coming. The girl was clutching an armful of small black boxes to her chest. She looked at the cops and at the crowd, and then she feinted forward, threw the boxes over the policemen's white helmets, and turned to sprint for the street.

She made it three steps before a cop laid her on her back with a baton blow to her throat. Then the rest of them were around her, bringing their batons all the way back and pitching forward as they swung at her. The girl's screams were lost in the cries of the women scrabbling for the boxes of Black Aria she'd scattered. Some of the vials had broken, and the heavy fragrance of perfume filled the air.

Carver scanned the swirling crowd until he spotted Mia. She was edging past the screaming girl, toward the Vendôme's entrance. He could tell she was hesitating, that she wanted to step into the circle and try to stop the beating. There was blood on the sidewalk, droplets of it on the storefront, where it had been flicked back from the ends of the batons. But something more important than the girl was driving Mia tonight. She passed without stopping, and soon was inside the revolving doors, a whirl of polished metal and glass.

Carver raised his phone to his ear.

"She's in," he said. "Jenner – you there?"

"Here."

"I'm going after her."

But first he went to the cops. He wished he had a badge. He loosened his jacket so his weapon would be visible in its shoulder holster, and then he grabbed the nearest officer by his shoulder and swung him around. The kid was wearing a white SFPD crowd helmet. His Plexiglas faceplate was down, and it was speckled with blood. The kid raised his club, but Carver caught his wrist. His eyes shot to the kid's breast pocket to read the silver nameplate.

"That's enough, Wilson. Look at me – you want to put that down."

He'd tried to say it the way Jenner would. So calm and low that the kid wouldn't know if he'd said it, or growled it. And to emphasize it, he twisted the kid's wrist and squeezed until the baton fell from his grip, clattering onto the pavement between their feet.

"Robbery and the patrol sergeant are ten-ninety-eight. They'll be here in a minute. And look at you – look at all of you."

"Who the fuck –"

The kid was half-crazed with adrenaline or Dexedrine, but when

Carver slapped the side of his helmet, he blinked and looked down. Next to them, the girl had begun shaking, her feet hitting the sidewalk in an arrhythmic seizure. The other cops had stopped and now stood above her, watching Carver.

He thought of what Mia had been trying to tell him. It hadn't always been this way. There was something wrong—wrong with the five patrol cops staring at him, with the girl on the ground, with the state of the city and the world they all shared. It hadn't always been so low. But it had sunk so slowly, the first subsidence so far in the past, he'd never noticed.

"She resisted, and—"

Carver hit the other side of the kid's helmet, using the base of his palm like a hammer.

"Shut the fuck up," he said. "And call an ambulance."

He went for the doors before any of them could ask another question. He didn't have to fight to get there: the crowd parted in front of him and closed behind him. There was complete silence until the sirens started on the other side of the square.

Carver came out of the revolving doors and pushed past a line of saleswomen who had come up to the front to watch the beating. There was Christmas music playing, and soft overhead spotlights picked out the display cases from on high. Handfuls of unset diamonds were scattered beneath each glass countertop. The air was shot with their radiance. An entire wall of Black Aria stood next to the escalators, the boxes individually wrapped in silk organza and tied with red ribbons.

He spotted Mia on the escalator, going up. She stood backward on the steps, scanning the room below her. Carver turned away before she saw him. Keeping his head down, he went deeper into the store. Only a fool would follow her up there. The escalators were a bottleneck, and she was watching her tail going up them. If her plan was to meet someone on one of the upper floors, she'd be able to do it out of his sight.

He moved toward the store's far corner, where the elevators came down from the top-floor restaurant. If she came down the escalators or any of the fire stairs, he wouldn't see her. But he could see the front doors from here, and he could watch the elevators.

He looked outside. There was no ambulance yet. The cops had

rolled the shoplifter onto her stomach and cuffed her wrists behind her back. He hoped that meant she was still alive.

His phone started to vibrate, and he answered it.

"She just came out the back door," Jenner said. "She's heading east on O'Farrell."

"On foot?"

"But walking like she means it," Jenner said.

Carver was already moving, winding through the store's intentional labyrinth, searching for the rear exit. It took him a minute to get there. When he reached the sidewalk he started to jog.

"She just crossed Stockton," Jenner said. "She's on the south side of the street and – I see you."

"Stay with the car," Carver said. "Keep our options open."

"You have her?"

"Not yet."

He reached Stockton and jaywalked. Most of the off-duty cops had drifted toward the front of the store to see the unconscious girl, and only one man yelled after him. He ignored it, then started jogging again, watching across the street to his right until he saw Mia.

"I got her now," he said.

"Good – I just lost her."

He ran across the street so he could tail Mia on the south sidewalk, keeping a hundred feet back. She took a quick right and he could see her through the two sets of corner display windows at the Marshalls department store. She joined a line of people waiting to board a bus.

"Better start driving," Carver said. "Pick me up on Market. She's taking a bus."

"This girl isn't joking," Jenner said. "What number?"

"It's a five, or a five L."

"Soon as she's on board, I'll come," Jenner said.

The bus was already full, and the line to board it moved slowly. Mia was shifting back and forth, perhaps thinking of abandoning the line and going for another taxi. But she stayed where she was, her fare clutched in her right hand. She was the last aboard, and the doors closed behind her.

Tailing the bus was relatively easy.

After picking up Carver, Jenner caught up to the bus and followed directly behind it, waiting there whenever it stopped to load and unload passengers. The only risk was that if Mia got out she might see them. But Jenner's car wasn't one she'd recognize, and his windows were dark.

They were moving west now, away from the city center. The buildings grew lower and darker. Dozens of people had exited at the early stops, but Mia hadn't been among them. The bus jogged to the left and a moment later they were passing through the bell tower shadows beneath St. Ignatius. Not long after that, Golden Gate Park appeared on the left.

The streets were quiet enough now that Jenner could follow the bus from a block back. When it pulled to the curb at the Fourteenth Avenue stop, Jenner hit the brakes.

Mia stepped out, keeping her head down. She was out of view as Jenner sped up and passed the bus. He took a right and stopped at the curb. Carver was already getting out.

"I'll circle back and tell you what she's doing," Jenner said.

Carver nodded and shut the door, then dialed Jenner's cell.

"She's heading into the park," Jenner said.

"All right."

At least he'd had fifteen minutes to rest in the car. Now he was running up the hill, stopping behind a parked car to watch for Mia. He saw her for a few seconds in the amber cone of a streetlight, and then she took a footpath that curved into the park through a grove of cypress trees.

Carver reached the path a minute behind Mia and put his hand against a tree trunk. He closed his eyes to let them adjust to the park's shadows, and then whispered to Jenner between breaths.

"Headed along a footpath," he said. "Near Shoreline Highway."

"That's close to the redwood grove," Jenner said.

"I know it."

He followed the path in the direction Mia had gone, walking off to the side so that his footsteps were muffled by the grass. He couldn't see Mia right now, but if she'd stuck to the path, then he knew where she was. She'd be passing fifty feet from the spot where they'd found Hadley Hardgrave's split and carved body.

"Why would she be going there?" Jenner asked.

"I don't know."

He went off the path and jogged through the trees until he caught up with the wrought-iron fence that bound the western edge of the rose garden. Then he followed that, at a full sprint, until he came to a wide clearing in the trees that led into the Fourteenth Avenue East Meadow. He stood at the edge of the meadow and looked across it. It was there, in that dew-soaked grass, that they'd found Hadley.

Of all the places Mia might have come, she chose this spot.

On the far side of the meadow, the path came out of the redwood grove where it crossed John F. Kennedy Drive. There was a working streetlight above the crosswalk. He knelt in the grass, breathing hard again, and waited. He began to wonder if he'd made the wrong move. She could be meeting someone right now, passing along the information she'd learned tonight at the Irish Bank.

But before he'd made up his mind to try to creep into the grove, she emerged from the trees, alone. She came to the crosswalk, following the edge of the light's pale reach, and started along the path to Stow Lake. This time when he followed her, he could keep her in view. She headed up to the boathouse and disappeared behind it. He went to the edge of the lake where he could see over the cattails and across the dark water to the docks. There were rowboats stacked on top of each other along the shore. She walked past them and went out onto the dock. It was quiet enough that he could hear her boot heels clicking on the wooden planks. She knelt down at the end of the dock and reached under it, then came up a moment later with a small cylinder in her hands. He watched as she unscrewed the cap from the cylinder and checked inside it with her fingers. Then she twisted it back together and replaced it.

She stood on the dock for five minutes, just staring at the water. He wasn't sure if he could hear her crying or not. Then she turned and retraced her steps, but this time Carver made no move to follow her. He dialed his phone again.

"Jenner?"

"Still here."

"She just checked a dead drop."

"She get anything from it?"

"I couldn't see," Carver said. "She's headed back out – probably to the bus or a taxi."

"You following her?"

"I need to check the drop, see if she left anything. Where are you?"

"Back at Fifteenth, where I let you out."

"Keep an eye on her when she comes back to Fulton," Carver said. "She's coming your way."

"Okay."

But Mia didn't walk out as fast as she'd come in.

She'd done whatever she'd left her apartment to do, and now her drive was spent. He watched her pass along the path above him. She was hugging herself, walking as if each step cost more than she could pay. When she was gone, and he could no longer hear the drag of her feet on the gravel-strewn path, he got up and came around the shoreline to the boathouse. He went out onto the end of the dock and fished beneath the cold lake water until his fingers found a short length of steel pipe attached to the dock with a spring clip. He pulled the dead drop out of the water, unscrewed the cap, and lit up the inside with his flashlight.

It was empty.

He put it back onto its underwater clip and sat on the dock, looking out at the lake as Mia had. After ten minutes, his phone rang and he picked it up. His hands were still wet, but he didn't care.

"She's just sitting at a bus stop on Fulton," Jenner said.

"She's done now," Carver said. "She's going home."

"What do you want to do?"

"Come pick me up. If we take Geary, we can beat her by half an hour."

"And then what?" Jenner asked.

"I don't know."

17

CARVER CAME INTO his apartment and went to the hall closet. He reached up to the shelf, feeling along it until he touched the leather case that held his backup set of picking tools. These weren't as good as the ones in his crime scene bag, but he wouldn't have time to go to the parking garage to get anything from his car. And he didn't really care how much damage he did to Mia's lock.

He left his trench coat and hat on their hooks, then went back to the hallway and crouched in front of Mia's door. It took him five minutes to open the deadbolt and another twenty seconds on the simpler lock in the doorknob. He put the picks back into his closet, then went across the hall and into Mia's apartment before he could change his mind.

"Mia?"

He didn't expect an answer and didn't get one. He closed the door and locked it. Then he went into the living room and sat at the wing-back chair by the fire. The window was behind him, and the chair's back rose above his head. She wouldn't see him when she came in.

She'd left the fire burning, and he was glad for it. He'd sweated through his suit while chasing her, and gotten wet kneeling on the ground. Now that he wasn't running anymore, he was cold. So he sat and let the fire warm him up, and he didn't move or open his eyes until his phone began to ring again.

"She's here," Jenner said. He was somewhere in the alley, down below. "You sure you don't want me to come up?"

"I'm sure."

"Climbing now," Jenner said, and then he fell silent. Carver could hear the wind in the alley and nothing else. "She's already on the first walkway, untying the rope. She'll be at the window in fifteen seconds."

"I'm ready."

"I'll hang in the neighborhood, if you need me."

"Go on home."

"I'll hang."

Jenner cut the connection and Carver put his phone into his jacket pocket. He listened for Mia coming up the fire escape, but wasn't surprised that she managed it without making any noise. The first sound he heard was the window sliding open, and then her boot on the wooden floor. A cold current filled the room when she parted the heavy curtains, and then the window slid shut and the air was still again.

He listened as she walked behind him, and then she came into view as she passed into the kitchen. He had his hand inside his jacket, on the gun's rough grip. He knew he wouldn't use it to threaten her, but he was ready to protect himself if she drew on him. But she didn't see him at all. She drank water straight from the tap, and then crouched at the wine cabinet and chose a bottle by the sticker on its base. She stood and set it on the counter, then turned to the cabinet for a glass.

"Better get two," Carver said.

She screamed and dropped the glass, which shattered in a spray when it hit the granite counter. He stood and came toward her.

"No, Ross—*please!*"

She dropped to her knees, falling hard on the broken glass. Her hands were out in front of her face. He looked at her, then down at himself. His hand was still inside his jacket, gripping the gun. She thought he was going to shoot her. He raised both his hands to the height of his shoulders, palms toward her, so she would see they were empty. But her eyes were closed.

"Mia," he said. "Look at me."

She looked up.

"I'm not here to hurt you."

"This isn't what you think," she said.

"What do I think?"

"That I had something to do with it—with what happened to you and Jenner. With the murders—all of it. But I didn't."

He took a step toward her to see how she'd react. She didn't shrink away from him. So he came the rest of the way to her and took her under her arms to help her stand. Once she was leaning against the counter, he crouched to look at her knee. There was glass stuck to her jeans, and a cut in the fabric, but she wasn't bleeding. He swept the glass off with the side of his palm and stood up, meeting her eyes. She was sobbing.

He'd meant to scare her, to be hard with her until she told him the truth. But he hadn't expected it to be like this. He went to the sink, dampened a hand towel, and handed it to her. She used it to wipe her face, and then she came up to him and slid her arms around his waist to hold him. Her hands were inside his jacket, and he knew if she tried, she'd be able to reach his gun before he could. But there was no tension in her muscles, no hidden potential waiting to spring. He was almost holding her up.

"Ross," she said. She was whispering into his shoulder. "I should've told you sooner. I didn't know how."

He put his arms around her then. He didn't know what to say. Instead, he let his right hand go up to her hair to stroke it, then let it fall down the length of her spine to rest above the waist of her jeans.

He thought of the teenage girl, tossing vials of Black Aria into the crowd. Men and women crying out and diving for the perfume while the off-duty cops pummeled the girl so brutally that everyone within ten feet had been hit by her blood. There'd been a woman who'd dropped to her knees just outside the circle of the beating, taking a broken vial and stroking its raised emblem with her fingertip. She'd been wearing a gray wool suit over a white blouse. Her hair was done up in a tidy bun. She might have just come from court, or a board meeting. She hadn't seemed to think anything was wrong.

How many times had he seen that same scene? How many times had he shrugged past it?

He cupped the back of Mia's head with his left hand and whispered into her ear.

"Somehow the world changed. It went dark a long time ago, but nobody noticed. Except you. You saw something, figured it out. And now you have to tell me what it is."

She held on to him tightly and spoke without lifting her face from his shoulder.

"I can't tell you everything," she said. "But I can tell you what I know."

"You're still shaking," he said. "You don't have to."

"After they got Hadley, it's all I do," she said. "They're looking for me, and when they find me, they're going to kill me the same way — or worse."

"You knew Hadley."

"I did," she said. "Of course I did."

She opened the wine and poured it while he found a broom and swept up the broken glass. Then she led him to the living room. She had her wine in one hand and the folder of tomography scans in the other.

He thought she was going to take the same chair she'd used before, but instead she sat on the rug in front of the fire. She drank her wine and he sat opposite her, watching as she calmed down. She was holding the folder on her lap.

"I used to have a different life," she said. "I lived in New York. I had a husband — for a while, we were trying to have a baby. I had two cell phones, and a tablet, and three or four laptops. We went to parties, and I went shopping with my friends. I had a job."

"You were a doctor."

She nodded.

"A neurologist. I'd finished my last fellowship, had taken an offer with a specialty group in Midtown. And on my first day, I saw a patient I couldn't figure out. We'll call him James. He'd been to a psychologist, a psychiatrist, a substance abuse therapist. And then he decided none of it was working, that his problem wasn't psychological. It was wired into his brain. So he came to me."

"What was wrong with him?"

She took a long sip of her wine.

"He'd been with the NYPD, was a retired detective. His boss — his lieutenant, I guess — wanted a new investigative division. A new task force. They had Robbery, and Homicide, and Sex Crimes. All the usual things. But this lieutenant wanted a new division. Do you know what they wanted to call it? Can you guess?"

Carver shook his head. He didn't know anything about the NYPD. It was hard enough to keep up with his own city, his own department.

"Brand Cults," Mia said. "The Brand Cults Special Investigation Division."

"Brand Cults?"

"You've seen them everywhere, for years. Why do you think ten thousand people would turn out for a perfume launch party? It's water and alcohol in a glass bottle, some scents cooked up in a lab. It costs pennies to make, and what are they selling it for? And people are paying that?"

Carver shook his head.

"It's a fad. People get excited for a new thing."

She touched his shirtsleeve.

"This is nice," she said. "Francesca Cavaleri. You got it in June."

"How—"

"Everybody got one in June. And then the company disappeared. Just like Black Aria will be gone before spring, and the hotels and the billboards and the flashing postcards in your mailbox will all be advertising something else."

She took another sip, smaller this time. She moved closer to the fire, which brought her up against his side.

"James worked in the Brand Cults division for three weeks before it got shut down," Mia said. "They were picking up the desperate cases. Not just the shoplifters, but the schoolgirls who were trading sex for spending money. The lawyers who zeroed their client's trust accounts and blew everything on trinkets. And what he found in the interrogation rooms is what he already knew."

"Which was what?" Carver heard himself ask.

Mia touched his chin to turn him toward her.

"It starts in your head," she said. "At first, most of them thought they could ignore it. But they'd wake up in the middle of the night, and they'd be aching. Haven't you ever wanted something so badly it hurts?"

She was speaking in the same tone she had been the first time he'd heard her voice—when he'd woken to the sound of her reading. There was a catch in her throat before the pauses, a reedy sound, like a woodwind instrument's taken to the vanishing point of silence. Carver remembered the way she'd put her hand on his forehead. He closed his eyes and held his wineglass, and listened to her.

"And it didn't just stay in their heads. It would spread from there, sweet and warm. Waves of it. It was like sex, how they described it to him. That same golden rush. Except the climax would last as long as they could stand to look."

"Look at what?"

“At the ads. Have you seen our neighbors, downstairs in the mailroom? Have you seen them go through a stack of glowcards?”

To keep his shame from her, Carver drank the rest of his wine in one go. He knew just what she meant and could not have felt more exposed. If Mia sensed it, she didn’t care. She inched closer to him and went on.

“It’s pure pleasure,” Mia said. “But not something most people are aware of—is it?”

“I guess not.”

“Some people just look at ads and throw them away, but he couldn’t—and it didn’t matter if he could afford what he bought. It was ruining him.”

“Did you help him?” Carver asked. “Could you?”

She shook her head.

“I didn’t make a dent—I didn’t understand the depth of it. I saw him for a year. The last time, I cut out his brain and put it in a cooler.”

“You did what?”

“He’d shot himself,” Mia said. “When he couldn’t pay his debts—when they were taking his apartment, he put a bullet through his heart. But first, he wrote a note.”

“Saying what?”

“That it was mine, his brain. That if I cut it up, maybe I’d figure it out.”

18

MIA PUT THREE glossy pages on Carver's lap. He looked at the first image she'd handed him, picking it up by its edges to study it. When he turned back to her, she read the question from his face.

"That's an MRI, looking in from the back. The white area, here —" she traced the spot with her fingertip, "— that's his hypothalamus."

"Okay."

"Look at these," she said. "Do you see them?"

She'd touched a pair of S-shaped tendrils. They glowed with a white light, brighter than anything else in the image. They reminded Carver of the filaments inside an old-fashioned light bulb.

"Is this magnified?"

"Magnified, fine-tuned — you have no idea how long it took to get this."

"The bright lines, they're part of the hypothalamus?"

"They run from the hypothalamus and tap in to the optic chiasm," she said. "But they shouldn't be there. They're not part of the hypothalamus; they're not part of James at all. Turn the page."

He lifted the top page and laid it on the rug next to him. The next image was another MRI. The filaments were there again, a brilliant resonance against the gray haze of the brain matter.

"That's looking down, from above," Mia said. "Now you can see the other legs."

"Are they implants?"

"They couldn't be," Mia answered. "They were buried at the center. The tendrils go to every part of his brain. If someone put them there, I'd have found scarring. I'd have seen lesions and nerve damage. But his brain was perfect. Except for these."

There were eight filaments, spreading outward from a central point. It looked like a spider, a delicate one holding itself high off the ground on gossamer limbs. In the blur, he could almost make out the thing's body.

"These are the first two?" he asked, touching two of the filaments with his finger. "But from above?"

"That's right."

"What about these other six?"

"They spread all over."

"How small are they?" he asked.

"Thinner than a nerve axon, but long. You wouldn't be able to see them at all, but I got them to shine."

"Shine?"

"I hand-tuned the coil until I got that. It's like looking for a harmonic on a violin—when you get it, it rings."

"But you wouldn't have looked so hard if your patient hadn't told you to," Carver said.

"I wouldn't have, no. We'd done MRIs before, and PET scans, while he was still alive. But nothing showed up—they were always there, but I wasn't looking the right way."

"What about this?"

He was pointing at the center, at the place where all eight strands came together. On the page, it was a spot of the purest white. The hint of a sphere shone through the nebular ridges and folds of the man's brain. It was a bright star behind a thin cover of clouds.

"This?" she asked, circling the center point with her fingertip. "It's the legs that really tell the story. This is a thousand times smaller than a pinprick. But if we backed out, if we followed the other six legs, they'd spread through the brain, to the pleasure centers. The ventral pallidum, the orbitofrontal cortex—all of them."

"Pleasure centers?"

"Some regions of the brain, if you stimulate them—if you go in with a wire and run an electric current—you can trigger intense feelings. Joy and fulfillment. Desire. Need, even."

He looked at the image, at the thin filaments spreading like the roots from a newly sprouted seed.

"These are wires?" Carver asked. "You're saying he had wires in his brain?"

"You could call them wires," she said. "They're made at least partly of metal. But they're not like anything you've ever heard of, because they're sheathed in protein. So you might say they're at least half alive."

"What do they do?"

"Specifically?" she asked. "I don't know."

Carver saw the evasion on her face but knew he could ignore it for now. He could circle back to it. The important thing was to keep her talking.

"The legs—you didn't say where they're coming from," Carver said. "What are they connected to?

"Turn the page."

He lifted the second page by its edges and started to move it aside, but Mia's hand fell across his.

"Wait."

He looked up at her.

"I've only shown this to a few people."

"All right."

"They're all dead now," she said. Her voice was barely above the whisper of the gas-fed flames. "Every single one of them. So if you want to forget all this, and walk away, then do it. Do it now, before we go any deeper."

He studied her face in the soft firelight. After a moment, he took her hand, lifting it from the edge of the page. Then he circled his fingers around her wrist and set her hand in her lap. If Mia had an answer, he needed to hear it.

"You know I can't just stop," he said.

"But you can't go back, Ross. Once you know this, that's it."

"Then show me."

He turned the page.

He was looking at a silvery sphere. On the page, it was the diameter of a tennis ball, but he knew that whatever it was, it had been magnified far beyond its true size. Its surface was grooved, marked with structures and meandering lines. It was like looking at a city map that had been curved into the shape of a teardrop. The eight legs came from its equator and disappeared out past the edges of the page.

"This isn't an MRI," he said.

"I got this with an electron microscope."

“And this was from his brain? This thing was in his brain?”

She nodded.

“The MRI showed me where to look. I cut in and took the hypothalamus. Then I made slices, and worked them under the microscope until I had it.”

He looked at it, at the hard metallic sheen of its outer shell. He thought about ticks, how they burrowed into you and didn’t start to feed until they were halfway under the skin.

“It built itself in place,” Mia said. “The wires were like roots, pushing until they found water. Vines, twisting up, for the sun.”

“You’re saying it grew there.”

“That’s what I think.”

“So it’s not a machine?” Carver asked. “It’s a living thing?”

“Not the way I think about life. Maybe it’s something in between.”

He tilted the page toward the fire’s light, studying the thing’s design.

“What does it do?” he asked.

“I’m still figuring that out.”

He lowered the page. She was balancing her wineglass on her knee, the way she had a few nights ago. Poised and lovely. There was still a glow of sweat on her forehead from climbing up the fire escape. He realized he didn’t know a single thing about her that he could rely on, except the fact that she was sitting next to him. She had appeared in his life at his lowest and most vulnerable moment. She was far too smart to let him see any guile. Maybe now she was telling him the truth, but the truth was an endless, dizzying labyrinth. She could misdirect him without ever telling a lie.

“What’s your best guess?” he asked.

She pointed at the two legs near the top of the page, tracing just above them with her finger.

“We’ll just call these wires, okay?”

“Okay.”

She’d had a fair amount of the wine by now, and judging by the new cadence to her voice, it was loosening her up. That was fine. Even if she didn’t say a single thing he believed, he might learn something from the direction of her lies.

“I think they’re hooked in to his optical nerves. Like a tap on a phone.” She traced back down the wires to the spherical body. “They sent an image of whatever his eyes saw up to this. It’s a processor of some sort, maybe a quantum computer built out of biological components. It interprets the optic signals and decides what to do. If it sees something it likes, it sends signals to the pleasure centers."

"Through these other six wires?"

"Through those, yes."

"When you say it sees something it likes – what does that mean?"

"That it's programmed. That it scans everything its host sees. And if it sees a trigger – something buried in an ad or a label – it reacts. You've heard of the EURion constellation?"

Carver shook his head.

"It was a tripwire embedded in European paper currency, a long time ago. It was supposed to look like the constellation Orion. You wouldn't notice it with the naked eye, because it didn't stand out. But if a counterfeiter tried to scan a bill, the scanner would see the constellation and shut down. We think there's something like that embedded into advertisements, hidden on billboards."

"And if this thing – this quantum computer – comes across a trigger like that, what does it do?"

"It makes you want whatever you're looking at. It makes you fall in love with it. You think there will always be a hole in your heart unless you have it. It aches, but at the same time, it feels so good, you can't bear to turn away."

She laid all the pages in front of him. They were glossy enough that from an angle, they reflected the fire. To see them again he had to lean over. He looked at each: first the spidery glow of the MRIs, and then the sharp, computer-generated topography assembled by the electron microscope.

Then he looked up at her.

If he'd just passed her on the sidewalk, he wouldn't have marked her as someone who picked the labels off her wine before she drank it, who used a security guard to order her takeout because she was afraid to use a telephone. She didn't look like a woman who talked earnestly about tiny machines that grew in your head, about things that spread roots through your brain and tapped in to your eyes to tell you how to think. And maybe she wasn't that woman. Perhaps there was another reason she needed him to believe this story.

"I'm not making this up, Ross."

He nodded at the folder in her lap. She'd only given him three documents, but there were dozens more inside it.

"You told me those were your scans," he said. He touched his finger to his temple. "*Right in here,* you said — that's why you left New York, why you came here."

She reached for the wine bottle and refilled her glass, then tilted the bottle toward him. He nodded and she poured for him.

"A lot happened, after I found it," she said. "I told you I was married?"

"Yes."

"My husband disappeared. Not like you're thinking. It wasn't the cliché, where he stepped out for cigarettes, for a carton of milk. I knew where he was — he was in the condo. Just sitting there, fading away. I could see what was left of him. But he'd stopped seeing me."

Carver drank some of the wine. It would hurt, he thought — to be loved so well and then forgotten. Most everyone he knew had a story like that. Maybe they had all become invisible to each other, but that wasn't any excuse.

"By then," Mia said, "I was waking up. I was fighting it but he wasn't. I tried to help him, tried to make him see. But he wouldn't let go. He said I was crazy. A paranoid schizophrenic. He'd say I was unfit to be a doctor, unfit to be a mother. And then he'd tell me not to stand in front of the television when he was watching. And then, eventually, he really did leave."

Carver used the base of his wineglass to point at the three documents on the rug.

"Did you show him these?"

"I didn't."

"Why not?"

"I was afraid of them — and I didn't trust him."

"But you trust me?"

"Do I have a choice?"

He had no answer for that. Twenty minutes ago, he'd broken into her apartment, carrying a gun. He looked at the tear in her jeans and thought of the way she'd fallen on her knees into the broken glass, her hands in front of her face. He understood, of course, that he'd been using his gun every day whether he drew it or not. People knew it was there, and that changed everything. It might skew everything they told him. That was part of the bargain.

"You were telling me about your husband."

"There wasn't any more to it — I asked too much of him, and he left. After that, it would've been easy to fall into it. To wander into Times Square and stand there gawking with everyone else. Look at the lit signs, the window displays. Pick a glowcard off the sidewalk and stand there drooling. But I fought it. I knew I had one too, like James. I thought it'd be easier to fight it if I could see it."

She turned back the folder's cover and handed him the first page. It was a three-dimensional image of a brain. Mia's brain. She had manipulated the scan somehow, so that the brain matter was nearly transparent, like cloudy glass. The things growing inside of her were blue and violet, like arcing electricity. There were three spheres lodged in her hypothalamus. Their wiry legs twisted around each other, spreading through the dark space inside her skull, the tangled roots of weeds.

"It's why you won't go out, unless you have to," Carver said. "Why you peel the labels off everything, why you won't look at a phone."

She nodded.

"I thought maybe if I took away what they wanted to see, I could starve them out. That they'd die off, like vines in a drought," she said. She pointed at the three pale-violet bodies in the image. "But they don't go away. They dig into the cortex, and wait, watching signals flash past. They never sleep, even when I do—they can see what I dream."

He thought of the flies in Patrick Wong's apartment, their lidless, opaque eyes watching from the walls and the ceiling.

"Why did you come here?"

"Because of the scans," she said. "That's how they found me."

"They?"

"I'd rented time on an MRI at Sloan Kettering, to scan myself. When I saw what I had, I ran out. I didn't bother to reset the machine—I left the coil tuned to find these," Mia said.

She took the page from his lap and put it back into its folder.

"Was that a mistake, to not reset it?"

"It depends on how you look at it. What I'd done wasn't a normal way to set up an MRI. It wouldn't have happened by accident. And the next man who used the machine saw the settings and happened to know what they meant."

"A coincidence?"

"Yes, but not an unlikely one. If our movement was going to start anywhere, it would have been someplace like Sloan Kettering. There were people with the knowledge and the tools, and some of them were awake enough to watch. So when this man saw what I'd done, he checked the lab logs and found my name. And then he came looking for me."

"He recruited you."

"That's right."

"Who was he?"

"Another neurologist, one who'd woken up. I knew him as George – but it doesn't matter. He's probably dead now."

"Because of this?"

She nodded, then finished the wine in her glass.

"He disappeared a week before they got Hadley."

"What did he get you into?"

"A network," she said. "There weren't many of us to start with, and now I think I'm the only one."

"This network – who was in it, and who were you working for?"

"We were doctors, working for ourselves," she said. She looked him in the face, her dark eyes catching the firelight. "We weren't afraid to remember the way the world used to be. To hope it might be like that again."

"But you don't know who they really were."

"I don't," she said. "I took a risk. I had to. You've seen it, how it is out there."

"Yes."

He'd seen it all his life, maybe. He'd seen the way it slowly built, one stone on top of another until the spires touched the sky and blotted out the sun. By now their shadows darkened everyone. It had been so incremental that he hadn't understood. This wasn't a city, but a tomb. Standing in the mailroom with a stack of glowcards, he'd thought every acquisition was as necessary as water or air. But with every finger swipe, he'd been losing what was most important. He couldn't even remember the last time he'd spoken to anyone in his family, the last day he'd spent with a friend.

"Then you know what I'm talking about," Mia said. "And you can't fight it in the open. You can't publish papers on it, or talk about it on the internet or the phones. You can't go to the FDA or the CDC, or any of the research universities."

"Why?"

“Because people who push just a little, who make a bit of noise – they might wake up like you. Smelling like burnt iron, their memories a mess. And if they push a little harder, they end up like Hadley.”

“You’ve seen other people who’ve had their memories erased?”

She shook her head.

“Not until Friday morning, when I found you. But I knew it could be done. George saw three cases in New York, and the symptoms you presented matched his files exactly, right down to the smell.”

“How well did you know George?”

“Face to face, it was just the one time,” she said. “It was too dangerous to meet any more than that. We had other ways to talk.”

“Dead drops,” Carver said. “Like the one at the lake.”

She looked up, but recovered quickly.

“You must be very good,” she said. “To have followed me like that, you’d have to be.”

“Jenner and I know our business.”

“And I don’t,” she said.

“That’s not –”

“Really, I don’t,” she said. “I’m a doctor. I’ve been playing at something else, but it’s not what I am, not what any of us were. George, too. I keep hoping he’ll turn up. That’ll he’ll tell me what to do.”

“That’s what you were doing tonight – checking for him.”

She nodded.

“He wasn’t in San Francisco, I don’t think. He sent me here, to run Hadley. I made sure she had money, and I kept her on the right track – I had more technical knowledge than she did, but she was better at getting close to people.”

“What about George?”

“If he needed something, he’d contact me through the dead drop, and I’d reach her through a different one.”

“He’d do it himself, or through someone else?”

“I don’t know. There was a sign if there was going to be a message – a piece of red cloth, tied to a rain gutter on the other side of the alley. If I saw that, then I’d go.”

“What if you needed to contact him?”

“I’d leave a crack in the curtains so the light came out,” Mia said. “Then a message the next night.”

"You know where they dumped Hadley, after she was killed?"

Mia nodded, slowly.

"So your mailbox might not be safe anymore. Did she know about it?"

"I don't know."

"Did she know where you lived?" Carver asked. "Could she have given you up? You know when they did all that to her, they were asking questions."

"No — god, no. We were careful."

"Not careful enough. You went back."

"I didn't know what else to do," Mia said. "I've been sitting here for weeks, waiting. Either to be killed, or for someone to pull me out. And there wasn't any other choice. I can't do this alone. I don't even know how they got to her, so I have no idea what's safe and what isn't."

"She wasn't just a nightclub singer, was she?"

Mia raised her glass toward her lips, then saw it was empty. She set it down.

"She'd been a medical student. She found her way to George, somehow. Or he found her."

"Did Johnny Wong kill her?" Carver asked.

"I don't know."

"But you didn't hear that name for the first time from me. You already knew about him, didn't you?"

"I knew she was trying to find him."

"Why?"

"We finally had a lead," she said. "Years in the dark, and then we thought we had a way in."

"Tell me."

"It's like what they said about J.F.K. You want to know who killed the president? List the world's best marksmen, and then find out which ones were in Dallas. Making these devices would be incredibly hard. We guessed only a few scientists in a few labs could do it."

"So you did your research, and then you made a list."

She rose from her place on the rug, went into the kitchen, and pulled another bottle of wine from the rack. The corkscrew was still on the counter, and as she was twisting the handle, she looked at him and spoke quietly.

"It wasn't a long list. And inside a year, we ruled everyone out, except for one man."

When she'd extracted the cork, she came back to the fire and settled next to him again. He shook his head when she tilted the wine bottle toward his glass, but she filled her own.

"Who was he?"

"No one knew his real name. He called himself the Master." She must have seen his eyebrow twitch upward. "Even in science there's an underworld. Scientists who go rogue – mercenary types, who'll set up a black market lab, or build you a bomb, or a missile program, or whatever it is you've got the money to pay for."

"And what was the Master's specialty?"

"Nanorobotics," Mia said. "He had warrants in ten countries, his own page on the Interpol website. We finally tracked him down, in Mexico, but he wasn't much help."

"Then you ruled him out, too?"

"Not exactly. When we found him, he was dead. Shot through the temple. Suicide, or at least it was supposed to look like it. There was a gun next to him."

"You were there, in Mexico?"

She shook her head.

"I got this from George. He was there. And he found something in the Master's house that tied him to Johnny Wong."

Carver stopped himself from leaning forward. He didn't want to look too excited or too interested. Not while she was talking this much.

"What did George find?"

"A painting – a Bridget Laurent painting. One of the ones missing from the Legion of Honor. And everybody knows Johnny Wong was supposed to have been behind that."

"That's it?" Carver asked. "That's all you had to connect them?"

"That's all."

"And so George sent you and Hadley here to try to do what Jenner and I, and the FBI, and the DEA haven't been able to do. Find Johnny."

"That's right," Mia said. "And I think Hadley found him."

That thought sat between them for a while. Mia drank her wine, and Carver pictured Hadley's body in the wet grass. Then something occurred to him and he looked up from the fire.

"If George is a fake name, then Mia Westcott's a fake too," Carver said. "Who are you?"

She leaned back, shaking her head. If there'd been any wine left in her glass, she would have spilled it. When she answered, she spoke as quickly as he'd ever heard her.

"I won't tell you," she said. "If you knew my name, you'd go across the hall and run a search for me on your computer. And that'd raise a red flag somewhere, wouldn't it? My name, searched from this city. From this building. If they dug at all, they'd see you were the one looking. Don't you think you're already in their sights?"

"Then how can I believe any of this?" he asked. He touched the folder with the base of his glass. "Those are just pictures. Pictures, and a story."

She came back to him, taking his hand from his knee and weaving her fingers into his. He didn't pull away.

"If you can get me into a lab with an MRI," she said. "I can show you."

She was drawing him closer to say something else when his phone began to vibrate. When he took it out to read the text message, she quickly turned to look at the fire. He read it, and then put the phone away.

"You have to go," Mia said.

"Jenner's worried."

"Then go talk to him," Mia said. "Tell him whatever he needs to know. But promise me you'll do it face to face. Not on the phone. Not by email."

He nodded, and she took his hand again. She brought it to her lips and kissed his knuckles.

"Knock later," she said. "If you want."

19

INSTEAD OF GOING to his apartment, Carver went to the stairwell. Up until now, he'd been talking to Jenner freely on the phone, because it was a burner. But after his conversation with Mia, he was more concerned than ever that his apartment might be wired. She'd had unlimited access to it for an entire weekend, to say nothing of the crew who'd brought him home. So he took the stairs to the top floor, and then climbed the steel ladder to the roof. He unlatched the trapdoor with his left hand, then held on to the top rung and used the back of his head and his shoulders to lift the door open as he climbed through it. The sky above the city was black and orange with the remaining streetlights' reflected glow.

He went to the balustrade at the roof's edge and looked down the rain-swept street. Above Union Square, a police helicopter was descending through the opaque cloud cover, its searchlight igniting the sky until it broke into the clear air and the rain. He could feel the thump of its rotors as it began searching west along Post Street.

He took out the burner and called Jenner.

"You okay?" his partner asked.

"I'm up on the roof now."

"Alone?"

"That's right – listen, did you stay in the neighborhood?"

"I'm in Pinecrest Diner, grabbing a bite. I didn't know –"

"Take your time," Carver said. "Where's your car?"

"Garage across from the Marriott. Third floor."

Carver leaned over the balustrade and looked down his street. Near the intersection of Grant and Sutter was an old-style gas motorcycle, its rear wheel facing the curb. He could tell the bike was running from the warm haze of exhaust gathered around it. But its rider was nowhere in sight.

"Be there in twenty. You know how to pull the fuse on your GPS?"

"Already did," Jenner said.

"I'll call you."

He hung up, then put his hands on the stone rail. When he looked up, the helicopter was circling back, its searchlight roving left and right as it swept toward the Vendôme. He waited to hear gunfire, or the sirens of radio cars converging on the square. But neither came. Maybe they'd lost their man.

He closed his eyes and pictured Mia, replaying the time he'd spent with her through the lens of the story she'd told him. He knew it didn't answer everything. Even if what she'd said was true, all it explained was her desperation. He still didn't know what had happened on Thursday night. He didn't know who had killed Hadley Hardgrave or Patrick Wong. Mia had only deepened the mystery. And there was still no one he could trust, except Jenner.

Before going back to the ladder, he checked the street again. The motorcycle hadn't moved.

He walked to Powell, then up toward Nob Hill. He heard a motorcycle's racing engine one block over. He wanted to turn around and check the sidewalk behind him, but he didn't let himself. He trudged up the steep hill, listening to the rattle of the cable in the track to his left. At the mouth of Fella Alley, the same girl he'd seen on Sunday night was leaning against a brick wall. Her robe was open, and in the cone of light from the streetlamp, he could see the rhinestones in the waistband of her black underwear. She'd dusted silver and blue glitter across the pale undersides of her breasts.

"You wanna date?" she asked.

He didn't answer, but stepped past her into the alley.

"You don't see anything you like down there, come see me," she said to his back. "You could get me in, if you wanted. They'll let me in if I've got a date. And I can't go home, unless I get in there."

He went halfway to the club's door to get away from the girl, and then he stepped close to the brick wall and called Jenner. It had been twenty minutes and he knew Jenner was either in his car or standing somewhere close enough to watch it.

"Tell it to me," Jenner said, when he picked up.

"Last year we caught that triple. Two girls and a pimp. You remember?"

"Go on."

"I'm at the scene, but I'll be coming out the other side. Going the way he went. Take about ten minutes."

"Someone following you?"

"I don't know," Carver said. "Just watch for tails. Motorcycles, maybe."

"I see one, I'll shake it."

Carver hung up. When Mia didn't want to be followed, she'd taken a fire escape and a taxi before dodging through the Vendôme. That had been very good. But she didn't know the city the way he did, hadn't devoted her life to finding its darkest places. He went the rest of the way to the door. It was flanked on each side by gas lamps, but they were broken. The letters spelling out the club's name had been pried off the door years ago by metal thieves. No one had bothered to replace them; a name was the last thing this club needed.

He could hear the music from down below, could see the purple light leaking from the gap at the door's threshold. He knocked three times, his knuckles hitting bare wood. Other men had worn away the paint. The door swung open and the bouncer stepped out. He looked at Carver and took a long drag on his cigarette, then flicked it over Carver's left shoulder.

"One fifty."

Carver gave it to him and the man stepped aside and opened the door. The staircase behind it led down. Under the building and under Nob Hill.

Once, this club had been something special. He believed the old men's stories because he'd seen their photographs. They'd called it a jewel box. A treasure—if you were lucky enough to know it was there. But it had been abandoned. Thieves had stripped its ebony floors, had carted away the piano and the chandeliers. In peeling that veneer away, they'd unearthed an old tunnel, a leftover from the even deeper past.

He crossed the small dance floor, brushing past a half-dozen unclothed women. Their pupils were as wide as the bullets in his gun. Canvas tarpaulins hung from the ceiling to make private spaces along the walls. From inside them, he could hear the rest of the girls. They were working, and their cries carried over the music. He went to the bar and leaned against it until a man came over. He wore a black

T-shirt and had clay plugs in his earlobes, and when he saw Carver he nodded slightly. They'd spent a day together in an interrogation room, and he hadn't forgotten it.

"Who called you?"

"No one," Carver said. "I came on my own. My own dime."

"You want a drink, order one," the man said. "You want a girl, they're right behind you."

"I want to go through," Carver said. "Is that still fifty, to go through and out the other side?"

"A hundred," the man said. "The girls don't like it."

"What's it to them?"

"They're living down there."

Carver brought out his wallet again. He had exactly one hundred dollars left. He wasn't sure if his informal suspension included getting paid or not. That could turn into an issue if he had to keep spending money like this. But he lifted the bills from his wallet and handed them over. The man pocketed them.

"You know the way."

The door to the underworld gave no hint at what lay beyond it. It was as squat and unassuming as a pantry door. It might have passed for one: it was built into the back wall of the club's unused kitchen. The door was ten or twenty years old, but the passageway beyond it ran back to the first Tong War. The bartender unlocked the door for him. Carver took out his flashlight and stepped through.

The narrow passage led down the side of Nob Hill, burrowing beneath basements and through the foundations of the buildings above it. There were side tunnels, and low stone chambers. The floor was strewn with trash, and the walls were marked with graffiti. Some of the scrawls were so old they were ghosting back into the bricks. He saw a living space that hadn't been there when he'd last been through. Mattresses on the floor, plastic bins filled with shimmery-thin dresses. High-heeled shoes were piled against the stone wall. He saw a child's denim jacket, saw a little girl's plastic doll on one of the shared beds, its blond hair carefully combed. All around the floor there were candles and oil lamps, but none of them was lit.

In the ten minutes he spent underground, he heard no voices. But once, from far back in a side tunnel, he heard the slap of bare feet on wet stone. Several pairs of them. Women and girls, he thought. They were running through the dark, to hide from him.

The door on the other side opened into the back of a storeroom. He came out from behind a metal shelf and stepped over a mop bucket. He opened the door and went up a set of wooden steps. He parted a red curtain and slipped quietly onto the main floor of the club. No one noticed him come out. Everyone in the place was watching the television, including the three desultory girls who were supposed to be dancing on the bartop.

He followed their gaze to the screen.

A vial of Black Aria was descending through an eternal night sky. If he could believe Mia, Black Aria was only the latest thing. It didn't matter what it was as long as people saw the hidden triggers and robbed their own savings to buy it. As he had done, too many times to count. The vial pierced layers of clouds, everything lit silver by the moon. Then a city spread out beneath it. A city with no ragged edges, no darkened districts. It was a glittering promised land. No child inside its borders had ever been shot over a bucket of bricks. Its men didn't gut their own homes for copper. Women didn't hide in the catacombs.

He wasn't sure how long his phone had been vibrating before he answered it.

"I'll be out front in one minute," Jenner said.

"Any trouble?"

"No."

He looked once more at the advertisement, and then around the room at the men watching it. Some of them sat with open mouths. One of the girls on the bar had stopped dancing altogether. Absently, she pinched her nipple. She had it between her thumb and forefinger, and as she stared at the television, she was pulling it out. Twisting it. If it hurt at all, her face didn't show it.

The strip club was on Waverly Place, in the heart of Chinatown. As the crow flies, it was fourteen hundred feet from the top of Nob Hill. Carver had probably covered twice that distance underground. Jenner's headlights lit the rain around Carver's legs when he crossed in front of the car and got into the passenger seat.

"You okay?"

He nodded.

"What is this?"

"I couldn't let you pick me up at my place. In case it's being watched."

"What's going on?"

"Drive," Carver said. "We can't just sit here."

"Where?"

"South," he said. "Hunter's Point. But don't hurry."

"What's in Hunter's Point?"

"Calvin Tran."

"I thought he was in Folsom."

Carver shook his head.

"Parole. A couple days ago. I had an alert pop up, in case I wanted to go to the hearing."

"All right," Jenner said.

He turned left onto Clay Street. The Ønske Pyramid was two blocks in front of them, rising above everything else in the Financial District. Tonight it was lit blue-green, the color of sea ice. The crown jewel, the beacon at the spire's tip, was shining through the windblown mist. That was the one light that never went dark.

"You gonna tell me about Mia, or what?" Jenner asked.

"It's why I told you to take it slow," Carver said. "Stick to surface streets. Keep an eye in the mirror."

"Who are you worried about?"

"Johnny Wong," Carver said. "Hernandez. What Mia talked about."

He told Jenner then. Before he finished, they were in the pitted, dark streets of Bay View. Jenner didn't say much while Carver talked. He took a winding route, pulling to the curb and waiting sometimes, his eyes on the rearview mirror. Then he'd take a U-turn and speed off. If they had a tail, it was a very good one. They saw nothing.

Jenner parked across the intersection from Tran & Tran Auto Body, and they sat in the car and watched the dark shop and the little apartment above it. There had been a car accident in the intersection. A minivan had T-boned a pickup. Both vehicles had been abandoned there, then stripped. At some point, they'd been set on fire. Now they were just black hulks. The asphalt around them had burned, leaving nothing but a circle of loose gravel. In a year, all this would be gone. In its place there'd be clean white concrete and glass-fronted warehouses. Lines of delivery trucks departing every fifteen minutes for points in the city, heavy with liquor and silk, with dry-ice-cooled cuts of meat. Carver finished his story and they watched the building in silence for five minutes while Jenner thought about it.

"Is she crazy?" Jenner asked, finally. "Paranoid schizophrenic, something like that?"

"If she is, she's got a category all her own."

"I just met her the one time," Jenner said. "I wouldn't have pegged her that way either."

"If she's not crazy, there's someone else in her network. She didn't think George was here in the city. But somebody would leave a sign for her when there was a message from him. And she could leave a sign if she needed to contact George."

"You're thinking we could find this guy. See if he and Mia tell the same story."

"I don't know," Carver said. "Maybe I'm just thinking out loud."

"Are you even entertaining this, that it's real?"

"I don't know."

"If she's not crazy," Jenner said, "then she knows something. But maybe it's not the same thing she's telling you."

A light appeared in one of the apartment windows. It stayed there a minute, then went away.

"Where's he fit in?" Jenner asked. "Calvin Tran."

"We got a tip," Carver said. "A note. It said we should look at Johnny Wong for Hadley Hardgrave."

"That was anonymous," Jenner said. "And two months ago, Tran was still in Folsom. How's he gonna slide a note under your windshield wiper?"

"The handwriting," Carver said. "I just put it together."

"What?"

"When we worked out the plea on Tran, we were in the DA's office. Tran's lawyer wrote the deal points on a notepad, handed the page to me."

"Eight years ago."

"After I talked to Mia, I was thinking about Johnny Wong and Hadley. Trying to remember everything about when we first made a connection. So I was thinking about the note, and when I pictured it, I remembered the other. The writing on the plea deal."

Jenner looked at Carver. The only light came from the red glow of the dashboard clock.

"The shit you hang on to, Ross," he said. "I mean – Jesus. You think he got a message to his lawyer, asked him to send us the note?"

Caver nodded.

"And that note, a lot of it checked out," Carver said.

"Sure."

"We were sure enough about Johnny Wong to swear out a warrant. But if Mia's telling the truth, then Hadley wasn't some two-bit torch singer. Johnny wasn't in her league, and neither was anyone else we know."

"That doesn't mean he didn't kill her," Jenner said.

"But it puts a different spin on it."

Jenner thought about that for a while. Then he checked inside his jacket, making sure his gun wouldn't catch on anything if he had to draw it. Carver did the same.

"All right," Jenner said. "Then we'll go ask him."

20

CARVER STOOD OFF to the side, in front of a cinderblock wall, where a shotgun blast couldn't hit him. He reached around, through the iron bars of the outer security door, and hammered on the inner door's wooden lock rail. He pulled back, then brought the phone to his ear.

"Anything?"

Jenner was in the scrap-strewn backyard, watching the other door.

"Nothing. I could hear you knocking."

"I'll do it again."

He put the phone in his pocket and was leaning to knock again when he heard a footstep on the other side of the door.

"Who's there?"

It was just a whisper from the dark.

"SFPD," Carver said. "We're here to talk with Calvin Tran."

"You can't," the voice said. "It's – I mean – you just can't."

When Calvin had gone up to Folsom eight years ago, he'd left behind a wife and a twelve-year-old boy. Carver guessed he was talking to the boy. He closed his eyes and reached down into his memory until he caught hold of the name.

"Garrett," he said. "That you?"

There was silence. But he knew Jenner wasn't going to wait. Until he came through, Carver had to keep the kid busy.

"Listen up," he said. "We've got business with your dad. You can let us in now and we'll talk in the dark, so it's private. Or you can stand your ground and we'll come back tomorrow with a bunch of guys in blue. In the daylight, when everyone can see."

Garrett Tran thought about it for half a minute. Then the locks started to turn. He'd opened the inner door but not the security gate. A flashlight lit up the weed-choked path leading up to him. Carver didn't step into view.

"I want to see your badge," the kid said.

Carver was considering how to respond when Jenner beat him to it. His voice came from inside.

"Give it to me, Garrett," Jenner growled. "Nice and easy."

Carver listened, waiting to hear a struggle. But then Jenner was talking again, low and calm.

"Like that . . . just like that," Jenner said. "That was good. Now open the gate."

Carver took out his phone. It was still on speaker, still connected to Jenner. He hung it up, then put his gun back into its holster. Garrett Tran opened the gate and Carver stepped inside.

Jenner had Garrett's sawed-off twelve-gauge in one hand. The flashlight was taped to the barrel. Its beam lit the waterlogged ceiling. Carver caught the set of lock-picking tools when Jenner tossed it. He put it in his jacket pocket.

"Trouble with it?" he asked.

"It was a little rough," Jenner said. "I never had your touch. These guys might have to buy a new one."

"Small price," Carver said.

He looked at Garrett Tran. He took after his mother, had her finer features. He might have been a handsome young man in other circumstances. Right now he looked as if he'd been shot in the gut. His face was bloodless and he was breathing in short, shallow gasps.

"How about we go see your dad?"

They had to cross the garage floor to reach the apartment stairs. A black Maserati GranTurismo was in the main workspace. Jenner and Carver each let their lights touch its sleek body. Its sapphire windshield sparkled in the dark. There was a terrycloth towel on the hood, and a laptop computer on top of the towel. Wires ran from it and disappeared through the car's open window.

"Don't touch that thing," Jenner said. "So hot, it'd blister your skin."

The kid didn't answer. He was wearing sweatpants and a thin T-shirt, had plastic slippers on his feet. He was shaking. From the cold, from exhaustion. And he was terrified of something. That was plain. The fear was spilling out of him, so thick Carver could almost taste it.

Jenner pointed to the stairs with the shotgun and the kid shook his head. But he led the way.

At the top of the stairs was a thin wooden door, and Garrett Tran opened it. Carver saw a wall switch and flicked it, but no light came on. The power lines serving this neighborhood had probably been stolen years ago when the eminent domain condemnations turned the neighborhood into a wasteland. They'd have gasoline generators in the garage, because they wouldn't be able to run their shop without electricity. But gas wasn't cheap, and was getting harder to find. So up here, in the apartment, they were using flashlights and candles. The air smelled of smoke and sickness. The unwashed stink of the dying.

In the corner by the dead TV there was an overstuffed recliner. Calvin Tran was asleep there, a blanket thrown over him. Though it was entirely dark in the room, he wore a sleeping mask over his eyes. Carver turned to Garrett.

"Where's your mom?" Carver asked.

The kid shook his head again.

Carver glanced at Jenner, who crossed to the bedrooms. He disappeared inside them and came back out a moment later.

"It's just us."

"Go ahead," Carver said. "Wake your dad up."

The kid looked at Carver, his eyes pleading.

"You shouldn't," he whispered. "It's better if you don't. You don't understand."

Carver stared at down at him, until the kid went trembling to his father's side. He knelt there, put his hand on the man's shoulder.

"Dad," he said.

There was a round table next to the recliner. On it stood a half-full bottle of water with a flexible straw stuck into it. There was some kind of mush in a bowl. Next to that, a pill bottle lay on its side. Its cap was off. Carver picked up the bottle, but it had no label. He looked at the pills and guessed they were oxycodone.

"Dad," Garrett said again.

Calvin Tran stirred awake. He raised his head but didn't take off the sleeping mask.

"He can hear you," Garrett whispered. "But he can't talk. I told you that already."

"What's with the mask?" Carver asked. "Hey, Calvin? Take it off."

The kid did it for his father. He was shaking as he stepped in front of his father and took the mask by its corners. He lifted it off, his body blocking his father's face. Then he pulled off the blanket and stepped away. It was only when he'd moved aside and Carver could see everything that he understood.

Calvin Tran's hands were gone.

His arms ended at his wrists, which were wrapped tightly in white dressings. Square patches of gauze were taped in place over his eyes. But the bandages were sunken. They covered vacant space, were sagging into empty sockets.

Calvin Tran opened his mouth and made a sound. It wasn't any kind of word.

Carver fumbled his flashlight, but caught it and steadied it. The beam jerked across Calvin's face. His teeth were bloody. When he opened his mouth to moan again, Carver saw the stitches on the stump of his tongue. It had been cut out at the base.

It took half an hour to calm him down. Later, Carver mostly remembered the moaning. The flashlight beams stabbing uselessly at the dark. He saw Jenner's face in the chaos. It was tight and gray, no different from how the kid had looked when they'd caught him downstairs.

Carver crushed two of the pills and spooned the powder into Calvin Tran's mouth. He put the bottle under Calvin's chin and tilted his head until his lips found the straw. After that, it was another half an hour until he was asleep.

Then they took Garrett back to the garage.

Jenner had found a battery-powered lantern, a bottle of Johnny Walker, and a glass. He put the lantern on the workbench and turned it up, and then he poured a shot of the whiskey for the kid. Carver thought he might take one for himself, but he didn't.

Garrett took the glass and winced each time he sipped from it, but he worked through the drink until it was gone. None of them had spoken yet.

"This ... everything that happened to Calvin ... to your dad,"

Carver said. He paused and swallowed, then tried again. "Did it happen in Folsom, or after he got back here?"

"Prison," Garrett said. He wasn't looking at Carver, just staring at the amber liquid in the whiskey bottle. "They don't know who did it."

"They said that?"

"To my face."

"That's bullshit," Jenner said. "Not you – them."

Carver nodded. It was absolutely bullshit.

"He spent eight, ten nights in the infirmary," Garrett said. "Then the parole came through. They dropped him off like this. Mom saw him and started screaming."

"Where's she now?"

"Maybe L.A.," he said. "Her sister's there."

"She didn't say anything to you?"

"Nothing."

"Did she pack stuff up?"

"I don't know," Garrett said. "I haven't looked."

"You're still getting work from Johnny Wong," Carver said. "The Maserati, that's a job for him. Right?"

The kid didn't answer. He looked at his empty glass, his face frozen. Jenner poured another shot into it. The kid drank it right away and wiped his lips with the back of his hand.

"Tell me about Johnny," Carver said.

The kid nodded. When he spoke, it was a whisper.

"After dad went away," he said, "our other mechanic took over. There was always work. He was looking out for us, if you know what I mean. The mechanic."

"Johnny Wong was looking out for you. Through this guy."

"I guess."

"And now?"

The kid nodded at the car.

"Nothing's changed."

"Even since your dad got back?"

"He sent the doctor, who brought the pills."

"You know how to get in touch with him?" Carver asked. "This doctor?"

The kid shook his head. If he knew, he wasn't telling. It'd be just as useless to ask him where to find Johnny Wong.

"Why'd you come here?" he asked.

"We knew your dad," Carver said. "He tried to help us. He'd done it a couple times before."

"Helped you how?"

"That's between him and us."

Carver looked up the stairs. They'd left the door open so the kid could hear if his father woke up.

"What are you going to do with him?" he asked.

"I don't know."

This time, the kid filled the glass himself.

They went up the block to the car. Jenner put the keys in, turned on the headlights, and did a U-turn. He drove two blocks to get away from Tran & Tran Auto Body, and then he stopped in the middle of the street. It didn't matter here. There was movement in the shadows on either side of the street, but there was no traffic.

"I don't know what to make of any of that. I've never seen anything like it. Absolutely nothing," Jenner said. He was squeezing the steering wheel. After a while he let go and looked in the rearview mirror again. "You want a coffee somewhere?"

"Yeah."

"Then what?"

"I just need to make a couple calls," Carver said. "From a pay phone."

Jenner thought about it a moment, then started driving.

"I know a place," he said.

Carver watched the darkness ahead, watched the fog roll out from between the ruined buildings. It whipped across the road in tendrils. There was only one explanation for what they'd seen tonight.

"Someone knew it was him," he said. "Knew he tipped us off."

Jenner steered around a pothole the size of a bomb crater.

"Johnny Wong heard it was Tran. So he put out the order to have him cut up," Jenner said. "Like what he did when he heard we were looking for Patrick. That's what you figure."

"Yeah."

"But when Tran got out, Johnny sent him a doctor. And he's taking care of the kid. How's that make sense?"

Carver could see the expressway ahead of them. Once they reached it, they'd be back in the light, back inside civilization's shrinking circle. But for now, they were pressed between gutted buildings and wrecked cars. Stray cats roamed through the ruins. From ahead, their eyes shone out of the dark like bits of green and yellow glass.

"It makes sense if you're Johnny Wong," Carver said. "If your goal is to break people down. To take away everything until you're the only thing left. So they need you."

"We should talk to the lawyer," Jenner said. "Tran's guy."

"He wouldn't give us a thing."

"Still," Jenner said. "He could let something slip."

"Anything with those guys, it's just a waste."

They went to a pancake house on Beach Street. It was nearly six a.m. when they sat at the Formica table. The waitress came and put down an aluminum pitcher of coffee. Carver poured for both of them. After he added cream, he drank half his mug. He'd been cold since they'd left Tran & Tran. Then he felt in his pocket for coins and brought out some change and counted it in his palm.

Jenner slid a handful of one-dollar pieces across the table.

"It's down the hall," Jenner said. "By the men's room."

"I saw it coming in."

"You want me to order for you?"

"Only if you're eating."

He pushed out of the booth and went to the pay phone. He started with his building's front desk. Glenn worked for a private security company and knew guards across the city. A lot of them were on the waiting list for the SFPD Academy. They might do a favor for a man like Carver. When they hung up, Carver counted his change, then picked up the receiver again and started making calls.

21

JENNER DROPPED HIM at the Embarcadero Center, across from the Ferry Building. The sun must have come up on his walk home, but he couldn't see it for the clouds. The cars that passed him threw arcs of runoff onto the sidewalks. Everything was glittering. The streets, the rising arches of the bridge to Yerba Buena. The raindrops, streaking through the dark.

When he walked into the lobby, he found a letter waiting for him at the front desk.

Something Glenn had signed for, had left with the guard on the next shift. A rare thing, getting something in the mail that wasn't printed on a glowcard. It was from the Personnel Unit of the SFPD Staff Services Division. The department's seal, in embossed print, took up the entire left side of the envelope.

He opened it in the elevator and read it while walking to his door.

Inside his apartment, he threw the letter in the kitchen trash. He poured a glass of bourbon and drank it neat. Then he poured a second over ice and took it with him to the shower.

When he'd toweled off, he guessed enough time had passed that Jenner would be home. He turned on both taps, switched on the exhaust fan for its added noise, and got the burner phone.

"Can you hear me okay?" he whispered.

"Yeah."

"You get one too?"

"The letter? I got it."

"Approved for duty. If a medical review board gives us a pass," Carver said. "You heard of anything like that?"

"I don't know."

"You know it's a code for something else."

"Psychiatric evaluation, I guess," Jenner said. "Are you going? It's next week."

"I'll call the union rep," Carver answered. "Push mine back. Say I need more rest."

"Will that look good?"

He knew what Jenner meant. It was a cowboy department, and had been since the day it was founded. Its cops were supposed to be resilient. Skin like saddle leather. An officer didn't need rest; he needed action. That's what the commissioners thought, and that's what their medical review board would be looking for.

"I'll chance it," Carver said. "I don't want to stop this. Not till we're done."

When he came out of the bathroom, he heard a knock at his front door. He went to the peephole and saw Mia in the hallway. She was in her white robe, and even with the distorted angles of the fisheye lens, he could tell she'd been up all night. He opened the door and stood so she wouldn't see all of him. He was only wearing a towel, but he wasn't worried about that. He didn't want her to see the gun in his right hand.

"I know you're tired," she said. "You want to sleep."

"Mia—"

"I'm so scared I can't even sit still."

She brushed her hair back from her face, hooking some of the locks behind her ears.

"Mia, it's okay."

"Will you—I mean—I don't even know how to ask. I'm embarrassed to ask. Do you mind?"

"It's okay," he said again. "I think I understand. Can you give me a minute? I'll come over."

"Okay."

He shut the door. He went into his bedroom and put on clean clothes. He put his gun into the waistband of his pants and pulled his sweatshirt over it. Then he got his phone and his keys and went across the hall. Mia opened her door before he knocked, and locked it behind him when he was inside.

He hadn't been sure what she'd had in mind, but understood when he got to the living room and saw the pillows on the rug in front of the fire. She'd put down blankets, too. There was an opened bottle of white wine in a stoneware chiller. A wooden tray next to it held two glasses. He looked at her and she glanced away, the color already rising on her throat.

"Like a sleepover," she said.

"If you had a couch, we could take the cushions. Put them around us and hunker down."

"That'd be good," she said. "Safe."

She took off her robe and hung it over one of the wingback chairs. Underneath it, she was wearing a blue silk slip. The hem, trimmed in black lace, came less than midway to her knees. He wasn't sure if she had anything on underneath it.

She crossed to the rug and knelt to take one of the blankets. After she'd put it around herself, she arranged two of the pillows so she could lean against the heavy chair. She took the wine and poured it into one of the glasses, and then looked at him. When he nodded, she filled the second glass.

He sat on the other chair and took off his sweatshirt. Beneath it, he had a white T-shirt. He pulled the gun from his waistband and folded it into the sweatshirt. She watched him do it.

"This is safe too," he said. "It's never let me down."

"I hope so."

He put the gun by the pillows she'd set out for him. Then he slid off the chair and onto the rug. The blanket she'd chosen for him was a down duvet. As soft as fresh-fallen snow. He put it over his legs, then leaned against the pillows and the wingback chair.

"Thank you, Ross."

She was holding her wineglass toward him. He took his glass, touched it to hers, and had a sip. It was like biting into a tart green apple. Like the first days of summer. Somewhere high up, where the nights are still cold.

He wondered if Calvin Tran could taste anything now. Surely he wouldn't live much longer. Sooner or later, his son would get on a southbound bus to join his mother in L.A. That would be the end of it. Calvin's only crime had been to roll up his garage door. He'd gotten a midnight call and he'd let the wrong people in. For that, he'd gotten ten years as an accessory after the fact on a pair of carjack murders. It seemed fair at the time. But he'd drawn a punishment worse than anything Carver had ever imagined.

"Do you want to talk?" Mia asked.

"Not really."

They drank their wine. She looked at the fire, and he watched her. When her glass was empty, she put it on the tray and settled under her blanket. She shifted onto her side, her back toward him.

"Hold me?"

"All right."

She pressed against him. He wrapped his arm around her and put his face into her hair until it brushed the back of her neck. She lifted her blanket with a sweep of her arm, bringing it over him. They were close against each other, sharing each other's warmth. He still didn't know if he could trust her. But he didn't consider pulling away for a second. His gun was just behind him, wrapped in the sweatshirt. He was sure if it came to it, he could reach it first.

Sometime around noon, he woke for a moment. The curtains blocked whatever daylight there might have been. Mia had turned around, had burrowed her face into his shoulder. In the fire's heat, one of them had pushed the blanket back. He carefully hooked his finger under her shoulder strap, lifting it to cover her left breast. Then he brought the blanket over her. He rolled away and sat up, leaning on the chair again. He reached to his right and felt the gun inside his sweatshirt. He lifted it, measuring its weight in his hand. The magazine was still full.

He put his left hand between Mia's shoulder blades. Without waking, she arched her back into his palm. And like that, he went to sleep again.

He woke again when it was dark, and made coffee while Mia dressed in her bedroom. She came out while he was washing his mug.

"I'm going now," he said to her. "Give me at least five minutes of lead. Let them have time to follow me, if they're going to follow."

He left before she could answer, and went across the hall to change clothes. At 6:45, he walked out the building's front door and got into the taxi at the curb.

"Where we headed?" the driver asked.

"Powell Station," Carver said. "But let's roll through Chinatown first."

"Somewhere particular?"

"Stay out of traffic, if you can," Carver answered. He turned to look out the rear window. "Keep us moving."

"You got it."

They'd stopped at the light and were waiting to cross Bush. The Dragon Gate faced them from across the intersection. The driver was watching him in the rearview mirror.

"Maybe none of my business, but you worried someone's following you?"

"I don't know."

"What are we looking out for?"

"Could be anything. A car, a van. I don't know."

"Must be something about this block."

"What's that?"

"Last night, I pick up a lady on Bush. Right around the corner from here. She had the same problem."

"Anyone follow her?"

The driver shook his head.

"Wasn't anything," he said. "Just nerves. Feminine vapors."

"You were watching?"

"She asked me to," the driver said. "You think I wouldn't?"

"All right," Carver said. He turned around again so he could see out the back. "Just drive. I'll watch."

The motorcycle came around the corner from Sutter just as the light changed.

It followed the taxi from three cars back, going under the Dragon Gate and up the hill that rose into Chinatown. It was an older bike, an Italian import that Carver hadn't seen since his first year of patrol. Instead of batteries or fuel cells, it still ran on gasoline. A full tank might have cost more than the bike itself. The rider was wearing a black leather jacket and a matte black helmet with the face shield down.

The cabbie went through the intersection of Grant and Pine without turning. But the motorcycle took a left on Pine, and after it was out of sight, Carver could hear the rider accelerating toward the Ritz.

"Take a right on California, then a left on Kearny," Carver said. He had enough experience following people to know the psychology. The longer it went on, the more paranoid the guy would get. But at the very beginning, he'd feel invisible. He might be feeling bold enough to follow the taxi through a few quick turns.

"Come into Chinatown on Washington?"

"That's fine."

Carver watched behind but didn't see anything until they were passing Portsmouth Square Plaza. There was a motorcycle between two parked cars, its rider astride it. They passed it too quickly for him to decide what he'd seen. It might have been a different bike, a different rider.

But when they turned off Washington onto Waverly Place, there was a motorcycle coming fast down Clay Street. He saw its dual, vertically stacked headlights, saw the reflection of the streetlights in the rider's face shield.

He took out his burner and texted Jenner.

At least one tail, maybe two. Motorcycles.

Jenner responded immediately.

Can you shake?

Carver looked out the back window. The motorcycle hadn't turned down Waverly. If the riders were following him, they either had an unnatural ability to guess where the cab would show up or they were getting help from above. It was illegal to fly an unlicensed and unlit drone over the city's airspace, but there was no way to police them. At night, the skies hummed with them. Sometimes, at his bedroom window, he could catch their flitting silhouettes against the glowing clouds.

All they needed was an eye above him and they could follow him on the streets all night. It wouldn't matter how many sudden turns his driver made.

"Let's go down to Powell Station," Carver said. "I guess no one's back there."

"You got it."

Carver turned back to his phone and typed out another text.

If I don't show, she knows what to do. But she'll have to do it to you.

If motorcycles were following him, they could be on Mia, too. Now he understood how reckless he'd been to go out with her, to the Fairmont and the Irish Bank. Anyone watching the building would have seen her with him, would have concluded that Mia was a part of whatever he was doing. Maybe tonight they should have just stuck together. As far as he knew, she didn't carry a gun, nor did she have a knife slipped into her boot. For Mia, it was running or nothing.

"Powell Station," the driver said.

Carver looked up. They were at the curb on Cyril Magnin Street, facing Market. He settled the fare with cash he'd borrowed from Mia, then exited the cab and went quickly across the brick-paved plaza to the escalator that fed into the underground station. As it carried him down, he heard a motorcycle racing up Market Street. He began to run down the moving steps.

He fed his pass card to the machine, then pushed through the turnstile and went to the next escalator, which led another level deeper. There were at least a thousand people on the platform, most of them watching the Fremont train as it spilled from the tunnel. The metal-on-metal cry of its brakes filled the underground room. He stepped off the escalator and turned around to watch above. A man in a black leather jacket stood at the top, looking down. He took off a pair of black gloves, then unzipped his jacket and reached inside it. Carver pushed into the crowd, moving away from the escalator and toward the Fremont train, which had come to a stop.

There wouldn't be much time. Surely the man had seen him.

When the train's doors slid open, the crowd on the platform began to push toward it. Carver boarded with a group of office workers, then went up the aisle between the rows of seats and stood where he could see through the passageway leading to the next car. He looked behind him and saw the man through the window, crossing the platform, shoving people aside. He boarded the train one car ahead of Carver. Carver hit the button to open the sliding door in front of him, then stepped through the narrow vestibule, and into the next car, elbowing through the crowd to propel himself up the aisle. The man in the leather jacket was just turning around when Carver reached him. He was fit, white, and in his late thirties. He had close-cropped brown hair, and eyes like brushed steel. His face had just tightened with recognition when Carver threw a right hook. He felt the man's jaw break in the follow-through. Before the man could fall, Carver flattened his nose with a shove of his left palm. The man crumpled like an empty can.

A woman screamed, then another.

Carver looked around. Up and down the car, passengers were scrambling to give him space. The man on the floor wasn't moving at all. Carver took out his phone, stepping sideways to block the doors from closing. One of the doors pressed between his shoulder blades, then slid back. The intercom gave a *ding*, before the train's computer spoke.

"Please step away from the door. The train is leaving the station."

He snapped a picture of the man's face, then knelt and reached into his motorcycle jacket, stretching backwards with one foot to keep the doors from shutting. The gun was in a slim shoulder holster, the phone in a zippered pocket. Carver slipped back onto the platform and heard the doors close behind him. The train was gathering speed before he got to the escalator.

Powell Station had nine exits to the surface, scattered across two and a half blocks. He'd gone underground at Hallidie Plaza, and he returned to the surface using the eastern stairs at Fourth and Market. He didn't run, didn't look back. Someone would have called the BART Police by now. He checked his watch and saw there was no time left. He hurried to Fourth and walked along the curb until the taxi pulled up beside him. Mia opened the back door and then slid across the seat to make room for him.

"Battery and Sacramento," Mia said, when she caught the driver looking at them in the mirror.

"But first let's go down Fourth," Carver said. "Past Caltrain, and then the ballpark — I want to see what's going on down there."

Mia understood and nodded to the driver, who took his foot from the brake.

"It's your meter."

Carver was watching out the passenger window, looking back toward the underground entrance, expecting patrol officers, or a second man in a motorcycle jacket. The cab moved forward until the intersection was out of sight, and then he leaned back. He felt Mia's fingers on his right hand. He looked down and saw the broken skin along the tops of his knuckles. Fresh wounds cutting through the layered scars.

"You're all right?" she asked.

He nodded. His hand didn't matter.

"If I show you a picture on my phone — it's just a picture — will you look at it?"

"Okay."

He brought out his phone and handed it to her so that they could look at it together.

"This happened just now? You did this?"

"On one of the trains."

The man's face was out of proportion. His jaw reached too far to the right, and his nose lay on its side. Carver had taken the picture quickly, before the real bleeding started. Mia studied the screen closely, then used her thumb and forefinger to zoom in. Finally, she handed the phone back to him.

"He's one of them?" he asked.

She nodded.

"He was there. In your living room."

Carver put his phone away, then got the one he'd found in the man's jacket pocket. It was risky to keep it. Even turned off, there were ways to track it.

"You got a paperclip in your purse?"

"I don't think so."

"That's all right."

With a paperclip he could have opened the memory card slot on the phone's side. Instead, he held the phone in both hands, down low where the driver wouldn't see it. He broke it in half down the middle, then picked the pieces apart and found the card. He slid it into his wallet, and dropped the rest of the phone into the foot well behind the driver. When he looked up, they were passing the shuttered ballpark. A lone prostitute leaned against the blackened ticket window, her cigarette tip and jewelry flashing in the dark.

The driver let them out on Sacramento Street next to a scrolling-poster kiosk. Carver watched the cab roll away. The poster changed from a backlit photograph of a nude woman draped in a sapphire necklace to a bottle of cognac and a pair of low snifters. One of the glasses bore a lipstick mark, the red so deep it was almost black.

Jenner crossed the empty street and joined them. He was carrying his briefcase in his left hand, and walked with his right hand inside his coat.

"Y'all okay?"

Carver nodded. He'd texted from the cab, so Jenner already knew what had happened in Powell Station. They shook hands, and then the three of them turned to look at the building. Bank offices took up most of the lower floors, and those had closed hours ago. Everything to the tenth floor was dark. Above the twentieth floor, where they were going, the building simply disappeared into the fog.

"You texted him already?" Jenner asked.

"Five minutes ago."

They went up the sidewalk and crossed through the bronze bollards that stood as protection against ram-raiders. Next to the glass door was a card reader and a thumbprint scanner. Beyond the glass, on the far side of a polished marble lobby, was the empty security desk. When Mia saw the CCTV cameras, she put her head down.

"What do we do?" she asked. "Knock?"

"He's expecting us."

They waited another minute and then the guard came into view from the elevator banks. He crossed toward them and used his card to unlock the door. He opened it six inches and stood looking at them. He wore a black windbreaker with yellow stenciling, and his bleached hair curled from beneath his black cap.

"Who sent you?" he asked.

"Glenn."

"All right."

He opened the door and they came into the lobby. He led them to the elevators, walking ahead so that his back was to them.

"Clinic's on twenty-six. Whole floor. No one's up there."

"You're sure?" Jenner asked.

The guard pointed toward the security desk without turning or breaking his stride.

"I've got motion sensors," he said. "Got thermal. It's clear."

"We need a master key?"

"I was just up there. It's unlocked."

The guard stepped into an elevator, which was waiting with its doors open. After he swept his card through the reader, its lights came on. Machinery above the steel ceiling hummed to action. He pressed the button for twenty-six and stepped back out. The doors began to close and he caught them with his foot.

"You don't need it to get down," he said. "Just hit the call button."

"Okay," Carver said.

The three of them stepped into the elevator, but the guard didn't take his foot away.

"Let me have it before you go up."

“I’ve got it,” Mia said. “It covers both of you.”

She brought an unsealed envelope from her purse and gave it to him. The guard opened it and thumbed through the bills. He pocketed it and handed back a yellow square of paper.

“She said tear it up when you’re done,” he said.

“I will.”

He let the elevator doors close, and then the car began to rise.

22

THE IMAGING CLINIC was dark when they stepped off the elevator and into the reception area. An exit sign glowed near the stairwell, and the floor-to-ceiling windows next to the leather couches let in the dull-orange blur of radiant fog. Mia took a moment to look around, and then she pointed at the door behind the receptionist's counter.

"It'll be back there."

They followed her down a hallway. Carver had never seen the inside of a clinic like this. He was used to linoleum floors and battleship-gray walls. Raised voices and wet coughing in the waiting room. But this place had hardwood paneling on the walls, and deep-pile carpet underfoot. When Jenner found a switch and hit it, accent spots glowed alight from the ceiling to illuminate framed paintings of brocaded koi, each fish floating in the negative space of an otherwise blank canvas.

"You worked in a place like this?" Carver asked Mia.

"Pretty much."

"You'll find what you need?"

"It won't be a problem," she said. She held up the square of paper the guard had given her. "I've got the console password, and that's the main thing."

She opened the door to a patient changing room. There was a cabinet in the back, and she pointed to it.

"Find a gown that fits. Take off everything else. Don't forget your watch. You can't have anything made of metal."

"Okay."

"I'll set up the machine," she said. "But first, let me give you this."

She went into her purse again and brought out a small glass vial and a new syringe still in its plastic packaging.

"What is it?"

"A paramagnetic tracer," she said. "It'll help us see what we need to see."

"Let me take a look at that," Jenner said.

He came into the dressing room and took the vial from Mia. He wasn't rough, but it was clear to Carver that he might have been if Mia had refused. If it bothered her, she didn't let on. She turned her back to him and opened the syringe, then set it on a tray. She knelt and found alcohol swabs in the cabinet beneath the counter. Jenner was turning the vial in his fingers, studying the label.

Mia looked around at him, watched him read the tiny print on the label.

"Don't open it," Mia said. "You don't have gloves and your fingers aren't sterile."

"This could be anything," Jenner said. "I'm supposed to let you stick it in him?"

"It's gadodiamide – the contrast agent. They've been using it forever. This clinic probably runs through it by the liter."

"It's fine," Carver said. "Let's do it. Give it back to her."

Jenner closed the vial inside his fist and stepped back toward the hallway.

"Ross, you don't know what this is."

"Make a list of everything we don't know," Carver answered. "How long would that be? What else can we do?"

Jenner took another step back.

"We could go take our evals next week," he said. "Pass them and get back to work. How much easier would this be with the cover of a badge? You're not thinking with your head."

"I trust her," Carver answered. It sounded true when he said it. "But it doesn't matter. I've got you. She's not injecting it in you. And you'll be with her, watching. She knows that. So it's okay."

"Ross –"

"Give it back to her," Carver said. "Then go help her set up the MRI."

"I don't know about this," Jenner said. "After last night – after Calvin Tran – I really don't know. Maybe we ought to step back."

"You mean quit."

"I mean step back. Think things through."

"That's what we're here for."

"Except that it has to work out. We just pulled a B and E, on camera. You beat down a man at Powell Station—"

"He was following me."

"—in front of a crowd," Jenner finished. "And your excuse is worth shit. All our excuses are shit. So if this is how we think things through, then what Mia told you better be true. And it has to lead somewhere. Or we're in trouble."

Jenner hadn't raised his voice, but that might not last. He was sweating at his temples, gripping the vial of gadodiamide as if he wanted to break it in his fist. Carver wanted to explain. They were in trouble, maybe had been for a long time. Now they might be at the threshold of finding out where everything had gone wrong. He didn't know if they could trust Mia, but there was nothing to stop them from using her to get a step closer. He needed to know what had happened to them. It wasn't just that the world had fallen so low: he'd been walking point, had led the charge into the darkness. The only thing that separated him from the copper thieves and the prostitutes was his job. He'd held on to it, and so he had a paycheck to spend. Which meant that every night for him had been the same: a maze of mirrors and flashing glowcards. If he managed to thrash awake and shake off the nightmare, the room just tilted and spun, and then he slid back into the dream. He was trapped. There'd been some clarity with Jenner, whole nights where their partnership had let him focus. But in the end, the only long-term relationship he had was with his phone. If there was even a chance Mia knew a way out, he was ready to risk anything to get there.

But if Jenner didn't already understand all of that, then explaining it wouldn't help. Maybe he was afraid that, like the addicts who slept in the abandoned blocks past the ballpark, they wouldn't be able to change anything. Maybe it was better not to know, to ignore the sting of the needle and lose themselves in the glowing lights.

"Go if you want," Carver said.

"I won't just walk out when you need me."

"I know it."

"Then you ought to know this isn't fair," Jenner said. "But you don't get it."

"I get it," Carver said. "I just don't have a choice. Give her the vial. Let's do this."

• • •

Carver was inside the machine's bore, looking at the curved white ceiling, listening to the banging hum as electricity pulsed through the gradient coils around him. A narrow mirror angled from a brace above his eyes, so that he could see Mia without lifting his head.

He watched her behind the glass, in the control room. A bank of screens lit her face in blue-green light. Jenner stood behind her, his arms crossed below his chest. She touched her fingers to the headset and brought its microphone to her lips.

"Five more minutes, Ross," she said.

Her voice came to him through headphones, barely audible over the noise of the MRI.

"You're doing just fine. Try to hold still."

He closed his eyes and waited. He thought about the darkness inside him, where every particle in his brain was now aligned to the machine's magnetic field. He thought of Mia, cross-legged by her fire, asking if he ever thought about what had gone wrong with the world. He wondered if the answer to that lay inside him.

In the elevator, coming down, Mia took the slip of paper with the password and tore it into pieces. She let them flutter into the guard's hand when he opened the front door for them, and then they were out in the misty rain on Sacramento Street, watching the halos around the taillights of passing cars.

"I know a place we can go," Carver said. "Four blocks from here."

"Old Saint Mary's," Jenner said, and Carver nodded.

It was the first time Jenner had spoken since returning the vial to Mia. But he'd been standing behind her in the control room, and he'd seen the images as they'd come in. Now he was carrying the small memory card with the scans, and when Carver started to lead them west down Sacramento, they walked three abreast on the empty sidewalk.

"Where are we going?" Mia asked.

"Carver's got this idea he can get people to talk if he takes them to the right spot," Jenner said. "And when you work a Chinatown murder, you need that. People won't talk at home, and you can't take anyone down to the station. You do that, everyone sees."

"It poisons the well," Carver said.

"Old Saint Mary's is a church?" Mia asked.

"Catholic," Jenner said. "Edge of Chinatown. And he's got a set of keys."

"I'm just borrowing them."

"Like in a museum," Jenner said. "Where the plaque says, 'On permanent loan.' That's Carver, borrowing something."

They crossed Sansome Street at the light, and when they reached the other side, Jenner touched Mia's shoulder and stopped. She turned to him, her head tilted and her face guarded with caution. A car shushed past on the wet street, throwing runoff to the curb.

"Look," Jenner said. "The way I acted up there —"

"It's okay."

"— I'm sorry."

"You were being careful," Mia said. She started walking again. "We owe each other that, at least. To be careful, all the time. You've seen what happens."

They cut down Kearny and then walked along California until they got to the church. On the bell tower, beneath the clock, was a brass plaque:

SON, OBSERVE THE TIME AND FLY FROM EVIL

The clock had been broken for decades. Frozen with rust, it marked an eternal midnight. Carver checked his watch. It was only a quarter of nine. They went up the steps to the paired wooden doors beneath the bell tower. Carver got out his key ring and sorted through it until he found the one that matched the church. He unlocked the door and pulled it back to let Mia and Jenner enter. Then he stepped inside the narthex, locked the door behind them, and used the same key to unlock the door that accessed the bell tower steps.

They took the ladder-steep stairs single file, winding up the tower until they came through the trapdoor into its highest room. The bell had been stolen long ago. The thieves had cut it down and then simply pitched it out. Now, in the empty space, there was a wooden table. Four plain chairs around it. An ashtray, because some of the men Carver brought here wouldn't talk unless they could smoke. But he always cleaned the tower before he left. Tonight, it smelled only of aged wood and wet bricks, and of the fog that wept through the wood-louvered windows. The only light came from the street.

"I'll get the lamp," Carver said.

He went to the corner and found the brass oil lantern, then fumbled on the floor until he touched the box of matches. When it was lit, he trimmed the wick and brought it over to the table. Mia was fitting the memory card into the reader slot on Jenner's computer.

"Why don't more people know about this?" Jenner asked. "Doctors, radiologists."

"You wouldn't see it unless you were looking for it," Mia said. She turned on the computer. "It's like taking a picture of a ghost. You have to set your camera just so. And even if you saw it, you might shrug it off. You might think you just had noise in the data. Dust on your lens."

"But you found it."

"I was looking a long time."

"What about autopsies? I've been to, what"—he looked up at Carver—"maybe four hundred? Every time, they get out the cranial saw. Take out the brain. Why don't they see it?"

"Four hundred?" Mia asked. "That many?"

"Easy."

"How many times did they use an STM?"

"Use a what?"

"A scanning tunneling electron microscope," Mia said.

She waited for Jenner to respond, and when he didn't, she leaned forward, her hands on either side of the computer.

"You'd have seen the ME cut slices of the brain and coat them with an atom-deep layer of gold."

In the second that followed, Carver knew what Jenner was thinking.

Half of their cases only got a glance from the medical examiner. Erika Alexander didn't need a microscope, or even a magnifying glass, to find a bullet hole. She could probe those with her gloved fingers. And then there were the knives, the blunt objects. They'd had a girl last month who'd been beaten to death with a two-quart saucepan. They knew the brand and the size of the pan because the text etched in its base was imprinted, backwards, all over the girl's pale skin.

"I haven't seen anything like that," Jenner said.

"Here," Mia said, pivoting the laptop so that its screen faced Jenner. "Type in your password."

Jenner tapped the keyboard, and bent to the screen for the retinal scan. Then he pushed the computer back to Mia. She accessed the memory card and opened the image files.

"Ross," Jenner said. "You'll want to see this."

Carver came around the table and stood behind her. The image on the screen might have come from the same batch Mia had shown him on the rug in front of her fireplace. Except this was his own brain. There was no doubt of that. Jenner had brought a blank memory card and had watched Mia use it on a machine she'd never accessed before tonight. He'd stood behind her and seen the scans come up on the screens in real time.

"This is your hypothalamus," Mia said. "We're zoomed in, close."

He stood behind her, one hand on the back of her chair as he leaned over to look at the image. There were four of them in his brain. Tiny, eight-legged spheres. His skin prickled with revulsion.

"And if you back out?"

He heard himself ask the question but didn't feel himself thinking it. It was a reflex, just a stall while his mind reeled backwards.

"That's the next one," she said. "Here – look."

The second image showed his entire brain, in three dimensions. He was looking down on it from above. She'd made it almost transparent, a hazy gray cloud. The wiry legs spread like lightning flashes through the space of his skull. But these were different from what he'd seen in Mia's other scans. The lines were broken, as if someone had dipped them in acid and let them dissolve. He could trace their paths through his brain, but they'd been severed somehow, broken into hundreds or thousands of short segments.

"What's wrong with them?" he asked. "Why do they look like that?"

"I don't know," Mia said.

"You haven't seen that before?"

She shook her head, then traced one of the broken lines with her fingertip.

"But it might explain something," she said. "How you've been feeling, since you woke up on Sunday."

"I don't understand," Carver said. "You've seen how I felt. I was weak for a bit, and then –"

"I'm not talking about that," she said. "I'm talking about how you think. What you think about."

She touched the screen again, drawing a circle through the middle of his mind.

"I've been . . . okay, I guess," he said.

"But you weren't before."

"No."

He could answer that without any hesitation. He thought of the dark tug of the night, the scattered lights that had dazzled him. He'd lost his bearings in the glitter of cask-aged bourbon and Black Aria, and a hundred other things that had captured him in years past counting. He couldn't even place himself in time. Everything before Sunday lay behind him in a shimmering blur. The life he could remember was just a shadow of what it might have been. His desires had been desolate and his satisfactions empty.

"Same for me," Jenner said. "Way I've been feeling, since Sunday."

"Your head's been clear."

Jenner nodded. He didn't get up when Mia came to stand behind him. She put her hands on the sides of his head, above his ears.

"Lean forward," Mia said. Then, turning to Carver, she pointed at the skin on the back of Jenner's neck. "Do you see them?"

There were three welts. Raised circles, slightly inflamed.

"You have them, too," Mia said. "The same pattern."

"What are they?" Carver asked. They looked like horsefly bites.

"They were clearer on you when I saw them on Friday morning."

"When you were taking care of him," Jenner said.

"So I got a good look at them when they were still fresh," Mia said. She let go of Jenner's head. "I think they're from a jet inoculation gun."

"A jet . . . what?" Carver asked.

He watched as Jenner used his fingers to search the back of his neck for the marks.

"They used to have them for mass vaccinations," Mia said. She took Jenner's index finger, guided it to the nearly healed welts. "Think of whole villages lined up, WHO doctors in hazmat suits. Jet inoculators are fast, and they're cheap. But they spread as many diseases as they stop."

"Mass inoculation," Jenner said.

Mia nodded.

"If they had to hit a lot of people in a hurry," she said, "they'd want jet inoculators."

"You're saying we wandered into that on Thursday night?" Carver asked. "A mass inoculation?"

"More than that," Mia said, returning to her chair. "I think whatever they injected in you, it went to work on the things growing in your brains. It tore them up, broke them down."

"Why would they do that?" Carver asked.

Mia thought for a moment, looking at the wooden beam that once suspended this tower's bell.

"If you made a living machine, something that could self-replicate, then maybe you'd want a kill switch," she said. "Think of all the things that could go wrong. Imagine a hemorrhagic fever, but with a virus made of metal. If it mutated, if you got a bad strain that didn't behave the way it was supposed to, you'd need to shut it down. They must have a way to do that."

"So they wiped us clean."

"And afterward, we felt like shit," Jenner said. "But we could think again."

Carver looked at his brain scan on the computer screen. He thought of the gossamer legs extending from each of the silvery bodies to his optic nerves, to the pleasure centers of his brain. Mia had called them quantum computers. He leaned forward, brought his hands to his temples.

"Ross?"

He was remembering a night down at the waterfront, near Fisherman's Wharf. A troupe of homeless men staged street puppet shows there, their cardboard theater dissolving in the rain. Now he understood. There was no difference at all between the wooden puppets and the starving men who worked their strings. And there was nothing to distinguish the men and women hurrying past the theater to reach the pier and its new shops. Their need was too great to pause and watch a show. They had to reach the shops, had to stand and marvel at the wares beneath the spotlights. But if they'd taken the time, if they'd watched the marionettes as they were tugged from scene to scene by invisible hands, they'd have seen themselves.

"Sit down, Ross," Mia said. "Quickly, now."

She got off her chair and turned it for him. He fell into it, and it was only her hands on his shoulders that kept him from tumbling the rest of the way to the floor.

23

"IT COULD BE the gadodiamide."

That was Mia's voice, behind and above him.

"You said it was just a contrast agent," Jenner said.

Carver realized he was right behind him. He could feel him there, could feel Jenner's big hands steadying him.

"It *is* just a contrast agent," Mia answered. "But it can cause dizziness. Make him lightheaded."

Carver was holding his face in his hands, had his elbows propped on his knees. The chair had been spinning, but it came to a stop. He opened his eyes and sat up. Jenner stood and gave him space.

"I'm okay. It wasn't what Mia gave me," Carver said. He nodded toward the computer screen. "It's that. Those things. It's all connected, isn't it? What's in our heads, and what happened Thursday night. Hadley Hardgrave and Patrick Wong."

It wasn't until he said it that he knew he was beginning to believe it.

"Calvin Tran," Jenner said.

"Him, too."

Jenner took his computer back and closed the image files.

"You knew, didn't you?" Jenner asked Mia. "When you saw Ross on Friday morning, saw the welts on his neck. You knew what he'd gotten into."

"I'd guessed it," she said. "After they got Hadley—after George disappeared—I was out in the cold. They rolled us up, our whole network."

"But you wanted to keep going."

"I had to keep going, and I needed a way in," she said.

"What do you want?" Jenner asked. "Suppose you find what

you're looking for — you figure out what these things are, where they came from. What then?"

"I want the world back. We don't even remember everything we've lost, but I want it all back. I want to shut them down, and I want to get their vaccine. I want to load it in a jet inoculation gun and line up the village."

There was a helicopter flying close enough that it shook the bell tower. Carver went to the window and bent to look through its angled wooden slats. A searchlight was probing the rooftops on the other side of the street.

"Are they looking for us?" Mia asked.

"I don't know."

The helicopter moved off, back toward the Financial District. Carver didn't realize he'd been holding his breath until it was gone.

"We should turn on the scanner," he said, and looked at his watch. "It's almost time — Houston and Roper are coming up on their dinner break."

"Then I've got to go," Jenner said. "Scanner's in my briefcase. Text when I need to pull the trigger."

"I'll come down," Carver said. "Unlock the door for you."

Carver was opening the front door when Jenner laid a hand on his wrist to stop him. The narthex was cavern dark.

"What is it?" Carver asked.

"This," Jenner said.

"You still don't believe her?"

"I know what I saw on the scans. I know she's not making that up."

"Then what?"

"It's easier up there, when we're all bent over the table. Looking at a screen and whispering. But I'm about to go out on the street. It's a kids' game for you and Mia, but it'll get real for me."

"I didn't hear her say anything that sounded like magic," Carver said.

"First of all, I don't know anything about brains or MRIs, and neither do you. And second, if it isn't true then our best hope is that she's crazy. Because if she's not, this could be a setup. Something so big, we don't even know the tip of it."

There was a noise from above in the bell tower and they both looked up. It had sounded like a footstep, weight slowly settling on a ladder rung. But the way up was empty. They waited for it to come again, and when it did, it was followed by a bird's soft coo, and Carver placed it. There were swallows nesting under the roof.

"So maybe she knows how to take a picture and get those tendrils, or whatever," Jenner said, his whisper as low as it went. "It doesn't mean they're what she says they are. You use a camera flash in a roomful of people at night, it doesn't mean they all have red eyes in real life. And this is real life, Carver."

"You ever talked to a witness, and ninety-nine percent of what he says is bullshit, but you keep listening to the guy for that one percent? Because the one percent is all you need?"

"But you trust her now."

"It doesn't matter if we trust her or not," Carver said. "She knows something. She knew about Johnny Wong. I have to keep her talking. If this is a setup, we'll have to see it coming."

"But how's it fit?" Jenner asked. "Up there, you said it's all connected. I'll give you Hadley, Patrick, and Calvin Tran. They go together, have the same thing in common. But you're fitting that in to what happened to us?"

"What I say to her, and what I really think—those two things aren't going to link up every time," Carver said. "But I'll tell you this. If you put Johnny Wong in, everything starts to fit. Hadley and Mia were looking for him. We were looking for him. Something happened to us, and then I woke up with Mia in my room. Johnny's the nexus."

"Sure," Jenner said. "I get that. Maybe Mia knew about him. But who doesn't? Everybody's heard of the devil, whether they've had any dealings with him or not. And what happened Thursday night? These things Mia says she found? Johnny Wong's a gangster—but that's all he is. He's nothing special. He runs girls and card rooms. He's got a protection racket. Sometimes he kills people."

"A lot of people."

"But this?" Jenner asked. He touched Carver's forehead. "This is too big for Johnny Wong."

"You're not seeing it," Carver said.

He waited for Jenner to protest, but his partner was silent.

"Hadley was looking for Johnny," Carver said. "She wasn't just singing in nightclubs. She was burrowing into the underworld. You look at the list of her gigs, and you can see it. She knew what she was doing, said all the right things. She climbed up the ladder and found him, and we know what happened after that."

"A lot of his acquaintances turn up dead. You said it yourself."

"It's not what happened to her that proves it. It's that she wanted to see him at all. If she was in Mia's network, then she was looking for Johnny because he knows about these things. There's a lot of difference between knowing about something and causing it. Maybe it's hard to buy that Johnny built these things, but is it so much of a stretch to think he knows about them?"

"How's he going to know a thing like that?"

"He owns all the bars and all the girls. He's got an ear in every cab and every limo. He probably knows what you're going to order at that club of yours before you've even seen the menu."

"And if Mia's network is a lie, if her contraptions are made up?"

"If she's lying to us, it's still all connected. It still leads to Johnny Wong. He's our key."

It was too dark to read Jenner's face, but Carver knew he was running the possibilities again, trying all the scenarios.

"I still don't know," he said. "But I guess it's like you said. What other choice do I have?"

"None," Carver said. He pulled the door open and Jenner stepped out. "This is the one thing we've got. So we run with it. But watch your back."

"You know it."

They shook hands, and then Jenner was gone.

Mia was waiting for him in the bell tower.

She'd trimmed the lamp's wick until its tiny flame gave off more smoke than light. The helicopter had made another pass, this time releasing its belly-pod of drones. Carver could hear the electric hum as they cut through the air outside the tower. Mia was leaning over the police scanner, her right ear to the chatter on the Central District police band. She'd set its volume as low as it would go.

"Adam-Five-David just called in. They're ten-seven-M," she said. "I don't know what that is."

"They're eating dinner," Carver answered. He pulled out the chair next to her and sat. "Or getting a cup of coffee, killing time. You catch where they are?"

"Seventeen oh one Stockton."

He closed his eyes to picture the city, running the blocks in his mind.

"That's Mama's, on Washington Square."

It was just a few blocks from the house on Filbert. He hadn't spoken to Houston since she'd left the confessional at the Irish Bank. But he knew she was following the plan he'd given her. She'd taken her dinner break on schedule, and she'd picked a perfect spot. When she got to her radio car and called a 10-8 to let dispatch know she was back in service, she'd be exactly where they needed her.

"Does Jenner have time?"

Carver looked at his watch.

"She'll be twenty minutes. And Jenner—he knows his way around."

"Did you find out anything about the house?"

"Just what's online, the public records," Carver said. He'd looked it up immediately after hearing the address on Fremont's recording. "The city tax map says it's owned by something called the MMLX Corporation. But I'd need a subpoena to get a list of its officers."

"So it's what—a front company?"

"I guess."

"Does that happen a lot?"

"I'm a homicide cop," Carver said. "Most people I meet, they're lucky to sleep indoors. They don't have holding companies."

"Anything else you found on the house?"

"It's forty-seven hundred square feet. The tax-assessed value is fifty times my annual salary. Three years ago, someone pulled an electrical permit to wire half a dozen four-forty-volt mains into the basement."

"All that's online?"

Carver nodded. "What could you do with electrical mains like that?" he asked.

"Run an imaging center, for one thing," Mia said. "An electron microscope. Take your pick of industrial lab equipment."

On the table, the scanner was still playing the exchanges between the dispatcher and the hundred radio cars she was running. Carver leaned toward the speaker and listened for a moment. It was a calm night, relatively speaking. There'd been an armored truck hijacking on the Embarcadero. A murder-suicide in a North Beach garret apartment. But there hadn't been any all-unit calls that would have taken Houston and Roper away from their dinner break and out of the area.

"Did you and George ever talk about how these things are getting built?" he asked Mia. "Where they come from?"

"It's all just guesswork."

"Tell me what you guessed."

"We think they start out like spores," she said. "Tiny things, smaller than bacteria. Small enough to pass through any safeguard, to slide past an FDA inspector. Are you following me??"

"You think they're putting them in the water supply. In the food."

"Just consider everything you let into your body. It could be in the water. Or it could be in ordinary table salt. Or a drug everyone takes, sooner or later – like aspirin. Maybe, thirty years ago, they sprayed it over the major cities like aerosol, and it's just waiting in the dust."

"You're saying it could be airborne?"

"It could be anything. It could be in your annual flu vaccine. You sign up for an immunization, but that's not all you're getting."

"But these spores – where would they come from?"

"If you wanted to make a nanomachine, something this small, you could use three-D printing."

"They'll print on that scale?"

"You could do it with an electron microscope – they do more than just make images. You can move atoms one at a time."

"One atom at a time?" Carver asked. "Wouldn't that be too slow? You have three of these in your head. I have four. And multiply that by how many billions of people?"

"What if you just had to make the first one?" Mia asked. "And then that one made a second. And those two made four, and then eight, and so on."

"You're talking about reproduction. Like they're alive."

She shook her head. "I'm talking about molecular self-assembly."

"A machine that can make a copy of itself – like when a cell splits in two?"

"Yes."

"That's possible?"

She nodded.

"My guess is that somewhere there's a lab with a breeder tank in it. The spores are in a solution. Carbon and hydrogen. Some rare earth elements, for the nanoelectronics. They gather raw materials and spit out copies of themselves, and when the vat's full, a technician does something to them. Activates them for the next phase."

"Which is what?"

"This is a machine with two modes," Mia said. "In the first mode — the breeder mode — all they do is split in half and reassemble. It's the machine version of cellular mitosis. They could do that forever, or until they ran out of raw materials. But the second mode is what they're really for — getting inside a human host. Growing their legs to wire up the brain, to tap in to your thoughts and feelings. You'd want them sterile before that. If they started multiplying inside a host, it'd be a disaster. So there's got to be a way to switch them off."

"How would you flip a switch on something you can't even see?"

"They might respond to an ultrasonic pulse. Or irradiation."

"So you have a vat full of breeding nanomachines," Carver said. "You blast them with x-rays, and they stop reproducing and get ready for phase two."

"But there's one other thing," Mia said. She was warming her hands around the lantern's glass globe, which threw the room into shadow. "This is what really worried us. What if someone accidentally released them into the wild and they hadn't all been sterilized? What if a strain got out that could make copies of itself while it was inside your body?"

"I don't know."

"One becomes two, and two becomes four," Mia said. "Do the math."

"Just tell me."

"Say one generation takes an hour. At the end of three hours, you only have eight. Not such a big problem when you're talking about something so small," Mia said. "But after twenty-four hours, you'd have sixteen million."

She held her hands closer to the flame, blocking it entirely. Now the only light came from the red dial of the police scanner.

"With that many packed in your head, you might be bleeding out of your ears. But if you somehow stayed around another day, you'd have so many, you'd need a mathematician to explain it to you. They wouldn't stop breeding until they ran out of raw materials. If something like that got out, there'd be a narrow window to eradicate it. Either you stop it in the first twenty-four hours or there'd be nothing left to save. Any organic matter they came in contact with would have turned to gray soup."

Carver looked at her in the low red light. When she'd knocked on his door to ask him to sleep over, she'd had the same expression on her face. Terrified by things beyond his understanding.

"You think that's what happened on Thursday night."

"I don't know," Mia said. "I don't know if it happened or not."

"But that's what you think."

"It would explain why they gave you something that broke the things apart and inoculated you against their own invention."

His face must have shown that he still wasn't following her. She started again, speaking more carefully this time.

"Start with what we know," she said. "You went to a house that had been converted into a lab. You were called there for a dead body. Houston and Roper were there, and they let you in. After you went inside, someone else came along and hit you with a jet inoculator gun. They erased your memories, too, but that wasn't the real point. They needed to kill the things growing in you before they could spread. They were trying to stop an outbreak."

Carver stood up and went over to the louvered window. Peering through the wooden slats, he could see the half-circle cuts in the sidewalk where the bell had hit. A woman ran past, holding her shoes in her hands. A moment later, two men came in pursuit. Their arms pinwheeled as they sprinted down the hill after their prey.

There was nothing he could do, and he didn't want to watch. He sat down again, pulling the lamp away from Mia's hands so that he could see her face.

"Everything you're telling me, this would be huge. Worldwide."

"It's everywhere."

"If these people can do what you're saying, they must be the most profitable outfit on the planet. They're not running it out of a basement on Filbert Street."

"Of course they're not."

"Then what is that house?"

Mia answered with a question of her own.

"If you'd built a machine this illegal, would you apply for a patent?"

"Probably not."

"And if you don't have patent protection, then the only way to protect what you own is to keep it a secret. But secrets can be stolen. And if a company was sitting on something that valuable, a person on the inside would have a lot of temptation."

"So you think the body on Filbert was an insider. A scientist who worked for the organization behind this."

Mia looked up and nodded. "He snuck something out of the lab but didn't know how to control it," she said. "Then you and Jenner wandered in."

Carver had nothing to say to that. If everything worked, they would know more about the Filbert Street house in a few minutes. If there were clues suggesting that Mia was lying, Houston and Roper would find them. He looked at his watch and saw that it was time. Jenner would need to make the call before Houston and Roper went back in service. It would take a minute for it to filter through the 911 center to Central Dispatch, then another minute for the police dispatch to pick it up and send it out. Houston and Roper had to be the closest available unit, with nothing else on their plate.

"It's time," Carver said.

"All right."

He picked up his phone. He'd already typed the text, so all he had to do was hit send.

Roll.

Jenner wouldn't bother to answer. By now he'd be getting out his second burner phone, the one he'd bought earlier today. He'd use it once and then toss it in the trash. Carver took Jenner's computer and logged in to the church's wireless network. He'd borrowed the password along with the keys.

When he had a working web browser, he went to the video conferencing site. He logged in to the chat room and then angled the computer so Mia could see the screen.

"Is it working?"

"She'll turn on video when they get the call."

"All right."

He leaned back in the chair and looked at the blank chat screen. Houston's voice came up on the scanner, clear and confident.

"Adam-Five-David, we are ten-eight."

"Ten-four, Adam-Five-David," the dispatcher answered. "What's your twenty?"

"Washington Square."

“Proceed to four fifty-seven Filbert for a possible ten-seventy,” the dispatcher said. “Complaining witness was on a cell phone. Walking his dog.”

“Ten-four.”

Jenner had timed it perfectly. He’d used his throwaway phone to call 911 and report a prowler outside 457 Filbert. He wouldn’t have been within sight of the house, but a block or two away. If the 911 dispatcher looked at her screen to see where his call originated, the GPS ping would make Jenner’s claims seem plausible.

From here on, it was Houston and Roper’s show. How they investigated it would depend on what they found on site. Houston understood what he wanted, and he knew she’d do it if she could.

“Here it comes,” Mia said. “She’s starting the feed.”

24

HOUSTON HAD TURNED on her body camera, which was wirelessly linked to her car's computer. From there, she'd uploaded the feed to the video chatting site. Carver and Mia could watch everything as it happened.

She was coming up Filbert Street, driving no faster than the traffic. A block from the house, she turned to the curb and parked by a fire hydrant. They watched her take the mike and raise it to her lips, saw her key the transmit button with her thumb.

Then they heard her voice over the scanner.

"Adam-Five-David. We are one block downhill from four fifty-seven Filbert. We will proceed on foot. If there's a ten-seventy, we don't want to spook him off with the unit. We'd rather catch him."

"Adam-Five-David – proceed ten-double-zero."

"Ten-four," Houston said. "Confirm will exercise all caution. Adam-Five-David is ten-seven-I."

"That's good," Carver said to Mia. "She just bought herself fifteen minutes off the air."

"Can anyone else see her camera feed?"

"Not the way she's patched it."

On the screen, he watched Houston put the mike back on its dashboard clip. She unbuckled her seatbelt and stepped out of the car. When she turned her head, Carver saw across the roof of the radio car. Roper was already out. He was a tall, good-looking kid. He nodded at Houston, and she came around the hood to meet him. They went up the sidewalk together, Houston walking slightly behind Roper so that he stayed in the frame.

When they reached the house, Houston stood on the sidewalk in front of it. She brought her head back to let the camera sweep from the front steps to the top floor. Carver recognized the basic outline from the images he'd seen on the internet. He'd expected a house that was extravagantly well kept. A postcard scene from the city he'd grown up in. But when Houston panned up, he saw burn marks around the second- and third-floor windows. Peeling paint, and dead plants in the flower boxes. The largest windows on the second floor had been boarded from the inside. The heat-crazed glass looked like it might fall out of its frame with the next strong breeze.

"Does this thing have audio?" Mia asked.

"Let me try."

He toggled the volume bar on the chat screen, then leaned toward the computer's pinpoint microphone.

"Houston?"

"I read you," she said. "You getting this?"

"We are."

"You can smell it," Houston whispered. "The fire, and that same metal smell. It's like they dumped barrels of it on the street."

"What are you going to do?"

"Ring the front bell," she said. "If someone comes, we'll try to talk our way in. Say we need to check for a prowler."

"And if nobody's home?"

"Then getting in will be a lot easier," Houston said.

She was definitely his kind of cop.

"All right," Carver said. "Proceed. But ten-double-zero."

"You know it."

She glanced down, and Carver saw she'd drawn her service weapon, had it in her right hand. Then she was going up the steps to join Roper. He spoke to her, but his voice was too soft to pick up on Houston's throat microphone.

"Do it," Houston said to him. "I've got you."

Now she was holding the gun in both hands, pointing it at the door. Roper hit the bell.

"It didn't ring," Houston whispered. "I think the power's been cut. He's gonna knock."

Roper stepped to the door and began to pound with the side of his fist.

"SFPD – open up!" Roper shouted.

He stepped away from the door and raised his gun. Carver counted to thirty while they waited. Then Houston was whispering again.

"No one's here," she said.

"Do a thermal scan," Carver answered. "Don't go in there until you've done it."

"Ten-four."

She gave the scope to Roper. For a moment, Carver could see Roper using it to scan the inside of the house, but then Houston stepped away and went halfway down the steps. She checked up the hill, and then down the street in the other direction. Then her gaze drifted along the row of houses on the other side of the street.

"You hear something?" Carver asked.

"Negative," Houston answered, falling into her usual style of radio speech. "Just making sure we're ten-twenty-six."

Mia glanced at him.

"She's making sure it's all clear," Carver said.

Mia nodded, and then Houston was whispering again.

"Roper says there's no one in there."

"All right. Ten-double-zero, Houston."

"Ten-four," she said.

She came back up the steps and took the scope from Roper.

"Kick it down," she said.

Roper had been laid out sick for the last week, but Carver wouldn't know it from what he saw on the screen. Roper holstered his gun and dropped into a crouch five feet out from the front door. Then he uncoiled, as fast as a striking snake. His boot hit the door next to the jamb. There was an audible crack as the door splintered and flew open. Roper drew his gun again and rushed inside, immediately swinging to the right to cover his blind spot. Houston followed, and the screen went dark.

It took the camera a moment to adjust to the near-black foyer. When it did, the grainy image that reappeared was composed in shades of gray and black. Carver saw a stone floor, a chandelier, a staircase. Houston was moving fast, checking each corner twice.

"Take it easy, Houston," Carver said. "Roper did the scan and it was clean. Get out your lights. We need to see this place."

"Ten-four," she said.

She switched on the small light that mounted to her gun, and Roper did the same. They let them rove along the walls, picking out the paintings hanging along the entryway.

"What's wrong with them?" Carver asked. "I can't make it out. It's not fire."

"Acid, maybe," Houston whispered. "It smells like it, anyway. The walls are blistered. It's like they sprayed everything with acid."

Her light touched a large frame at the end of the hall. Houston was about to move on, but Carver stopped her.

"Wait, Houston," he said. "Go back. I want to see that one."

She stepped up to the painting and let her camera pan across it. The colors had dissolved. The paint had run in a bubbling cascade over the lower portion of the frame and down the wall. In a few places, the acid had eaten through the canvas entirely. Carver could see all the way through to the wooden wall behind it.

"It looks like there's a plaque on the frame," Carver said. "See if you can wipe that stuff off and read it. But don't touch it with your fingers."

"Ten-four."

He watched on the screen as Houston used a pocketknife to scrape at the plaque. Then she bent close and held the light to the words. The camera pulled in and out of focus before it caught.

Ocean Beach, with Sea Glass (IV)

—

Bridget Laurent
Oil on canvas, 2017

Mia was leaning forward and staring at the screen, her hands clenched together in her lap. Carver killed the computer's microphone with the mute button.

"Did you know about this?"

"No."

"But it's not exactly a surprise."

"Not after Mexico."

Carver reenabled the microphone. Back on Filbert Street, Houston panned across the painting once more before settling the camera back on the plaque.

"Does it mean anything to you?" she asked.

"Yeah. It's ballsy, putting it by the front door," Carver said.

"Say again?" Houston whispered.

"Before your time," he answered. "You wouldn't know it. That painting was stolen out of the Legion of Honor. Job of the century—an entire exhibition. I didn't work it, but some of my friends did."

"Not much left now," Houston said. She let the camera glide across the ruined canvas once more. "You done here?"

Mia slid toward him, put her hand on his shoulder, and whispered in his ear.

"We should see the basement."

Carver leaned back to the computer.

"Houston?"

"Go ahead."

"You guys see a door to the basement?"

She pivoted and the camera sped along the walls. Carver saw a blur of blister-cracked wood and melted artwork, and then the screen held still on a steel-trimmed door.

"Roper," Houston said. She kept her light pinned on the door. "They want us to check the basement. I think that's it."

If Roper answered her, Carver couldn't hear it. But he came into view and crossed the room to the door. He tried the handle, then opened the door and pulled it back.

"I got your back," Houston said.

Roper went through the door and disappeared into the shadows. Then Houston went through, her gun in front of her, aimed to Roper's right. The camera was struggling with the darkness again, but in the grainy blur, Carver could see the concrete steps leading down.

"The smell's really strong in here," Houston whispered. "Acid, or something."

"You okay?"

"There's no ventilation."

She stopped and turned to look at the door. It was a dim rectangle of light above her.

"Houston—you okay?"

"No," Houston breathed. "But I can handle it, for now."

Her voice sounded like it was being played through a vinyl record. On the screen, vertical bands of snow sliced through the video image. The feed had been fine until she'd started down the basement steps.

"You read me, Houston?"

"Barely," she said. "You're ten-oh-one."

"I'm having a hard time seeing. Is there a wall next to you?"

"Yeah."

"Show me," Carver said. "Get close."

"Like this?"

She must have slipped on the stairs when she turned to the wall. There was a jerk and a thump, and then her hand was visible in the frame. It was trembling. She caught the wall and steadied herself against it. Then she brought the camera close. There was a steely-gray blur until the camera caught a point of focus. Now he was looking at the wall as though standing six inches from it. It was covered with some kind of wallpaper. Snowflake patterns, etched in silver ink, glittered in the light.

"That's radio-frequency-blocking paper," Carver said.

"Say – what?"

Even with the interference, he didn't like the way she sounded.

"Houston, can you tell me your badge number?"

"My what?"

"Get Roper. I want you two out of there. The air's not doing you any good –"

"– it burns, in my nose –"

"Get Roper. Get out."

"– and there's spots, green spots –"

There was a loud bang from somewhere down in the basement, but Carver couldn't tell what it was.

"Houston?" he said. "You catch what that was?"

She didn't answer.

He watched her push off the wall. Mia put her hand on his shoulder and squeezed.

"It doesn't matter, Carver. Get her out."

On the screen, they saw Houston catch her bearings. She looked back up the stairs to the half-opened door, then at her feet. Then she was going down again. One step. Two at a time. With every step into the darkness, they lost more of the signal.

"Houston –"

She tripped and fell, and Carver heard a clatter that he knew was her gun on a hard tile floor. Houston spun her head around in the dark. A short beam of light stabbed at the floor nearby. It must have been the light on her gun barrel.

"Houston, get Roper and get the fuck out of there."

The angle on the screen changed. She'd made it up to her knees. Her camera adjusted to the darkness. The screen passed through a grainy filter. He saw a spinning image of machinery. Smashed lab equipment. Broken glass. An entire wall of computer monitors that had been pried open and burned. Houston began to cough, and the camera view shuddered with her body's spasms.

When she turned again, Roper came into view. He was on his back, and even in the dark Carver could see the black spatter of blood around his head. There was something on the floor next to him, but Carver didn't have time to make it out. A sledgehammer, maybe. But Houston had begun to scream, and now she was scrabbling backwards on the debris-strewn floor. Carver saw the naked beams in the basement ceiling.

A light came on. The screen went entirely white, then eased back into washed-out color as the camera adjusted again. Houston froze, and went quiet.

A figure in a silvery, heat-resistant spacesuit came into view. Carver assumed it was a man based on his size and his stance. But he couldn't be sure. The suit's faceplate was like a piece of stainless steel. Carver could see Houston reflected there. She was on her knees. Her gun was nowhere in sight, but the man in the spacesuit was armed with something that Carver didn't recognize right away. He raised the nozzle-gun in his heavily gloved hands. A hose led from the gun to the tanks strapped to his back. Carver saw the blue flicker of the pilot flame there at the tip of the nozzle, and then he understood.

In the faceplate, Houston raised her hands above her head.

When the man in the suit hit the trigger, there was an instant when Carver could see the flames rushing toward her. They spread and mushroomed, yellow and white. When they swept around her, Houston never made a sound. The screaming, Carver realized, was Mia. She was squeezing his shoulder hard enough to draw blood through his jacket.

The screen went white.

For ten seconds, he didn't dare touch anything. Then everything went black. A small pop-up window appeared.

Thank you for trying OmniChat!
Now try:
Black Aria

The pop-up window dissolved and a bottle of Black Aria replaced it. It hovered in a dark sky and then began its descent. Layers of moonlit clouds appeared below it. Mia reached out and slammed the laptop screen shut.

Carver was still trying to understand what had just happened. Houston and Roper were dead. He'd sent them down to the basement, and now they were dead. Their reflexes had been dulled by the noxious air, and then a man in a flameproof suit had incinerated them. The suit was clearly insulated to protect him from heat, which must have made him invisible to Roper's thermal scan. He must have been in there to make sure the house was clean and that whatever threat it had been hiding was gone.

"I have to warn Jenner," Carver said. "If there was a man in the house, there could be others in the neighborhood."

"Hurry."

He dialed and brought the phone to his ear. Jenner always answered by the end of the first ring. Especially on something like this, when the situation was fluid and they had to stay in close contact. He'd keep his phone in his hand so he'd feel it vibrate even at a dead run.

But not this time.

"What is it?" Mia asked. "What's happening?"

Carver set the phone on the table, then put it on speaker.

"He's not picking up."

They watched the phone. The seventh ring cut off mid-tone, and Carver saw the call timer begin to count. But Jenner didn't speak.

"You there?" he said. "Can you hear me?"

The timer counted the seconds.

"You there?"

"Yes . . . *yes* . . . I'm here," a voice said.

It wasn't Jenner, and it sounded almost subhuman. The person using Jenner's phone was speaking through a voice changer.

"I . . . can hear you. Is this *Carver?* Am I speaking to Inspector Ross *Carver?* Is there a Miss Mia *Westcott* there too?"

"Put Jenner on."

"I . . . can't."

"You sonofabitch. Put—"

Mia reached out and hung up the phone. Then she took it and smashed it against the edge of the table. Three quick blows and it was shattered.

"Mia, for fuck's—"

"They'll use it to pin us down, Ross."

"They've got Jenner."

"And you won't get him back on the phone. They'll just string you along. Then they won't just have Jenner. They'll have us, too."

Her face was wet with tears. He didn't know if they were for Houston, for Jenner, or for herself. But she was right. Maybe she wasn't telling the truth about everything, but she was right about the danger.

"We have to get out of here," Carver said.

25

HE HAD JENNER'S briefcase and a flashlight in one hand, and Mia's arm in the other. They were running down the bell tower stairs. When they reached the bottom, she turned toward the narthex and the front door, but he pulled her in the other direction.

"Ross—"

"Not that way," he said. "It's not safe."

They went down the main aisle of the church, between the pews. He led her to the right, into a gallery off the east transept. There was a small office here. His key didn't fit the lock, but the door was flimsy and splintered along the jamb with the first kick.

"Ross, what are we—"

He kicked the door a second time and it swung open. He didn't bother looking for a light switch, but went in and shined his flashlight along the walls until he found the key rack. He grabbed all the keys off their hooks.

"Church van," he said. "This way."

There was a green exit sign above a wooden door at the far end of the transept. He unlocked it, and then they were in the tiny courtyard with two white vans parked side by side, facing the cast-iron portico gate. Carver hit the key fob, and the closer of the two vans flashed its lights as the doors unlocked.

He went around the hood and climbed in. Mia was already in the passenger seat, buckling her seatbelt.

"What about the gate?"

"It's fine."

He drove toward the gate and then stopped under the arched brick entryway. There was a keypad mounted on the wall. The church let him park in the courtyard, so he knew the code. He leaned out his window and punched in the five digits, then looked through the windshield to watch the gate as it swung open.

"Where now?" Mia asked.

He was trying to grab ahold of the situation. They needed to find Jenner, but that was impossible.

"I don't know—give me a minute, unless you can think of something."

"The voice on the phone, he—*it*—knew my name. It won't ever be safe to go home."

"But it's not really your home, is it? It was some kind of safe house."

She'd told him that after she got recruited, she'd been sent to San Francisco under a fake name. Running Hadley, she might have had to leave at any time. They'd go wherever their investigation took them. They didn't have to worry about jurisdiction. He couldn't see her buying a place, hiring a moving company.

"It belongs to the network," Mia said.

"Were there others?"

"There's one," she said. "I've never been to it, but George told me how to find it. There's a key somewhere, hidden in a laundromat in the Outer Sunset. I could use it in an emergency. After Hadley died, I'd been planning on going there—and then I met you."

"But George knew where it was," Carver said. "So maybe Hadley did too."

"Maybe."

He heard the idea wilt in her mind as she spoke.

"It's not safe anymore," Carver said. "We don't know what happened to George, but we do know what happened to Hadley. So we should assume they've got whatever information she had."

"All right."

"Is there anyone else in your network? Someone we could go to?"

She thought about it while Carver drove. They reached a stretch of road where the street lamps were missing, and he had a hard time seeing anything at all until he realized he'd never turned on his headlights.

"There must be someone who was helping pass the messages," Mia said. "An intermediary between me and George."

"But you don't know who."

"No."

"We'll have to think of something else."

"It's no use going to Filbert Street," Mia said. "If that's what you're thinking. Houston's already dead."

"I know," he said.

It had been his idea to send Houston there. He'd thought she'd be safe, that they wouldn't dare hurt a uniformed officer who came to the house. She'd been sent by dispatch. When she walked up and rang the bell, the full weight of the SFPD was behind her. But it turned out that none of those rules applied. And if they could take Houston and set her on fire, he was terrified to think what they might be doing to Jenner.

"Slow down, Ross," Mia said. "There's police ahead."

"Shit."

He took his foot off the accelerator and let the van blend with the traffic again. If he made a single mistake, Jenner's chances were all gone. He knew that. He also knew it was useless to think Jenner had a chance. They hadn't put him on the phone. And wouldn't they have put him on the phone if they'd wanted Carver to keep talking?

"Just take it easy," Mia said. "Stay inside the lines, under the speed limit."

The cops Mia had spotted were a pair of motorcycle officers from Traffic Patrol. They were parked along the curb below Grace Cathedral, and they didn't even look up from their cell phones when Carver drove past them.

"Where are we going?"

"To see Fremont – you got any money?"

"Five hundred."

"Can you get more? Do you have an ATM card?"

"Yes."

"We'll stop for cash in the Richmond District. We'll each get as much as the machine will let us take."

"You're worried they'll freeze our accounts," she said. "Track us if we keep using them."

"Aren't you?"

"I don't know," she said. "What about this van? How long till the church reports it stolen?"

She was right to worry about that. The police wouldn't have a hard time spotting it once they knew to look for it. *Old Saint Mary's Cathedral – Holy Family Chinese Mission* was written in foot-high letters down both sides.

"We'll ditch it in a couple hours," he said. "Find something else."

"Do you have an idea about that?"

"Maybe."

Carver parked the church van in front of the karaoke place on Noriega. The club's neon sign was gone, and its windows were broken. There had been a fire, and its roof had collapsed onto the restaurant floor. Charred timbers pointed into the rain, like the bones of a whale. The pizza joint on the other side of the street was now the only point of light in the neighborhood. It was still in business, and meant to stay that way. A man sat on a folding chair out front, a shotgun across his knees.

"If they burned this place down too, it could be too late. The strain got out, and it's spreading. They'll try to contain it, but—"

"It's not what you think," Carver said. "It's just copper thieves. When they screw up and don't shut off the mains, this is what happens."

"That's what the people on Filbert Street are telling themselves."

He got out of the van and met Mia on the sidewalk. It was raining, but he could still smell the smoke. Black water flowed out of the ruins and across the sidewalk. Mia took his hand and they walked together to Fremont's garage apartment.

There were no lights in the windows, but when Carver knocked with his fist, the bulb next to the door came on.

"That you, Carver?" Fremont asked.

"That's right. And my friend."

"What do you want?"

"Another job. It's quick."

The door opened and Fremont stepped out. He was wearing sweatpants and a white T-shirt, and had on fingerless weight-lifting gloves. His face was covered in sweat.

"What job?"

Carver took out the memory card he'd retrieved from the motorcycle rider's phone. He held it between his thumb and forefinger and brought it up so Fremont could see it.

"I got this off a suspect—"

"I thought you were suspended."

"If I could take it to the lab, I wouldn't be here."

"Except I asked about it," Fremont said. "This suspension. Called some guys. Nobody knows anything. There's a lockout notice, but there's no entry of suspension, no hearing."

"It's informal," Carver said. "You got equipment to read the data on this?"

"If it's encrypted, forget it."

"Two hundred – if you can get whatever's on there, put it on my laptop."

"Three."

"Three, then. And for that, you don't call your friends about me anymore. You don't know me."

Fremont opened the door and let them in.

"What happened to you guys?" he said as Mia passed him. "You look like shit."

"Nothing you need to know about."

Fremont turned two deadbolts and put the chain on the door. Then he gestured at the couch.

"I'll do this in my bedroom," he said. "You want coffee, there's a shop on Fortieth."

"Thanks."

"Unless it's been firebombed," Fremont said. "You look at this city, and it's like SFPD surrendered everything west of Twenty-Second."

He went into his bedroom and shut the door.

From outside, there were three pops of gunfire. Five, maybe six blocks away. Carver went to the couch and pushed aside a pile of unfolded laundry. He sat, and Mia took the space next to him. They waited for Fremont for half an hour, and in that time they heard a dozen more shots but not a single siren. Probably no one bothered to call anymore.

He couldn't blame people for losing faith. His own partner had just been kidnapped. He'd witnessed, on screen, the murder of a police officer. Yet he hadn't called anything in. There'd be no point to it. He had nothing solid to give and the police would do nothing in return. He had no confidence that the man in the spacesuit wasn't acting on Lyndon Ivies's orders.

He turned to Mia.

"I didn't understand, until just now, how they knew your name. How they knew you were with me."

She nodded, her eyes welling up again. She understood; she'd already figured it out. They might not have known her name an hour ago. But once they had Jenner, everything changed.

"Ross — there's nothing you could've done."

"They'll have to pay it back," he said. "Whatever they did to him."

"Stay with me, Ross," Mia whispered. She put her arms around him and pressed her face against his neck. "I know what he means to you. But don't let yourself go there. Not right now. It won't help."

Mia let go of him when Fremont came out of his bedroom office. He crossed the small room and sat on the end of his weight bench. Then he handed Carver the memory chip and a portable hard drive.

"Most of what you want — call logs, text messages, email — is encrypted. The FBI, maybe they could do something. But not me."

"Was there anything you could get?"

"His camera roll — two hundred pictures. Some video clips."

"Pictures of what?" Mia asked. "Did you open them?"

Fremont nodded at the briefcase. In the time he'd been gone, he seemed to have shed most of his arrogance. He looked like an old man, a lonely soul trying to keep a light burning as the world around him slipped into darkness.

"You got a laptop in there? Take a look."

Fremont went to his kitchen and found three unmatching glasses. He reached up toward his collection of Kinclaith and took the opened bottle. He poured a finger's worth of the scotch into each glass and brought them back. He set two of them on the coffee table and then went back to the weight bench, the only other place in the room to sit.

"You said you got it off a suspect," Fremont said. "The memory card. You didn't say he was the guy who did Hadley Hardgrave."

"That's what's on here?"

Fremont brought the glass to his nose and breathed in. Then he took a sip and let the whiskey sit on his tongue for a moment.

"I never saw a snuff film before," he said. He looked at Mia. "You might not want to watch this."

The gunfire outside was farther away now. Ten blocks, Carver guessed. He watched Mia take a glass of whiskey from the table, watched her drink it. She turned to him.

"I don't want to watch it," she said. "But I guess I have to, don't I?"

Carver inserted the portable drive and opened the folder of video files. The file names were just meaningless numbers assigned by the man's cell phone. But there were file creation dates, and those meant something. The first video was shot the day Hadley Hardgrave had gone missing. She'd sung four nights in a row at the San Lung Lounge and was supposed to come for one last performance. But she never showed up.

Carver double-clicked the file. A media window opened. There was a still image of Hadley Hardgrave's face. Her eyes were closed and she was screaming. Her lips were fully intact, hadn't yet been carved into that Cheshire grin. If that didn't happen in this video, it would be on the one after. Carver hit play, and felt Mia's grip on his arm. She was bracing herself against him, getting ready for it.

They both knew what was coming.

26

THEY LEFT FREMONT'S apartment and went up the street in the blowing rain. Carver had the briefcase in his left hand, and his right arm was wrapped around Mia's waist. He was ready to push her aside if he had to draw his gun, but the streets were empty. It was dark in every direction until they reached Noriega and turned the corner. The pizza place was still lit, but the man with the shotgun was gone.

That should have told him something, but it didn't occur to him until later. He was thinking about the man on the train. The right hook that had smashed his jaw like a piece of damp plaster.

"I had him," Carver said. "Had him on his back. I could've put a bullet through his head. Could've stepped on his windpipe and been done with it."

"You didn't know."

"I might not get another chance."

"It's not just him," Mia said. "He's part of it, but he's just the tip."

"He's a psychopath."

"And a useful one," Mia whispered. "He might've enjoyed what he did to Hadley. But they let him do it – they let him keep doing it – because it suits them. It keeps my people underground. It keeps us running."

They finished the walk to the van in silence.

Thirty minutes ago, he would not have thought it possible to believe Houston was lucky. But she had been. Her pain ended in seconds. He didn't think that was true for Jenner. He thought of the high-pitched, scratching voice on the phone. If it had been the man from the train, the man from the videos –

"Ross?"

"In the bell tower, when Houston and Roper were in the foyer, you said they should look in the basement. You told me to send them to the basement—"

"Ross, I—"

"What did you know?"

Mia took a step away from him so that she was backed up against the van. She spoke carefully, her eyes on the gun in his shoulder holster.

"Only what you'd told me—that someone pulled an electrical permit. That someone put four-hundred-forty-volt mains into the basement. And if you wanted to run a lab, run something with the kind of machinery that could print nanomachines, you'd need a steady foundation. You couldn't put it on an upper floor."

"That's it?"

"I promise you, Ross."

She was holding her hand out to him. Jenner was gone and there was nothing he could do about it. He had one lead but no way of following it, and he still didn't know whose side Mia belonged to. So nothing had really changed. He had to keep her close until he figured it out. He used the remote to unlock the van, then opened the door for her. That was his second mistake—to help her inside, to hold her elbow as she stepped off the debris-slick sidewalk and up to the passenger seat. He didn't see the men come out of the ruined restaurant, didn't notice anything amiss until the five of them were already behind him. He started to turn, but stiffened when he felt the gun's muzzle pressed against his spine. Someone pulled the briefcase away from him. He didn't turn around to see who'd done it.

"Put up your hands."

He raised his arms, laced his fingers over the top of his head.

"Tell the lady to get out."

Mia climbed back to the sidewalk, her hands up.

"Turn around, Inspector Carver."

He turned and faced the five young men. They wore black slacks and black woolen coats. Their faces weren't covered, and he recognized some of them from their mug shots, the Gang Intelligence photos. When they were tracking Patrick Wong, Jenner had kept a folder of them on his desk.

One man stepped forward, shoving a gun in Carver's face. A second man patted him down, taking his weapon and then his keys. The man moved to Mia, and Carver had time to think of his first two mistakes. Then he thought of a third.

He should never have let Fremont go into his office and close the door.

"Sonofabitch," Carver said.

The second man had just finished checking Mia and they both looked up at him.

"That sonofabitch just sold us to Johnny Wong," Carver said.

"And he'd like a word with you," said the man with the gun in Carver's face.

A dark limousine rolled out of the fog and came to a stop in front of them. Its windows and bodywork were the same smooth black; the whole thing might have been cut from a single piece of polished volcanic glass. The chauffeur stepped out and came around to the rear. He opened the door and extended a white-gloved hand to Carver and Mia, as if they were guests on their way to a costume ball.

The man facing Carver was less discreet. He jerked his gun barrel at the open door.

"Get in."

Mia went first, and Carver followed her. He expected the other men to climb in after him, but the chauffeur shut the door.

Carver was on a wide leather-bound seat, looking down the length of a wet bar. The liquor bottles were illuminated from beneath by soft incandescent bulbs, their combined light filtering easily through the glass because every label had been removed. The air was thick with cigarette smoke, and through the haze Carver could see the glowing tip smoldering across the car. Once his eyes had adjusted, he saw it was held by a man sitting in one of the rear-facing seats.

He wore a well-cut suit and had a submachine gun across his knees. The cigarette was pinched between his left thumb and forefinger, so that his pinkie stuck out. He'd let that nail grow long. A sign of wisdom, Carver had heard.

"I've seen a picture of Johnny Wong," Carver said. "You're not him."

"There's a picture of Mr. Wong?" the man asked. He half smiled. "I thought we'd found them all. Removed them, one way or another. We should look harder?"

Carver didn't answer. The man took another drag on his cigarette, then twisted it into the ashtray next to him. The limousine started to roll. On the street, the five gunmen were piling into the church van. The man with the submachine gun must have seen the direction of Carver's eyes.

"A clean vehicle," he said. "Mr. Wong, I'm sure, will thank you."

At the end of Noriega, the chauffeur took a right. They were going north along Ocean Beach. The water was invisible in the fog and the dark. Twenty blocks of wasteland lay between them and any street where they might reasonably hope to see a policeman.

"You've heard a story about Mr. Wong," the man said. "Maybe it went like this: A man is called to see Mr. Wong. Naturally, he's terrified. They stuff him into the limousine – this limousine – and offer him a drink."

The man waved his hand above the glowing bottles.

"Calvados? Or maybe a vodka. We have Russian, of course. But if he doesn't want to support the Russians, he can support the Finnish. Or the Swedes."

Carver watched as the man dug a cigarette case from his left pocket. He put it on the seat next to him. He used his single, elongated fingernail to stroke the etched silver lid.

"Of course, this man accepts a drink. He's too frightened not to take what Johnny Wong offers. One must be courteous. But ultimately, the drink is not what soothes him. What sets him at ease – what sets them all at ease – is the blindfold. Because that is how he knows he isn't going to die. That Johnny Wong intends for him to walk away from the meeting."

The man took another cigarette from the case and put it between his lips. Then he pulled a lighter from his lapel pocket and lit the cigarette. He did this all with his left hand. His right hand never left the stock of the gun on his lap.

"You've heard this story?"

Carver had heard a hundred versions of it. He'd heard it in interrogation rooms, and in the alleys behind bars. He'd spoken to men who'd actually taken the blindfold, who'd sat across from Johnny Wong and lived to tell about it because they'd never seen his face. His voice was supposed to be like a good single malt poured over frozen stones – smooth and golden, and cold. And there were women around him, all the time. The men Carver interrogated had never actually seen one, had never heard so much as a feminine whisper in Johnny's presence. But they'd revealed themselves in passing. Trails of perfume, whispers of satin.

Carver nodded slightly at the man.

"I know about that story."

"Then would you like a drink?" the man asked. "Pour your own. My hands, obviously, are full."

"No," Mia said. "We don't want a drink."

The man smiled again.

"That's all right, miss," he said. "That's very good. And Mr. Wong said you wouldn't need blindfolds, either. In fact, he told me not to bring them. Maybe, since they were never a possibility, I shouldn't have brought them up."

They followed the ocean to the northwest tip of the city. At the corner of Lands End Park, he saw the Legion of Honor in the fog. He looked at the man across from him.

"Everyone said Johnny Wong was behind that job. Was he?"

"What job?"

"The Laurent show," Carver said. "The beach and glass paintings. They said it was Johnny's money, and his crew. But no one could make anything stick. He was untouchable, invisible."

"Who said that?" the man asked. "What are their names?"

He took a long pull on his cigarette and blew the smoke across the illuminated bottles.

"And where do they live? Maybe I should see them later."

The man put out his cigarette and used his left hand to pour himself a drink. With the label missing, it was impossible to tell what he'd chosen.

They cut away from the shoreline, back onto city streets. They merged with Geary Avenue, and by the time they passed George Washington High School, the traffic signals were functioning again. Streetlamps glowed above the sidewalks, and lights shone from the windows of the houses they passed. If civilization had a bare requirement, Carver thought, it was a light to burn in the nighttime.

Every day that circle grew smaller. Soon they'd all be in the dark.

The limousine stopped in front of a club on Columbus Avenue. There was a green canvas awning, and above that a backlit marquee surrounded by chasing lights. Carver had driven past this club when the names of bands, sometimes half a dozen in a night, were spelled out in red block letters. Hadley Hardgrave's name had been up there. But tonight, the sign was simpler.

CLOSED

The chauffeur came around and opened Carver's door. This time, he had a slim automatic pistol in his left hand and he'd taken his gloves off.

"He'll show you and the lady inside," the man across from him said. He was tapping another cigarette out of his case. "Mr. Wong, I'm sure, is waiting."

Carver stepped from the limousine and waited for Mia to slide out after him. She took his arm and they walked together up the steps to the club's front door. The chauffeur followed from ten feet back.

"Open it," he said.

Carver took the handle and turned it. The door was heavy, made of steel thick enough to stop anything. The club itself was made of poured concrete, and had no windows. No one on the street would hear anything that happened inside. If he wanted to try anything, the time was now. They might hesitate to shoot here. The street was twenty feet away, traffic rolling past. Once they got inside, there would be no witnesses.

"It'll be her," the chauffeur said.

Carver turned around. The man had raised the gun, was holding it in both hands so anyone would see it.

"Right in her neck," he said. "So I'd open the door – or don't you like her?"

Carver pulled the door open and held it for Mia. Before she went inside, she leaned up and kissed him.

The chauffeur followed them down the entry hall. There was a palm-flanked fountain, a statue of a nude girl sitting astride a goldfish in its basin. Carver wasn't sure if she had been carved from marble or cast in concrete. They crossed a hundred feet of red carpet, went under a low-hanging chandelier, and through a wide door to the bar.

A bartender was polishing glasses with a white cloth. In a velvet-lined booth, there was a man with his back to the door. He was the only other person in the place. His close-cropped hair was a mix of white and gray, but his shoulders were broad and muscular. He wore black suspenders over a white dress shirt; a dinner jacket lay across the back of the banquette.

The chauffeur hadn't come into the bar. He closed the door, so that Carver and Mia were sealed in with the bartender and the man in the booth. Carver looked at the closed door, at the bartender, and then at Johnny Wong.

"You must trust your people," Carver said. "Sitting with your back to the door. I don't even do that."

"Then you need better people."

"Maybe so."

The man still hadn't turned. The bartender set down one glass and picked up another. If he'd been following the conversation, he gave no sign.

"Go see Sam," the man said. "Get a drink. Then come sit, and we'll talk."

The bartender put down his glass and his cloth. He wiped his hands on his apron and then set them on the bartop. He looked at Carver.

"What's yours, friend?" he said. "And how about the lady?"

Carver didn't answer. Behind the bartender, there was a fish tank. It was built into the back bar, just beneath the mirror. It held the usual things – coral castles, sunken ships. But in the center there was a small screen. It couldn't have been more than six inches across. On the screen there was a woman. She appeared to be swimming across the satin sheets of a circular bed. Her naked legs kicked lazily. She rolled over, one forearm draped demurely across her bare breasts as she swam.

"If they don't tell you what they want," Johnny Wong said, "just pour two of what I'm having."

"Yessir," the man said. "And how are you doing? You need another?"

"That'd be fine."

The bartender bent and came up with a bottle. A plain glass bottle, no label of any kind. Carver glanced at the back bar. None of the bottles had labels, just as it had been in the limousine. There were no advertisements in the bar. Just polished glass and shimmering wood. Red and black damask on the walls.

The naked girl in the fish tank swam across her sea of silk.

The bartender poured a long measure from the bottle into a shaker of ice, then strained it into three martini glasses. He garnished them with lemon twists, cutting each slice from a different lemon. If he had a gun, it was tucked into the back of his pants, or somewhere out of sight behind the bar. But if he had a gun, it was secondary to his role. The man was a bartender, and a good one.

"I'll bring them," he said. He turned to get a tray. "Just sit."

Mia still had Carver's arm. She led him to the booth. She slid onto the seat and Carver sat beside her. She touched his leg, a gentle but deliberate brush, and then folded her hands on the table.

Johnny Wong watched them, his fingers pinching at the bit of lemon peel on the rim of his empty glass. He was the man in the picture Carver had seen. The same age as Carver, and the same build. Like a boxer. But his shirt might have cost a thousand dollars at a bespoke Hong Kong tailor, and his gold cufflinks, when they clicked across the tabletop, sounded as heavy as bullets.

"The girl you see in the tank, she's really in the basement," he said. "She's got a dressing room down there. Over the bed, it's all optics. Like a periscope on a submarine. Takes her image, projects it into the fish tank. No electronics at all."

He looked at Carver and waited, but Carver gave him nothing.

"Don't you like that? Isn't it nice, the way they used to do things?"

The bartender came over with the tray. He set down Mia's drink first, then Carver's. He served Johnny last, took his empty glass, and left.

"When I took this place over, the girl, Dolphina—they've always been Dolphina, since maybe 1930—she asked me, 'What am I going to do?' And I told her, 'Honey, you keep doing what you do best. Seven nights a week, as many hours as you want, whether anyone's here or not.' And she tells me she's never swum better."

Johnny picked up his drink, ran the lemon peel along the edge, and took a sip.

"What do you want?" Carver said.

"I could ask you the same thing," Johnny answered. "What do you want?"

"I was minding my own business. You brought us here, guns in our faces."

"Please," he said. "Minding your own business—you've been

looking for me. You were all over town. Asking about my nephew, asking about me."

He took another sip of his drink. Carver glanced at the bartender. He was polishing glasses again, not watching them at all.

"You went to Patrick's place, the San Lung Lounge," Johnny said. "You tore it up, cracked the safe. And you left your calling card on the table."

He took Carver's business card from his breast pocket and laid it on the table between them.

"After you found Patrick, you went to see Calvin Tran," he said. "So, really, it's me who should be asking you: 'What do you want?' Except that I know."

"You know what?"

"That you think I killed Hadley Hardgrave. That I got nervous when you were looking for my nephew, so I killed him. His mistress and his neighbor. You think I was upset when Calvin sent you a message about something he'd heard – something that isn't even true."

"Upset," Carver said. "That's what you do when you're upset?"

"I didn't cut off his hands and take out his eyes. I didn't pay anyone to do it, and I didn't ask anyone to do it as a favor. I didn't do Hadley, or Patrick, or Calvin. That's what I brought you here to say."

Four hours ago, Carver wouldn't have believed a word. He might have reached across the table to throttle the man. Grabbed his three-hundred-dollar tie and slammed his face into the table. But everything was different now. Jenner was gone, and he and Mia had until sunrise to find a sanctuary. He'd watched the snuff film on the memory card he'd taken from the motorcyclist's phone. He knew for a fact that Johnny Wong hadn't killed Hadley personally, and Wong wouldn't have brought him here just to deny a story Carver couldn't prove.

"You've got men in the Department, men on your payroll," Carver said. "So maybe you know it's pointless to talk to me."

"I heard you got suspended. You and Inspector Jenner," Johnny said. "But you're still working a case."

"What else do you know about Jenner?"

"The usual – the ex-wife, the young daughter. He's honest. He's good with his fists, when it calls for it."

"You know he's missing?"

"Since when?"

"Since tonight."

"I didn't know that."

"Your men were looking for me. Were they looking for him, too?"

"Nobody was looking for anybody until we got the call. Then we didn't have to look."

"Fremont, you mean. He's the one who called."

"Fremont," Johnny Wong said. He finished his drink and waved for another. "He's a friend. He was a more useful friend before he retired. He thought we should talk, you and I. I think, when we're done, you'll agree."

"Hadley Hardgrave," Carver said. "That's what he wants us to talk about. I heard she stole a hundred thousand dollars from you."

"Hadley never took anything that I didn't give her," Johnny said. He pointed around the bar. "This place? I'd have given it to her like that. It'd have been perfect for her."

"Calvin Tran's note—"

Johnny stopped him with a sideways wave of his hand.

"The thing you don't get is Calvin's got ties to my wife. They're second cousins. Maybe they didn't like how I spent my money. But the fact is, I gave it to Hadley. And it was mine to give."

"But she didn't come to you for money."

"No," Johnny said. He leaned back and let Sam switch his old glass for a new one. "She came for information. She took the money first, because she didn't want me to think she was after something else. It was a long seduction. She was seducing me while I seduced her. Different aims, the same methods—but if she'd just asked, the first time we met, I'd have given it to her."

"Asked for what?" Mia asked. "What did she want?"

"She wanted to know about a job, ten years ago."

"The Laurent show," Carver said. "The Legion of Honor. It was your crew, your money that backed it."

Johnny looked up from his drink and studied Carver. He might have had a man at every substation, and he might have a line open to Fremont. But he couldn't possibly know everything Carver had seen in the last week.

"The crew," Carver said. "Three men and a woman. The woman's on point. Two of the men are white and one's Asian."

"That's right."

"One of the white men, he's psychotic. Out of control."

Johnny nodded. Under the table, Mia took Carver's hand. When she squeezed his fingers, he knew what she was thinking about. The man had cut Hadley Hardgrave to pieces, but he hadn't broken her. He'd only wanted one thing. He'd promised to stop, had promised to end it with an easy bullet if Hadley would just give it to him. But she'd died without ever saying a word to expose Mia.

"Tell me what you talked about," Carver said. "You and Hadley."

27

"THE FIRST THING you have to understand," Johnny said, "is that this wasn't really my crew. They weren't my people. I hired them for the job — the Laurent job. These people, they were in from New York. Came with a recommendation. That's all they were to me."

"Whose recommendation?"

"It doesn't matter," Johnny said. "You get what I give you. That's it."

"It's your place," Carver answered. "You make the rules."

"I'd heard you're smart," he said. He pointed at the three martini glasses. "Drink if you're thirsty. They're all from the same shaker."

"I don't know what was in the glass before he poured it."

Johnny Wong leaned around the edge of the booth.

"Hey, Sam — you poison the glasses?"

"No, sir."

"See?"

Johnny reached across and took Carver's glass. He used it to refill his own, which he then drank.

"I was saying . . . They weren't my crew. A guy I trust said they'd get the job done. But that's all I knew."

"You didn't know their methods, is what you're saying."

"I didn't expect it to go like that," Johnny said.

"The body count."

"You don't go into an art job thinking twelve dead. Women missing."

"But you didn't wash your hands, either."

"I didn't," he said, without turning his eyes or dropping his voice. "I had a deal."

"What was your take?"

"My place," Johnny said. "My rules. Or did you forget?"

"All right."

"The second thing you need to understand is, it wasn't my idea. The Laurent job. Someone approached me, asked if I could put it together. Asked how much it'd cost."

"This was a flat-fee operation," Carver said. "You put in a bid. You didn't need a fence, because you had a client who wanted the paintings for himself."

"Not for himself—he wanted to give them as gifts. Rewards, for a job well done."

"Some reward," Carver said. "What did you think they were worth?"

"I figured they were priceless. But the guy just wanted a quote for the job, so he got one," Johnny said. "He said okay, and then we had a deal. I went and found a sub."

"This East Coast crew," Carver said.

"After it was done, they dropped out of sight."

"Except you heard where they landed," Carver said. "The client from the Laurent job picked them up. Didn't he?"

Johnny nodded.

"I heard it around," he said. "Don't ask where."

"That's what Hadley wanted to know—the client's name?"

"I don't know where she heard everything else," Johnny said. "She knew about the job, knew where the crew had gone. She was good."

Mia looked like she was about to say something, but stopped herself.

"Or she got around," Johnny continued. "That's a skill too, isn't it? Not that it's a bad thing. And I'm not putting her down—I liked her. I *appreciated* her, all the more after I figured out her game. That's why I'm helping you."

"Then tell us what she wanted to know," Mia said.

"The only thing she was missing was a name. That's all she needed."

He finished his drink and poured some of Mia's into his glass. Then he slid hers back across the table.

"His name was Alex. We met three times. He said he was negotiating for himself. That when we talked, it was principal to principal. But I saw through it."

"Saw what?" Carver asked.

"You meet a man ready to pay that kind of cash, for a thing like that, and he acts a certain way. You meet his second, his go-between, and you see something else."

"What's that?"

"Hesitation."

He looked at Carver, his eyes flicking from his worn-out suit to his cheap, steel-banded watch.

"You know what I'm talking about," he said. "And it's not about money. It's position. You've got that – or you had it – so you know. It doesn't even matter if you speak the same language. You meet a man, a woman, with position, and you know. You see eye to eye."

"So you dealt with Alex," Carver said. "He wasn't the real guy. But you must have given Hadley more than that, or she wouldn't be dead."

"It was a year after the job," Johnny said. "After the crew dropped off and I'd heard the rumors about who picked them up, I saw a picture in the news. A man getting an award, and behind him, like a lackey, was Alex. That's how I knew who I'd been dealing with – I saw the hand inside the glove."

Carver waited for him to go on.

"You wouldn't believe me if I told you."

"Try me."

"That's a name I won't say out loud," Johnny said. He glanced around the room, then dropped his voice to a whisper. "If they can get into your head, think what they can do on the outside. You can't sweep for bugs anymore. Not when they can burrow and walk. I won't say his name as long as he's alive and looking for me."

"So what are you going to do about it?" Carver asked.

"It's more about what I won't do. I won't show my face on the street, because there are cameras everywhere. These days, you don't know if a bird's a bird. It could be something else. And it's worse than just worrying about cameras. The feds have old wiretaps sitting in a file, so if he's looked, he's got my voice signature. And that's why in here, I don't even speak in my own voice."

He loosened his tie and undid his shirt's top button. A band of black fabric circled his throat, tight and slim, like a priest's collar. It was interfering with his vocal cords, probably bringing his voice down an octave and changing the entire signature. Anyone could buy an illegal voice band in the backroom of a Chinatown shop. But the one Johnny was wearing was so good, Carver hadn't even realized it was there.

"All it would take is one mistake," Johnny said. "I'll show up like a blip on a radar screen. I know who he is and what he's done, so you don't have to think hard to guess his next move."

"If you won't say his name, then what do we do?"

"Your briefcase is still in the car. Everything I gave Hadley, it's in there. My driver will take you wherever you want to go," Johnny said. "Don't open it until you're somewhere safe."

He pushed up his left cuff and looked at his watch.

"You're not holding anything back?" Carver asked.

"This is for Hadley," Johnny said. "I owe her."

Carver looked at the rows of unmarked bottles around the fish tank. Someone had taken the time to peel all the labels off, then wash off every trace of glue. This was a throwback nightclub, a gangster hangout. But the only thing Carver could think of was Mia's apartment.

"It was a give-and-take, wasn't it?" he asked. "She got what she was looking for. You would've let her have it for free, but she gave you something back. She told you why she needed it."

"And it helped—it really did," Johnny said. "Knowing that it wasn't just me. That there was something wrong with the world. That I could control it, even just a little."

He finished his drink. Carver had lost count of how many he'd gone through. But his face wasn't flushed and his speech was sharp and perfect. It occurred to Carver that he might not be drinking anything stronger than mineral water.

"There's one more thing," Carver said. "A request."

"All right."

Carver looked toward the fish tank. The bartender had his back to them. He was watching Dolphina as he polished the last of his glasses.

"I want Sam to drive the car," Carver said. "He and I, we get along just fine. But I can't say the same about your other guys."

They got out of the limousine on Baker Street, across from the Palace of Fine Arts. Spotlights in the gardens lit the dome, and its reverse-image shimmered on the surface of the lagoon. They watched the limousine disappear, and then Mia turned to him.

"You didn't say where we're really going."

"I didn't want them to know," he said.

He gestured toward the marina, which began across the street from them.

"When I was a kid, I had a friend who lived over there on Bay Street. His dad's pushing ninety now. But if we knock in the middle of the night, he'll let us in."

"It's not a place they'd think to look?"

"He's not family," Carver said. "We don't email, don't talk on the phone. I come now and then, see how he's doing. Bring groceries, make dinner. That kind of thing."

"You must have been close, to stay in touch so long."

Carver shook his head. They hadn't stayed in touch the entire time. He started walking with her along Baker Street. There were stray dogs ahead of them, but there was no traffic.

"It was fifteen years ago," he said. "Henry sent me a note. He'd heard I was a homicide inspector. Maybe he saw something in the paper. He thought we could meet now and then. Discuss cases."

"He was a detective?"

"He was the chief medical examiner. But when I was a kid, he had to resign. He'd made a mistake—a bad one."

People had died, including an assistant ME and three cops. Even fifty years on, he was a pariah. Out of the entire San Francisco Police Department, only Jenner knew of Carver's friendship with Dr. Henry Newcomb.

"If someone tracks us there, he'll get hurt," Mia said.

"Henry's seen hurt. He can handle himself."

"All right," Mia said. "If there's nothing else."

It was the only place Carver could think to go. Every hotel would ask for an ID except the shooting galleries in the Tenderloin. Carver didn't know who or what was hunting them, but if it wasn't safe to talk on the phone or send an email, he wasn't about to put their names into an online guest registry. And Mia would attract more attention in the Tenderloin than they needed.

Carver led them between the silent row houses of the marina, then under the rhododendrons lining Divisadero. There was no tail that he could see, but he was thinking about what Johnny Wong had said. A bird might not be a bird anymore. And what about rats? There were plenty of them, sliding along the street gutters. If he worried too much about what he couldn't control, he'd never get anywhere. So he led them to Henry's house.

Carver climbed the steps and knocked. Mia stood next to him, facing the dark street.

"Will we wake him?" she asked.

"If we have to."

But it didn't sound as if they'd woken him. Carver could hear him coming. It was three in the morning, and the neighborhood was as still as the dead streets around Calvin Tran's garage. Carver heard the creak of old floorboards, the arthritic gait. Then the locks were turning. Four deadbolts and two chains. The door opened a crack and there was a sliver of Henry's face. The oxygen tube ran across his cheek and under his nose. The rest of it was hidden behind the door.

"Ross — are you in trouble?"

"I need help."

"You better come in."

He stepped back, pulling the door open, and then he saw Mia. She didn't move at all, but Henry looked as if he'd taken a blow to his gut. He took four steps back, knocking a stack of books from the entry table. Carver went through the door and took hold of Henry's arm and shoulder.

"Take it easy," Carver said. "You've got to breathe."

Henry looked at him as he recovered, his nose struggling against the oxygen tube. Finally, when he could breathe well enough to speak, he turned to Mia.

"Miss Westcott," Henry whispered. "You were never supposed to come here. You need to get inside. Right now."

28

AT FIRST, CARVER wasn't sure what Mia would do. She looked as if she might bolt down the steps and then flee up the street. He was ready to chase her, if it came to that. She was frozen as she weighed the danger. Henry pushed himself back up and brushed Carver away from him. He held out his hand.

"Mia, please," he said. "You can't be out on the streets. Not like that. They're looking for you. They must know who you are by now."

"Henry," Carver said. "What is this?"

"And the cameras, they're everywhere," Henry went on.

If he'd heard Carver at all, he didn't care. He was focused entirely on Mia.

"If one caught your face just right, don't you know they'd have you in a minute?"

Mia looked once more at the street. Carver didn't understand what was passing between Henry and Mia, but he knew what Mia was thinking. She couldn't run from this. There was no distance she could travel that would take her safely beyond its reach. She wanted her life back, but the only way toward the past was by pushing forward. She stepped through the door and Henry closed it behind her. He threw the deadbolts and hung the chains.

Mia walked out of the entry hall and into the drawing room. There were bay windows facing the street. She pulled the curtains closed, then stood before one of the stuffed chairs facing the fireplace.

"I don't understand," Carver said. "You know each other?"

"She doesn't know me," Henry said. "We've never met."

"But you know who she is."

"Don't you get it?" Mia said. "He's George's man in San Francisco. There was someone who gave the signal when George wanted to reach me. Someone who watched for my sign, if I had something to send."

Carver looked from Mia to his old friend. Henry was shuffling into the drawing room. He wore heavy wool socks under his dressing robe. The oxygen cylinder was inside a black canvas satchel strapped around his waist.

"Is that true, Henry?"

"I didn't know him as George," Henry said. "He had a different name for me. But otherwise . . ."

"Why didn't you tell me?"

"Why the hell would I tell you a thing like that?" Henry said.

"You didn't trust me?"

Henry slowly sat in the chair opposite Mia.

"You'd have thought I was crazy, and that was too much of a risk. Then you'd stop coming, and I needed the information."

"About my cases."

"One more way to keep our fingers on the pulse," Henry said.

"How long have you known?"

"About the devices?" Henry asked. "Decades. Thirty-nine years. I found out a decade after I left the ME."

"How did you find them?" Mia asked.

She sat down, using no more than an inch of her seat's cushion.

"Lawyers," Henry said. "Plaintiffs' lawyers, guys with money to burn. They hired me to find a link between brain lesions and prescription drugs. These patients, they'd all died showing Creutzfeldt-Jakob symptoms—"

"Say that again?" Carver asked.

"It's a degenerative neurological disorder," Mia said. "A prion disease—it turns your brain into sponge."

"There were two clusters of people with symptoms," Henry said. "But they didn't test positive for any prion disease. So the lawyers were looking for anything and anyone to pin it on."

"Where?" Mia asked. "The clusters, where were they?"

"One was near Death Valley. The other one was up north. A village in Humboldt County. The sorts of places you'd go if you wanted to test something dangerous."

"What did you find?" Mia asked.

"I didn't do MRIs," Henry said. "George showed me yours, and they're the best pictures we have. I didn't have anything like that.

I was running tissue samples through a mass spectrometer, looking for drug metabolites bound to the lesion sites. But I was finding things that shouldn't be in the brain. Shouldn't be in the human body in the concentrations I was seeing."

"Like what?" Carver asked.

"Rare metals – tantalum, niobium. Stuff you see in superconductors and electronics. I knew something was there, but I didn't know what. I'm sure Mia can guess what I did."

"You started prepping samples for an electronic microscope. You wanted to see it with your own eyes."

Henry nodded and looked at the lithograph above the fireplace. It was a signed Magritte, *The Treachery of Images.* Carver knew he used to keep it in his office. He also knew that in his bedroom, Henry had a framed Laurent. A view from Angel Island, done in oils. He didn't keep it where visitors could see it, where they might ask him how he'd come to own it.

No one came by a Laurent lightly.

"Mass spectrometry is blind," Henry said. "It's just numbers and graphs. I wanted to see it, wanted to know what I was dealing with – I've still got it, the first one I found. It's here, in the house."

"You found one of the spheres," Carver said.

"They weren't as round back then. They've evolved. They've gotten smaller, and they've gotten better. Someone must have worked out the early problems, because those clusters – the people dying of lesions – you don't see those anymore."

"Or they got better at covering them up," Mia said.

"Or that," Henry said. He looked at Carver. "It isn't magic. It's not like they drifted down from space. They built them in a lab and let them loose. We didn't know what they were for until later, when MRIs showed us what they tapped in to. Now we know. It's just greed – pure greed."

They were in Henry's kitchen, sitting around the breakfast table. Carver had made coffee, letting Mia tell their story as he worked. When she was done, he poured a mug for each of them and passed them around. She stirred cream and sugar into hers, then drank it down all at once.

"What happened to George?" she asked Henry. "They got him, didn't they?"

He nodded.

"I saw a pair of stories in the news," Henry said. "The first was a day before they got Hadley. A man – a neurosurgeon – was missing in New York. And then, a week later, a body in the Meadowlands."

Henry's nose was red where the oxygen tube chafed at it, and his eyes were tired. What little hair he had left was as white as new paper. But he was strong, still. Carver had no doubt that he would have checked Mia's window every day, would have relayed messages and gone to the dead drop in Golden Gate Park. He'd never hidden his disappointment with the world, and now Carver understood that it wasn't just the idle talk of a bitter man. Henry hadn't lost hope that he could make things better. That there was time to amend his mistakes.

"You're sure it was George?" Mia asked.

"There was a name," Henry said. "The stories had a name. I hadn't heard it, but I had a bad feeling. I looked him up online and found a picture."

"You knew where Mia was," Carver said. "And that she was in danger. Why didn't you warn her?"

"The moment they got Hadley, Mia knew the danger," Henry said, and she was nodding before he was done. "And if they got George, their next jump would be me – because we talked directly."

"If you'd tried to warn me," Mia said, "you might have just led them to me. And if they knew about me but not you, it could've worked the other way. It was the right thing – and what were we supposed to do?"

"Another thing helped," Henry said. He looked at Carver. "I knew who lived across the hall. That made it easier."

"Which was no coincidence, was it?" Carver asked.

Now he realized, finally, what had happened. Everything had been set up from the beginning.

"You and George did this," he said. "You put her next to me for a reason."

Henry stalled before he answered. He picked up his coffee and took a sip, then set it down and stirred more cream into it.

"I don't know what George was thinking," he said. "It wasn't his call. But I know what I thought. You're a homicide inspector. We knew they killed people to keep their secrets. The chances of you running into this were close to one hundred percent. I thought it could be another way in."

Carver turned to Mia, who was studying the undissolved sugar at the bottom of her mug.

"Did you know that?" he asked her. "That I was part of your job?"

"Ross – everything I've told you has been true."

"You're not answering the question."

"I never lied to you. And I never did anything to put you in harm's way."

Carver couldn't look at her. He put his hand on Jenner's briefcase, which lay on the table between them. He knew they were watching him. Watching to see if he could set Jenner aside and focus. To see if he would accept the role they'd chosen for him, if he could believe what they were telling him. He hadn't been able to cross that line for Mia because he'd only just met her. But he'd known Henry his entire life. He was an old man now, bent with regret. But he wasn't a liar. The only thing that kept him going was his honesty.

"You asked why I didn't tell you," Henry said. "But it was the same for all of us. We only get recruited when we've already joined. When there's no other choice."

"Recruited to what?" Carver asked. "What did you make me join?"

"A good cause," Henry said. "At least, what's left of it."

Something touched Henry's eyes for a moment, and then bled away. Carver couldn't be sure what it had been. He hadn't seen Henry Newcomb smile in fifty years, so he doubted it was that.

"Open the briefcase," Henry said. "Find out what Johnny Wong gave us."

Mia lowered the blinds at the kitchen window and Henry dimmed the light. Carver pushed their coffee mugs to the side and opened the envelope that Johnny Wong's men had put into Jenner's briefcase.

There was a single piece of paper inside. A photograph printed from an online news article, blown up to fit the page. Seven people stood on a low stage in a hotel ballroom. Two men were shaking hands for the camera, one of them holding a small wood and brass plaque. The men and woman behind them on the dais appeared to be clapping. Someone had drawn a circle around one of the faces in the back row. That would be Alex, the man who'd approached Johnny Wong for the Laurent job.

There was nothing incriminating about the photograph. It was just an awards ceremony. Yet Hadley Hardgrave had died for this, because of what Johnny Wong had told her. He could tie Alex and the man holding the plaque to the Laurent job, and to twelve murders. But that wasn't all. Add what Hadley knew, and it could stop the world mid-spin. The paintings hadn't been about money. The man pulling the strings had more than he could ever spend. The Laurents had been gifts for a job well done, for work that had infected and darkened the world.

Carver laid the photo on the table, then took a step back so Mia and Henry could study it. After a moment, Mia pulled away and turned to him. Henry was still bending close, holding himself against the table's edge with both hands. His eyes wouldn't focus past a few inches.

"I don't understand it," Mia said. "I mean, I see the man Johnny Wong circled – Alex. And the one next to him is the man you knocked out – he killed Hadley. But who are the rest of these people?"

Henry shook his head, but Carver stepped back between them. He touched one of the faces in the back row.

"This woman – Lieutenant Hernandez, from Homicide."

"Your boss?" Henry asked.

"She suspended us. Pulled us off the case."

He moved his finger to touch the head of the man who'd just presented the plaque.

"This is Lyndon Ivies. Nine years ago, he'd just gotten on to the police commission. There's seven commissioners, but it's like Hernandez always says – only one of them matters. Ivies."

"And the other people?" Mia asked.

"This guy, in the back, he was a federal judge. Dead six years. Next to him, that was the President of the University of California. I forget his name. I think it was Thomas Skidmore. He cut the ribbon when we opened the new joint forensics lab. He shook my hand."

"Is that who I think it is, getting the award?" Henry asked. He was squinting through his glasses. "My eyes aren't what they were."

"That's Sheldon Lassen."

"*The* Sheldon Lassen?" Mia asked.

"There's only one I know about," Carver said. "I met him, too.

Same day as Skidmore—it was Lassen's company that built the forensics lab."

"Ønske," Henry said. "It makes sense."

Henry unzipped his belt pack and twisted the knob on his oxygen bottle to give himself more of the gas.

"It has a medical division," Mia said. "Laboratory equipment. Pharmaceutical research."

Carver looked at the photograph. Sheldon Lassen was wearing a pinstriped suit and a black bow tie. His curly hair was silver-gray and went past his collar. He looked like a philanthropist, the kind of man used to accepting awards and cutting ribbons. But he'd stolen an entire collection of Bridget Laurent's best work, and in doing so had paid for twelve deaths. The man standing behind him would eventually film himself killing Hadley Hardgrave, who had discovered Lassen's greatest secret. She had followed the trail from the Laurent job to the things eating through her mind. She'd known that if she solved one crime, she'd solve the other. None of this would have been enough for Carver to get a warrant. But Hernandez had taken care of that problem by suspending him. He didn't need a warrant.

Outside, a lone dog began to bark. Within the space of three seconds, the night erupted with their cries. There was a crash, and one of the dogs began to howl and yip in pain.

Carver pushed past Henry and went to the drawing room. He stood to the side of the bay windows, put his fingers at the edge of the curtains, and pulled them back far enough to see.

An old woman stood on the opposite side of the street. She wore a grime-slicked raincoat over a housedress. A knocked-over trash can lay at her feet, its contents scattered in the street and the gutter. She was surrounded by a dozen stray dogs, but they kept their distance. They were afraid of her stick. One of them was turning circles on the asphalt, its hind leg broken.

The scavenger woman began to drag a trash bag toward an ancient station wagon parked in the street. After loading it, she went quickly to the driver's seat. As soon as she closed the door, the pack went for the spilled garbage. The injured dog began a low keen as three of its littermates closed in around it.

Carver looked up and saw Henry and Mia at the other window. Henry let the curtain fall back.

"Thirty-nine years," Henry said. "Decades, they've been in

our heads. And what happened to us, to our invention and drive? Shouldn't we be farther along? This company, Ønske, it progressed. But the rest of us? We lived in the dark, and stared at pictures, and bought every shining thing we saw."

On the street, the entire pack had turned on the wounded one. It was shrieking from beneath a pile of writhing, mud-caked hackles. By sunrise, if that ever came, there would be nothing left.

"What do we do?" Mia asked.

"We'll start with what we know," Carver said. "With the people we can reach."

"Your boss," Mia said. "Hernandez."

"Right now, she's at Bryant Street—the headquarters. When she gets home, it'll be light. Better to catch her on her way back out."

"You shouldn't wait here," Henry said. "It's not safe, all of us together."

"I'll think of a place," Carver said.

"I have one. And you can take my car."

"The safe house?" Mia asked. "We can't—"

"Hadley knew about that," Henry said. "None of us should go there. I've got something else."

"Then come with us," Carver said. "If we're not safe here, neither are you."

"I've got a lady who looks after me," he said. "A nurse. She'll be here at seven. I'll leave with her."

"We can take you."

"I can take care of myself. But you—Johnny Wong's men took your gun, and they didn't give it back. That's a problem."

"You've got one?"

"A friend's. His name was Kennon. I think you've got his old desk," Henry said. "It's got ammunition, but it's fifty years old."

"How many bullets?"

"Whatever was left," Henry said. "Kennon didn't get off many shots the last time he used it. It's in my bedroom. Wait, and I'll get it."

29

HENRY'S CAR WAS black and boxy, and looked as heavy as a city bus. But he'd kept it maintained, and the batteries were full. They could drive all the way to Los Angeles on the charge, if they had to. Carver let Mia in, and then looked back up the garage steps to Henry.

"When your lady comes, don't have her take you to the Tenderloin hotels. They'd roll a guy like you in a second."

"An old guy like me."

"I'm serious," he said. Then he raised the paper bag of food Henry had given him. "And thank you for this. For all of this."

"How do we get in touch?"

"We don't," Carver said.

He looked at the car, wondering if Mia could hear their conversation. He turned away when he caught her eyes in the side-view mirror.

"In twenty-four hours, we'll know where this is heading."

"You won't be careful, is what you're saying," Henry said. "Don't mince words, Ross. I haven't got the time for it."

"Then hope for the best," Carver said. "Vicki would be proud of you."

Henry double-tapped his fist over his heart, and Carver repeated the gesture. Then he walked around the back of the car and got in. He hit the remote to open the garage door, waited for it to roll up, and drove out.

He parked in the public garage on Beach Street, across from Pier 39. Even now, the boutiques on the wharf were crowded. Inside a jeweler's showroom, a reception was under way. Waiters roamed the store, carrying trays of champagne and plates of canapés. A string quartet played in the center, surrounded by glittering display cases. They stopped on the pedestrian bridge and watched it.

"I've seen it for years," Carver said.

"But did you really? Did you really see it?"

"I never wondered what was wrong—why we let ourselves get to this."

"You've been in that crowd. Or one just like it."

"A hundred like it."

He started to lead her toward the water's edge, where there was a locked gate and a gangplank that went down to the docks. But she stopped him and turned him back to the crowd lined up outside the jeweler's reception.

"Look at them," she said. "See that girl? Maybe she'll buy a diamond ring. A necklace. She'll bring it home in a black silk bag and never wear it. When she wakes up, she won't even remember what she bought."

"Until she sees the label."

"She'll hold it until she falls asleep tonight, and she'll be so warm—you know what I'm talking about. It might sustain her a while. To hold it, to look at it. But then someday the switch will flip and it won't do anything for her."

"There'll be something else," Carver said. "Whatever's next in line."

She nodded and pulled his arm around her. When she was up against him, he could feel the tension in her. She was caught at a balance point between desire and revulsion. She wanted to break away from him and go toward the lighted store. Toward the soft music and the sparkling gemstones, and the promise that drifted from the open doors like a low whisper. Inside, you could find everything you had ever lost. Things would be all right again. You just had to come inside. Instead she put her other arm around him.

"Let's go."

"It's this way," Carver said.

They went to the gate and Carver punched in the code that Henry had given him. They walked down the gangplank and along the docks. In a moment, they were far enough into the marina that it drowned out the city's noise. There was just the wind. It stirred up ripples that lapped against hulls, and set a halyard beating against a sailboat's mast. The air was wet and heavy with fog. When Carver turned to look back, Telegraph Hill was just a blurry glow.

Jenner might be in any of those shadows. Until tonight, that had always been a comforting thought.

He tried to push it away, but it was useless. He saw Calvin Tran's face. The sunken bandages over his eyes, the black stitches where his tongue had been cut out. If they'd done that to Jenner, if they'd done anything at all to him –

He stopped in front of a wooden trawler.

"I think this is it."

"You're sure?"

"It's been a while."

Some of the bronze hardware had disappeared from the gunwales, and Henry had replaced it with cheaper aluminum. But otherwise, for a century-old boat, she looked good. Even in the dark, Carver could see his outline reflected in the teak. He stepped to the deck, then slid Henry's key into the cabin door's lock. He must have the right boat. He opened the door and Mia followed him into the salon.

There was a brass sconce above the dinette. Carver turned the switch, but nothing happened. It could be the bulb, or a dead house battery, or something with the shore power. Maybe there was an electrical panel somewhere.

"Do you mind the dark?" he asked.

He set Jenner's briefcase on the floor and Henry's bag on the table. There were windows all around the cabin, and they let in a bit of light from the pier.

"It's fine," Mia said. "I bet there's a candle somewhere. Sit down. I'll find it."

He sat at the dinette, put his elbows on the table, and rested his head against the heels of his palms. He closed his eyes, listening as Mia went through the galley drawers. Then she was coming across the salon, sliding onto the seat across from him. He heard the sandy scratch when she tried to light a paper match. A bite of sulfur followed.

"They might've gotten damp," she said.

She tried three more, and when the last one came alight, he could feel its heat against the backs of his hands. He raised his head and watched her light the votive candles. She'd also found a bottle of Laphroaig and a pair of tumblers.

"What do you think – would Henry mind very much?"

"I doubt it."

She pulled the bottle's stopper and poured for them. Then she opened Henry's paper bag, and brought out the bread and the rest of food he'd given them.

"We'll feel better if we eat a little," she said. "A glass of scotch, and dinner – and then we'll sleep."

She handed a tumbler to him, and he brought it to his lips.

After they'd eaten, Mia took one of the candles and found her way down the steps to the forward stateroom. He poured a second glass of the scotch and took out the gun Henry had given him. He'd heard of the make and model, but had never seen one. It was a compact automatic. Its magazine was designed for eight rounds, but it held only five. There was one in the chamber.

Henry's old friend, Inspector Kennon, had managed two shots before he died.

Carver hoped he would get as many, but he wasn't sure about the ammunition. The brass casings were pitted with corrosion. He lined the bullets on the table, then took the gun and racked its slide. It was stiff, and the action was rough. Nothing that couldn't be fixed by stripping it and cleaning it. He had a sip of the scotch and then picked up the candle. On a boat like this, he was sure to find a set of tools and an oily rag.

It was her hand on his shoulder that woke him.

He'd fallen asleep at the table, his head resting against his folded arms. Kennon's gun, reassembled and reloaded, was in his right hand. He raised his head and looked around. The candle had gone out, and the sun hadn't yet risen. Rain lashed against the windows, and the dock lines groaned against their cleats each time they went taut.

"What is it?" he asked her.

"You should come to bed," Mia said. "Come on – stand up. I'll help you."

"I'm all right."

He pushed up from the dinette, tucked the gun into his waistband, and looked at her in the dark. Though he was shivering from the cold, she wore nothing more than a half-buttoned shirt and a pair of black panties. She put her hand on the side of his neck.

"Come with me," she said.

She began leading him toward the stateroom, but he stopped before he reached the steps. He leaned against the captain's chair at the steering station. He looked at the wooden wheel, at the ancient electronic navigation instruments.

"What is it?" she asked.

"Henry put you across the hall from me," he said. "I know how Hadley got things from Johnny Wong, how she—"

Mia put her other hand on his collarbone, then came in close enough that she had to look up at him.

"If George had told me to, I wouldn't have done it just for him. Do you understand?"

"No," Carver said. "Say what you really mean."

"I did what I wanted. And that's all. It doesn't matter what George told me, or what Hadley did. I did what I wanted. And right now . . . this—this is what I want."

"All right."

She led him down the steps and closed a door behind him. After that, it was too dark to see her. There were hatches over the bed, but there was no light at all in the sky. She came behind him, and then her hands were at the lapels of his suit jacket. She pulled it from his shoulders, helped him out of it. In a moment she was close to him again. The length of her body pressed against his back.

She reached around him and began unbuttoning his shirt.

"Is it safe, do you think?" she asked.

"If it wasn't, they'd have taken us already."

"Then can we?" she whispered. "Will you?"

It wasn't a question he could answer aloud. He'd never learned to talk that way. But he could show her. He turned around. The gun was still in his waistband, but he tossed it on the bed before they came together.

She was trembling, but she wasn't cold.

In the dark, he found the last two buttons on her shirt. When he undid them, she let it slide down her arms to the floor. He'd never been with a woman he knew so little about. He didn't know her age or where she was born, or what her family was like. He didn't even know her real name. But now she was undressing him, leading him in increments toward the bed.

He thought he knew why this was happening. Why Mia was stretching across the duvet and pulling him down to her, why her hand on the back of his neck was leading him into this kiss. They'd lost everything. This was the most they could give each other. It might not carry them through tomorrow, but they had to try.

30

SOMETIME IN THE afternoon he opened his eyes and looked at the smoke-gray sky through the glass hatch above his head. Rain pounded the deck, heavy and cold. He stretched to touch Mia, but only found the gun. He took it and rose from the bed, following the three steps to the pilot house.

She wasn't at the dinette, but she must have used it at some point. She'd found a pen and a pad of hotel stationery in one of the drawers, and those were sitting on the table next to a packet of red envelopes from a Chinatown shop. He thought there would be a note on the pad, but it was blank. She wasn't aboard the boat, and must have taken her purse with her. He knelt next to the table and opened Jenner's briefcase. The laptop was still there, and Johnny Wong's photograph was inside its envelope.

He dressed in the stateroom, then returned to the salon to sit at the table. He checked his watch and told himself he'd give her half an hour. After that, he would look for her. But in five minutes he saw her coming along the dock, and then the boat rocked gently as she stepped to the side deck. She opened the door and came inside with a gust of wind. She was soaking wet from the rain. She crossed to the galley and set down two bags from one of the grocery stores on Bay Street.

"I thought I'd get back before you woke up," she said.

"How long were you out?"

"Twenty minutes."

"Did anyone follow you?" he asked. "Did you check?"

"I was careful," she said.

She took off the hat she'd found. Her hair spilled around her shoulders again. He got up and she came and put her arms around him. He held her tightly against his chest.

"I wake up, and you aren't here."

"I'm sorry, Ross."

"What were you writing?" he asked. "You got out a pen, that stationery."

"Nothing – I was going to write you a note, but I decided not to."

He held her by her shoulders and looked at her. The pen and the stationery made sense if she planned to write him a note. The envelopes didn't fit. There should have been ten of them in the cellophane-wrapped packet. He'd counted nine.

"Did you mail a letter?"

"No," she said. "Please, Ross."

He couldn't afford to doubt her now. If she was holding something from him, then he could only hope she had a good reason. Every time he held her, it felt inevitable. As if he'd been ordained to do it now because he'd done it ten times before in lives he couldn't remember. He didn't understand it at all. He knew they were drawing near to something. He wanted to rush in and find it; he wanted to take Mia and run as far as they could go.

"All right," he said.

He let go of her and nodded to the rain-soaked bags she'd set on the counter.

"What's so important you had to go out in this?"

It was raining even harder when they got to Noe Valley. Carver parked on Diamond Street, three blocks from Hernandez's apartment. They walked down the hill, sticking to the shadows cast by the condemned houses on the left. Hernandez's apartment building was on the right. Someday soon, it would be across from another new mall. To the east, every house for a half a mile was slated for destruction. Already, the thieves had taken whatever they could pry loose. You could walk through the missing front doors, but every step past the threshold was perilous, because the floorboards were all gone. If you wanted, you could balance on a joist in a space that for a hundred and fifty years had been a bedroom. You could look up through the rafters and see the sky. Feel the rain on your face.

When Carver saw Hernandez's car, he led Mia up the steps of the nearest empty house. They stood in the crossed shadows of its naked beams, where they could watch the street. He drew the gun and racked the slide to chamber a round. He'd reloaded the magazine so that the best-looking bullet was first. He didn't want to pull the trigger, but if he had to, he wanted something to happen.

He checked his watch, and then they waited. There was a pile of garbage balanced on the floor beams above them, and it blocked some of the rain. Mia stood close to him. Her hair, wet again, still smelled of cedar. He put his arm around her waist, and remembered being a boy. He'd gone with Henry and his son, a half day's drive to the redwood groves along the north coast. He remembered standing in a rough circle of trees so tall that their crowns had touched the clouds and brought down rain. People always said that losing the trees had been the price of progress, but there hadn't been any progress. The world hadn't moved anywhere.

"Is that her?" Mia whispered.

He saw Hernandez coming along the sidewalk on the other side of Diamond Street.

"Stay here."

He touched his finger to her lips, then went down the steps and across the street. He timed it so that he reached Hernandez as she was opening the car's door. When he put the gun's muzzle against the back of her head, she went stiff.

"Hands on the roof."

"Carver?"

"The roof, Hernandez. I'm not saying it again."

She did it, and he swept his left arm quickly along her chest and sides until he found her holster. He took her service weapon and put it in his waistband. He knelt quickly and patted the rest of her down. He'd seen her using a .25 auto on the range, and thought it might be on her ankle. But there was nothing. He took the phone from her hip pocket and the keys from her right hand.

"I'm not being as thorough as I could be," Carver said. "You weren't the worst lieutenant I ever had — so I respect you enough to stop short. But you know what that means?"

She didn't answer, so he went on.

"If you reach for anything, I pull the trigger. And after you're down I'll find out what it was."

"What do you want?" she asked.

"Jenner. To start with. That's just the beginning."

"This isn't the right way, Carver," she said. "If you and Jenner want —"

He spun her around and put the gun under her chin.

"If Jenner and I want to do what?" he said. "What do you know about Jenner?"

"He missed his psych evaluation," she said. "And so did you."

She didn't do herself any favors by sounding so calm. He thumbed back the hammer and pushed the muzzle against the soft flesh under her jaw.

"Ross?"

He hadn't even heard Mia walk up.

He stepped back from his lieutenant, a gun in each hand. When he gave Hernandez's weapon to Mia, she eased the slide back and held it in place with her thumb and forefinger around the barrel. Then she used her index finger to check the chamber for a round. It was the cleanest press check he'd ever seen. She released the slide, thumped the base of the magazine to seat it, and aimed the gun at Hernandez's chest.

He hadn't thought she knew how to shoot. There was so much about her he still didn't know.

"Hernandez drives," he said. "You take the back. Get in—I'll sit up front."

After Mia was in the car, Carver motioned Hernandez to get behind the wheel. Mia put her gun against Hernandez's neck.

"I've got this," Mia said. "Check under the seat, and in the door. Make sure she doesn't have anything."

He knelt on the pavement and felt under the driver's seat, then brushed his fingers through the cup holders and the storage compartment in the door. He found a ballpoint pen and tossed it over his shoulder. He shut the door, then came around the front and got in next to Hernandez.

"Your hands stay on the wheel."

He leaned across and put the key into the ignition, then watched the car's systems come up. When the GPS screen blinked on, he used the butt of his pistol to smash it in. Then he took Hernandez's phone from his pocket, swiped the screen, and came to the password prompt. He entered the four-digit number without looking up.

"We always loved your memory," Hernandez said. "The way you sweep things up, and save them. It's what makes you special."

He didn't answer her. Everything he saw stayed with him. It had always been like that. He hadn't realized she'd known that about him. Nine months ago he'd been next to her in a court elevator. She'd taken out her phone to check her email, punching her password with her thumb. He'd learned her address more or less the same way.

"Who should we start with, Hernandez?" Carver asked. "I bet Sheldon Lassen doesn't take your calls. I bet, to him, you're just a speck. Let's think of someone closer to your level."

"What are you talking about?"

Carver went to the phone's contact list and began scrolling through it.

"Or we could start with your friend, the guy who killed Hadley Hardgrave – is he in here?"

Hernandez didn't move. Her hands were locked tight on the steering wheel, and she was staring at the glare of raindrops on the windshield. Either she was waiting for something, or she was looking for a way out of the box.

After ten seconds of silence, she tilted her eyes toward Carver. She didn't turn her neck at all.

"You should've come to your psych eval," she said. "Maybe we could've done something for you. Maybe we still could. And we could set the record straight. I don't know what she's been telling you."

Carver waited to see what else Hernandez had to say about Mia, but she must have been done. She looked out the windshield and kept her mouth closed. He checked the back seat. Mia still had the gun to Hernandez's neck.

"You got it?" Carver asked. "I want to show her."

Mia switched the gun to her left hand and reached into her jacket. She took Johnny Wong's envelope and passed it to him. He slid the photograph out, then switched on the dome light. He looked at the picture for a moment before setting it on Hernandez's lap.

"Pick it up," he said. "Take a good look."

She took the photograph and held it in front of the steering wheel. There was no surprise on her face. As he watched her look at it, her phone began to vibrate in his hand. She didn't seem very surprised about that, either. The caller's number was blocked. Hernandez tossed the photograph onto the dashboard and put her hands back on the steering wheel.

"Answer it," she said. "It's probably for you."

"What?"

"They called to warn me," she said. "After they picked up Henry Newcomb, they knew you'd be coming here."

The phone was pulsing in his hand, its screen flashing. Everything went silent, and his mind dropped into a blurring race. Outside, the raindrops hung motionless in the car's headlights. She'd used Henry's name. If she knew his name, then it couldn't be a lie. They had him.

"If you want Jenner to live," Hernandez whispered, "then answer the goddamned phone."

Now there was no choice at all. But as soon as he answered the call, everything belonged to them. It would be their initiative, and their terms. It made him sick to imagine it, but he knew what he had to do. He looked through the windshield at the night. He answered the phone and brought it to his ear.

"This is Carver."

As soon as the words left his mouth, he put the phone on mute, stuck his gun in Hernandez's kidney, and turned to face the back seat.

"You have to get out," he said to Mia. "You have to go, right now."

"Ross," Mia whispered. "Don't—"

"Out," he shouted. "Run. I'm not leaving Jenner and I'm not taking you to die. You have to live."

She didn't move, and again, there was only one way forward. It was clear to him. He took the gun from Hernandez's side and put it in Mia's face. He'd carried a gun just like it every day since he was twenty-two years old, but this was the heaviest weight he'd ever lifted. His hand shook from the strain of it.

Beside him, Hernandez didn't move. The muzzle of Mia's gun was still pressed against her neck.

From the phone, a machine-altered voice was squealing into his ear. He paid it no mind.

"Get out," he said. "You're the one good thing. So go."

"How do I find you?"

"You don't. Not if you want to live."

She tried to say something, but couldn't. When she stepped from the car, her throat was struggling with whatever was caught there. She still had Hernandez's gun. At least there was that. He wasn't taking her to die, and he wasn't leaving her with nothing.

She slammed the door, and he took the phone off mute. He shoved the gun against Hernandez's temple, hard enough to make her bleed. She cried out, but he didn't care. From the street, Mia caught his eyes. She touched her fingers to her lips. Then she walked back into the ruins on the far side of Diamond Street. He watched until she was gone. It was so dark, it didn't take long at all.

He put the phone against his ear.

"I didn't catch that," he said. He didn't sound calm. "Say again?"

"I . . . said . . . do you want to *hear* Jenner? Do you . . . want . . . to hear him . . . *talk?*"

It sounded like the metal-on-metal screech of a train racing into one of the city's outer-limit stations. A place where the lights were gone, where children crept through the shadows.

"Just tell me what you want," Carver said.

"Jenner . . . wants to *tell* you."

"You sonofabitch."

" . . . *yes* . . ."

He heard the phone change hands, and then he heard three loud slaps. He pictured a palm hitting Jenner's face. Rousing him, maybe.

"Ross."

"Where are you?"

"Go with Hernandez," Jenner said. His voice was quiet, his growl slowed either by pain or by drugs.

"And then what?"

"Time to take our psych eval."

The connection went silent. Someone had taken the phone from Jenner, had ended the call. It had lasted twelve seconds. But the entire landscape had shifted, a fault line splitting across it.

"I wouldn't have thought you'd get into something like this," Carver said. He put her phone away. "I thought you were a good cop."

Hernandez leaned away from the gun and looked at him.

"When they come for you, you don't have a choice," she said. "You know that."

"Drive, then," Carver said. "Wherever you're supposed to take me."

She put the transmission into gear and began turning the wheel to the left so that she could pull away from the curb. As she took her foot from the brake and the car began to roll into the street, Carver heard three gunshots from across the way. At the first shot, he jerked to look out the back window. He saw the second and third muzzle flashes.

"Mia didn't make it very far," Hernandez said. "It was a good idea, though. Trying to keep her out of this."

There were two more shots, and then a scream. He couldn't tell if it was a man or a woman. He yanked the emergency brake and the car lurched to a stop. Then he put the transmission into park, pulled the keys from the ignition, and took Hernandez's thermal scope from the clip between the seats.

"You don't want to do that," she said. "Jenner doesn't have much time."

"Shut up," he said. "And stay put."

He shot out her left kneecap.

Inside the enclosed car, the gun blast was deafening. Hernandez's mouth flew open, but he couldn't hear her screaming. He stepped out of the car and slammed the door. Everything was muffled and cottony except for the ringing in his ears. He put the keys in his pocket, then ran up the hill. There was no movement, and he heard no more gunfire.

When he was one door down from the house where he'd seen the muzzle flashes, he crouched at the rear bumper of a parked car and turned on Hernandez's thermal scope. There was no one moving on the first or second floors. But at the street level, in what had probably been the garage, there was the red-orange heat signature of a person laid out on the cold concrete floor. He put the scope down and got out his flashlight, then went up the steps and through the shattered front door. He picked his way across the exposed beams in the living room and then aimed his light down.

There were droplets of blood on the beam. A body in the rubble down in the basement. Mia had shot him up here, and then he'd fallen through. It was the man he'd punched on the subway, the man who'd killed Hadley Hardgrave. His right eye was black and swollen nearly shut, and his nose was covered in medical tape and gauze. His left eye was gone; Mia had shot it out. Another bullet had gone through his throat.

A car door slammed, and Carver looked up. He almost lost his balance on the beams, which would have sent him tumbling into the basement to land on the dead man. He caught himself by stepping sideways to the next beam and dropping to a crouch.

Now he could hear feet scuffling on the gravelly pavement outside. Not out front, on Diamond Street, but toward the back of the house. There was silence, and then a woman's stifled cry.

Carver picked his way across the living room, went through the remains of the kitchen, and then turned off his flashlight. He approached the dining room window, which looked out the back of the house. The glass panes were missing, and the rain blew in. He stood to the side of the window frame and looked out in time to see two men pushing Mia into the back of a car. Her hands were bound behind her. He saw the glitter of steel cuffs. One of the men climbed in after her, and the other got into the front passenger seat. The car began to roll into the alley before the second man had even closed his door.

Carver raised his gun and aimed at the silhouette in the back window, but he couldn't pull the trigger. It would have been too easy to miss, to hit Mia. Instead, he turned and ran back to the front of the house.

31

HERNANDEZ HAD GOTTEN out of the car and was sitting on the street with her back against the front tire. She'd taken off her jacket and twisted it up as if to wring water from it. She'd tied that like a tourniquet above her knee. He stood above her so she'd have to look up the barrel of his gun when he spoke to her.

"Where are they taking Mia?"

"The same place they have Jenner, and Henry," she said. "Where I'm supposed to take you."

"Then let's go," Carver said.

She looked at him, not sure what he was telling her to do.

"Jesus, Lieutenant. It's only the one leg. You can drive."

He watched her get up, pushing off the pavement and then using the car's hood as a crutch. She hobbled around the open door and fell into the seat, then used her hands to pull her wounded leg inside. Carver shut the door and came around. He got in next to her and put the keys in the ignition. The car smelled of gunpowder and blood.

"Go," he said. "Take us there."

He put on his seatbelt and leaned against the door to put as much distance between them as possible. He had the gun on his lap, pointed at her kidney.

"You were there that night, weren't you?" Carver asked.

"What night?"

She was sucking air between words, and her face was covered with sweat. She put the car in drive and released the parking brake.

"Thursday night, Friday morning. Filbert Street," he said. "That was you on the radio, at the end."

She came to a stop sign and took a left turn. Now they were going east on Twenty-First Street, down a steep hill. The houses on both sides of them were completely destroyed, but in a few blocks they would be past the footprint of the future mall and back into a neighborhood where the houses were intact and the power was still on.

"It was you," Carver said. "It was your voice."

"What if it was?" she asked.

He saw a bulge on her jawline when she clenched her teeth.

"We all had a job to do that night," she whispered.

"What was yours?"

"To see that you got processed. Handled the right way. When that call came in, I didn't know what was inside—if I had, I wouldn't have sent you. When I started getting details through the backchannels, I wanted to be there."

"A good lieutenant, looking after her men."

"I thought so."

"They decontaminated you, but they didn't touch your memory," Carver said. "No need to mess with yours, since you're on their side. But that's why we smelled it, the burnt metal, in your office."

Hernandez turned north onto Dolores, and they followed under the shadows of the date palms until they passed the old mission. Priests with candle-lanterns stood their nightly vigil around the building, pacing to keep warm in the rain, holding up their lights to warn back the thieves.

"What happened that night?" Carver asked.

"I don't know."

"An Ønske scientist lived in that house, didn't he?"

"You honestly think they tell me anything, Carver?"

"And he'd been stealing secrets. Maybe to sell, maybe to strike off on his own. He'd set up a lab in his basement—"

"You're crazy, Carver."

"—and something went wrong. He didn't know what he was doing," Carver said. He waved the gun at her. "How much do you know about the machines? The things in our heads."

"I don't know about that," Hernandez said. "You've been talking to crazy people. Spies."

Her voice had been very quiet when they'd started driving, but it was coming back now. And she was driving a straight course, not weaving through the street. Either she was getting on top of her pain or she was good at faking it. He was ready to grab the wheel if she passed out.

"You do what Lyndon Ivies tells you," Carver said. "Isn't that right?"

She nodded.

"So you stood there and let this happen."

"It wasn't like that."

"Then what was it like?"

"You're not responsible for anyone but yourself, so you wouldn't understand," Hernandez said. "And it had already happened—happened a long time ago. All we did was step up. The world was already made. Plus, Lassen gave us a deal."

"You pay your dues, stay in line, and they won't hurt you. That's the deal?"

"More or less."

"How's that any different from Johnny Wong protecting a strip joint?"

"They won't hurt any of us. Anyone with a badge. Including you."

Of course they would have had a deal with the police, he thought. They were tearing the world to pieces, but they needed it to run smoothly until it was gone. They didn't care if the outer edges fell apart. People's urges were pricing them out of life, and that tended to run down everything around them. But Hernandez's bosses needed lights burning all night in the shopping districts. They needed the neon signs to glow and buzz. The phones had to work, the banks had to stay open, and the trains had to run. And for all that, they needed the police to go out into the night and see the city through until the sun rose again.

"What about Houston and Roper?" he asked. "Did they get the deal?"

Hernandez shook her head.

"I don't know."

"That's above your pay grade too?"

"I just don't know, Carver. It shouldn't have happened like that."

She took a right onto Market Street, and they were going northeast toward downtown. Hernandez was using her left hand to clench the makeshift tourniquet on her thigh. He thought about Johnny Wong's man in the limousine, the story of the blindfold. Hernandez was driving him to meet something even worse than Johnny, was answering all his questions. And she hadn't offered him a blindfold.

"What about Johnny Wong?" Carver asked. "Why bother setting him up? You could've just killed Hadley and made her disappear."

"Wong's a gangster," Hernandez said. "They knew Hadley was meeting with him. They knew she could find him."

"But she didn't talk, did she?" Carver asked. "I saw the video. So then you were back to square one. You hit Patrick, and that didn't help either. Because nobody can find Johnny Wong unless he wants to be found."

"You could, after you were suspended," she said. "Then he thought it was safe to reach out. You never would have found him if he hadn't come to you. We made it so he wanted you to find him."

"You set us up, from the beginning," Carver said. "Even the dream Jenner had, about talking to Patrick. You put that there, planted it in him. You started us down the path and then just stood back and watched."

"You found Johnny, and in the process led us to everyone else we'd been looking for. People we'd needed a long time. It was a successful operation."

A successful operation. One that had swept up Henry and Mia, and left Hadley Hardgrave in pieces. They had cut out Calvin Tran's tongue and eyes so he couldn't tell Carver that he'd never sent the note. He wondered where they put Jenner on their ledger. Was he just an acceptable loss, a fair trade to eradicate a few problematic people?

He raised his gun and pressed it to Hernandez's temple.

They were at a red light. He wouldn't even have to worry that she'd crash. He grabbed the parking brake and yanked it up, so that the car wouldn't roll when she went slack. She closed her eyes and her shoulders sagged, and that was the only thing that saved her. He thought of Mia, the way she'd fallen to her knees in her kitchen. Her hands in the air, begging.

It was for her that he lowered the gun. He had to find her, and he couldn't do it without Hernandez.

"Drive," he said.

He released the parking brake. Above the intersection, the light turned green. Hernandez opened her eyes, then set the car rolling. When they passed under a set of working streetlights, he saw how pale her face was. He wondered how much blood she'd lost.

• • •

They were going east down Clay Street, and in front of them, the beacon atop the Ønske Pyramid flashed blue-white in the falling rain. Far past that, a wall of fog was swallowing the Bay Bridge. Then they were coming down the hill, walled in by the row houses, and he could see nothing.

Hernandez stopped in front of the electronic gate that guarded the Ønske Pyramid's underground parking lot. A hidden sensor must have recognized her car, because the red lights in front of them switched to green and the bronze bollards blocking their way began to retract into the pavement. At the top of the ramp, a steel gate was spooling into the concrete lintel above the automobile entrance. The light that shone from beneath its ever-widening crack was as white and sterile as the noonday sun.

When the ramp was clear, Hernandez drove down it and into the garage.

There were only three vehicles on the level where they parked. One of them was Johnny Wong's black limousine. It was riddled with bullet holes and sat on four flat tires. All the window glass was missing. The chauffeur was slumped against the steering wheel, blood running out of his ear and down his cheek.

Then there was the tow truck, which must have brought the limousine to the garage after the ambush. And in the space next to it was the car he'd almost fired on, the one they'd used to take Mia.

Hernandez parked next to it.

"Stay there," he said. "Don't get out."

He took the keys and stepped out, then looked into the windows of the car in the next space. The white upholstery behind the driver's seat was smeared with blood, and there was a pool of it in the foot well. They must have shot Mia below the knee before they'd caught her. He looked at the floor and saw the trail of blood leading away from him. It went in drops and dashes across the clean concrete and the newly painted yellow parking lines. It stopped at the elevator bank.

He went back and got Hernandez out of the car. He shut the door and she leaned against it.

"Can you walk?"

"No," she said. "I really can't."

"All right," he said. "Put your left arm across my shoulders."

She did, and he held on to her wrist. He pressed the gun at her back, above her right hip. He had seven bullets left, but he doubted they added up to even one chance.

"Let's go see your bosses."

32

WHEN THE ELEVATOR doors closed behind him, he stepped away from Hernandez and scanned the room. Floor-to-ceiling glass panels boxed in the area around the elevator. The wall directly across from him was screened with an opaque film that shimmered like the surface of the bay. He looked at the floor and saw where the blood trail picked up at the threshold to the elevator. It turned left and went under one of the glass walls.

Whatever lay beyond the glass box might have been a clean room. Everything that wasn't blinding white was made of stainless steel. He let go of Hernandez and she leaned against the smooth wall, using it to ease her way to the floor. She sat with one leg bent and the other straight out in front of her.

He followed Mia's blood to the glass wall. It went straight under it, reappeared on the other side, then curved off to the right. One of the panels had to open, but he couldn't see any mechanism that would allow it. As for the blood trail, it curved away, and the opaque film covering the main wall kept him from seeing where it ended. He hammered his fist against the glass, but it did nothing. It felt as solid as a brick wall. He touched his finger to the joint between two of the panels, and it was as hard as concrete. He took a step back from the glass wall and raised his gun.

"I wouldn't try that."

He looked up. He couldn't see the intercom speaker. Maybe it was hidden behind one of the recessed lights.

"Why's that?" he asked.

"It'll ricochet," the speaker said. "It could hit you, or your lieutenant. By now I would think you'd know better."

He recognized the voice and the accent. He'd heard it several times on television, and once in person. He was looking at the ceiling, but turned when he heard a knock on the glass behind him. Sheldon Lassen stood on the other side. He wore a long physician's coat and had a paper surgical mask pulled down so that it hung around his throat. His hair was whiter than Carver remembered, but it still turned into curls where it fell past his collar.

"It's always such a pleasure to see you, Inspector Carver."

"I want to see them," he said. "Mia and Jenner."

"Or what?"

Carver glanced at the gun in his hand, then nodded toward Hernandez where she sat against the wall.

"You won't do that," Lassen said. "Don't waste our time."

"Why not?" Carver asked. "It's the first shot that's the hardest. We're past that."

"I'll grant you, you've gone pretty far this time. But you've always liked Lieutenant Hernandez. Always worked well with her."

"What are you talking about?"

"Look around you, Carver," Lassen said. "This is practically your second apartment."

He hit a button on his phone, and the glittering film on the main glass wall began to fade until it was transparent. The space beyond wasn't a clean room. It was an operating theater. There were three stations set up in the middle of the floor. White robotic arms sprouted from the ceiling above each bed. Some of them held imaging devices, or mounted high-powered lights. The rest were bristling with tools and machinery beyond Carver's capacity to guess.

He focused on Mia.

She was in the middle bed, and Jenner was to her left. She was lying unconscious, an oxygen mask strapped over her face, and multiple intravenous ports in her forearms. Her legs were covered with a blue sheet, and he couldn't tell whether she was wounded or not.

The same went for Jenner. On his left, two men and a woman in green scrubs studied a bank of monitors. Another man came through a set of sliding doors. He was pushing a crash cart, which he left between Jenner and Mia. No one paid any attention to Carver. Maybe the glass was only transparent in one direction, or maybe they simply didn't care.

Mia's vital signs scrolled along the bottom of three monitors behind her bed. He didn't know what most of the lines meant, but he could see her pulse and it was steady. He'd seen what they'd done to

Hadley after strapping her to a bed like that. Maybe they were just waiting for Mia to wake up.

"Nothing?" Lassen said. "Nothing coming through?"

"Where's Henry Newcomb?"

Lassen stepped closer to the glass.

"We didn't need him," he said. "He was useless. Miss Westcott, though – she's something else. Truly a great find. So many possibilities."

"What are you doing to her?"

"You know about the house on Filbert Street?" Lassen asked.

Carver didn't respond. Whatever he had learned about the house was irrelevant now, and they both knew it. And talking to Lassen was as useless as holding a gun on Hernandez. This would end however Lassen chose to end it, and no words from the inside of a glass box were going to make a difference.

"What we did for you, the decontamination truck – that's just a mobile facility. It's not equipped like this room. We can go deeper here. We can scrub harder. If we plant something, it always takes root."

He raised his phone again and scrolled through a menu. Then he hit another button and looked at the ceiling behind Carver.

"They won't feel a thing," Lassen said. "And neither will you."

Carver couldn't hear the gas, and couldn't see where it was coming from, but the air was suddenly too sweet. He looked at Lassen and took a step back from the glass.

"Lieutenant Hernandez has the right idea," Lassen said. "Sitting down, I mean. It's better to sit, so you don't fall – of course, she remembers. A luxury, in here."

"She remembers what?" Carver asked.

"I always enjoy these conversations. Especially with you – you've done so much for us. For this city."

"I've never done anything for you."

"You are the saddest thing – really, you are. A man who deserves accolades but can't be recognized. Not even by himself. It's all erased, scrubbed clean," Lassen said. "And it has to be. There's no other choice. But if I put stars on a wall to mark my greatest officers, yours would shine the brightest. And never doubt it. You're not SFPD. You work for Ønske, and you belong to me."

Carver backed up and leaned against the glass. He was taking shallow breaths now. The gas coated his throat like melted candy. He looked at the lights and saw a glowing halo around each of them. When he turned back to Lassen, the air dazzled with electric-blue sparks. He couldn't blink them away.

"How many?" he asked. "How many times?"

Lassen looked at his left hand as he thought about it. He tapped his thumb twice against each of his fingertips.

"Eight," Lassen said. "Eight times, we've stood here. Just like this. Always this glass between us, or I'd have shaken your hand. I'd shake your hand now, if I could. What you've done for us – my god – the threats you've eliminated. The problems you've buried. You don't even remember going to New York and taking care of that doctor – I believe you know him as George. Two behind the ear, and you were sure he deserved it. He did, of course. He was trying to destroy me."

Carver raised the gun, pointed it at Lassen's head and started pulling the trigger before the man had a chance to react. He meant to empty the magazine, but the fourth shot was a misfire. All three bullets ricocheted off the glass and whined past his face. He heard them hit the marble wall around the elevator doors.

Lassen hadn't moved.

Now he put his finger to the other side of the glass and traced it behind a leaden streak. The bullets hadn't done a thing. Not a chip or a crack. Lassen walked away, bringing his phone to his ear.

By then, Carver's airways might have turned to sugar crystals. Sweet granules had gathered in his throat, were sifting like dust into his lungs. He dropped the gun and slid down the wall until he was sitting. He was across from Hernandez, and she pulled her head up with some effort and watched him. They were both taking shallow breaths. He tried to think of something to say to her, but found nothing.

If he'd come to the floor facing the other direction, then he would've been able to look through the glass and see Mia. But turning himself around was an impossibility. He had only the strength to stay sitting up, to keep his eyes open. He tried to gather his memories, tried to wrap his arms around them and hold them tight to his chest where Lassen couldn't pull them away. They had taken Mia from him once already tonight, but now they meant to make it permanent. They were going to reach inside of him and pluck her out, and when he opened his eyes again, it would be as though she'd never existed.

His chest was burning.

It hadn't been dust falling into his lungs, but smoke and blowing embers. Now there was a smoldering fire inside him. He fell into a spasm of coughing. The only way to stop it was by holding his breath and picturing Mia.

There was no way he could tell her now. No way to explain that he understood what she had tried to do for him, that even here, as he fell back into the tumbling nightmare, there was one bright light and it came from her.

She'd known this might happen. She'd done what she could to prepare him.

He closed his eyes and let her take him again, let her lead him down the steps to the stateroom and undress him in the dark. He was with her in the berth, and her hands were on his shoulders. He was moving inside her, moving with her, and then she pulled him close and began whispering into his ear.

Hold on to me, Ross. Hold everything close. Everything we have together. You have to hold tight to everything you see and never let it go. So remember this — this, right now — remember me, doing this —

— Mia, wait —

Don't you let go of me, Ross Carver — like that — don't you let go of me.

— Mia —

You can't forget me. I won't let you forget me.

— never, Mia, I'll never —

You can't. You can't ever.

— I won't, Mia, I can't —

Hold on to me Ross. Hold me now.

— I am —

Touch me — touch me everywhere and breathe me in — it's coming — it's coming soon and you have to be ready — so kiss me, taste my skin, put your hands in my hair and —

Yesterday, he hadn't understood at all.

Mia hadn't been gasping in the dark. She didn't talk that way every time she made love. She'd been building a defense by placing markers in every corner of his mind. She'd known they were both going back into the darkness, but she thought she could leave him with something that would resonate. A light that would shine with enough brilliance to lead him back. So she was etching herself into the oldest pathways of his memory: the scent of her hair, and the taste of her skin. The rush of her breath across his ear as she guided him. Memories that would awaken at any brush and blossom into longing and need. She wanted him to wake from this with a hole in his heart, something that couldn't be filled unless he found her. She didn't want to be taken away—

A rattling, wet cough roused him.

He looked up in time to see Hernandez slump facedown into the pool of blood that had gathered around her.

He turned to the glass, where Lassen had been. No one was watching them.

Now Hernandez began to spasm, her body shuddering against the floor. Her hair was a dark spill around her head. He pulled himself toward her, clawing at the slick marble until he reached her. He turned her on her side, put her head onto his knee. He watched her bubbling breath come back, and he tried to remember what he'd been thinking about a moment ago.

He'd been on the other side of the glass box, had been drifting down into the dark with something very important gripped to his chest. But he'd lost it in the suddenness of his awakening. He'd been startled, and then he'd lost his hold.

When he knew he couldn't hold himself up much longer, he lay down along the wall. His eyes blurred in and out of focus until they came to rest on an empty shell casing a few feet from his nose.

A glowing tendril rose from the tarnished brass, wavering like a candle flame.

He still couldn't remember what he'd been thinking, what had been so urgent a moment ago. He looked at his fingers. They were glowing with a light so soft and so cold that he thought of snow. A gray winter's morning, and the feather-tap of snowflakes against a window pane. He counted along his fingertips, touching each one with the pad of his thumb.

Eight times, he'd been here. Lassen wanted to shake his hand, wanted to congratulate him for his good works. Mark his efforts with a star on a wall no one could see, where it would shine so brightly, and illuminate nothing.

It had all been so useless.

33

FOR A WHILE after he woke, he lay under the blankets with his eyes closed and listened to the woman's voice while he tried to place himself. There had been rain pattering on a window, but the window was far from the bed. The mattress was too hard and the blankets too thin. He didn't know where he was, but it wasn't his apartment.

He listened to the voice and he drifted with it, hoping to catch hold of something.

"No—I told you already—Yes, because nobody's switching for anyone else's shift and we're still shorthanded—Yes—Yes, he'll be back on in the next couple of days—I don't know, maybe because he needs some rest? I mean, what do you think? Maybe I'll take a day off too—No, forget I said that—Look, just give me Bodecker—Then tell him to call my cell—Yes, goddamnit, Cleve. I'll be back by then."

The sheet was tucked under his chin and smelled like it had been washed in pure bleach. It was as crisp as a shirt collar. He heard something go wheeling past his room, and understood then that he was in a hospital. He opened his eyes and saw Lieutenant Hernandez sitting next to his bed.

"They said you'd be waking up soon," she said. She put her cell phone onto her lap.

"They must've been right."

"I wanted to be here," Hernandez said. "Wanted to be the first to say thanks."

"Okay."

"Do you remember what happened?" she asked.

He had to think about that. She inched the chair a little closer. He hadn't noticed it was a wheelchair until she used her arms to move it. Then she was so close to the bed that he couldn't see what was wrong with her legs.

"Most of it," he said. "Jenner and I went to the pier, after we got the call."

"You saw me in the lookout?"

He nodded.

"The door at the loading bay was unlocked – it was supposed to be. We went upstairs to the office."

"You thought you were meeting Patrick."

"We thought we'd finally get the sit-down we'd been looking for. But we walked in on Johnny Wong and three of his guys."

"He'd already killed Patrick," Hernandez said. "His mistress and his neighbor. They'd been dead for weeks."

"He set us up?" he asked. "That's what you're telling me?"

"Those messages with the bartender, that was just to get you to the warehouse. Patrick was out of the picture."

"You're sure about that?"

"We found him three days ago."

"What day is this?"

"The nineteenth."

That didn't mean anything to Carver. He wasn't even sure of the month, but he didn't want to say it. This was the police department; he was supposed to be tough. He couldn't let his lieutenant see him rattled by a little smoke. He tried sitting up and found that he could. Hernandez reached behind him and moved the pillows.

After he leaned back on them, he saw her leg for the first time.

She was wearing a navy blue suit and the skirt had climbed above her knee. The bandages looked an inch thick.

"I remember you coming in," he said. "You must've heard the shots."

"I left the lookout, came running."

"You got it in the knee."

"That's right," she said. "Do you remember how the fire started?"

"I remember a fire."

"But that's all?"

He remembered the smell of the burning bodies, and the flames climbing the warehouse's clapboard walls. He'd been gasping for air when he crawled to stop Hernandez from choking. Sometime near the end, when Hernandez's head was resting on his knee, and her blood was all around them, he remembered hearing the first cracks as the roof started to collapse.

What he couldn't understand was why he was in the hospital if she was out.

"Hernandez –"

He stopped and reached with both hands to feel his face, fingertips carefully probing the skin, afraid for the first time since waking.

"Relax, Carver," she said. "It was just smoke inhalation. Fumes from all that crap they had in there. You were touch-and-go, a couple days. You smelled like an ashtray. But that's all. Look, I'll show you –"

She twisted in her chair and took her purse from one of the push handles. She found a compact mirror, opened it, and handed it to him.

"You see?" she said.

He looked at himself. He remembered the burning in his chest, could see Hernandez writhing next to him. They'd made a tourniquet of something. Her jacket, maybe. But in the mirror she'd handed him, his face was fine. There wasn't anything wrong with him at all. Someone had even shaved him that morning. He tried to focus, tried to let all the images and memories stick together.

"Jenner?" he asked.

"Back at work – partnered with Bodecker till you get back. He's already bitching about it."

He leaned back and closed his eyes. Jenner was all right, and that was the main thing. That was what he'd been worried about the most. He didn't remember much from when he was out, but he remembered not knowing about Jenner. He wasn't sure how they'd gotten separated, though that wasn't something he was going to bring up with Hernandez.

"Who wouldn't bitch a little?" he asked. "Jesus, Hernandez – this is Bodecker we're talking about."

Hernandez turned her chair to face the door.

"I've got to go, Ross," she said. She reached up and caught his hand. "But I needed to thank you. You saved me – you truly did."

"It's nothing."

She let go of his hand and straightened her jacket.

"It's a lot to me," she said. "And here – you can read about it. It's got all the details. Anything you might've forgotten, it's in here."

She put her copy of the *Chronicle* on his lap and pushed herself halfway across the room. Then she stopped and looked over her shoulder.

"Take as long as you need," she said. "When you're ready to come back, call me."

"Thanks, Lieutenant."

She wheeled herself to the door and turned the corner. He heard the chair go down the hall, and after a moment, the elevator's chime. He looked at the window on the far side of the room. It was impossible to tell if it was morning or evening. The light was gray and sleepy, and the rain washed against the glass every time the wind stirred.

He brought his fists to his forehead and closed his eyes.

They'd followed the leads to the warehouse and Johnny Wong had come out shooting. They'd come away from it with their lives, but Johnny hadn't, and neither had his men. Carver remembered his last shot, the one that ended it. The fire was already going by then. It had just been an accident, probably. No one in there would have wanted to start it.

He flipped through the paper, but it didn't matter what it said. After a while he tossed it on the floor, where he couldn't see it. Nothing in a newspaper was going to fill what was missing in his chest. He looked at the gray light and listened to the rain, and waited for someone to come and tell him he could go home.

When he woke the second time, it was dark outside and even darker in the room. He sat up and swung his feet to the floor. He wasn't sure what it would be like to stand, but when he tried, it wasn't a problem. He crossed to the window and leaned against the metal sill. He was looking down at Parnassus Avenue, from about five floors up. The rest of the medical center was across the street. Hard to see it for the rain.

He went to the bathroom and washed his face. The water never got warm and his bare feet were freezing on the tile floor. Then he went back to the bed and found a plastic bin underneath it. Inside it was a clear bag. He took it out and held it toward the window to read the printing above the UCSF Medical Center logo. Someone had written his name with a black marker.

He set the bag on the bed and ripped it open. They'd put his keys and badge inside his shoes, had rolled his pants and boxers into a ball. Someone had made a half-decent but pointless attempt to fold his shirt and jacket. All of his clothes smelled strongly of smoke, and when he held the pants up, even in the window's vague light he could see the dark bloodstains.

At least they hadn't cut his clothes off. He'd had that happen, and then he'd had to choose between walking down Parnassus in a backless hospital gown or waiting for Jenner to bring him something. He dug into the bag again and found his wallet and cell phone. His gun was missing, but that was probably in ballistics. They'd need to check it against the rounds they dug out of the warehouse walls and Johnny Wong.

He pulled off the hospital gown and dressed in his suit. Then he took the phone and turned it on. There was still one bar left on the battery. There was only one person to dial, and he picked up on the first ring. He always picked up on the first ring.

"You're calling," Jenner said. "That's gotta be a good sign. At least you're up."

"That's about all I can say."

"Hernandez went to see you. This morning."

"She told me you're already back at it."

"Bodecker," Jenner said. "Sweet Jesus. Two days of him."

"I've been here that long?"

"Longer," Jenner said. "They brought us there five days ago. I got out in three. I came and saw you yesterday. You remember?"

"A little, maybe," Carver said. "Did you read something?"

"You were sleeping," Jenner said. "I said hello, and that's about it."

"I remember someone reading to me. I guess it wasn't you."

"They had you drugged to the sky. You sound okay now."

He felt okay now. Every muscle in his body ached, but that didn't concern him. He'd been horizontal for too long.

"Where are you?" he asked.

"Bryant," Jenner said. "Paperwork."

"Can you meet in half an hour?"

"We could get a bite, if you're up for it."

"I'm starving," Carver said.

He walked to the window and looked down at the street. There was an ambulance parked in the turnabout beneath him. Light from the main entrance spilled out and made the raindrops flash as they streaked toward the black pavement.

"I'll go down the block, wait at Fifth and Parnassus. I shouldn't stand out front."

"You're not asking if you can go, is what you mean. You're not waiting to get released."

"I just want to get the fuck out of here."

"I hear you," Jenner said. "But you keep doing this, next time they might put a chip in you. Sound an alarm when you go out the front door."

A nurse passed him on the way to the elevator, and before she recognized him as a patient, he reached into his jacket and showed her his badge. He put it a foot from her face and then snapped the case closed.

"Carver," he said. "Homicide. You see which way Dr. Newcomb went?"

"I—"

"Forget it. I'll find him."

He stepped past her and pushed the elevator button. He listened to her go down the hall, and when her footsteps stopped, he knew she was at the door to his room. He'd left the hospital gown on the floor, next to the empty plastic bag that had held his things. It took the nurse about a second to put it together.

"Sir?"

He put his phone against his ear and didn't turn around. The elevator doors opened and he got into the car.

"Sir!"

He punched the button for the lobby, and the doors rattled shut in front of him.

When he saw Jenner's headlights, he came out of the shadows and stood at the curb, and then got into the passenger seat when the car stopped. Jenner didn't pull back into the lane right away, but sat with one hand on the wheel and looked him over.

"Shit, Ross."

"I know."

His suit smelled like it was still smoking.

"You look like—We'll find a casual kind of place. What do you think?"

"There's Mel's, on Geary."

"That works," Jenner said. He checked his mirror and then did a U-turn, taking them down Parnassus toward the ocean. "That Hernandez's blood all down the side of your leg?"

"I think so."

"She doesn't need that chair, I don't think. She could get by on crutches. It'd be faster, plus she could do stairs."

"I wouldn't know. I never got shot in the knee."

"She says you saved her," Jenner said. "You remember it?"

"Not really," he said. "Some flashes."

"It's all in the paper, her story."

"I saw it."

"What do you think?"

"I haven't been up very long," Carver said. "I haven't thought about much."

"Are you going to?" Jenner asked. "This time?"

"I don't know."

"I've picked you up like this before," Jenner said. "It's a thing we do, once or twice a year. I'm just saying."

Carver didn't have a reply to that. He'd just been doing his job, this time and all the others. He sat and watched the streetlights as they came through the Inner Sunset and then crossed Golden Gate Park. Jenner had the heater on, and from the vents, Carver could smell the wet grass and the redwood trees. They weren't far from the meadow where they'd found Hadley Hardgrave.

"At least we got him," Jenner said. "There's that."

"There's that," Carver said. "Do we get to keep Hadley's file open?"

Jenner shook his head.

"They closed it."

"Who?"

"Hernandez, the chief. The commissioner," Jenner said. "Shit—even the mayor dropped by. But he was just looking for a photo."

"Suddenly they're all as sure as we were."

"Guy's dead," Jenner said. "It's a good time to be sure."

They reached the north end of the park, and Jenner waited at the light for a chance to turn right on Fulton. Down the sidewalk, in the shadow of a cypress tree, there was a bus stop. A woman stood beneath its glass shelter, arms clutched against her chest. He turned as they passed her, something like hope expanding in his chest and pressing hard against his lungs. But when he saw her face, she was no one he knew. He didn't understand what he'd expected to see.

"Doesn't this sort of thing worry you, though?" Jenner asked.

Carver turned away from the window.

"What sort of thing?" he asked.

“I don’t know. What we’ve been seeing on the streets, the stuff we’re up against. It’s not like it used to be.”

“People are getting harder,” Carver answered. “That’s all. They wear down the world around them because they’re too rough for it.”

“I’ve heard that one,” Jenner said.

“Heard it where?”

“From you. Every time we do this.”

34

IT WAS PAST midnight when Jenner stopped in front of Carver's building. A motorcycle went past, shot across Bush, and then disappeared under the Dragon Gate and up the hill into Chinatown. After it was gone, the street was empty except for a flock of sparrows that swirled out of the darkness and settled onto the roof of a parked car.

"If you don't feel good, call me," Jenner said. "I know you won't call the hospital."

"I'm fine."

"You coming in tomorrow?"

"I might take a day," Carver said. "Unless you and Bodecker close everything. Then I'll take two."

"There'll be plenty left."

"There always is."

They shook hands and Carver stepped out. He watched Jenner drive off, and then he went to the front door and into his apartment's lobby. Glenn was asleep at the security desk, his head down on the glass-topped monitors. Carver crossed under the chandelier and stood where he could look down at the sleeping guard.

His forehead was on his crossed arms, and the back of his neck was visible. There were three red welts in a tight triangle.

"Glenn."

He didn't stir, but his breath was fogging the glass beneath his nose.

He exited the elevator on his floor and was coming down the hall when a man stepped out of the apartment across from his. He came out backwards, pulling a hand truck loaded with cardboard boxes. A Japanese guy, late thirties. He wore slacks and a dress shirt, the sleeves rolled up. When he saw Carver, he glanced back inside the apartment he'd just left, then continued down the hall to the elevator. They passed each other without speaking.

As he unlocked his door, he could hear more people across the hall. A man and a woman, talking quietly as they loaded boxes. His neighbor had only moved in a few months ago, and she'd never had a friend come over that Carver had seen. She'd kept to herself, mostly. He couldn't remember her face and wasn't sure if he'd ever known her name. But whatever her story was, it wasn't odd to move out in the middle of the night. People did that all the time.

He showered and changed into clean clothes. He stuffed his suit into a garbage bag and put that in the trash can under his kitchen sink. His apartment was spotless. There was a service that came by once a week and cleaned everything but his study, which he kept locked. They must have come while he was in the hospital.

Everything was perfect. Dust-free, lemon-scented, and utterly empty. He went to the window and looked through the slat blinds at the Neptune Hotel's neon sign, blurry in the rain. He walked into the bedroom and looked at his bed, which was made up. The down duvet had been untouched for so many days that it looked six inches thick. But he knew he wouldn't sleep. He got a jacket from his closet, got his wallet and keys, and went out.

His neighbor's door was closed now, and there weren't any voices coming from behind it. He went down the elevator and went across the lobby without waking Glenn. He turned left on Grant and left again into the alley, hurrying now because of the rain.

There were a dozen people sitting at the bar in the Irish Bank. He took a stool at the end, away from everyone else. He looked at the bottles on the back bar and stared at the advertisements on the mirrors. After a while Cathleen came over.

"Jenner's on his way?"

"Not tonight."

Her eyes moved past him, to the confessional.

"It's open, if you need it."

"No one's coming."

"All right – it's none of my business," she said. "Pint of Harp?"

"But first bring me an Oban."

"Neat?"

He nodded.

He watched her go along the shelves until she found the bottle. She brought it back with an empty tumbler, put it in front of him, and poured.

"I saw the paper," she said.

"Yeah?"

"Did you just get out?"

He took a sip of the scotch and turned his face away from her as he breathed out through his nose.

"Left tonight. Jenner brought me back."

"He's okay?"

"Yeah."

"I close at two. If you can stick around—"

"I don't know, Cath."

"I'm sorry," she said. "That came right out of nowhere, didn't it? And let me fix that—it was a bad pour."

The bottle of Oban was still on the bar. She pulled out its stopper and added another finger's worth of scotch to his glass.

"That's on me," she said. "I'll go pull your pint."

He'd come to the Irish Bank looking for company. But when he'd found it, he'd pulled back. If Cathleen had said anything like that to him a week ago, he was sure he would have stayed until she closed. He didn't understand what was going on with him. He felt so hollowed out, he could almost hear the rush of the emptiness inside him. It was the blank sound at the mouth of an elevator shaft.

He had no idea what would fill that hole, no sense of what he was looking for.

It had stopped raining while he was in the bar, but there were still deep puddles in the alley. He wasn't drunk but he knew he would be in about ten minutes, when the rest of the whiskey worked its way into his bloodstream. He stopped and leaned against a dumpster and looked at the fire escape. He could climb it, could climb up to the roof and come down to his apartment through the trapdoor to the fire stairs. The thought took shape in his mind, gathered momentum. He stopped himself halfway across the alley when he realized there was no way to catch the last ladder. There was no reason to sneak into his apartment through the fire escape, no reason to even be thinking about it.

Maybe the whiskey had gone farther than he'd thought.

From the outside, looking in, he could see Glenn was still asleep. He opened the door and went across the lobby to the mail room. He dug out his key ring, and opened his box.

The mail pushed out and fell onto the floor, a dozen glowcards lighting up when they sensed the impact. He had to kneel down and gather what had fallen. Then he stood and took the rest of the mail from the brass box. He tucked it under his left arm and went to the elevator.

Glenn had raised his head. His eyes weren't tracking together.

"You okay?" Carver asked.

"Okay."

"You need a doctor?"

"I'm good."

"All right," Carver said. "You remember my extension?"

"Six fourteen."

"You need anything, you call me."

"Okay."

Glenn put his head back down and Carver hit the elevator button. It wasn't the first time he'd seen Glenn like this. By any measure, the man was unreliable.

In his kitchen, he knelt and took a bottle of bourbon from the liquor cabinet and poured an ounce over an ice cube. He set the bottle on the counter without corking it, and took the stack of mail.

At the top of the stack was a dimming glowcard. He took a sip of the bourbon and turned the card over, shaking it to wake it up. It began to play a video of the Fairmont Hotel, the entire building wrapped in silk and tied up with red ribbons. Strings of Chinese paper lanterns wound through the gardens, wavering in an invisible breeze. Two words slowly superimposed themselves across the face of the card.

Black Aria

He felt it start somewhere inside him, a building wave that had traveled a thousand miles through deep water and was now rising to greet an approaching shore. He set the glass down and held on to the counter to be ready for it. The wave curled and broke, and washed across him. As it receded, there was peace. He stared at the shining lanterns in the boxwood hedges, the glittering lights behind the thin silk wrapping. After a while, he took another sip of the bourbon and set the glowcard aside so that he could look at it later. There was still a whole stack of mail to go through.

The next in line was a red envelope. The kind of thing you could pick up in Chinatown, ten in a packet. A gold-leaf dragon was intertwined with a phoenix along the bottom edge. The address was handwritten in black ink. A woman's script. The postmark showed a zip code near Fisherman's Wharf. There was no return address.

He couldn't remember the last time someone had sent him a letter. He took a knife from the rack next to him and used it to slit open the top. When he pulled out the three small sheets of paper, they came with a faint scent of cedar, an even lighter touch of jasmine. He thought of the woods up north he'd gone to as a boy, the oldest trees gathering the fog and sending it down as rain. Those groves were all gone now. Everything was gone.

He turned the pages over.

The letter was written on stationery from the St. Francis Hotel. Small, careful handwriting took up both sides of each page. A woman's writing.

Dear Ross,

This letter is my life insurance policy. If you're reading, it means I'm gone. You'll only believe it if I show you something first. I know I have to prove my bona fides. So let me tell you what I know. Either you just got out of the hospital, or you woke up in your own bed and there are days you can't account for. It doesn't matter which, because they marked you. Reach up and touch the back of your neck. Go ahead and do it, but be gentle. You'll find three swollen welts there, and when you touch them, they'll sting—

He stopped reading, setting the letter on the counter. Slowly, he reached back with his right hand, using the pads of his middle and index fingers to trace the nape of his neck. What he found just above his collar felt no different than the marks he'd seen on Glenn. A triangle of swollen skin, hot beneath his fingertips. Leaving the hospital, his entire body had felt beaten and sore. He hadn't noticed anything about his neck until he touched it. Now it felt like he was wearing a freshly burned cattle brand. He looked at his fingertips, but there was no blood. Yet all the same, she was right. They'd marked him.

Turning back to the letter, his eyes caught and held in the middle of the third paragraph:

> *– so I told you to put your hands in my hair. I told you to touch me everywhere, to taste me. I couldn't let you forget me. I knew it wouldn't work, but I had to try. I was desperate, and I'm sorry. The best I can do is point you in the right direction. We get recruited when we've already joined. Henry said that. I hope you remember him. But if you're the only one left, you'll have to do everything yourself. It won't be easy, because you belong to them. And they watch –*

The air had already left his lungs. Now it went out of the room altogether. He hurried into the living room and sat on one of the chairs before he fell down. He brought the pages close to his face, and when he finally got a breath, he could smell her. He had no memory of her face, or her name. No idea when or how he'd known her, or if he'd ever met her at all. But then –

> *hold me?*
> *all right*

– for a moment, he could see the rich spill of her hair and the touch of flowers at her throat, the full length of her body warm against his. The memory was almost close enough to touch, and then it dissolved into the dark.

He tried to reach for her again, but all he came up with was a flickering image: looking at the dawn sky through a square of rain-beaded glass. He closed his eyes and tried again, and this time he could almost hear the reedy whisper of her voice, beautiful and calm in the pauses as she carefully chose her words.

> *Do you ever think there's maybe something that's gone wrong with the world?*

He didn't know where the words came from, or where they went after running across his thoughts. But he knew the answer to her question: Of course there was something wrong. A flood of desire and fear washed into him. It made no sense that he could be so overwhelmed by both feelings at once. And yet he'd never felt so empty. He read the rest of the letter. When he reached the end he slid out of his chair and to his knees. With his eyes closed, he counted slowly and waited for the world to come back.

When he could breathe again, he read the letter twice more.

He'd already memorized it, but he wanted to let her words play through his mind, wanted to see what she might set loose. He didn't know anything about her. Not her name, or where she was born, or how she carried herself when she walked into a room. She said they'd spent one night together, though that could be a lie. Either the letter was full of misdirection, or nothing Hernandez told him in the hospital was true. In the letter, the woman was telling him to find Johnny Wong again. The envelope was postmarked the day Hernandez had told him that he and Jenner shot Johnny dead; but according to the letter, he'd sat across a table from Johnny that same day and made a tacit peace with him. He had no memory of that, or the shooting, or the warehouse fire. It was all a wasteland. More empty spaces than solid structures.

And if Hernandez was the liar, where did that leave Jenner?

He tried to think, tried to find some way to make the shattered pieces fit into something he could use. It took him a while before he was ready. He knelt on the rug for ten minutes, but he'd known all along what he had to do. There was something wrong, he was sure of that. He'd been denying it for years, had dismissed Jenner's doubts just tonight. But he couldn't go back to that now, not after reading the letter. It would be better if he could forget. Better if he could get back to denial. He'd probably live longer that way. But on the other hand, at least now he had a purpose.

He took the fire stairs to the top floor and then climbed the ladder and went through the trapdoor to the roof. It was raining a little, but not enough to stop him from doing what he'd come for. He went to the corner of the building and stood at the balustrade, looking out across the intersection of Grant and Bush. The sky was dark in patches where the clouds were too thick to catch and burn with the city lights. Where it was brighter, he could see the silhouettes of drones darting past.

The letter and the butane lighter were in his jacket pocket, and he took them out.

She hadn't signed her name on it. Not her real name, nor whatever name he'd known her by. It was too dangerous for him to know either one now. In a weak moment, he might search for her. Then they would know what he knew, and that would end it. He had to be silent, and he had to be strong. He had to bury her deep, and carry her in secret.

He tried to picture her. It was too dark to see her face. But he could feel her hands on his shoulders, could feel the curve of her back as she arched forward to meet him. He had been with her, let her undress him in the dark and lead him to bed. But why could he remember that, when everything else was gone? Everything up until he'd woken in the hospital, floating through a halfway haze, carried along by Hernandez's voice.

How many people had been whispering to him in the dark, and for how long?

He opened the lighter's hinged lid and struck a flame. Then he held the corner of the envelope over it and watched it catch. He kept it below the level of the balustrade, where the flames would be safe from the wind. When his phone began to vibrate, he took it from his pocket and checked the screen.

It was Lieutenant Hernandez.

He thought of smashing the phone against the stone rail, throwing the pieces into the street. The flames had half the envelope now. He tilted it so they would spread up toward his fingers. He had to answer. That was the way it worked, the way it would have to be from now on. He swallowed once, to calm his voice. Then he brought the letter up and let the wind take it. He stood against the rail and watched it twist through the air, burning as it fell. High above the street, the letter had broken into four pieces. One of the sheets made it almost all the way to the Dragon Gate before it dissolved into ash and flickered out. There was nothing left but the dark city spreading out beneath him, and Hernandez waiting for him to pick up.

He couldn't let her hear any doubt in his voice. She had to think he believed the world had no problems so great they couldn't be fixed with a badge and a gun, and a stiff drink at the end of the day, standing alone in the kitchen with the mail spread out and glowing in front of him. All the shining things that blinked and promised and glittered in the dark – then moved out of grasp like sparks dancing away on the wind.

He brought the phone to his ear.

"Carver," he said. "Homicide."

Acknowledgments

I have always thought of *The Poison Artist, The Dark Room,* and *The Night Market* as a three-panel painting of San Francisco — a single work, loosely connected. So with this last book, which completes the story of a city and an interrelated group of characters, you'd think I might have something to say about it. But I finished this book almost a year before I finished *The Dark Room,* and so I said most of what I have to say about this series (if *series* is the right word) in the acknowledgments to that book.

Speaking of acknowledgments, there seems to be a long-standing tradition on the last page of novels (at least those written by male authors) in which the author thanks his wife for typing the manuscript — something you could get an enterprising kid to do, for a reasonable fee. Maria doesn't type my manuscripts. What she does do is talk to me about my stories, read them and critique them, and give me insights and guidance. I'd be afraid to send something out without her comments, and I don't think I could find anyone, for any fee, who could do what she does.

For the last four years, I've been blessed to have Alice Martell as my agent. She has opened doors for me that I wouldn't have even knocked on, has gotten my books published in seven languages, and has somehow managed to sell every single thing I've sent her, including short stories. Thanks to Alice, I also have some truly fine editors. Naomi Gibbs and Alison Kerr Miller at Houghton Mifflin Harcourt, and Bill Massey and Francesca Pathak at Orion have been superb.

I live in Hawaii now, and I often write at outdoor bars that are close approximations of paradise. I'm not kidding: it's eighty degrees in the sunlight, the wind smells like plumeria, the waves lap on the beach with Diamond Head in the background — and my head is in a San Francisco fog. I used to live there, in the late nineties, and after the turn of the millennium. At the time, I had a writing teacher named Thomas Cooney. He and I have stayed in touch, so that he has given me something like nineteen years of encouragement in my writing. To say that I am grateful – to say that he has taught me a lot – would be an understatement.